The Vosto
By
Christopher Cartwright

Copyright 2022 by Christopher Cartwright
This book is protected under the copyright laws of the United States of America. Any reproduction or other unauthorized use of the material or artwork herein is prohibited. This book is a work of fiction. Names, characters, places, brands, media and incidents either are the product of the author's imagination or are used fictitiously. All rights reserved.

Chapter One

Module B, Vostok Research Station – Antarctica

The first shot quietly whizzed past her head.

It landed in the aluminum wall just eight feet away.

A few stray strands of hair, brushed aside by the pressure wave in front of the bullet as it whipped across the side of her face at a supersonic speed, was the only indication it had been there at all. If it had been another few inches to the left, she would be dead already.

Anastasia Utkin raised a hand to her cheek.

A mild expression of wonder animated her gunmetal-gray eyes. More a curiosity than any real expectation of a threat. She could have sworn a gnat had touched her face. It was impossible of course. The Antarctic midge – the only endemic fly on the icy continent – was in fact flightless.

So what had touched her face?

She tilted her head just slightly, trying to somehow determine what it was. There was a strange sound associated with the feeling, too, but she couldn't quite place it.

Then, a split second later, she heard it again.

It didn't really sound like gunfire.

More like the crisp staccato of ice hammering against the aluminum walls of the newly built research station, driven there by the gale force winds that routinely ripped through the Central Antarctic Plateau at 150 miles an hour. It was a soft, almost melodic, sound.

A flicker of what might have been fear crossed Anastasia Utkin's face like a shadow for the first time. She sat back from her computer desk and exchanged a glance with Pavel, a fifty something year old geologist. Pavel was still beaming from their recent, extraordinary discovery of a thriving, hidden eco-system some two miles below the surface, locked away from the outside world by more than 15 million years of snowfall.

It was more than that, though.

Technically, it was an Alien Biosphere.

Albeit a microscopic one that even Stephen Spielberg might struggle to get the general global population enthused about. But for the small scientific community in Antarctica, this was like having the winning ticket in the greatest lottery ever played.

The scientist looked happy, almost child-like with a big, unsuppressed grin. She smiled back at him. Everyone was still on a high. She glanced at the two other scientists in the room. Like her, they were both typing away on their computers, putting together a paper to address the scientific community concerning their remarkable findings.

No one seemed flustered or concerned by the varied and numerous sounds outside. And why should they? The Vostok Research Station was under a constant barrage of ice, pummeling against its structure at more than a hundred miles an hour.

Welcome to Antarctica.

It was all perfectly normal.

Only, somewhere in the reptilian part of her brain – developed more than 400 million years ago – a warning alarm fired in Anastasia's mind. Something didn't belong. Not today. Something was different. Her pulse rate increased almost imperceptibly. Her pupils widened, and her gunmetal-gray eyes intensified.

The auditory cortex and brainstem struggled but failed to make sense of it all. Only a few split-seconds passed before her hippocampus solved the riddle. The curved, seahorse-shaped organ on the underside of each temporal lobe was responsible for memory, learning, navigation, and perception of space.

And right now, it just identified that the crisp, rasping sounds that were entirely normal outside the research station, originated from *within*. Right here, where the living quarters were housed.

Her eyebrows cocked. Like a primitive animal, she was finally beginning to make sense of it. The auditory cortex kicked into gear. It matched the sound with another sound she'd previously heard...

Gunfire!

Yet it couldn't be gunfire...

No, that noise wasn't quite right, was it? Her brain struggled to confirm the sounds she'd only ever heard in the movies. Did they match? Surely it didn't really sound like gunfire in her tiny research station? Or maybe they sounded exactly like machinegun fire, but the shots were so far out of place, that her brainstem simply couldn't make sense of it.

The Vostok Research Station was one of the most isolated places on earth. Just shy of twelve hundred miles from the coast and nearly seven hundred from the nearest research station, they were multiple days travel away from anyone. Even if someone had made the treacherous journey, there was no reason for anyone to fire a gun. It wasn't like there were any animals in the region to shoot. Even if there was something for someone to shoot outside, it was impossible.

Nobody could reach them right now. Not here.

It was winter in Antarctica.

That meant Vostok was locked in the most inhospitable place on earth, shrouded in a 24-hour-a-day permanent darkness, with icy winds that could kill a person within minutes. The swelling sea ice that surrounded the continent grew, doubling its landmass in the winter and prohibited even the strongest steel ships, the massive icebreakers designed for such a region, from reaching any harbor. The frigid air was so cold, and the runways so dark, it became nearly impossible for any aircraft to reach the continent, let alone land or takeoff again.

It was this absolute isolation that she loved most about the place.

Gunfire outside Vostok in the dead of winter?

Impossible.

A moment later, a round of bullets came through the doorway, landing just shy of her head. It was only luck that none of them hit her right between the eyes. She hardly registered the mild noise the bullets made as they zipped past her face and lodged in the heavily insulated wall behind her.

Primed by her primitive, lizard brain, Anastasia Utkin was the first to react. She ducked down beneath her desk. Taking refuge, she concealed herself at the very back of the alcove traditionally reserved for one's feet, and hoping to hell no one came close enough to notice her.

The door opened.

She could hear Pavel's voice. "Who the hell are you?"

"*Bonjour,*" a man replied.

"What is the meaning of this?" Pavel asked.

No answer was given.

Instead, she heard someone open fire.

The wash of bullets that followed ripped through the science room with the clack-clacking speed of a propeller in a Red Bull air race.

The shooter fired a series of short bursts at each person. Nikolay and Constantine swore as they tried to move away from their desks, but were mowed down before they could even cry out. A narrow grouping landed on Pavel's torso. He fell forward, twisting onto his back, and landing just behind Anastasia. His face, animated just seconds earlier, was now lifeless. His open eyes stared vacantly at the ceiling.

The shooting stopped.

Heavy footsteps followed, as someone stepped into the room.

Anastasia pulled her knees to her chest, crouching in a ball, thankful for the first time in her life for her small stature and petite frame. Blood hammered in the back of her ears, but she held her breath, terrified that any sound might give her away.

A man's voice called, "*Dégager*."

The single word was spoken in French and meant, "Clear." The man walked through the computer room, and out through the next door, into the biolabs, where water samples from the Vostok Lake were still being analyzed. He was followed by another two men. Dressed as winter soldiers, they wore white balaclavas, snow jackets, and were carrying weapons with a short barrel and one of those over-sized ammunition magazines.

Anastasia assumed they were submachine guns. These men and their weapons looked like they belonged in a bad action film from the 1980s in Hollywood – not the Antarctic.

All three men passed through the computer room into the biolabs without taking a cursory glance in her direction. They looked confident, efficient, and nonplussed. Why wouldn't they be? They were clearly professional soldiers, armed with military weapons, attacking a remote research station filled with unarmed polar scientists.

Anastasia froze, unable to move.

Carefully, she drew in a shallow breath.

Two more bursts of shots rang out in the biolabs. She pictured Alyona studying her water samples, concentrating on the finely detailed microscopic world through her slides. With her AirPods playing heavy metal, she would have shut out her external world, allowing her to concentrate on the microscopic one instead. Unaware of the massacre taking place, she had likely just been shot dead.

It was enough to shake Anastasia out of her stupor.

Coming out of shock from the initial attack, her prefrontal cortex suddenly came to life. Specializing in a person's cold, unemotional, and rational thought processes, it was here that her immediate needs came to light. A team of elite soldiers were inside Vostok. They wanted to execute every scientist.

If they found her, they would kill her.

Ergo, she needed to get the hell out of Vostok.

Her eyes furtively darted toward the door leading toward the biolab. No one was there. She could hear the sound of someone tapping away at the keyboard of one of the bio-computers. Whoever they were, they knew exactly where to find what they were after.

She took a deep breath.

Anastasia quietly crawled out from under the desk, and made her way back through the living quarters. Running on pure adrenaline, she didn't even glance at any of her dead colleagues, many of whom she'd spent the past three months living, and working alongside.

Then she heard heavy footsteps echoing through Module B.

She pictured the attackers making their way through the engineer module with its labyrinthine network of metal steps and platforms that spread like spider-like lattice over the electric generators, boiler, and water treatment systems.

The engineering module was unoccupied.

That meant it wouldn't take long for her assailants to get through the northern most end of the Vostok Station. How long after that before they turned around for a second sweep through the research labs? No, she needed to get going.

Right now!

Anastasia stood up, and began to move quickly.

She tread as softly as possible. Placing each heal down first, and slowly rolling her feet toward her toes along the outer edges of her shoes, she made her way south through the living quarters that made up the rest of Module B. She passed the medical labs, which included a make-shift operating theater.

Fighting against her will to run, she stepped inside and retrieved an Iridium satellite phone, charging on the wall. It was unlikely to save her life. A rescue mission would take days if not weeks for anyone to come get her out of this mess. But that didn't matter, she only needed the satellite phone to make one, vitally important call…

Then she could die.

Besides, she would feel better that someone knew what really happened here. Better than waiting until the end of the Antarctic winter, and far better than the other possibility – that no one would ever find out about the attack on Vostok. That their bodies, removed after death, would be replaced by a permanent mystery for their loved ones.

Sitting next to the satellite phone, she grabbed a small, red medical bag with a large white cross. It contained the basic equipment needed to save a person's life under normal situations, including a portable defibrillator, an array of drugs, needles, and trauma dressing. She strapped the bag onto her shoulders and kept going without giving it much thought.

For some reason, she felt better about having it with her. Like some kind of innate, altruistic urge made her do it in the off chance she was still capable of saving just one of her colleague's lives. But that thought seemed doubtful. She'd watched firsthand what her attackers could do. They weren't spraying the scientific grounds with bullets indiscriminately. They were professionals, working each room systematically, and making perfect kill shots.

She passed through into Module C.

This was the living and leisure quarters.

In the mess room, Vlad lay dead, slumped backward in his chair, a modern spy-thriller open next to his untouched dinner on the table in front of him. There was a closely knitted array of bullet-holes that no longer bled from the center of his chest. Congealing blood pooled beneath the table. At a glance, she knew he was dead.

She kept going.

Past the gymnasium.

Orlov lay dead on the bench press rack, a heavily loaded bar compressed across his bloodied chest, his eyes staring upward. She shook her head and kept walking, her brain barely able to comprehend her new reality.

Anastasia stopped at the sauna.

Her good friend, Mila, a double PhD graduate from Moscow Institute of Physics and Technology, who maintained overall authority and command of the Vostok Research Station, sat inside the heated sauna. The thick, insulated door was closed and undamaged. Through the small glass window, Anastasia spotted her friend's face. She wore expensive, American made, noise-cancelling headphones. Her eyes were shut, and she looked like someone enjoying their much-needed Rest and Relaxation time.

Anastasia's heart made a double beat.

Could Mila have survived, blithely unaware of the attack unfolding around her beloved research station?

Anastasia opened the door.

"Mila," she whispered.

But the physicist didn't move.

Anastasia's eyes landed on the small grouping of bullet holes at her friend's lower chest. She swallowed down the fear that rose like bile in her throat, and turned around. She had seen enough. Whoever these people were, one thing was certain, they were experts who had moved quickly and efficiently, killing everyone in each module.

It wouldn't take them long to reach the end of the research station, and then how much longer before they doubled back and found her? No, she needed to get away before they returned.

Anastasia kept moving.

She crossed through Module C into D, which housed the second engineering Module, including the electric generator, boiler, and technical rooms. Her pace remained constant, not stopping to search any of the workstations for survivors.

Anastasia crossed the bridge into Module E, which was basically an oversized garage, used to house the heavy machinery used for drilling core samples, along with a small fleet of snow vehicles. If she could reach one of them, and open the doorway, she might just get away. Carefully and silently, she closed the door behind her. Taking stock, she stared at a couple of snowmobiles, and four PistenBully 300 Polar-Antarctic vehicles, two Tucker Snow Cats, lined up in a row. A red, Antonov An-2, single propeller, biplane from the 1940s was parked at the very back of the garage. The antique aircraft was reliable, even in the extreme cold of Antarctica. It was stored for emergency medical evacuations. Just what she needed right now, if only she could fly the damned thing.

Escape…

It was the first time she'd considered the thought long enough to contemplate her next move. She glanced at her watch. Only a measly eight minutes had passed since the attack had commenced on the Vostok Research Station. Eight minutes since all her colleagues had been killed.

Running on adrenaline alone, driven by that powerful, autonomic response known as flight or fight, all she had been doing was trying to escape. But now, she had to consider where she would go. Vostok was the coldest, driest and most geographically isolated place on the planet. All snow vehicles here were slow moving, designed to overcome the substantial obstacles of the Antarctic landscape by using heavy metal caterpillar tracks.

Powerful but slow.

No way was she going to be outrunning anyone in one of those.

She considered the snowmobiles, however they weren't going to be much use to her. They were light and nimble but carried minimal fuel. Certainly nowhere near enough to reach the Mirny Research Station and Vostok's supply station on the Devis Sea some 600 miles away.

Where would she go?

Even if she hid somewhere for a while, there was nothing to suggest that whoever attacked them would be leaving anytime soon. What if they planned to stay there for a week or longer? Then what would she do? Stay out in the icy plains and freeze to death long before she starved? No, given the hostility of an Antarctic winter, there wasn't any chance of rescue, even if she was able to get a call to the outside world.

No, she needed a more permanent plan for escape.

She ran her eyes along the array of expertly parked heavy machinery in the garage of Module E, dismissing each vehicle for its unsuitability, before eventually landing on a Kharkovchanka.

The machine was a relic from the 1960s.

Its name literally meant "Woman of Kharkov" and was the first Antarctic off-road vehicle made in the Soviet Union, designed and built by the Kharkov Transport Engineering Plant. It was based on the AT-T tractor platform, which was itself based on the T-54 tank. In December 1959 two of them, number 21 and 23 were delivered to Antarctica and reached the South Pole. Number 23 was lost down a giant crevasse, but 21 had ended up at Vostok, where Nikolay, their chief mechanical engineer had spent the last two years restoring the historical vehicle out of love.

She stared at the machine with a newfound interest.

The massive off-road snow vehicle had a small galley, toilet, oven, and eight beds. She could load it with food supplies and use it to escape across the Antarctic all the way to the coast.

Anastasia opened a supply cupboard at the end of the room, and retrieved a large backpack filled with MREs – Meals Ready to Eat – ration packs, or Ratpacks. They were brought in by bulk from a supply company that served the US, French, Australian, German, and Russian bases.

She stepped across to the massive Kharkovchanka and climbed the external ladder, putting her feet on the steel caterpillar tracks to help her. It was like climbing into one of those oversized mining vehicles, with a large grab bar on the side to hold on as you worked the door handle. She pulled on the seventy-something-year-old latch and the heavily insulated door swung open. Anastasia tossed the bag of ratpacks inside, followed by the medical kit. Then she clambered in, closing the door behind her.

The hatchway opened to the driving compartment. A big, oversized chair was placed behind a large steering wheel that gave it the appearance of one of those RVs the Americans seemed so fond of, like a Winnebago or Jayco. Behind which, were two bunkbeds, followed by a small doorway that extended into the dark, internal living spaces of the vehicle.

She threw the ratpacks on the bunk bed along with the medical kit, and then went to find the fuse board that housed all the switches.

It was at the back wall of the polar exploration vehicle.

Anastasia opened the orange, metal cover that protected the fuse box. A small array of switches, not too dissimilar to what one would find on the side of their house, lined the internal wall in a neat little row.

She found the one labeled "Master" and flipped it to "On."

The background light to the various controls oozed a faint yellow glow as the Kharkovchanka slowly came awake from its frozen hibernation.

Anastasia ran her eyes across the various switches, turning on the internal heating, and intentionally leaving the cabin lighting set to "Off." Next, she found the main battery switch, and turned the dial until it directed both primary house batteries toward the starter motor.

She was ready to go up-front and start the monstrous polar vehicle. It only took a few seconds to navigate through the narrow compartment ways, across a steel grate, and into the driver's compartment. At the controls, she scanned the instruments. They were rudimentary with just three gauges. A Speedometer, Fuel Gauge, and an Oil Temperature indicator. A single starter button appeared to the right of the instrument consoles.

Anastasia reached toward it, ready to start the vehicle.

Her fingers nearly touching.

At the last moment, her fingers stopped.

Her ears, sharpened with fear and primitively attuned to any sound that might indicate danger, heard footsteps outside the Kharkovchanka, where someone opened the door to the garage of Module E.

Heavy footsteps followed.

Anastasia carefully slid the internal latch that locked the Kharkovchanka's only external hatchway, and then silently slipped into the hidden living quarters at the very back of the vehicle. She made a silent prayer that she hadn't yet switched on the Kharkovchanka's power. To anyone searching the garage, the Kharkovchanka would appear to be the seventy-year-old relic, and the last vehicle anyone would choose to use to escape.

A man spoke loud and clear. *"Nous vous trouverons partout où vous vous cachez..."*

Translated, he said, "We will find you wherever you hide..."

Chapter Two

Drake Passage – 300 Miles South of Argentina

Sam Reilly felt the aircraft drop with a sudden jolt.

Inside the massive cargo hold of the US Air Force Lockheed C-5M Super Galaxy, he sat upright and listened to the four GE CF6-80C2 turbofan engines change pitch, drawing every bit of their 50,580 pounds of thrust, as the pilot nosed up, gaining altitude. The entire aircraft buffeted from violent turbulence, and the not-so-tiny high-frequency disruptions in airflow that sent shock wave oscillations through the aluminum frame. The aircraft, he knew, was built for it. Still, it was still taking one hell of a beating.

Suddenly, the entire world lit up with a lightning-like flashing explosion.

It was followed by a simultaneous clap of thunder, which echoed throughout the cavernous hold. There were no windows within the cargo bay, but as the entire aircraft shuddered Sam could imagine the pilots fighting to climb out of one hell of a cumulonimbus for which the Drake Passage was renowned.

The Super Galaxy continued to climb.

Its entire body buffeting and shuddering, the aircraft's high strength aluminum alloy frame vibrated like a rocket before takeoff. The high-frequency instability came from airflow separation or shock wave oscillations from one object striking another. A random forced vibration, it was caused by the sudden thrust of increasing load. Generally, this affects the tail unit of the aircraft structure due to air flow downstream of the wing.

Sam pictured the cumulonimbus clouds outside. Those menacing, multi-level clouds, extending high into the sky in towers or plumes. Colloquially, they were known as thunderclouds – the only type capable of producing hail, thunder, and lightning. He imagined the chaotic and capricious eddies of air like threads of rising smoke, breaking up into ever more disorganized swirls.

And then they were out of it.

The Super Galaxy broke free of the disturbed air. The pilots leveled out and once more the only sound to permeate the cargo hold was the constant, reassuring drone of the engines.

Sam blinked away the grogginess in his eyes from what little hours of sleep he'd managed to achieve on the long flight. Next to him, along a row of fold down seats that hugged the side of the fuselage, were the rest of his team of stow-aways.

Elise, one of the greatest computer whizzes and hackers alive, adjusted her position to keep her open laptop from falling off her knees as she worked to establish current satellite data of the region. Next to her, was Tom, Sam's right-hand man, who, despite the violent turbulence as they traveled through the Drake Passage, remained sound asleep. Genevieve, Sam's weapons expert, appeared more concerned by the weather, but kept working on oiling a series of weapons, ensuring they were ready for the harsh, icy environments in which they were about to be employed.

At the end of the row was Hu Qingli.

He was casually reading a well fingered copy of Sun Tzu's Art of War.

Qingli was the newest member of their team. He had descended from the 75 generations of Youxia, who had sworn to protect the ancient burial tomb of the first Chinese Emperor, Qin Shi Huang and prevent the deadly element known as Dragon's Breath from being released upon the world. He had dedicated his life to the protection of Dragon's Breath, studying philosophy and the art of fighting with both traditional and modern weapons. After the destruction of the last piece of Dragon's Breath, he felt at a loss for what to do with his life. It was Sam's idea, that Qingli join his team and as he watched him now, Sam knew he'd made the right choice, for Qingli's talents could be put to good use.

The plane shifted again, leveling out above the turbulent pocket of air.

His eyes took in a cursory glance of his surroundings. The internal cargo hold was what interior decorators might call spartan functional. Despite its cavernous dimension of 120 feet in length, 19 feet in height, and 13.4 feet in width, the walls were stripped bare, with minimal insulation and an array of wiring and hydraulics clearly visible along the aluminum frame. It could accommodate up to thirty-six 463L Master

Pallets – the standardized pallet for airlifted cargo – or a mix of palletized cargo and vehicles. The nose and aft cargo-bay doors could be opened the full width and height of the cargo bay to maximize efficient loading of oversized equipment. Full-width ramps enable loading double rows of vehicles from either end of the cargo hold.

Over the years, Sam had seen the C-5 Galaxy move just about every type of military combat equipment imaginable, including bulky items such as the Army armored vehicle launched bridge, at 74 short tons, from the United States to any location on the globe, or another time, six Boeing AH-64 Apache helicopters or five Bradley Fighting Vehicles at one time. The flying machine was, without doubt, a monster transporter.

The military carrier was operated by a crew of seven, including two pilots, two flight engineers, and three loadmasters. They were enroute from Hawaii to the Amundsen–Scott South Pole Station, Antarctica under the auspices of transporting a series of supplies. The flight came under the heading of Operation Deep Freeze, an historic codename by the US Air Force for any mission operating in Antarctica.

Fifteen 463L Master Pallets, carrying food and supplies for scientists working at the Amundsen–Scott South Pole Station lined the cargo hold, along with a specialist ice drilling machine, and the engine for a bulldozer. At the very back of the cargo bay, parked at the very tail end of the aircraft, and facing outward, almost as an afterthought, was a hovercraft. Painted white, it had a matching rubber skirt, with an equally bland four-bladed propeller at the back of the machine.

Painted along the side of the hull were the words, *Global One Antarctic Relay Team.*

Inside, the hovercraft was big enough to carry Sam's five-person team, along with enough fuel to reach the Vostok Research Station. Elise had set up a website, including social media feeds, which had been superimposed on older accounts in order to make the entire set up appear like legitimate posts from earlier. It even included a YouTube channel that showcased the events of the past few weeks of the crossing.

The end result was that it appeared that Sam Reilly was heading up a winter arctic relay team to break the record for the fastest land-crossing of Antarctica in winter.

As of today, the websites all indicated that the relay team were in trouble and needed assistance. Elise had utilized a top-grade social media trending company to control the story, until it had progressed from an artificially trending to an organically viral story. They had uploaded videos via their satellite phone, showing their hovercraft had been involved in an accident, causing it to roll. They had fortunately survived the crash, but were in the process of limping into Russia's Vostok Research Station for medical assistance.

Sam opened his laptop and kept working.

He read through the dossier containing the background on the Vostok Research Station, along with the various data collated about the unfolding discovery that would inevitably lead to a disaster.

Researchers working at Vostok Station produced one of the world's longest ice cores in 1998. A joint Russian, French, and United States team drilled and analyzed the core, which was 11,886 ft long. Ice samples from cores drilled close to the top of the lake have been assessed to be as old as 420,000 years. The assumption is that the lake has been sealed from the surface since the ice sheet was formed 15 million years ago.

Drilling of the core was deliberately halted roughly 300 feet above the suspected boundary between the ice sheet and the liquid waters of the lake. This was to prevent contamination of the lake with the 60-ton column of freon and kerosene used to prevent the borehole from collapsing and freezing over.

A moratorium on further drilling until a means of doing so without contaminating the lake had been in place ever since, and the Vostok Project had been mothballed.

At the end of last summer, the head of the Russian Antarctic Expedition made a statement that they had reached the last fifty feet of ice. The researchers then switched to a new thermal drill head with a "clean" silicone oil fluid to drill the rest of the way. Instead of drilling all the way into the water, they said they would stop just above it when a sensor on the thermal drill detected free water. At that point, the drill was to be stopped and extracted from the bore hole. Removal of the drill would lower the pressure beneath it, drawing water into the hole to be left to freeze, creating a plug of ice in the bottom of the hole. Drilling stopped at a depth of 12,200 ft so that the research team could make it off the ice before the beginning of the Antarctic winter season.

In the wake of this plan, the following summer, the team was to drill down again to take a sample of that ice and analyze it. The Russians resumed drilling into the lake and reached the upper surface of the water. The researchers allowed the rushing lake water to freeze within the bore hole and months later, they collected ice core samples of this newly formed ice and sent it to the Laboratory for Glaciology and Environmental Geophysics in Grenoble, France, for analysis.

The results of that report showed a hidden eco-system thriving in marine life, locked some two miles below the surface, and protected from the atmosphere for more than 15 million years.

The discovery was fascinating from a biological and evolutionary perspective.

Astrobiologists, who studied the possibility of life on other planets went berserk, arguing this was proof that life almost certainly might exist on planets with similar unique frozen environments, such as Uranus and Neptune, which are filled with "icy" materials like water, ammonia, and methane, under incredible heat and pressure. Or even Saturn's moon Enceladus and Jupiter's moon Europa, which both appear to have salty, liquid oceans covered with thick layers of ice at the surface, and volcano-like geysers that routinely erupt with ice.

Yet, it was the chemical composition found within the water which had really sent the scientific, and military communities into a frenzy. They had found trace elements of aluminum, copper, magnesium, manganese, silicon, tin, nickel and zinc. According to the think tanks advising the Department of Defense, although all of those elements occur naturally, the unique composition was most commonly found in one specific industry...

Aerospace.

In the absence of other information, every nation privy to that report was currently asking the same question...

Did lake Vostok hold the remnants of extraterrestrials? Perhaps even a 15-million-year-old spacecraft? And if so, what were they willing to do to secure it for themselves?

Chapter Three

Gengenbach, Germany

He's nearby here, somewhere.

Detective Tobias Fischer was certain. He knew it. He could almost sense the psychopath living among the picturesque medieval villages in rural Germany. The man was a ghost, but Tobias had been hunting him for a long time, and he'd learned that even ghosts leave trails. He had a feel for how the man thought, how he acted, and what sort of things he might like. And this was just the right place for The Ghost to bring her.

It had become an unhealthy obsession.

Cost him his marriage.

That cost him his kids who were old enough to judge him like the schmuck he was. It led him to a string of antisocial behaviors. Loneliness, which led to prostitution, which only served to lead him to a greater dissatisfaction in life, and further loneliness. It made him mourn the loss of the things that had been good in his otherwise unhappy marriage.

Of course, he'd tried seeing a psychologist.

The Bundespolizei – Federal Police Force – practically insisted on it. But it did no good. What the hell did a thirty-something year old psychologist, barely out of university know about what he was going through? How could she help him come to terms with the fact that he'd been tracking a serial killer for more than a decade? That just once, he'd almost caught the guy. The man – if it even was a man – had slipped away.

Tobias had him backed against a cliff.

He should have shot him dead.

But, in Germany, along with the rest of the civilized world... even criminals have rights, and shooting someone with their hands up, was a crime.

The psychopath had turned at the last minute and dived into the Upper Danube River.

Police divers searched that river for weeks, but the body never turned up. Neither did any of the bodies of the twenty-three young women who kept going missing. Every one of them was young. Beautiful. With their whole lives ahead of them. It was suspected that the perp ran some type of sex-trade syndicate for wealthy people. But unlike so many sex-trafficking systems around the world which prey on the weak and vulnerable, this one seemed to focus specifically on high profile women from rich, well supported families in Europe. Daughters of prominent businessmen, politicians, celebrities. You name it, they were part of the list of women who went missing. Age wasn't really a thing, too. A lot of them were eighteen to mid-twenties. But some were thirty or forty.

None of them were under eighteen.

That was the one thing The Ghost had going for him. He never touched children. Go figure.

Detective Fischer felt the pain of every single one of the victims, as if he were personally responsible for their loss. After all, if only he'd just taken that damned shot, every one of them would still be around today, living whatever extraordinary lives they were supposed to live.

There was only one victim who ever escaped.

A Russian woman.

The daughter of a senior politician.

He tried to interview her, but she shut him down and refused to talk. She asked if he was holding her as suspect. He told her he wasn't. She then just up and left the precinct. He tried to follow her, but she disappeared and like her captor, became a ghost. There was no sign of where she went. Her Russian passport hadn't been used to leave the country.

Nothing.

She too, was a ghost.

In turn, like so many cops before him, Fischer took to the bottle. Alcoholism barely served to keep his demons under control, so he'd progressed to a wide swathe of prescription medications to help take the edge off things. Sleeping tablets. Antidepressants. Even stronger medications. All of it.

Unfortunately, these coping mechanisms didn't work too well with the job. In the end, the legal stuff became inadequate for his needs. Recently he turned to illegal drugs. Amphetamines to keep him alert when he needed to be. Opioids when he needed to switch off from reality.

All in all, he knew his life had become pretty much one lousy mess.

But none of that mattered.

Because, if he was right about this place...

Hannah Zimmerman, who had been abducted twelve hours earlier, might still be alive.

The charcoal Audi A6 Quattro unmarked police car drove along the 294 Motorway as it hugged the Kinzig River. At the wheel, Tobias was alert, searching the verdant countryside, as though he alone might just spot the offender.

Even he knew it was unlikely.

But dammit.

This was the first time in more than a decade of chasing his tail that they had managed to get lucky. There was no way he was going to let the monster slip through his net again.

Sitting in the passenger seat next to him was his "partner" Andrea Jordan. She had been forced on him. She wasn't even a real cop for God's sake. She was a criminologist with a PhD in profiling. Twenty-something years old, she was a vivacious brunette that perpetually seemed far too happy and much too excited to be on the case. To him, she felt like a kid he was obliged to look after. Then again, she was almost certainly younger than any of his kids, so maybe there was something in that too. Fischer didn't know. But the big brass had told him he needed her and that he could thank them later.

This case was by far too high profile for him to say no.

Hannah Zimmerman was an 18-year-old French beauty. Her uncle was a wealthy merchant banker who specialized and brokered in the Russian-German oil and gas trade. He'd spent a huge proportion of his wealth supporting her father, Mykel Zimmerman, to become the German Chancellor three years ago. Her father had lost at the elections, but retained his position as an MP in the Bundestag, and his portfolio of Minister of Defense and Aerospace. Hannah's mother was Vivienne Laurent – as in the famous actress and Europe's undisputed sexiest woman alive.

And Hannah was a spitting image of her mother at that age.

That's how they had gotten lucky.

A homeless drunk, searching for food scraps in a dumpster in Waldshut-Tiengen, swore he spotted Vivienne Laurent getting dragged from a car into a yellow DHL delivery van, and called it in. Said he would have remembered that flock of red ringlets anywhere. The driver wore one of those athletic hoodies, Nike or Adidas, and looked like he'd been out for a run. The only thing he could recall about the driver was that he had creepy, gold eyes… whatever the hell that meant? He also reported a partial license plate number. The first three letters.

GFH

Although, he wasn't even sure about that. He thought possibly they were in the other order, *HFG*. Said he was pretty confident the F was in the middle, but that's about it.

Tobias had contacted DHL who had reported two delivery vans stolen this week with license plates starting with the letters GF, but none with an H.

All in all, it was something, but not a lot.

The homeless guy didn't even know what direction the yellow DHL van headed.

This brought in Andrea Jordan, criminal profiler and rising star, with what sometimes appeared to be little more than a pseudoscience, capable of predicting a serial killer's next move. In this case, Andrea matched the last known location of the DHL van, and then identified areas that such a person would want to take his victims.

She came up with several possibilities.

But the little town of Schiltach, set on the eastern side of the Black Forest, at the confluence of the Schiltach and Kinzig rivers seemed just about the most likely of all of them. As he drove south, following the Kinzig River, he had to admit, he tended to agree with her. The area was classed as rural. There were a few small estates, but for the most part, the houses were set back on large blocks, with plenty of privacy.

Just what every predator desires in their real estate.

So, instead of running everything from the Special Operations headquarters, Tobias and Andrea had jumped in an unmarked patrol car and raced to the countryside, where they could take phone calls and issue orders while patrolling. Every set of eyes helped.

They entered the quaint, idyllic town of Schiltach.

The Schiltach confluence flowed beside the main street, lined with flowerbeds of red and white flowers. The water sparkled and ducks played merrily under darkening clouds. Rows of three-story white houses with terracotta roofs popped up sporadically along the river, behind which was a mountainous forest of conifer trees that disappeared far into the ominously dark sky.

A few seconds later, there was a crack of thunder, and the threatening heavens made good on their promise. Sheets of water fell from the sky. Thick pellets of rain splattered the windshield making it impossible to clearly see the streets. The Audi's automatic headlights switched on.

Detective Tobias Fischer shook his head. He just couldn't get a break with this guy. This is just what they need to assist their hunt! He set the windshield wipers to work on the heavy raindrops.

He wasn't impressed. Dumped with a kid straight out of the academy, while following his closest lead in a decade for a serial killer who had haunted his dreams. Andrea was vivacious and tenacious, always trying to make chitchat that he didn't appreciate. Nothing seemed to shut her down.

"So tell me… Toby, how long you been a cop?"

"It's Tobias…"

"Okay, Tobias."

"Only my friends call me Toby." He suppressed a grin. Maybe he was being a touch hard on her. It wasn't her fault the Police Force had given him a kid to catch a killer. "And I've been a cop since you were learning to walk."

She rolled her eyes. "Tobias. I'll keep that in mind."

He continued driving in silence. The rain eased, and infrequent beams of sunlight began to break through the clouds.

After a few minutes, she said, "You know… I realize you're not too happy about me being here, but I do have a PhD in criminology, and I've spent the last ten years becoming an expert in profiling. Do you even have a degree?"

He made a theatrical sigh.

Didn't look at her, even once.

Then he shrugged. "Yeah, well, the whole time while you were learning to catch criminals, I was out here trying to catch this asshole."

Her mouth was set in a hard line. Full of defiance. The edges just slightly curved up, like she wasn't quite sure if she should be taunting the snake. "Yeah, well how did that work out for you? Maybe that's why the brass brought a kid in here to use modern policing techniques based on forensic sciences that were on this side of the millennium."

Tobias opened his mouth to give a retort, but was interrupted...

Ping. Ping. Ping.

The ALPR sounds on the dashboard of their unmarked patrol car. The Automated License Plate Reader was a high-speed, computer-controlled camera system. In addition to their vehicle, they were also mounted on street poles, streetlights, highway overpasses, mobile trailers, and all police squad cars. ALPRs automatically capture all license plate numbers that come into view, along with the location, date, and time. The data, which includes photographs of the vehicle and sometimes its driver and passengers, is then uploaded to a central server.

It was set to specifically search for any configuration of a license plate starting with *GFH.*

The computer mounted on the dashboard flashed red.

A hit.

Andrea leaned forward in the passenger seat and checked it, hitting the silence button in the process.

Tobias frowned. "No luck?"

She shook her head. "False alarm."

The automatic license plate readers aren't perfect. Es are often mistaken for Fs, Os are mistaken for Ds, Ls for Is, etc.

It's all just a game of luck.

They were searching for the veritable needle in a haystack.

Tobias kept driving.

When they reached the end of Schiltach, he looked to Andrea. "What do you think? Do we circle back or keep heading southeast on to Dunnigen?"

Andrea bit the top of her lip. "There's a dirt road that comes off the main street and leads to several homesteads dispersed through the conifer forest. Each one is set on acreage. What about driving there?"

Tobias frowned. "That's what... five... six houses? Seems unlikely to me."

"Sure, but so does the rest of this. We've got patrol cars at each town along the way. If something comes by, they'll pick it up. Let's clear Schiltach."

"All right, sure."

Tobias hit the blinker and turned left onto the unmarked, narrow dirt road. The laneway was hooded by tall pine trees. They passed a couple private driveways that led to large, gothic style houses. Dark storm clouds still flooded the sky, and what light managed to get past was stopped by the massive trees surrounding them.

The dirt road ended with a large, electronic gate. It must have been at least ten feet high, and built of wrought iron. Twin sandstone gargoyles, bigger than an adult, stood watch over the gate. Tobias ran his eyes left and right. The fence was made of solid sandstone blocks some ten feet high. The gravel driveway continued deep into the recess of the large block, lined by rows of pine trees, before reaching a three-story gothic house.

While the house looked medieval on the outside, that's where any semblance of 16th century architecture ended. Tobias could spot not less than six motion-detected cameras that traced his Audi, as it approached the gate. This was far more security than one could possibly need for a country house set deep in rural Germany.

Tobias exchanged a glance with Andrea. "What do you think?"

She shrugged. "Someone's a little security conscious."

"I'll say."

"It's not a crime, you know?"

"Yeah. Neither's keeping a secluded property."

Andrea smiled. "I'm hearing you. If I wanted to keep abducted women somewhere, this place certainly ticks all the boxes."

Tobias eased the Audi up to the gate.

Andrea said, "What are you doing?"

"Seeing if we're right." Tobias opened his side window and pressed the intercom button.

The electronic bell rang several times and then stopped.

Tobias shrugged and pressed it again.

Andrea laughed. "What? You think they didn't hear you the first time?"

"I don't know."

The rain began to fall harder once more, and the windshield wipers went up another notch. An ice-cold wind blew through the open window, and Tobias quickly closed it again.

He shifted the Audi into reverse and made a three point turn on the narrow dirt road. Returning back the way they had come, they came face-to-face with a red van.

The ALPR pinged.

The license plate didn't start with anything even close to *GFH*. And it wasn't a yellow DHL delivery van either. It was red with heavily tinted windows.

But the guy driving it was in a gray, Nike hoody.

Tobias stopped the Audi.

He threw it in park and pressed the hazard lights, leaving his vehicle stopped dead-set right in the middle of the narrow dirt road. Just to see what the driver of the van would do.

The driver slowed nearly to a complete stop.

His eyes fixed straight ahead, as though he hadn't seen them, or didn't want to acknowledge their existence.

Tobias looked up at the driver, perched in the van, as he slowly maneuvered around them. Its tires crunching the thick foliage of pine needles as it went by. The man was close enough that if their windows were open, he could have reached out and touched the guy.

The driver's eyes were fixed up ahead.

But there was no mistaking it. He had, for want of a better word, creepy, deep-set eyes of an unusual pale green color with flakes of gold.

Tobias inadvertently held his breath.

A second later the moment had passed.

He exhaled.

Turning to Andrea. "Any chance that guy's just an asshole, unwilling to stop and help out a stranger?"

"No, way!" She shook her head. "That's our guy."

Tobias threw the gear into drive, planted his foot on the accelerator, and made a sharp U-turn. Up ahead, the driver of the red van gunned the engine, and sped off down the narrow dirt road.

And Tobias hit the gas.

There wasn't a snowballs chance in hell that he was going to let this monster escape a second time.

Chapter Four

Sam watched Tom sit up and stretch from the impossibly tight position he had managed to squeeze his six-foot-four frame into. Tom rolled over, and looked at Sam.

Tom's voice was gravelly. "We there yet?"

"Nearly," Sam said with a smile. "Did that earth shattering turbulence finally wake you?"

Tom tilted his head, cracked his neck, and spread his arms. "Turbulence? What turbulence? I just got hungry, that's all."

Sam laughed. "Only you."

"Right," Tom peeled back the aluminum seal on a ratpack, dipped the attached spoon into the mess, and started eating without any apparent interest in what was inside. He took a couple bites, and then sat down next to Sam, giving his laptop a cursory glance. "Did you find out anything more about what's happening in Vostok?"

"Not yet. Apparently, the Russian scientists have found trace elements of aluminum, copper, magnesium, manganese, silicon, tin, nickel and zinc in Lake Vostok."

Tom shrugged. "Any chance those elements naturally occur in these parts."

Sam cocked an eyebrow. "And through some sort of rare geological event all of them have melted together to form one of the most prolific alloys used in the aerospace industry?"

"Right, it does seem a little far-fetched."

"More than far-fetched," Sam admitted. "Aircraft manufacturers prefer to use high-strength aluminum alloys – primarily alloy 7075 – to strengthen aluminum aircraft structures. Alloy 7075 has copper, magnesium and zinc added for extra strength. But one of the components found in the water sample is nearly identical to an experimental alloy dubbed GRX-810."

Sam paused, and exchanged a glance with Tom, checking to see if he knew about the material.

Tom returned a somewhat blank expression, then smiled. "Go on."

Sam said, "The alloy, dubbed GRX-810 could revolutionize space travel, according to NASA as it is capable of withstanding far harsher situations than existing materials used in rocket engines. At 1,093 degrees – that's Celsius, not Fahrenheit, by the way – the alloy offered twice the strength in resistance to fracturing, three and a half times the flexibility of what they're using now."

"So, what we're finding down there inside Lake Vostok is our best current aerospace materials?"

Sam nodded. "It's not just an alloy commonly used in the aerospace industry... it's a class known as super alloys, and this one in particular is new. I mean, state of the art, experimental technology. According to the scientists who have examined the data, this might hold a clue that was missing in GRX-810 that would make it roughly ten times as durable."

Tom took another bite of the dark and gluggy mixture of God knows what he'd found in a ratpack designed specifically for those serving in Antarctica. He washed it down with a can of Dr. Pepper he had found in a crate of supplies heading to Amundsen–Scott South Pole Station. "Okay, so if it didn't form naturally, how else did particles from the modern-day aerospace industry find their way into a lake, sealed in ice for more than ten million years?"

"Fifteen," Sam corrected him. He closed his laptop. "Well, there's only one explanation... but I still don't believe it."

"Hey, don't leave me wondering. What do the fine people at the Pentagon think it is?"

Sam drew a breath and sighed. "They've ruled out several probable possibilities, leaving just one, highly improbable one."

Tom met his eye. "Which is?"

"There's a spacecraft down there, preserved by its icy tomb for nearly fifteen million years."

Tom's eyes narrowed. "Do you think it's true?"

"I don't know what I believe yet."

Tom gave a coy smile. "That's surprisingly vague, coming from you, Sam. What are you thinking?"

Sam shrugged. "On one hand, the Secretary receives some of the best intel on the planet. It all filters through the heads of countless departments, trickling down through the eyes and minds of a great many analysis experts, whose job it is to wash away the relevant from the irrelevant, fact from fiction, until eventually, what arrives on the Secretary's desk is generally pretty much pure gold intel."

Tom nodded. He and Margaret Walsh, the Secretary of Defense, went back a long way to a time when his father, now a retired Naval Admiral, Dwight Bower, and she first worked together on a secret experimental submarine program, called Omega Deep. Back when Tom was still a kid. Tom knew just how good the US Secretary of Defense happened to be at her job.

"Okay. And on the other hand?"

Sam nodded. "This report reads like something straight out of a science fiction novel."

Tom said what they were thinking out loud. "A spacecraft resting at the bottom of a subglacial lake, untouched for nearly 15 million years."

"Yeah, like I said, it seems a little far-fetched."

"Yet, if it's true… you can imagine how many nations will try and secure that spacecraft. Alien technology capable of interstellar flight 15 million years ago, could provide a treasure trove of technology."

"Exactly."

Tom said, "Anyone who wields such information might gain an impossible military advantage that will reshape global relations and landscapes with a ferocity unseen since the dawn of civilization. I mean, in terms of research and development boons, this one could put the victor at the sort of advantage equivalence of bringing an Uzi to a duel with a Colt Single Action Army Revolver."

Sam frowned… "More like bringing a nuclear bomb against the spear throwing aboriginals of Australia 75,000 years ago."

"Yeah."

"All right, we're under no misapprehension about the priority of securing that spacecraft."

Tom shook his head. "Just out of interest, how did the Secretary find out about its existence?"

"We have a spy working in the Vostok Research Station."

Tom looked skeptical. "In case they came across a 15-million-year-old spacecraft? It sounds more like Russian propaganda than legitimate intel."

"Yeah, well, that's what we're here to find out."

"Why not ask the spy?"

"We can't. Without being there, it's hard to know whether we're being fed propaganda or not."

"Why do we even have a spy at Vostok?"

"It's a low-level spy. First and foremost, a glacial scientist or geophysicist, or something, I don't know what. We apparently recruited him or her years ago to keep track of Russian scientific developments."

"We do that?"

Sam shrugged with indifference as though the specifics were irrelevant. "Apparently it helps with National Security."

"How many do we have?"

"I don't know. By the way the Secretary of Defense was talking, I guess we have a lot of them."

"Okay. So we have this scientist-cum-spy agent working in Vostok, keeping us up to date with scientific discoveries." Tom paused. "And then when they found the possibility of alien technology…"

Sam nodded. "We hit the jackpot in espionage terms."

"Okay, so who's the spy?"

"We don't know."

Tom laughed. "What do you mean you don't know? How do we make contact with them by turning up under the ruse of a crashed hovercraft?"

"Spies are valuable. Their handlers are careful. It's a dangerous game. To protect our operative, the Pentagon sets up a closed loop system. At every step of the game, there's a lockout."

"Makes sense. You don't want one agent to get captured, only to reveal the location of dozens, if not hundreds of other agents."

"Yeah, something like that."

"Okay, so how do we find this spy?"

"We don't."

"No?"

"No. He or she finds us."

"How?"

"The Pentagon has sent a coded message to the agent at Vostok, informing them that we'll be coming. He or she will make contact with us."

"Right. Let's hope the agent hasn't been compromised, or we're just about to find ourselves in the middle of a deadly trap."

Sam exhaled slowly. The same thought had crossed his mind. "We'll do what we can, but that is definitely a possibility."

Tom asked, "Why doesn't the Pentagon just send in a team of Navy SEALs?"

Sam raised his brow. "To secure a secret discovery made by the Russians?"

Tom sighed theatrically. "I can see how that could be a political nightmare."

"What do you think the Secretary of Defense wants us to do instead?"

"Let me guess." Tom spread his arms. "If there's a spaceship there, then she's happy to risk World War III to retrieve it. If not, she'd rather deny everything and pretend nothing ever happened."

Sam grinned. "And that, my friend, is why we're about to turn up at the Vostok Research Station unannounced, seeking help for our recently crashed hovercraft."

Chapter Five

Inside the Vostok Research Station

In theory, *Hide and Seek* is a primitive response built into our DNA.

It might be a favorite children's game, but it had been played since the dawn of mankind and was built into and programmed into every single one of us, dating from our earliest Hunter-Gatherer days. Back when the winners got to live another day, and the losers became someone else's dinner. We've been primed, like our ancestors to hide and take shelter against predators. Small lessons learned over generations, formed through thousands of years, have been stored in our DNA.

Anastasia couldn't tell you why, but it was these primitive lessons that made her hide underneath the lowest bunkbed in the middle of the Kharkovchanka. Like a child, afraid of monsters in the dark, she took refuge under a bed. She didn't choose the row of three bunks at the very back of the vehicle, or the three at the front. Instead, she picked the ones in the very middle, where her breathing and any sound she made, would have to travel the farthest to be heard outside, and any stray bullets were least likely to land on one of her vital organs.

Outside, she heard the banter in French as what appeared to be three or maybe even four men searched the garage of Module E. She could hear the opening and closing of various doors to bulldozers, snowplows, and drilling machines.

The words turned to Russian. "Come out, come out, wherever you are..."

Her heart accelerated. It felt as though it was beating double time.

Everything went silent for a few minutes.

Anastasia could hear the rush of blood pounding in the back of her head as she imagined her attackers stalking her outside, listening for any sound that might reveal her hiding place. She found herself unintentionally holding her breath.

The quiet hush was heavy and thick.

Finally, and almost mercifully, like a bulldozer plowing through a line of sports cars, the silence exploded into loud, hard pieces as machinegun fire sliced through it.

The bursts of shots were sporadic. The massive dome of Module E echoing with the report of multiple gunshots. She heard some windows shatter, followed by the pinging sound of bullets hitting metal as they whizzed through the air at supersonic speeds.

Anastasia didn't want to die.

She pulled her legs to her chest, and covered her head with her arms in the hope that her position would reduce the likelihood that a stray bullet would hit a vital organ. She was a scientist, and the honest simplicity of mathematics always appealed to her. Yet she was human too, and that meant fear and her need to survive thrived strongly within her. The scientist would admit that her meager attempts to shield her head and vital organs were almost entirely useless, but the human side of her never would.

After a couple of minutes, the firing stopped. Her ears rang, but other than that, she was left in a deep shroud of silence once more. A minute or two later, the raking sound of machine guns started up again. They opened fire, shooting at anything and everything in the garage.

She adjusted her position, compelled to move farther away from the side where the sounds originated.

A small burst of just three bullets ripped through the weak, aluminum shell of the Kharkovchanka, and whizzed past her, leaving three distinct holes in the wall where her head had been just seconds earlier.

Anastasia wanted to scream...

But she held it in.

And the firing stopped once more.

Her heart was pounding in her chest like she'd just run a marathon. She felt compelled to open the single hatch in the Kharkovchanka and run. But that was insane. The sort of thing a bunch of pigeons might do after a dog barked at them, drawing them into the firing line of a bunch of aristocratic hunters.

She forced herself to slow her breathing.

Stay silent...

...and wait.

A full three minutes passed.

A man spoke. *"Allez, elle n'est pas là. Nous avons dû la manquer dans l'un des modules précédents."*

It meant, "Come on, she's not here. We must have missed her in one of the earlier Modules."

Anastasia waited, expecting that to be yet another ruse to draw her out into their line of fire, but as the minutes wore on, she couldn't wait any longer...

She moved to the driving cabin.

There, sitting on the dashboard was a little electronic remote, no different than one might find to activate their own car garage.

She pointed it toward the garage sensor and pressed the button.

A little red light glowed, and the massive garage door creaked, as its hydraulic struts began to compress. The door gave way a few inches and stopped. The garage door's electric engine's pitch went up a notch, the door grinding against some sort of external force, before an internal safety system caused the entire thing to shut down.

Anastasia swore.

She pictured Nikolay on the portable snowplow in the days before opening the garage door for the first time after winter. The process usually took him a couple of days to free the giant door from its icy crypt.

There was no way around it.

She needed a new plan.

Anastasia grabbed her medical kit, throwing in some of the Meals Ready Made, Ratpacks.

Stepping out of the Kharkovchanka a voice came over the Vostok Research Station's speaker system. There was a fast exchange of French between three or possibly even four men. She tried to follow it, but they spoke too fast for her to follow with her limited French. She was only able to get everr third or fourth word.

Vostok Manifest...

Names...

Lists...

Finally, the speaker stopped and someone new began to speak.

He spoke perfect Russian.

"Anastasia Utkin, geophysicist."

This was followed by a short burst of French banter, too fast for her to keep up.

After a minute or two, the man spoke in Russian again. His voice was loud and crisp, like an officer giving out an order to a soldier. "Anastasia Utkin. I am afraid your comrades are all dead. I have Vostok's crew manifest. Every name on that list is now dead, except for you. We know who you are, and we're coming to get you."

Chapter Six

Schiltach Germany

Tobias gunned the Audi A6 Quattro.

The all-wheel drive system kicked up gravel and mud in his wake, as he quickly raced to follow the red van. Hannah Zimmerman had been kidnapped twelve hours ago. If this was the same creepy guy who had abducted her, it meant she might still be alive.

None of The Ghost's other victims were ever found.

Alive or otherwise.

The van was a Mercedes Sprinter. Definitely without its regular cargo, it moved much faster than one would expect. Judging by the ease with which the driver handled the turns and terrain, he must have been local.

Andrea got on the radio. "PolAir19, we have a probable sighting of our suspect. He is in a red van heading east along a dirt road at the southern tip of Schiltach. We're in pursuit and are requesting an airship to help track the vehicle."

"PolAir19. Understood. We're roughly six minutes out from your coordinates and on our way."

"Copy that, ta."

The narrow dirt road made a sharp dog-leg curve, before dipping down and across a shallow ford that crossed a creek feeding the Kinzig River. The van jolted from left to right as its driver fought to prevent the entire truck fishtailing out of control. The Sprinter hit the water at speed, sending a spray of water some twelve feet into the air, before shooting up the crest of the ford.

His foot on the gas, Tobias didn't slow down at all.

He leaned heavily on the Audi Quattro's strong roots in rally car racing, as its all-wheel drive system hugged the dirt road like the rails of a rollercoaster. The wheels struck the ford, and water sprayed across the windshield like a reverse waterfall.

The windshield wipers went up another notch.

They climbed out of the crest and the dirt road straightened out for another few hundred feet, before turning sharply and meandering along the base of the Black Forest. The road began to climb, winding a few hundred feet up the mountainside. It looked like an old service trail that hadn't seen much use in a very long time.

The van didn't slow down.

Andrea put her hand on Tobias. "Give him some room."

"No way," Tobias said, staying right on the Sprinter's taillights. "I'm not letting him get away from me again."

"We won't," she said emphatically. "But if you keep driving this hard, you're likely to force him to crash, and if Hannah's still alive in there, we're just as likely to get her killed in the process."

Tobias struggled not to scream at his youthful partner.

He fought back the urge to tell her that he cared more about capturing the serial killer than saving Hannah's life. He knew that was wrong. But this wasn't about right or wrong. It was about the truth. And the truth was, if he let this guy escape again, maybe another 23 women would end up dead.

No, Tobias intended to get him this time.

He eased off the accelerator.

But Andrea was right.

No point in forcing him to crash.

PolAir19 was already airborne, coming up from Dunnigen. In less than five minutes, they would have overhead visual. They were still in rural Germany. No chance was this guy getting away.

"All right, you're right, I'll give him some breathing space."

He dropped back and watched the van from a distance of ten or so car lengths. They kept following. The van driver must not have gotten the memo. If anything, he somehow managed to speed up. The Audi kept pace with ease.

Tobias exchanged a quick glance with Andrea. "Tell me you have a sidearm?"

"Yeah, a SIG-Sauer P226 9mm. Standard issue." Her tone was abrupt, like she didn't need his damned condescension right now.

"Can you use it?"

"I passed field training."

Tobias arched an eyebrow. "This is about to get very serious. I need to know, can you shoot the damned thing or not?"

She hit the dashboard with her hands. "Yes! I shoot."

"Good."

The dilapidated trail crept back down the mountain. Small temporary streams began to form up ahead, meeting in the middle to form a waterfall that threatened to take out what was left of the road up ahead.

Any minute the whole trail was going to fall like a landslide.

The van driver must have seen it too.

At the last minute, just before the road disappeared, the driver jerked the van to the left, and turned down a very steep trail that ran straight down the mountain.

Tobias' eyes narrowed. "Where the hell does he think he's going?"

"Beats me," Andrea replied. "Maybe he knows something we don't?"

Tobias jammed on the brakes.

The Audi's four wheels dug into the soft soil and Tobias worked hard to keep it from fishtailing off the cliff. He didn't want to follow the van down what appeared to be much too similar to a cliff.

But he was moving too fast to pull up in time.

He was going to have to make a decision.

Through the massive waterfall, or over the cliff?

His brain changed gears.

Up ahead, an eight-foot gash opened up along the dirt trail, where the torrent of water had ripped through the soil, tearing apart its foundations.

A split second later, the entire trail disappeared, taking with it a jagged crater from the mountain along with it. More than a dozen fully grown pines trees fell with the impending destruction.

Tobias swore.

He swerved the Audi perpendicular to the rough roadway, and against his best instincts, followed the van off the near vertical cliff, straight down the mountainside.

The Audi dropped off the cliff, like a skateboarder entering a halfpipe.

Its undercarriage scraped the rocky ground, sending sparks in all directions. Through the downpour streaming across the windshield, Tobias could only just make out the faint outline of the abandoned trail.

All he knew was that it must exist. If the van driver could keep the Mercedes Sprinter upright, the Audi Quattro could do it too.

Beside him, Andrea gripped the sides of her seat so tight her knuckles turned white. Tobias held onto the wheel, gripping it like the frame of a lifeboat. Eyes focused up ahead, he touched the gear paddles behind the wheel, and dropped it down a gear to try and maintain some semblance of traction. His gut seemed to rise, as the ground fell away.

The Audi bounced around, but Tobias somehow managed to keep it upright.

Gaining distance up ahead, the van kept bouncing around the trail, the driver expertly maneuvering it so that the Mercedes Sprinter didn't tip over.

It took no more than ten seconds to reach the plains below.

The trail leveled out, then opened up.

Tobias planted his foot to the floor, and the Audi quickly made up any distance he'd lost over the speeding van.

The dirt trail became more of a road.

Up ahead, the van began to slow down.

Tobias exchanged a glance with Andrea. "What the hell is he doing?"

She tilted her head to the left, her eyes narrowed. "I don't know. Maybe he's got a flat tire, or all those driving stunts he's pulled have ripped out the inner workings of his Sprinter."

He drew a breath and exhaled slowly. "If that's the case, let's just hope he doesn't do anything stupid."

"Yeah, we can only hope."

The van slowed right down to a crawl.

Andrea said, "Give him space."

Tobias eased off the gas. "I will. Just be ready to use that handgun of yours if he tries to make a run for it on foot."

She unclipped the SIG-Sauer P226 9mm from its holster. "He's not getting away."

The trail ran parallel to the Schiltach River. Up ahead, the dirt road intersected with a railway crossing. The tracks crossed the river over a small, iron bridge. There was no sign of a ford or bridge for cars.

The van pulled up to the railway tracks.

Its engine revved hard.

The driver accelerated, the van's tires jumping the small lip between the dirt trail and the iron railway tracks. He turned the wheel to the left, and the van managed to mount the train tracks.

Tobias' eyes narrowed.

He slowed the Audi down, mentally preparing to follow.

The van's tires bounced along the wooden railroad ties, some fifteen feet above the Schiltach River. It was a delicate feat of driving, but the driver of the van had already shown that he wasn't afraid to put the Mercedes Sprinter through its paces. There were no railings or sides to the bridge. Just the train tracks.

Tobias slowed the Audi to a near stop, turned the wheel hard to the left, and gave the accelerator a curt tap. The Quattro all-wheel drive system launched the Audi up and over the iron tracks, spinning the car 90 degrees, and landing onto the wooden railroad ties, two car lengths behind the van.

Andrea face hardened. "Careful now."

"I've got this," Tobias said, his voice full of a confidence he didn't really feel.

Andrea smiled, revealing a perfect set of evenly spaced, white teeth. The tip of her tongue touched her top lip as though she was trying hard not to break into laughter. The van got halfway across the bridge and stopped. She exhaled. "Yeah, I know... you've been chasing the bad guys since I was a kid."

Tobias nodded.

The van came to a complete stop midway across the railway bridge. The mist coming from the exhaust stopped, suggesting the engine had been turned off. Well, shit. This was perfect. Now all they needed was a train.

Tobias pulled the Audi up to a complete stop just before the bridge.

Andrea said, "What the hell is he doing?"

Tobias shook his head. "I've no idea."

They waited for three or four minutes.

Tobias tapped the steering wheel, his eyes never leaving the van. He felt the steady beat of his heart hammering in his chest. The van driver could take all the damned time he liked. They had a clear view of the van on the bridge. No way he was going to sneak out. And PolAir19 was getting close. Nowhere for him to go. If he gets out of the van, he's dead.

Nowhere for him to go, he repeated the thought.

Except in the Schiltach.

His mind returned to that nightmare, nearly a decade earlier, when the same man jumped in the Upper Danube.

Tobias unclipped his seatbelt and withdrew his service pistol.

Not this time.

If the driver as much as steps out of the van, Tobias would take that shot, consequences be damned. If it cost him his job, he could live with that. If it cost him his personal freedom... well, he could live with that too.

Another minute passed.

Andrea opened the door. "Screw this... I'm getting out of the car. You stay here in case he moves."

"Sounds like a plan." Tobias kept the engine running. "And Andrea..."

"Yeah?"

"Be careful."

She smiled. "Sure thing. Dad."

"I mean it."

Andrea grinned, raising the SIG Sauer up into a two-handed firing position toward the van. "I know. I will be."

She closed the door.

A second later, the entire railway line started to vibrate.

The lines across Tobias's face etched deeper into a frown. "Now what?"

Up ahead, far in the distance, the Eurostar approached.

Andrea spotted it at the same time. She turned her hands upward. "What the hell is he doing?"

Tobias shook his head.

Then they both got it.

Simultaneously.

Tobias said, "He going to commit suicide rather than be taken into custody!"

He opened his door and jumped out of the car.

Together they approached the van.

Wind and rain pelted down on them.

Andrea spoke into her portable radio. "Dispatch. Suspect is on the railway bridge crossing at Schiltach. There's an oncoming train. We need to have the Eurostar stopped."

Dispatch acknowledged, but it was unlikely the line of communication could pass down the chain in time to stop the unfolding rail disaster.

She exchanged a glance with Tobias. "What do you want to do?"

"There's still a good chance Hannah Zimmerman's still alive in there." Tobias approached the van. "We have to do something."

"Agreed."

They moved up toward the van.

Tobias motioned to the right. "You go that side, I'll go this side."

The Eurostar kept moving.

Andrea reached the back of the Mercedes Sprinter. She tried the rear door. It was locked. Tobias moved to the driver's side of the van.

No one was visible inside.

"He's going to kill her!" Tobias shouted. "Move, move!"

They both threw caution to the wind.

Tobias tried the driver's door.

Locked.

The train kept coming.

It was getting closer.

Probably too close to stop.

Tobias aimed his SIG Sauer at the driver's window and squeezed the trigger. A small star formed in the fractured glass. He squeezed two more rounds. Another two splinters formed.

He shook his head.

The damned van had bullet-resistant windows.

A man sat up from behind the driver's wheel. He turned to face Tobias. His eyes wide, his lips spread wide with the sardonic grin of a madman.

The driver shook his head and made a tsk, tsk sound.

The loud, train whistle erupted.

It sounded like one of those old-fashioned air horns popular with clowns in the eighties. Tobias' eyes darted between the train and the driver.

The Eurostar was getting close.

The van driver turned the palms of his hands upward, in a gesture of surrender. He seemed to smile harder. *What's a guy gonna do?* Then he mouthed words. "Better go."

The driver turned the key.

The Mercedes Sprinter's twin turbo diesel kicked into life. The driver floored the accelerator and raced off straight toward the oncoming train.

Tobias looked at Andrea and shouted, "Run!"

Tobias and Andrea were closer to the other side of the river than the one with their Audi still parked. They both looked at the oncoming train and made the simultaneous, split decision. There was no way they were making it back to the Audi in time.

With that thought, they bolted toward the far side of the river, running at full speed.

Ahead of them, the van picked up speed.

The driver looked like he was playing chicken with the train. Death by train was just as fatal as death by cop. Judging by the look in the driver's eyes, Tobias doubted he cared one iota whether or not he lived or died.

At the last second, the van reached the far end of the bridge, and swerved.

The train driver blasted its horn.

And Tobias and Andrea jumped.

Another heartbeat passed in silence.

It was broken as the Eurostar collided with their unmarked Audi sending wreckage flying. Erupting in a cacophony of grinding metal and glass, the flash of metal upon metal showered the train in sparks.

Chapter Seven

Tobias hit the water hard.

It was shallow, and his feet slammed into the gravelly riverbed. He kicked equally hard and made his way to the surface, taking a deep breath as soon as he'd cleared the water. His ankles hurt like hell. Sprained at least, but most likely fractured.

But who cares?

He was still alive.

His eyes darted all around him.

The Eurostar was still making that *thump-thump* sound as its wheels softly rocked the wooden railroad ties. It carried on, undisturbed – the Audi barely registering as an impediment in its progress. Then there was a squeal of metal on metal, as the driver pulled the emergency braking system.

Elation turned to terror.

Where was Andrea?

A few seconds later, she surfaced. A little more dazed than himself. Blood coming from a small gash on the side of her forehead.

She was breathing hard.

Her eyes were staring vacantly at him. Some sort of concussion preventing her from focusing on anything in particular. It seemed to be taking all her energy just to keep afloat and every few seconds she would dip beneath the water, breathe in a mouthful, which would then trigger a primitive cough response, and she would start swimming again.

Tobias swam toward her to help.

He was breathing hard, too.

In between breaths, he said, "You all right?"

She nodded. "I'll live."

He filled his lungs with oxygen.

Savoring the air.

Tobias turned around in the water, and glanced up at the wreckage of the Audi, which had been knocked off the tracks. It had rolled up-hill for twenty or thirty feet and stopped. But gravity had finally overcome kinetic energy, and the car was now rolling down the embankment toward the river...

Heading straight for them.

"Andrea!" he shouted.

She turned to meet the car rolling toward her, but didn't seem to register the threat. Or, if she did, she didn't seem to have the mental faculties to do anything about it.

Tobias grabbed her and pulled her back.

The Audi continued rolling toward them.

He kicked hard like his life depended on it – which it did – heading for the stone pylon of the railway bridge. The wreckage hit a boulder at the edge of the river, flipped twice, and flew through the air. It was heading straight for them.

Tobias dragged Andrea behind the pylon.

Their eyes locked for a micro-second. He said, "Hold your breath."

And then pulled her under the water.

The Audi slammed into the side of the pylon, before landing on the river with a massive crash, sending a shock wave of water in all directions.

The muffled sound of metal crunching on the sandstone pylon echoed through the water.

Tobias kept hold of Andrea, pulling her to the side, swimming hard underwater – putting distance between them and the burning wreckage.

Soon his feet touched the bank of the river.

He and Andrea stepped up onto the rocky shore.

Andrea shook her head and blinked her eyes. She turned and glanced at the smoldering wreckage of the Audi, which had begun to float downstream.

Her head turned to face him. "You saved my life."

"You're welcome," he said, making sure she was out of the water. "Are you going to be all right here? I want to keep going after him."

"No. I'll come with you."

"Are you sure?"

"You bet. I want to make this guy pay."

"I agree."

They both clambered up the bank of the Schiltach.

Tobias reached for his radio. Thankfully it was water-resistant. "PolAir19 we've lost the suspect. Any chance you can find a red Mercedes Sprinter delivery van heading east through Schiltach?"

"Copy that. We're searching for it. We'll let you know if we get a hit."

Tobias was still holding his Sig Sauer in his right hand.

He holstered it and stepped onto the main road.

An old BMW 7 Series sedan slowed down. Tobias crisscrossed his arms and flagged the driver down. He ran over to the driver's window, showed the elderly woman at the wheel his badge, and told her he needed the car.

She opened her mouth to protest. Not her car. He could commandeer some other poor fool's car. But she was too rich and too old to have her car taken. She spoke with the defined, natural authority of Germany's aristocracy.

Tobias tried to argue the point in his most assertive, yet polite, voice.

Andrea wasn't having any of it.

She opened the passenger door, sat in and pointed her handgun at the driver. "Ma'am. There is a really bad man getting away right now. Get out of the damned car."

The old lady, opened her door and got out, adjusting her full, wide skirt, traditionally known as a dirndl. Not to be beaten completely, she said, "Fine. Take my car. But I expect to be financially reimbursed."

"As I'm sure you will, ma'am," Tobias said, adjusting the seat to accommodate his large stature.

He pushed the gear stick into drive and accelerated hard.

Andrea got on the radio. "PolAir19. Any luck finding our van?"

"Afraid not..." The radio was full of the background hum of the helicopter's rotary blades *whump, whumping* through the air. "Wait... I've got eyes on the red Mercedes Sprinter heading south-east out of Schiltach."

"Don't lose that van!"

"We're on it," returned the voice of Ben, the spotter on board PolAir19.

Tobias gunned the old BMW. Its V12 made a surprisingly smooth grunt as the heavy machine, picked up speed like a much smaller, spritely sport car. He overtook several cars and a truck, meandering between both sides of the road, as he made his way through the quaint town, driving the BMW Flagship more like its Formula One equivalent.

The radio made an inaudible, garbled sound.

Andrea said, "PolAir19, you were unreadable. Can you repeat?"

"The van has turned north along a dirt road at the end of Schiltach, and is heading down a conifer lined, narrow road. There are about six large estates that come off the road."

Tobias and Andrea exchanged a glance.

Laughing with relief and excitement, they both spoke at the same time: "He's heading back to the gothic house!"

Chapter Eight

Tobias raced down the narrow dirt road.

Hooded trees flickering by them, as he drove as fast as possible. The heavy all-wheel drive, 7 Series BMW sent mud flying in all directions.

They reached the end of the road.

The electronic gate was just closing. The two sandstone gargoyles looked menacing as they guarded any would-be intruders. Tobias kept his foot planted on the accelerator.

"Toby!" Andrea shouted. "What are you doing?"

"Hold on!"

They hit the steel gate at forty miles an hour.

The heavy BMW carried through the metal without breaking stride. Sparks shot off in all directions as the gate hit the hood, flying over the windshield.

Tobias didn't ease off the gas.

He kept driving hard.

Right up to the old, gothic homestead.

The driver of the van was already out of the vehicle. He was holding a woman hostage in his arms, using her as a shield to protect his body. A gun in his left hand was pointed at the girl's head. At a glance, Tobias could see her mother's signature fiery red hair.

Hannah Zimmerman.

He pulled up just behind the van.

Without a word, he got out and went to the left. Andrea went right. The rain was still coming down heavily. PolAir19 circled overhead.

Tobias said, "It's over."

The man shook his head. "No, not even close. You have no idea who you're dealing with or how high up this thing goes."

"Maybe. But for you it's over."

"No," the abductor said, shaking his head. His eyes were wide and intense. "You have no idea what's going on here. I'll walk away from this, and there's nothing you can do to stop me."

There was something about the man's expression the way he said it. Maybe the kid was delusional. But it sounded more like he knew something that Tobias didn't. The abductor was protected by someone powerful. Or worse still, he was the weapon of someone who wielded plenty of power.

There was very little cover or concealment.

To increase their chances, Tobias and Andrea split apart, making it impossible for the kidnapper to shoot both of them.

"Let go of the girl."

The first shadow of fear washed over the kidnapper. "You have no idea what he will do to me if I lose her."

It was the first time Tobias saw any indication that this man wasn't just a sexual predator or psychopath. He was a mercenary. He worked for a VIP. An elite, wealthy, and powerful man.

But who?

And why would they want to capture the daughter of a movie star?

"You're trapped." Tobias said, "Let's make a deal."

"Oh no… there's no room for deals." There was now genuine fear in the man's striking eyes. "I'd rather be dead than make a deal. By the time he got through, I'd beg to die."

"There has to be something we can do."

"There isn't."

There were soft tears in Hannah's eyes. She mouthed the words, "Help me…"

The kidnapper moved with lightning speed.

He fired straight at Tobias.

A ring like fire seared through his chest.

The shot had hit him, a sharp stab to the thorax.

Tobias drew a breath and it hurt like hell. Blood poured out of the wound. It was mixed with bubbles and he knew it had pierced his lung. He placed his hands on the wound. Every breath he took seemed to produce a sucking sound at the bullet wound.

He pointed his gun.

If he was going to die, he wanted to make damned sure he took the kidnapper with him to hell.

Simultaneously, Andrea took the next shot. It hit the kidnapper in his left shoulder and the pain reflex made him drop his pistol. Realizing he had lost his weapon, he gripped Hannah tight with his right arm, leaving an impossible kill shot for Tobias or Andrea.

Pulling Hannah Zimmerman backwards, the kidnapper moved quickly into the house.

Hannah, realizing that her attacker was no longer armed, turned and bit his right forearm. The man screamed, let go of her, and quickly disappeared inside the front door of the house.

Andrea took another three shots at him, but he was already inside.

Hannah quickly ran to her.

Andrea grabbed her in her arms and directed her back toward the modest protection of the BMW. "Are you hurt?"

"No," she said. "Just scared."

"All right, come with me."

She came and squatted down next to Tobias.

"You look like crap." It was a statement, not a question. She leaned into her radio and said, "PolAir19. We have an officer down, my partner's been shot. Requesting urgent medical assistance."

There was a short burst of crackles over the radio, but Tobias couldn't quite make out much of what was being said.

After a minute or so, he heard PolAir19. "There's an Intensive Care EMS flight enroute to Munich being diverted. Hang in there Fischer. They'll be on the ground in six minutes."

"Copy that," Andrea said, squatting next to him.

Tobias was breathing slow, shallow breaths, through pursed lips. As he met Andrea's eyes, despite the pain, his mouth curved into an unrestrained grin. "You can shoot!"

Another statement. Not a question.

Andrea shrugged. "First in my class."

"Well done. You're all right, you know, for an academic..." He closed his eyes and eased back into the excruciating discomfort. "....and for a kid."

"Thanks, old man."

She helped him shuffle back toward the minor safety behind the BMW.

Andrea turned to look back at the house and then back to him. "Are you alright here?"

"Yeah, yeah… go get that son-of-a-bitch!"

Andrea didn't need to be asked twice.

She turned and carefully entered the house, with her weapon drawn. She was a sharpshooter, and the kidnapper was unarmed. But there was always a chance her perp had more weapons inside.

Tobias cursed when she disappeared inside the house.

It was a stupid risk.

PolAir19 was circling. If the kidnapper tried to run, he would be spotted in two seconds flat. Specialist police teams were on their way to breach the house.

Stupid now to risk everything.

But that's what adrenaline does.

It makes you keep going, keep running, and when the scent is on, the hunter must catch his – or in this case, her – prey.

Tobias just wished her luck.

Two minutes passed.

Maybe three…

Tobias heard the high-pitched sound of the house alarm being triggered. Only, somewhere in the back of his head, he knew that wasn't right. He couldn't quite place it. Then it hit him.

That was a detonator's alarm.

With his own adrenaline running fast, and an almost primal paternal instinct triggered, he stood, despite the burning pain in his chest, and ran toward the house.

He shouted. "Andrea! Get out! Get out now!"

Tobias almost reached the front door when the explosion erupted in a whoosh of heat and fire. The air then quickly sucked into the house, and the entire building imploded on itself.

The air and heat blew Tobias back several feet.

He looked back at the house.

No way anyone survived in there.

The medevac helicopter landed.

Tobias tried to stand up.

The medical team coaxed him back to the ground. "Stay there... we've got this, sir."

Tobias said, "Andrea! We have to help her!"

The Trauma Doctor turned to look at the blazing fire that now engulfed the gothic mansion. His lips were set in a hard line. "I'm sorry. There's no one could have survived inside there."

Tobias tried to fight reality.

He couldn't.

There was no more energy left.

The Trauma Doctor inserted an intravenous line and gave him something for physical pain. Nothing could be given for grief and despair. Tobias struggled to remain conscious, trying to protest as he watched the mansion make its journey toward being razed to the ground.

A moment later, the pain became too great, and he mercifully passed out.

Chapter Nine

Ministry of Defense, Whitehall, Westminster, London

Leo Green had been in the game too long.

In the past forty years he'd gambled everything that was his to risk and equally as much that wasn't, while in Her Majesty's Service. Luck had mercifully been on his side. More often than not, the cards landing where he wanted, and he had reaped the benefit of that good fortune for decades.

But he'd stayed too long.

What was that they say? The crimes of the youth…

He gave an indifferent shrug.

Who knows…?

Whatever the saying… his transgressions were sure as hell coming back to haunt him right now. It wasn't the first thing to come back to bite him, but somehow this seemed different. This seemed infinitely more real. The stakes were certainly higher, that was sure. But it was more than that, the stakes had always been life and death – they had been for more than forty years.

So why did it bother him so much now?

He stepped out of the MoD and headed west toward St. James Park, still pondering the question. In his left hand, he carried a single brown, paper bag.

Despite his age, and the appearance of an elderly man taking in a casual stroll in the park, he still viewed the world with the eyes of a spy. Under his composed mask he was hyper-alert. Hyper-aware. Taking in every miniature detail. Who is walking in what direction? Where are they heading? Is someone following me? Who doesn't belong in this picture? He commanded everything to memory where he could recall the entire scenery with ease. It was a skill, long developed as a secret agent, but in Green's case, it had come naturally to him.

Unlike most people, he really saw the world.

Not just the small bits and pieces that he chose to take in.

But all of it.

More than years of training. It was simply the way he was built.

He looked up at the midway sun. It was an unusually warm summer's day, and London looked splendid. The scent of flowers filled the air. He gazed across the sea of nodding yellow daffodils. A small squadron of pelicans waddled along the footpath, blithely indifferent to an elderly couple who held hands. The pelicans acted as though they owned the place. A concept not entirely false. They were protected by royal decree, after they had been first introduced to the park in 1664 as a gift from the Russian Ambassador.

Birds chirped. And people – tourists and Londoner's alike – swarmed.

Green glanced at three young women in their forties, wearing skirts and tank tops. A few years ago, he would have been horrified to see women dressed like that this close to Buckingham Palace. He drew a breath, allowing his eyes to linger maybe a second or two longer than they should, savoring their young, supple bodies.

Ah to be young again...

Green sighed and kept walking.

He was getting old.

At least, he felt he was. At sixty-eight years of age, the game was getting harder to play. Despite a lifetime in the Service of Her Majesty. It wasn't just his looks. He genuinely felt every one of those years. His joints hurt. He had more injuries and wounds than he cared to think about, and the simple fact was, he was now paying the toll for the abuse he'd given his body.

He stopped at a park bench.

In the ten years since he'd taken a bureaucratic role at the Ministry of Defense as a consultant on foreign affairs – which was a euphemism for, "should we be worried about the potential influence a particular country might have on Great Britain?" – Leo Green had eaten at the same park, more often than not, the same bench, and looked at the lake, regardless of the weather.

He exchanged a glance with a fifty-year-old woman reading a book. She smiled politely, and told him she was about to leave, offering him the bench. Green smiled, thanked her, and took a seat.

Green placed the brown paper bag on his lap, and carefully folded back the sides, one at a time, until the egg, mayonnaise, and watercress sandwich on rye bread became visible. He did this, along with everything he did, with absolute precision.

He returned to the original nagging question…

The sins he'd committed from his clandestine days of a Cold War era spy, were coming back to haunt him.

He was in one hell of a tight squeeze.

But he'd been in trouble before.

The stakes were usually life and death.

So why did this feel different?

Leo took a bite of the sandwich. Egg and mayonnaise. He smiled as he savored the taste. It was just about as British as one could get.

He was a cliché.

So what?

He was damned proud of his heritage.

If he wasn't, he wouldn't have spent his entire life in the Service of Her Majesty.

He took another bite.

That's when it hit him.

The answer to his question.

It was different now because the game had changed. No, not the game. As much as he hated to admit it, the game was just the same as it had always been. It was him. He had changed.

And he no longer found the game fun.

He wanted out.

And this was his ticket to a retirement befitting James Bond. He figured he'd paid a fortune many times over in his Service to Country. Now it was his time to enjoy the fruit of such labor.

Only damned Vostok was about to threaten everything.

He finished his sandwich, and was about to get up when a man sat down beside him. The newcomer wore a tailor made, perfectly fitting suit. He was good looking. Maybe fifty. Blue eyes. Blond hair. Strong jawline. He could have been Nordic, Scandinavian, possibly even Dutch, but Green intrinsically knew that nothing would ever lead him to find the truth.

No, he was too much of a professional for that.

They sat in silence and watched as a couple kids fed the pelicans food that clearly wasn't part of their natural diet.

When the man did finally communicate, he spoke perfect English with just a trace of a European accent. Despite Green having a good ear for languages and accents, he couldn't place the accent, and even if he could, he would discredit it. The stranger, he knew, hadn't survived in the game this long by being careless. If he'd revealed an accent, it would have been intentional, and most likely to take one down the wrong path.

Green knew him as Merc.

It was not the man's real name. Green imagined the pseudonym to be short for Merchant, or Merchant of War, or possibly Mercenary? It didn't really matter. It was just a name. He knew the man and the man was invisible. In fact, in some circles, Merc was simply known as The Ghost. A dangerous arms dealer, who provided high end weapons to private armies, specialist forces, terrorist groups, and governments who didn't want to get their hands dirty. He specialized in supplying armaments that were on the International Humanitarian Law, including the UN and Geneva Convention list of banned weapons.

After a few minutes, Merc broke the silence. "We were close."

Green nodded. "Very close. We would have reached it any day now, and none of this would have mattered."

Merc kept his eyes on the lake, but his voice was directed at Green. "If the truth gets out…"

Green raised a placating hand. "I know, I know…"

"Yes." Merc nodded. "I wished we could change the narrative."

Green arched a thick, salt-and-pepper eyebrow. Hopeful. "You think we can spin this somehow?"

Merc was emphatic. "No chance in hell."

"That's what I thought."

Merc said, "What are you going to do?"

"Me? I thought you had plans in place to have the entire misadventure fixed?"

"There were… some… recent setbacks." Merc shrugged as though it were part of being in the business they were in. "What about you? What have you done about it?"

Green said, "I have a clean-up team containing the disaster as we speak."

"You had better hope to hell they don't leave any survivors, or we're royally screwed."

Green met his eye, displeased by the use of such profanity this close to Her Majesty's Palace. He nodded. "They won't."

"And if they do?"

Green nodded. "I've taken secondary precautions to deal with it."

Merc got up. "Yeah, well, I thought you'd taken care to ensure this thing didn't come back to bite us years ago. Ten years ago, to be precise! So I hope you don't take offense when I say I'm not all that relieved by your precautions."

Green shrugged and took another bite of his sandwich. He remained silent, but his expression said, *You don't have much choice, do you?*

Merc turned to leave. "I'll pull whatever strings need to be pulled to make sure this disappears."

"What can you do from here?"

"Exactly. That's the first thing I one hundred percent agree with you on, but I can't do anything from here. I'll head there tonight."

"Where?"

"Antarctica."

"In the middle of winter?" Green asked without hiding the skepticism in his voice. "Nobody comes or goes from the frozen continent this time of year."

Merc smiled. "That's where you and I are different."

"Really?" Green almost grinned. He was enjoying the dance. It felt like being active in the field again. "How so?"

"I'm rich." Merc turned, his eyes landing square on Green. "I don't have to play by anyone's rules."

Chapter Ten

Halley VI Research Station – East Antarctica

It looked like one of the wagon trains that belonged in the old movies of the wild west.

Only instead of wagons, there were a total of eight research modules made of lightweight and heavily insulated, composite materials designed to house a large team of polar scientists. Seven blue and one red. Each one set upon a series of skis designed to systematically climb out of the falling snow. The entire habitat was on the move.

Halley VI's eight pods (like the carriages of a train) could be disconnected as needed. The individual pods – which sit on skis – can be uncoupled and towed across the ice using specialized heavy vehicles.

The station was designed and built to provide first-rate laboratory and living accommodations that were capable of withstanding extreme winter weather, of being raised sufficiently to stay above thirty feet of annual snowfall, and of being relocated upstream periodically to avoid calving events as the floating ice shelf moves towards the sea.

For the past twelve years Halley, the British Antarctic Survey research station, had been located on the floating Brunt Ice Shelf, which moves roughly 1,200 feet per annum toward the sea. Halley VI was the latest version of the British most Southern scientific research lab.

In 2002, BAS realized that a calving event was possible which could destroy Halley V, so a competition was undertaken to design a replacement station. The current base, Halley VI officially opened in February 2013 after a test winter. It was the world's first fully relocatable terrestrial research station, distinguishable by its colorful modular structure built upon huge hydraulic skis.

Just now, Halley VI was being moved.

It was a routine process. At a minimum, the science station needed to be shifted at least 1,200 feet back, to prevent it eventually being swallowed by the sea. But in addition to that, sometimes the station was moved several miles along the Brunt Ice Shelf.

This time was different.

This journey had already taken six weeks.

There were another two weeks to go.

Halley VI was enroute to the Davis Station, an Australian base, to start a five-year joint, Australian and British research meteorological project.

All in total, the massive train of research modules was being towed by six bulldozers, and a giant Polar PistenBully 600 leading the pack.

Rhys Jones sat at the controls in the cockpit.

The driver's cabin for the PistenBully 600 looked more like an oversized computer console with virtual reality adjuncts. A single joystick controlled all movements. To his right were several buttons that adjusted the diffusion of weight around the entire caterpillar tracks, including the ability to widen, narrow, or extend the tracks themselves.

To his left, was a ten-inch touch screen that controlled and monitored everything from engine gauges through to internal heating, and a large array of warning systems that measure the thickness of ice, including active sonar, and ground penetrating radar designed to alert the driver if they were about to drive over a crevasse.

The beam truck's powerful headlamps penetrated the darkness. A soft glow nudging the sea of white ahead. The wind pummeled the 180-degree-wide windshield. The windshield wipers worked like a metronome, sliding side-to-side in a constant, comforting, rhythm.

It was minus 80 degrees outside.

Not that you would know it from inside the cabin. Rhys had the heater cranked up and the thermostat read 76 degrees Fahrenheit. A Hawaiian hula girl adorned the dashboard. Rhys wore a matching floral, Hawaiian shirt, and navy cargo pants. He might be just about the farthest place on Earth to Hawaii, but that was no reason to feel that way. The cabin interior was balmy. The speakers played an old Enya soundtrack.

In a bunkbed housed behind the cockpit, Rod Jenkins slept peacefully. The two men took turns to keep driving the Arctic machine 24 hours a day. It was long, slow, and boring work. But that was how Rhys liked it. Far better than the potentially life-ending excitement when things went wrong.

A blue light flashed on the dashboard.

It indicated there was a call from the satellite phone. The entire road train was connected via Wi-Fi for local communications. It meant that if a call was coming in from the satellite phone. Someone was calling from outside the convoy, and more like, the frozen continent.

Rhys picked up the phone handle. It was wired to the cabin, and connected to a large satellite dish housed on the vehicle's roof.

He greeted the caller with a welcoming, "Hello?"

The caller spoke in a clear, urgent, tone.

Rhys listened without saying much at all.

He took down the GPS coordinates of their new destination.

Behind him, Rod Jenkins sat up. He ran his fingers across his forehead and then through his hair. His mouth was set with a sort of half-smile, his eyes sparkled with mild curiosity. There wasn't a lot of change when you're driving across the icy continent. A phone call from the other end of the world was a welcome break in the monotony.

He climbed up front into the passenger seat. He put his hand on Rhys' shoulder. "What's going on?"

"We have new orders."

"Oh yeah... how so?"

"That was someone who had been put through to us from the MoD."

"Ministry of Defense?" Jenkins smile turned incredulous.

"Yes, the MoD, as in Whitehall."

"What the hell do they want with us?"

"Change of plans," Rhys said, inputting the new GPS coordinates into the computer.

"Oh yeah?"

"Yeah, we're now headed here."

Jenkins ran his eyes across the map, taking in the location some thirty miles west of Vostok. "Why?"

"I don't know. There's trouble at Vostok and our assistance has been requested."

"So then why the hell aren't we being ordered to head to Vostok?"

Rhys spread his hands outward. "Beats the hell out of me."

Chapter Eleven

The US Air Force Lockheed C-5M Super Galaxy flew over the South Pole.

The pilots traced the Transantarctic Mountains until they reached the Amundsen–Scott South Pole Station, and turned left, heading in the general direction of the Vostok Research Station. The aircraft's four GE CF6-80C2 turbofan engines went quiet, as the Super Galaxy made its descent into the Antarctic Plateau.

Silence was replaced by a slowly rising series of vibrations through the fuselage and frame of the enormous aircraft, as it was beaten by the fine disruptions in airflow above the snow field. The oscillations shuddered through the aircraft.

At the back of the cargo bay, the eight-foot tall four-bladed propeller of a hovercraft began to turn. It picked up speed, churning the air inside the aircraft, and the machine's skirt began to inflate on a bed of air. Inside, Sam and Tom were up front. There were three seats in the back. Genevieve, Elise, and Hu were all lined up in a row as if they were in a typical family sedan.

Sitting at the controls of the hovercraft, Sam glanced over his shoulder. "Everyone strapped in tight? This is gonna be a little bumpy."

Next to him, Tom gripped a holding bar to brace himself and nodded. "Compared to last time when Elise was driving, and we fell some two hundred feet onto the 80-degree slope of the side of a mountain… this will be a breeze."

Elise wasn't taking the bait. "Complain all you want, but I doubt either you or Sam could have made the mental calculations quick enough to land it alive had either of you been at the controls."

Sam shook his head, a smile on his face. "Can't argue with that."

Genevieve grinned. "I'd feel safer if Elise was driving."

"Duly noted," Sam said, his eyes landing on Hu. "What about you, Hu?"

Hu shrugged. His lips curled into a wry, stoic smile. "I'm good. I'm just coming along for the ride."

"Good man." Sam drew a breath. "Any minute now."

The plan was based on a modified version of the Low-Altitude Parachute-Extraction System – known as LAPES – that was popular during the Vietnam War. It employed a tactical military airlift delivery method where a fixed-wing cargo aircraft could deposit supplies in situations in which landing is not an option, in an area that is too small to accurately parachute supplies from a high altitude. The practice was no longer used in the USAF.

Sam listened to the hydraulics of the landing gear doors opening, and the wheels coming down. The pilots had no intention of landing, but they were going to be flying awfully close to the ground not to have some sort of protection underneath their belly.

A moment later, the massive cargo bay door extended outward.

The hovercraft began to shake under heavy mechanical vibrations as the Super Galaxy descended toward the infinite ice sheet ahead.

With its massive tailgate wide open, the military cargo plane skimmed across the icy surface, preparing a touch and go landing and takeoff.

The Loadmaster stood at the doorway, harnessed to the fuselage. With his hands, he indicated the height to the ground.

Ten.

Eight.

Five.

Three.

Sam drew a sharp breath. "Here we go."

He pressed a red button, and the tie-downs that gripped the hovercraft released their hold.

One.

He slammed the joystick forward.

The hovercraft's massive propeller directed the majority of its airflow at a 80/20 split between the horizontal and vertical axis, giving it a sudden burst of forward propulsion.

Sam kept the rudder fixed dead ahead.

The hovercraft, released from its heavenly confines, flew out the back of the Super Galaxy, landing softly on its massive cushion of air.

Fine snow and ice clouded their vision, as the downwash from the

Super Galaxy hammered them for a few seconds, before it ascended, moving steadily away.

By the time the downwash had subsided, the hovercraft's GPS had located enough satellites to triangulate their position.

Sam glanced at the GPS monitor.

It had already calculated and displayed the fastest route to Vostok. Sam rotated the hovercraft on its axis, until it was set on a direct line.

Sam pushed the throttle all the way forward. "Next stop, Vostok Research Station."

Chapter Twelve

Anastasia had to get outside of the research station.

Inside the maintenance office at the western end of Module E, she quickly donned a freezer suit, designed to keep her alive in the extremely dangerous Antarctic winter. It consisted of three layers of clothing: A woolen internal one, followed by a layer of quilted duvet, and lastly a thick, synthetic outer layer needed to keep the wind-chill from ripping through her body. She pulled a balaclava over her head, covering her mouth with the thick wool. It was designed to trap the warmth from her breath, making it possible to breathe outside, before finally bringing the hooded exposure suit over her head.

She needed to escape to survive, that much was certain. Yet Anastasia had no doubt that what she planned to do was equally deadly. It was the middle of winter in one of the coldest, driest, places on Earth. There was nothing outdoors which she could use to build protection from the elements.

It was cold outside.

Really, insanely cold.

She thought back to the morning's meteorological reports, which she had glanced at with only mild interest just an hour earlier, but now seemed to hold the difference between life and death over her future. It indicated temperatures of minus 118 degrees Fahrenheit. To put that in perspective, carbon dioxide turns to a solid – AKA Dry Ice – at minus 109 degrees Fahrenheit. Add to that the gale force winds pummeling the near-flat landscape, often at speeds in excess of 100 miles per hour, Anastasia knew that life outside the research station would only be livable in short bursts.

To the north, the doorway opened from Module D, and one of her adversaries stepped out.

Anastasia cursed under her breath.

She drew a lungful of air through the thick cloth and held it. Her eyes glanced to the eastern side of Module E, where an internal stairway led to an external door. In the middle were a series of snow vehicles, with the Kharkovchanka at the far side.

It would be nearly impossible to reach the external door without being seen.

Her eyes darted to the north. A moment later her patience rewarded her with the first real glimpse of the single attacker. He was short, and muscular, in a white snow outfit with matching balaclava. He wore one of those neck microphones, attached to his throat. She'd seen Russian Special Forces and Police use them in movies. They were designed to allow voice activated transmissions, popular in specialized operations around the world. In his hands, was a large weapon with a short barrel. A type of submachine gun that could likely shoot 500 rounds per minute. The balaclava seemed to trigger something primitive in the back of her mind. It didn't make sense.

They were in the middle of an Antarctic winter.

No one for hundreds of miles.

Why bother covering your face?

Her eyes narrowed with the realization that she'd learned something. Whoever they were, they didn't want to be recognized.

The man moved slowly, but determinedly. He was heading right for her.

Silently.

As though he seemed to think he might have heard or seen something, but wasn't confident enough about it to call on the rest of his team to help him flush out his prey.

She looked to the door that led outside.

It was her only option.

She held her breath.

And imagined her attacker spotting her running across the open ground.

No, it was too risky.

She would never reach the external doorway.

Anastasia needed somewhere else to go. A place to bide her time. Her eyes swept the ground floor of Module E, landing on the Kharkovchanka. It was still the best option. She ducked down, glanced up at her attacker –

still making his way down the series of steel stairs toward the ground floor – and bolted toward the Kharkovchanka.

She ran past three snowmobiles and the back of the PistenBully 300 Polar vehicle, used during the assembly of the massive Vostok Research station. A massive Hiab hydraulic crane, folded on the back.

In seconds she was back inside the safety of the archaic Kharkovchanka.

She closed the door and clambered to the back of the driver's cabin. Before retreating to her previous hiding place, she turned to the front of the driver's cabin, and took one last, quick, reconnaissance of the garage of Module E.

Her heart leaped into her throat by what she saw.

Anastasia's eyes landed on the Kharkovchanka's dashboard.

Where a vintage bobblehead still rocked back and forward. It was a Babushka Soviet Girl with a hand painted red floral dress. An innocent girl, who now risked giving her away. It was so small, but to her it seemed to stand out like a Neon sign. She considered moving forward to stop it, but a second later, heard the definitive change in footsteps landing on the gravel that lined the garage.

Had he seen the moving bobblehead too?

Anastasia retreated to the back of the Kharkovchanka.

She heard the crunch, crunch of footsteps on the gravel outside the cabin. The sound came to a stop toward the driver's cabin. She pictured her attacker standing there watching the tinny movements of the Babushka Soviet Girl bobbling back and forth.

Her pulse hammered in her chest.

A few seconds slowly passed in absolute silence.

Afraid of making a sound, she was unable to breathe.

And then the silence was broken by the distinctive noise that came with lifting the large, metal latch to the Kharkovchanka's only external door.

"Oh look, this one's unlocked…" the man said, speaking in her native Russian.

Her attacker made no attempt at silence.

And why should he?

She was trapped.

Chapter Thirteen

Anastasia's eyes frantically searched her surroundings.

A weapon, a way out, a place to hide... anything.

The entire Kharkovchanka had been stripped to bare necessities, more like the prized artifact at a museum than a working arctic exploration vehicle.

There was nothing here!

Wait, not nothing.

A Maglite – one of those powerful flashlights – was strapped to the wall for emergency power outages or if one had to leave the vehicle in the darkness of night. She pulled it off the wall. It was heavy and about a foot long.

It wasn't much, but she might be able to use it as a club.

Better than being totally unarmed. She was bringing a flashlight to a gunfight.

She heard footsteps inside the driver's cabin. They were followed by the man's words, that chilled her to her spine.

"Come out, come out, wherever you are little mouse..."

She turned around, searching for anywhere to hide. There was a small grate. It went through a narrow steel passageway that led to the engine room. There was even less room to move once inside. She hated the thought of being utterly trapped. But wasn't that what she already was? It wasn't much of a hiding place, but it was one more chance to survive.

Anastasia opened the grate, carefully closing it behind her.

She crawled on her hands and knees through the metal tunnel into the engine bay. She used the Maglite to see in the darkness.

The engine bay was tiny.

Only just enough room to stand at the middle of the room. There were solid moving parts and a cursory glance confirmed it didn't lead to an external hatch for the Kharkovchanka. The space was cramped. Even for her, and she was petite.

She fixed the light on the engine.

Malyshev Factory 12 was stamped into the cylinder head.

A Malyshev 12-cylinder, 520-horsepower diesel engine was put in place, with twin superchargers that could get the engine up to 900 HP. Like the American Snow Cruiser, this Soviet vehicle was completely self-contained, allowing a crew to work on the engine from inside. They also used the engine to keep the crew quarters warm.

She circled around the engine.

The entire place was made of solid metal. There were moving parts of the original engine, all surrounded by various bits and pieces designed to keep it working. The floor seemed softer than the rest of the vehicle, which seemed to be solid metal throughout.

She flashed the beam of her light on her feet.

There was a thick rubber mat. It was presumably to protect the mechanic who worked on the engine. She kneeled down on it, trying to keep her breathing as silent as possible, and removed the small medical bag off her back.

There wasn't time for niceties.

She poured the entire contents out onto the mat, like a stack of scattered toys in a kid's bedroom. She searched through the kit looking for a lifeline. Something that, instead of saving a person's life, might help her to end it.

There was a large array of medical drugs and needles. She knew what the important ones were used for, such as adrenaline and morphine. Unfortunately, the other ones, the ones used to anaesthetize a patient, she had no idea.

She wished she'd paid better attention during her mandatory training before coming out to Antarctica. But they had an actual medical doctor on the base, so why would she need to learn the names and uses of surgical drugs?

Anastasia ran her eyes across some of their names.

Rocuronium…

Vecuronium…

Suxamethonium…

Somewhere in the back of her memory banks she recalled that these put people to sleep, or knocked off their nervous system, so they were unable to move. But she couldn't recall which ones did what. And even if they did knock someone out, how long would it take to work, and what were the chances she could do so before this man aimed his weapon at her and shot her dead?

Not much.

No, she dropped the drugs.

She needed a better option…

There were a couple of scalpels. They were like a cross between a sculptor's chisel and a razorblade. She picked one up and tried to imagine herself using it to kill a man. It was light and short with a blunt sort of tip. Much too short to use as a stabbing weapon. As she considered the practicalities, she realized that the weapon was only a little better than useless to her and she was likely to be better off using the Maglite as a club to maybe smash her attacker's skull in as he climbed through. She shook her head, once more considering the merits of the scalpel. Even if she was strong enough, and got lucky, the question remained, where should she place the blade to do the maximum amount of damage?

In an eye? Or slit the throat?

Probably the latter.

It would be difficult and there was no way it would kill the man before he had time to aim his gun and pull the trigger.

No, she needed another way.

That's when she saw the Zoll defibrillator. One of those electrical devices designed to start a heart after it had stopped beating… or was it to stop all the aberrant electrical pathways from going into overdrive in what they called ventricular fibrillation?

That might be it.

Whatever…

It didn't matter.

The point was that it was capable of delivering high levels of electrical charge. Even without any medical training, she knew what that did to an otherwise well person. Anastasia smiled.

Goodnight attacker.

Chapter Fourteen

Anastasia peeled back the cover on the defibrillator pads.

She plastered the silicon semiconductors onto the metal passageway through which she'd just crawled, which led to the engine room, and switched the Zoll defibrillator on. The machine consisted of a lithium-manganese dioxide battery, attached to two electrodes, coated in silicon semiconductor pads via a small copper wire. It was designed to discharge 200 joules of electricity and was set to automatic, which meant the machine only discharged if there was a shockable EKG rhythm known as ventricular fibrillation or ventricular tachycardia.

Anastasia fixed the flashlight on the defibrillator.

Her eyes narrowed on the few control buttons and single dial.

She switched it to manual mode, meaning that you could shock any rhythm you liked, or in this case, no rhythm at all. Then she turned the "joules" dial as far up as it would go, until it reached its maximum discharge of 360 joules.

Just about enough to permanently stop a person's heart.

Anastasia hoped.

Her own heart fluttered in her chest like a trapped bird. She finished what she needed to do, switched off her flashlight, and waited. It didn't take long. No more than a minute or maybe a minute and a half later, the soft sound of footsteps landing on the floor of the living quarters outside the engine room crept silently closer. Anastasia squatted down at the farthest point from the passageway. She gripped the medical scalpel in her right hand, keeping it as a last line of defense.

The beam of a flashlight flickered through the small passageway leading into the engine bay, sending shadows across the massive Malyshev V-12 diesel engine.

"I know you're in there, Anastasia," came a man's soft, teasing voice, in perfect Russian.

She inadvertently drew in a breath and held it.

"Tsk, tsk… there is no point hiding. Give yourself up. I know you're in the engine bay and we both know there's no other way out of there. We both know you're unarmed, otherwise you would have tried to shoot me dead already, no?" He drew a loud, theatrical sigh. "All right, if that is how you want to play this, I'll come in and get you. But I'm warning you, I'm going to make you suffer for it."

She listened to the sound of her attacker getting down on his hands and knees, ready to make the narrow crawl along the passageway into the engine house.

Anastasia hit the defibrillator's charge button.

The low-flow, continuous current obtained from the defibrillator's batteries slowly filled the capacitor. This acted like the electrical equivalent of a bucket by collecting the low-flow current from the batteries. Once full it was ready to release as a brief, high-flow current. Her eyes watched as the small, digital display registered the joules stored in the capacitor as it increased, until they reached the maximum potential output of 360.

The defibrillator flashed orange.

The machine was ready to discharge a single burst.

In the darkness, Anastasia saw a hand on the ground along the metal crawl space. A shadow of a handgun flickered on the engine bay.

Her attacker was now inside the metal passage.

Anastasia pressed the shock button.

360 joules jolted through the crawl space.

Her eyes fixed on the body that kept moving slowly toward her like a monster in one's nightmares.

It failed.

The machine didn't electrocute him.

She hit the charge button again.

Seven seconds…

Until the machine was ready to shock again.

For a split second, she wished she'd paid more attention in her physics classes, rather than being enamored by glaciology. What was wrong with the damned equation? She was missing something basic. It was like trying to find the answer in an exam – only, in this case, a wrong answer meant death.

Five seconds.

An image popped up in the back of her mind.

That's how it worked in exams for her.

Something about a bird on a wire…

They don't get electrocuted.

Not unless…

That's it.

Something about an electrical potential difference…

Her attacker was on the entire steel bridge.

He still wore a balaclava, but she could see his eyes. They were a type of gray, like a cold, wintry sky, and hard as titanium. They flashed with intelligence. Underneath which, there was something else there, too. Something wild and passionate, and far more disturbing – barely constrained – a type of sadistic pleasure in watching her squirm.

Three seconds.

He drew the pistol, aiming it straight at her.

Anastasia pulled her body in as close to the engine as she could, but at this range, it was difficult to imagine a professional marksman missing.

He grinned.

One second.

He motioned toward her with the gun. "Come, come. Come here *now*, bitch…"

Zero.

Beneath his balaclava she could see the outline of his lips curling upward into a twisted smile. He licked his lips. "Now I'm going to have my fun with you, before you die…"

The Zoll defibrillator started flashing orange, indicating it was ready to shock.

She leaned back, just out of his reach.

He placed his hand on the rung next to the engine mount and pulled himself toward her.

She pressed the shock button.

This time was different.

He was crawling on the metal bridge.

His hand touched the steel bar to the side of the engine bay.

Her attacker gave a sharp jolt.

360 joules ran from the iron bridge to the engine bay, through the shortest conductible route. In this case – his body.

The shock didn't look like much.

Nothing like it was in the movies, where someone gets electrocuted. More like a small jolt, or a nervous twitch. But it was enough to knock him out cold.

Anastasia exhaled and drew a silent sigh of relief.

Potential difference! She thought, strangely remembering an early science lecture from school.

His handgun had fallen to the ground.

She flicked on her Maglite and scanned the engine bay. The weapon was laying just beside her attacker. She studied him intently. The man didn't seem to be breathing. Maybe the shock killed him? Or perhaps it just sent his diaphragm into a spasm. Who knows? She sure as hell wasn't going to stick around to find out.

Anastasia reached down to pick up the handgun.

With one touch, she was surprised she recognized it. No, more than that, she *knew* this weapon! It was a Heckler & Koch P7, German 9×19mm parabellum semi-automatic. Straight blow-back. Originally designed and manufactured in West Germany. The P7M13 was fed from a double-stack box magazine with a capacity of 13 rounds.

Her right hand expertly clasped the handle, her trigger finger was ready to fire.

Then the synapses in her brain exploded

And a flood of memories she'd spent years suppressing out of existence, filled her mind, washing over her like a tsunami.

Chapter Fifteen

Anastasia felt dizzy.

She shook her head, tried to zoom in. Focusing her attention on the handgun – a weapon she was once expertly proficient in – instead of getting sucked under by her past. A past which she only just now realized, was all coming back to haunt her.

The weapon felt light in her hand.

The P7M13 variant weighed 30 ounces. A full magazine added an additional 18.88 ounces. All in total, less than 50 ounces. A lightweight handgun. Almost imperceptible. But for someone with her experience, noticeable as soon as she gripped the handle.

She pointed the weapon at the seemingly dead man lying on the ground.

Anastasia frowned.

She'd like to put a bullet in his head just to be sure, but then again. The weapon seemed light.

In a fraction of a second, she turned the P7 over, drew back the slide. There was a single round in the chamber. She withdrew the magazine. It had two rounds left. Three, including the one in the chamber. She reinserted the magazine and hit the squeeze-cocker, drawing back the bolt, and putting the weapon into a ready and set position. She tucked the weapon into her thermals.

All of this, she did in under a few seconds.

It was automatic.

Based on muscle memory alone.

From a time when she was a different person, entirely.

Anastasia picked up the scalpel again. Holding it in her right hand, she carefully stepped over the body, and quickly clambered through the passageway into the living quarters of the Kharkovchanka. She reached the end of the tunnel and then pulled herself through and out using the stand to a makeshift dining table on the other side.

She stood up quickly.

Took a step.

But her leg was trapped.

She felt the fingers of a hand clasp around her left ankle, and her foot held down firm like it was stuck in primordial mud.

Her eyes darted toward the hand and muscular forearm. She twisted her body, and swung her right hand downward at speed. In it, she held the medical scalpel firm. The blade struck the man's forearm, severing tendons as simply as if they were strings of a violin.

Putain! The man swore in French.

Anastasia made a run for it.

She headed toward the Kharkovchanka's cockpit, kicked the semi-open door all the way open, and jumped out onto the gravelly ground of the garage.

Behind her she could hear her attacker's voice, barking a series of orders into his radio, no doubt alerting the rest of the attack force to Module E.

Her eyes darted around the garage.

The approaching voices of her adversaries were already traveling down Module D.

She needed to get out of Vostok, despite the lethal outside temperatures… and the winds.

Anastasia swallowed nervously. Meteorology studies indicated katabatic winds were common this time of the year in Antarctica, but even for this region, they were far more volatile and dangerous than normal. The katabatic wind was a drainage wind, a current of air that carries high-density air from a higher elevation down a slope under the force of gravity, giving it the colloquial name, "fall winds."

In this case, the drainage wind fell from the Transantarctic Mountains, causing speeding currents of air to cross the Polar Plateau. The Polar Plateau is a thousand plus mile radius along East Antarctica. At an average height of 9,800 feet, the high elevations of the Polar Plateau, combined with its high latitudes and its extremely long, sunless winters, meant that the temperatures here were the lowest in the world in most years, sometimes falling as low as minus 134 degrees Fahrenheit.

It made for a lethal environment.

Yet to survive the temperature and the winds, first she had to escape these men, and get outside.

Preferably without being shot.

Anastasia ran across the remainder of the garage floor until she reached her original destination. A ladder that led to a series of doors and metal landing platforms, stacked one on top of another in a vertical row. Each one a couple feet above the next, with the final one nearly thirty feet high. They were designed so that the scientists housed at Vostok could leave the compound at any time of the year, no matter how much snowfall had blocked their egress.

She climbed to the first one and tried the door.

It opened inward.

A solid wall of ice precluded her from escaping.

She closed the door and kept going.

When she reached the second platform someone shouted at her. She barely heard the words. It didn't matter. She knew what they meant – someone had followed her – they knew where she was heading, and she was probably going to die.

Anastasia opened the door.

She was greeted by a world of white and wind.

A blizzard, the likes of which she'd never seen in two years at Vostok, was harrying the station. Even with her sub-zero survival suit on, she knew she couldn't live outside the habitat very long.

Next to the door was a wooden shovel, about six feet long. It was used to clean up ice and snow from around the door frame and regular snow maintenance by the scientists.

Anastasia grabbed it, closed the door, and slid the shovel through a metal latch on the door, making it impossible to open again without breaking the shovel. She shook the door handle, seeing if it would hold. Already, her attackers had reached the exit and were kicking at it.

It looked solid.

She turned to run.

Directly ahead, some six hundred feet, were a series of deep crevasses that led to a small labyrinth of ice-caves. If she could reach it, she could stay alive long enough to make a single call on the satellite phone. Then she would probably freeze to death.

The wind was so powerful, she needed to duck all the way down, and exert all her strength just to make any progress whatsoever. It was like in one of those dreams where you're being chased, but just can't seem to run as your feet are caught in something heavy. She made twenty feet and heard someone shout.

It was the sound of pain, not an order.

Anastasia ducked down to the frozen ground. Her head snapped round to see her pursuer. It was another attacker – dressed the same as the one she had cut, his face concealed by a balaclava, but without a doubt, not the same man. Having been unable to break through the door, this man had climbed to the next level and then jumped the small distance to the ground.

It was probably only ten feet.

But snow can be deceiving.

It can look like a fluffy cushion.

And when the katabatic winds ripped across it at 150 miles an hour, snow turned to ice – rock hard ice.

The attacker had landed on that solid surface.

The weight of his body, weapon, along with his backpack containing ammunition, was more than his bones could take. He snapped one, or possibly both of his legs on impact.

He fought through the pain and managed to sit himself up enough to see her, regaining control of his submachine gun. Still focused on his mission, he scanned the icy alien world, his gaze landing on Anastasia. She was no more than twenty feet away from her enemy.

Close enough to watch the man's adrenaline-fueled pain turn to malice. To see intense loathing burning in his dark gaze.

Anastasia drew the P7M13 and fired three shots in quick succession.

The first two went wild.

The third found its intended target.

Right between those hate-filled eyes.

Chapter Sixteen

Anastasia raced toward the ice caves.

Less than five hundred feet from Vostok's Module E, and impossible to see until you were right up on it. Then the flat landscape opened up into a narrow crevasse.

The winds screamed like the fiendish man she'd just killed, after he'd broken both his lower legs trying to make a ridiculous jump onto solid ice. Snowdrift raced along the icy plains at speeds well in excess of a hundred miles an hour. The only reprieve was that the landscape was so dry that few pieces of snow formed larger than the tiniest flakes. Otherwise, even a small piece of ice could become a lethal projectile.

She pulled the hood of her exposure suit over her face for protection.

The windchill brought the temperature somewhere in the vicinity of minus 120 degrees Fahrenheit.

Even in her exposure suit, those sorts of temperatures spelled imminent death.

She had to crouch down just to make progress through the blizzard. The muscles of her thighs and calves burned. It seemed to take all her effort to make little more than a few feet of forward progress. The wind was deafening, and soon it blocked out all other sounds, leaving her with her own thoughts.

Behind her, internal ruminations were broken by a distinctive sound.

Snap.

Her head turned back to face the way she'd come. The door at Vostok burst open as the wooden shovel splintered in several pieces.

Three angry men poured out of the open door, including the man she had cut, who appeared to be nursing a wound to his forearm.

She wished she had cut him deeper.

Anastasia swore.

A moment later, the howling wind was pierced by another sound. Something sharper and altogether far more deadly. This one, she was now well attuned to recognize.

It was the sound of submachine gun fire.

She dropped to the ice cold ground.

The rounds flew over her head.

She had no way of knowing how close they were getting to her. And there was no way she was going to risk a sneak peak behind her by lifting her head.

Anastasia kept going.

Moving fast, in a sort of commando crawl, she scurried toward the crevasse that led to the ice caves – and her only chance of survival.

Up ahead, she caught the first flicker of moonlight reflecting off a shard of ice. It had become like a mirror, behind which, concealed a hollow void that fell deep into the icy crust.

It was the only sign of an opening.

Most of it had been covered up, concealed by ice during the Antarctic winter. A thin layer, no more than a few inches thick at most, had completely entombed the tip of the crevasse and entrance to the ice caves.

She reached the opening and tried to push through it.

The task was impossible by hand.

Her gloved hand gripped a portion of the ice, and pulled.

The shard of ice didn't budge.

Anastasia turned around, dug her gloved hands into the smooth surface to gain as much traction as possible. Then, in utter desperation, she began kicking the ice as hard as possible. The first two kicks didn't do much. Over the noise of the turbulent wind, she could make out the rat-a-tat-tat of more gunfire.

She was running out of time.

Anastasia tried to drive her foot into the ice. When training she'd learned that the key to a good punch was to aim somewhere a few inches past where you wanted to hit. She imagined aiming to plant her foot somewhere several inches past the sheet of ice.

She kicked hard.

Really hard.

No luck.

She tucked both her knees up to her chest and then gave it everything she had.

Anastasia could still hear the sound of submachine gun fire. It was getting closer. Now she started to kick at the ice like a crazy person, a trapped animal locked in a cage.

Ten seconds later.

Maybe fifteen.

A small crack began to form at the far end of the ice, where it began to fracture. Not even close to where she'd been kicking.

She kicked again.

Then the entire sheet of ice shattered.

Another round of bullets raked the snow beside her.

Not beside her.

Right at her.

The rounds had whipped through the ice.

In that instant, she realized it wasn't her feet that had kicked in the ice cover. It was a series of 9 mm Parabellums, traveling at supersonic speeds from submachine guns.

The floor beneath her gave way.

Anastasia felt the contents of her stomach rise up in her throat as she fell deep into the crevasse. She should have been trying to arrest her fall with something. But what did she have? Besides, wherever gravity might take her was better than the surface where four armed men pursued her with submachine guns.

In her downward plunge, she quickly picked up speed.

Anastasia felt like she was on a luge. Not the successful one, but more like the version depicted in the 1993 Blockbuster, Cool Runnings, where John Candy coached the first Jamaican bobsled Olympic team. The one where they crashed horribly on their final run.

Sliding at first, she broke through a mound of snow, before falling

She slipped into the crevasse.

Gravity dragged her downward…

Toward freedom.

Ordinarily, she would have been wearing crampons – those boots that ice-climbers use to find purchase on ice – along with a pick-axe, a harness, and a rope bolted to a bomb-proof anchor.

This time, she let herself go with it.

She slid down the first few feet, and then dropped really fast, and equally as hard. Smashing through a second, thin layer of ice, before free-falling past a series of ladders left there from an expedition in summer.

The white icy world shot by.

She fell more than fifteen to twenty feet, before coming to a stop wedged between two sections of the crevasse.

Her head slammed into the side of the chasm.

For a moment her world flickered.

She blinked away the haze.

High above her, she heard someone shout, "Allez après elle et assurez-vous qu'elle est morte…"

It meant…

Go in after her, and make sure she's dead.

Chapter Seventeen

Anastasia got up slowly.

She half-expected to find she'd broken several bones. Her entire body ached, but everything seemed to work. Her arms and legs still bent in all the right places and there were no new articulations that weren't there before.

Rolling over, she reached into her backpack, fumbled in the darkness, and eventually retrieved the Maglite. She switched the powerful flashlight on, taking in her alien environment for the first time. She was surrounded by the narrow incline of the icy crevasse. She'd fallen to the bottom of the first of many chambers in the seemingly infinite labyrinth of ice caves. At first impression, it appeared that she'd reached the bottom of the entire cave system and was now trapped in a dead end. But a narrow opening to the west of where she had landed, led to a tunnel that extended far into the subterranean ice world.

Dark, menacing shadows danced across the freezing cold chambers above her. Each one was more than ten-feet tall and carrying clubs, like some sort of fiends from the underworld. In reality, the clubs were three-foot long submachine guns.

She could hear their banter in French.

The way they spoke made her think they had come from the French Special Forces. They were so efficient and confident. There was also a certain amount of bravado. As though, despite their confidence, they still knew they were entering a potentially deadly environment. A place where luck and skill played equal roles in granting a chance of survival.

The end of a rope fell beside her.

Her eyes darted toward the rope and the opening high above. They had found a rope much faster than she expected. Maybe someone had been carrying one with them? They all wore backpacks. She shook her head. It was a moot point. The fact was, they had a rope, and had dropped it down beside her.

Any minute, they would be here, too.

It was just the right amount of motivation she needed to get a move on.

She stood up, and carefully walked to the end of the crevasse, where the two massive sheets of ice – probably some thousands of years old – narrowed into a small tunnel.

It was small enough that she had to get down on her hand and knees to crawl through. She knew where the tunnel went. She'd explored it when she first came to Antarctica three summers ago. She and Pavel had spent several days exploring the ice-cavern, rigging ladders, and ropes to explore its icy depths.

She ducked down and crawled through the tiny passageway.

It went on for at least a hundred feet, possibly a little more, and kept narrowing until it felt more like a traditional cave crawl. If her pursuers, who were much larger than she was, wanted to keep coming after her, they would need to drag themselves along on their tummies.

The tunnel tapered into its narrowest point in the middle.

Anastasia got down on her tummy, and pulled herself through, before the ice tunnel began to widen once more. She crawled farther along on her hands and knees, before eventually being able to stand up again.

Now the narrow confines of the tunnel gave way to a massive ice chamber.

She flashed the beam of the Maglite into the open space. It reminded her of a natural cathedral. The majestic cavity glowed with the cool blue tone of ice with otherworldly features, shapes, and crystal formations. Traveling in an east to west direction, the chamber was approximately forty feet wide, by at least a hundred long, with an abyss so dark it suggested it fell to the deepest recesses of the earth. A large block of ice formed a natural bridge between the north and south side of the cathedral. The bridge was no more than three or four feet wide, as it spanned across the void. Her eyes drifted from the darkness below to the ceiling high above.

Massive ice stalactites covered the roof like teeth lining the giant maw of an ancient beast. Some of the stalactites were as much as fifteen feet in length, and two or more feet wide at their base. Others, along the walls, had joined to form stalagmites in a process that had probably taken thousands of years to form. The stalactites were formed by drips, as droplets of water freezes when they lose heat to ice-cold air. It starts with a few frozen droplets and after reaching a certain size drop begin to drip along the side of the structure turning into a pointy stick-like form. At some sections the two met to form solid icicles.

Anastasia adjusted the beam of her flashlight, taking in the entire chamber. Beams of light radiated through the vast room, turning the walls blue. The ancient glacial ice was formed by snow, compressed over hundreds – if not thousands – of years. During the compression, air bubbles were squeezed out, so ice crystals enlarged. Without the scattering effect of air bubbles, light can penetrate ice undisturbed. In ice, the absorption of light at the red end of the spectrum is six times greater than at the blue end. Thus, the deeper light energy travels, the more photons from the red end of the spectrum it loses along the way.

The glaciologist in her made her appreciate that unique blue glow at a deeper level.

She imagined the water molecules vibrating under the different modes of light. The red, orange, yellow, and green wavelengths of light were absorbed so that the remaining light is composed of the shorter wavelengths of blue and violet. This is the main reason why the ocean is blue. Water owes its intrinsic blueness to selective absorption in the red part of its visible spectrum. And the blue ice was just a more powerful, spectacular version of this unique phenomenon.

Voices followed her from behind the tunnel.

It spurred her out of her reverence of the pure beauty of the ancient glacier. Her eyes darted around the icy cathedral. There was a small pathway east to west, but it was so narrow that she wasn't willing to risk it.

That left just one option.

She needed to cross the ice bridge.

A rope had been left along the span of the bridge. Something for the scientists studying the glacier to clip their carabiners into and secure themselves as they make the dangerous crossing. Only right now, the rope was buried in ice that would take her the better part of a day to reach, and even if she could reach it, she didn't have a carabiner or a harness to clip into.

Anastasia dug her boots into the ice. It wasn't much better than skating without ice-skates. What she wouldn't give for a pair of crampons right now to grip her feet into the ice with.

Behind her French voices accelerated her heartbeat, driving her to keep moving.

They were coming for her.

She took another, tentative step...

...and nearly slipped off the bridge.

Anastasia dropped down to her hands and knees. She shuffled forward. It was painfully slow, but at least she was alive and making progress.

At the halfway mark, her entire world erupted in submachine gun fire. The sound of bullets traveling at supersonic speeds, whizzing through the frozen vault, filled the cathedral.

Anastasia swore.

Forgetting the risk of falling, she scrambled across the bridge.

The trailing bullets raked the ground behind her, as she ran, sending shards of fractured ice splintering in all directions.

She reached the opposite end of the bridge and clambered through a small opening that seemed to lead upward. It was steep, and from previous experience mapping the cave system, she knew it led to a second chamber.

Moving quickly, she ascended the narrow tunnel, using her hands and feet to press against opposing walls, in a technique climbers use known as stemming. At the top of the tunnel, she pulled herself up and onto the icy mantle.

This chamber was a mixture of ice and rock, leading to a plethora of ice and mineral speleothems. The entire void was filled with crisscrossing stalactites, stalagmites, rocky flowstones, cave draperies, cave curtains, and crystals.

She fixed her flashlight on the wall of ice behind her. A thirty something foot ladder, bolted into the ice, extended all the way to the ceiling. There a small alcove formed between the two chambers, like an ancient bubble. It reminded her of a sort of subterranean, castle turret, or the crow's nest on a pirate's ship.

It would be a good place to make a stand.

But the question remained, without a weapon, what was she going to use to fight? She had nothing at all. Being there was no help at all.

The alternative was to keep going deeper into the cave system. The problems was, how far could she go? How long could she survive?

And the greatest problem with continuing to run was that the next series of chambers were all horizontal, with few places to hide, and even fewer that provided some sort of means from which to attack.

No. She needed to make a stand where she was.

This was as good as it was going to get. An old climbing rope had been fixed to a large ice stalagmite. The rope was still coiled up on itself, ready to use to descend into the lower depths of the ice caves.

Anastasia, grabbed the rope and threw it down the chimney she'd just climbed up, offering her pursuers an easier means to follow.

In her right hand she held the scalpel to the rope.

In her left, she touched the rope, and waited.

Then she switched off the Maglite and waited in total darkness.

Chapter Eighteen

The rope went taut.

Anastasia counted to ten, waiting for her pursuer to climb a little way.

The flicker of her attacker's headlamp danced on the ceiling of the passageway. She could hear his heavy breathing as he pulled himself up the rope.

She placed the scalpel on the rope and cut.

It wasn't a static abseiling rope, but a climber's dynamic rope, meaning in addition to nylon and other materials, the rope is highly flexible.

The first attempt cut through the outer layer but made no change to the inner layers. Panicked, Anastasia kept cutting, but it was too slow, and within seconds knew that she would never sever the rope in time.

She considered her next move.

Maybe now she should try and make a run for it?

No.

There was no time left.

A second later, the decision was made for her.

A gloved hand gripped the rope, almost at the very top of the ice chimney.

Anastasia, took the scalpel and cut the man's hand. In one sharp, fast movement, she sliced right through the extensor tendons located at the back of the fingers. It caused a reflexive spasm in the flexor tendons.

The fingers automatically opened.

The French attacker screamed.

And fell backward.

His face a white rictus of fear, his arms began windmilling as he slipped.

He slid all the way down the ice chimney, along the side of the bridge and into the void. His voice echoed as he fell into the icy abyss.

His throaty scream was filled with terror, growing distant until it mercifully ceased to exist, as his body slammed into the ground far below with a deathly crunch.

Chapter Nineteen

It had been ten years since Anastasia had killed a man.

Now she'd killed two in the past hour, and badly injured a third. She felt like she was getting the hang of it again, as though she'd never had a break. Just like riding a bike, it was all coming back to her in waves of silent efficiency. So was the pleasure that came with it, too.

She'd always been good at it.

Mentally, she imagined how many French attackers were still left.

Did she see three or was there up to five people who exited Vostok?

There was the one she'd shot and the one she'd just killed. Did that leave three? Could she even be certain there were only five people to begin with? Maybe a second team? Or more than five people in the team?

Not that it mattered.

She could kill another three as easily as she could kill ten.

That brought her back to her next move.

What was she going to do about the next men who came for her? There were a series of ladders that reached the bottom of the abyss. She could always climb down and then retrieve the submachine gun. But then she would be below her attackers, and that was never a good idea in any situation, especially in the ice.

Then again, they wouldn't be expecting it.

In the darkness, Anastasia heard the voice of the man she'd tried to kill inside the Kharkovchanka's engine room. If she had to guess, she would assume her attacker was the leader of the team that attacked Vostok.

The man spoke in Russian again. "Anastasia… you're gonna regret that."

Anastasia, grinned. It felt almost like she was enjoying the game of life and death again. "Come get me and we'll find out."

She snatched the rope and quickly coiled it up. There was no way the next attacker was going to be dumb enough to fall for the same ruse. She dug her feet into the ice, making footprints that led down, deeper into the mixed rock and ice chamber.

She then backtracked, taking cover in the darkness.

A large speleothem curtain formed at the opposite side of the chamber. The calcite formation had produced what eerily looked like a wavy or folded sheet hanging from the lower roof. It had been formed by water running down the roof at a steep angle – roughly 45 degrees. As a result, the water ran down the wall, always using the same path. As it did, it lost carbon dioxide to the atmosphere of the cave, thereby depositing calcite in a thin vertical line on the wall. The line had grown and grown, until there was a small rim.

Anastasia's mind flashed on all she knew from her previous experience mapping cave systems. Curtain formations grow drip by drip – so they are normally very thin. And as they consist of small calcite crystals, curtains are translucent.

When the weather on the surface changes, so does the amount of water in the cave. All variations in the amount of water alter the amount of calcite and iron oxide, and therefore change the color of the depositing calcite crystals. As curtains grows in layers, stripes are formed. Normally you can follow them from the beginning to the end of the curtain. This characteristic of curtains led to names like "bacon" or "bacon and rind" formations.

This knowledge gave her an idea.

Anastasia concealed herself behind the bacon. She picked up a clump of ice. When the first flicker of a headlamp rose from the ice chimney, she threw the clump of ice down toward the faux footprints, hoping to mislead her attacker.

Smiling, she watched their reaction from behind the curtain.

It was translucent enough to make out the outline of his shadow and the glow of his headlamp, but little else, and she hoped to hell that he couldn't see her or the whole game was over and she was dead.

The fighter stepped toward the footprints but jerked and crouched taking cover when he heard her clump of ice hit the ground.

He stopped

His head on a swivel, he turned around, taking in the entire third chamber in a slow, circular reconnaissance. His eyes and weapon carefully, and aggressively swept the icy vault.

Anastasia held her breath.

The fighter, seemed to accept that she had moved deeper into the cave system, or if she hadn't one of his partners would come through and find her. With decided intention, he began to follow the chamber in a gently downward slope, moving toward the sound and location of where she'd thrown the clump of ice.

He'd taken the bait.

She exhaled.

And moved in quickly.

She was operating in the dark.

Her attacker's headlamp facing forward was the only light visible.

Anastasia stalked her prey with a practiced silence. Long held muscle memory coming back from a decade ago where these movements had seemed so natural to her. She might have chosen to relinquish her old life, but the old life had never fully left her.

Within seconds, she reached her opponent.

Like a wraith emerging from the darkness, she slid her left arm over him, wrapping it around his neck.

In a split-second, her forearm was lodged firmly between his chin and chest.

His hands reflexively went up to protect his throat.

She wrapped her arm tightly around his neck, holding him in place. Her right arm locked on the back of his head, and her left hand locked on her right bicep.

It was a classic sleeper chokehold, designed to cut off blood supply to the brain.

The attacker knew this, and went berserk.

Thrashing like a wild thing, he arched his back and threw his weight backward, trying to dislodge her. But he wasn't the first person she'd tried to kill this way. Anastasia comfortably planted her feet, pulling him backwards, and taking her attacker's weight in her legs. It only served to choke him faster.

Behind her, another attacker arrived having scaled the chimney.

Anastasia swore.

Her attacker squeezed the trigger of his submachine gun, tilting it upward, in a vain attempt to dislodge her.

She turned around, swinging him with her.

The burst of submachine gun bullets ripped through the second attacker before he got a chance to fire a shot.

The second French attacker fell backward, dead.

This spurred on the man she was killing and he went ballistic, slamming her into nearby walls. He knew, as well as she did, that he didn't have long to live. Ten seconds at best, and the sleeper hold – true to its name – puts someone unconscious.

He writhed and kicked.

Baring his teeth, he tried to bite her. It was impossible. She was too much of a professional to relinquish her forearm from beneath his chin.

Ergo, there was no way he could sink his teeth into her.

The French attacker realized this.

He knew he was just about done.

Instead of leaning backward, he suddenly changed direction, pulling her forward. Using his weight, which must have been closer to twice that of hers, he managed to flip her over his head, in one sharp move.

Anastasia fell to the ground.

She landed with a violent crunch on the ice.

The man, seeing her vulnerable, but still dazed himself and not thinking clearly, moved in to strangle her with his bare hands.

In that instant, he could have killed her.

He should have shot her.

But he didn't.

Call it male ego. Or stupidity? Or simply the blood rage of someone in the midst of a fight. Either way, he came at her with his bare hands. Diving at her, he threw all of his 200 plus pounds of solid muscle in her direction.

Anastasia's right hand reached backward.

He fingers clasped around an ice stalagmite. It was roughly twelve inches long but thousands of years of slowly dripping water had tapered it into a sharp point at the top.

She twisted her wrist, snapping the ice at its base.

Anastasia brought the stalagmite up to her chest, its point as sharp as a spear.

The French soldier landed on her.

The ice blade went straight through his chest.

His own weight drove the ice inside him, piercing his heart. Her adversary's gaze landed on hers with a mixed expression of disbelief and respect, before his eyes rolled back in his head, and his body slumped forward.

She pushed him off her.

The man began to slide down the ice chamber.

Anastasia tried to stop it, but there wasn't a lot she could do to arrest his rapidly building momentum on the ice.

The body kept sliding, disappearing down an unmarked void. The man's headlamp drifted into the darkness, before vanishing completely.

She drew a breath and exhaled, making another silent curse. She would have liked to have taken the man's machinegun, pistol, and knife. He undoubtably had an entire armory on his person. Weapons would have made it easier. She found her Maglite, switched it on, and shined the bright beam of light down the opening.

The light disappeared down the void.

No way was she going down there to retrieve whatever the man had with him to inflict bodily harm.

Still on the farther side of the bridge, she heard the leader swear in French. If she was thinking, she probably could have made the mental translation, but she wasn't thinking. At least not about languages. Right now, she was trying to work out how to get a weapon.

That's when she realized she could reach the first one.

The guy who she'd knocked off the ice bridge.

It was about six ladders according to her memory, but they were all there, bolted into the wall of the massive ice crevasse. Just now, she was shivering from the cold. She could probably use the exercise to warm up.

She heard the leader speak in Russian again. "Who the hell are you?"

Anastasia ignored him.

He then said, "You're no scientist. That's for sure."

She made her way to the southern end of the chamber, where the first ladder was. It started at the end of chamber 3 and the start of chamber 4. She shone the beam of her flashlight down, and took in the row of aluminum ladders.

Anastasia made a mental picture of each of her next steps, gripped the top rung of the first ladder, and then switched off the Maglite, securing it in her backpack once more. She could easily climb in the dark and the last thing she needed during the downclimb was to meet her remaining attacker.

With that thought in her mind, she quickly descended the first twenty foot of ladder, before pausing long enough to feel the start of the next one beside it. Confident that her hand was clasped on the rung of the second ladder, she switched across, and continued making her way down. All in total, it took her less than five minutes to reach the ground.

The darkness was absolute.

It enveloped her in blindness.

She retrieved her Maglite and flicked it on once more.

The bottom of the ladder led to an opening to another chamber that descended to the even deeper chamber with the ice bridge.

Spread out along the entire ground was more than a thousand ice stalagmites. It was just as she remembered. These ran anywhere between three and six feet in height. Each one was pointing upward at odd angles, like some sort of deadly booby-trap inspired by an old Indiana Jones film.

There she found a grizzly scene. Impaled on a particularly large spike was the attacker who had slid off the ice bridge. His head was twisted in a disturbing angle. His neck was attached by a thin tether of skin with white broken bone and a severed spinal cord hanging out. The ice stalagmite had pierced his abdomen and chest, reducing his corpse to something barely human.

Anastasia didn't wait, or revel in her victory.

Unemotionally, her mind on practicalities, she carefully stepped through the maze of ice stalagmites, and searched her attacker's body. She found his submachine gun. She recognized the weapon, although had never fired one specifically. It was an MAT-49 submachine gun. Developed by French arms factory Manufacture Nationale d'Armes de Tulle (MAT) for use by the French Army back in 1949, and still in use today.

Picking up the weapon, she examined it.

The MAT-49 had a short, retractable wire stock, which when extended gave the weapon a length of 28 inches. The magazine well and magazine could be folded forward parallel to the barrel for a parachute jump or with a 45° angle, hence allowing a safe carry until the magazine well was brought back to a vertical position before opening fire.

The MAT-49 was blowback-operated and box magazine-fed, with a rate of fire of 600 rounds per minute on full auto. The weapon incorporated a grip safety, located on the backside of the pistol grip. The rear sights are flip-up and "L"-shaped, and marked for a range of 55 and 109 yards. It had a 32 round Sten magazine of 9×19mm Parabellum.

Securing the rifle, she searched through the man's uniform, and retrieved a second magazine. Then she searched his backpack and found another magazine. If he had any other weapons, they were likely lying nearby.

A voice activated (VOX) radio crackled.

She heard the leader checking off who was alive and who was dead. To her relief, no one seemed to be answering the persistent piece of dog shit. It had been five men pursuing her. Four down, one to go.

She leaned forward to pick up the dead man's VOX.

Anastasia grinned as she spoke. "It's just me. And now I have your friend's submachine gun. I'm coming for you, asshole."

Chapter Twenty

Anastasia slung the MAT-49 submachine gun over her shoulder.

It took her ten minutes to climb the series of ladders in the dark. She unslung her weapon and slowly edged through the gap between chamber 4 and chamber 3. She waited for her eyes to adjust to the new chamber.

No light was visible.

She blinked.

Still nothing.

Her adversary either wasn't there or had already moved through to one of the other chambers. The hairs on the back of her neck stood at attention.

There was another possibility.

He was still there in the darkness, with his own headlamp turned off, waiting to take an easy shot as soon as she arrived.

Anastasia considered that, waiting patiently for several minutes.

But time wasn't on her side.

It was somewhere in the vicinity of minus 90 degrees Fahrenheit in the caves. A little warmer than topside, but even so, too cold to remain still for very long at all. Even with the exposure suit on, hypothermia was slowly rearing its ugly head.

Anastasia mentally pictured the outline of chamber 3. It was riddled with stalagmites and pockmarked by deep craters that likely dropped fifty or more feet.

No, there was no chance she could simply navigate it in the dark.

She backed up against a giant stalagmite. Then, with a quick motion, she switched the Maglite on and flashed the chamber from right to left.

Only shadows of stalagmites flashed back at her.

She switched the flashlight off and quickly moved six paces, taking refuge behind the cover of a row of bacon curtain.

Once there, she waited again.

In silence.

And listened.

She tried to make out the sound of her attacker's breathing, but she couldn't. The only sound she could hear was that of her own heart pounding in the back of her head. She had to stay and be still longer. It was a game of cat and mouse. Whoever waited out the other one, had the greater chance of survival.

Her teeth began to chatter in the cold.

Hypothermia was doing more than creeping in.

She had to make a move.

Anastasia switched her flashlight back on.

Screw this, she thought.

She quickly scanned the rest of chamber three, keeping the light in her left hand, the weapon in her right. She held the Maglite along the barrel of the MAT-49 submachine gun, ready to shoot in the direction of the light.

Damnit.

There was nobody inside the chamber.

That meant he was either deeper in the system of ice caves, in which case she should make a run for it now, retreating back to Vostok.

Or, and this was the more likely case, her attacker was waiting for her on the other side of the ice bridge. The one point, he knew she had to cross to climb out of the cave system. And either way, none of that mattered. The fact was, she was freezing to death and needed to reach Vostok.

She made a decision to go the fastest route and be damned with the consequences.

Her attacker would get one shot.

That was all.

The second shot, if she were still alive, would be her bullet hitting him. That was all she needed. She was an expert markswoman and knew that it would only take one shot.

She reached the ice stalagmite with the coiled rope attached. Anastasia tossed the tail end of the rope down the chimney. She waited and listened for any sound from her adversary. There was none. She drew a breath, mentally prepared herself for what was most likely to be her moment of truth. If she survived the next few minutes, she would reach

Vostok and live.

There was an alternative, but she didn't feel like thinking about it.

Once more she slung the MAT-49 submachine gun over her shoulder, grabbed the rope, and switched the flashlight off. She then quickly clambered down the chimney in the dark, using the rope hand-over-hand to guide her.

At the bottom of the chimney, she looked toward the cathedral chamber. There was just enough ambient light drifting down from the starlight above and through the thin layers of ice to make out the shape of the bridge.

With her flashlight still off, and the MAT-49 submachine gun in her hands, ready to fire, Anastasia slowly made her way to the narrow pathway.

She took the first step onto the icy bridge.

It was slippery as hell.

Just like she remembered it.

She ducked down to a crawl, taking a small shuffle forward.

On the third movement, her hand touched something.

The tripwire went taut.

Click.

It was the distinctive sound of a grenade's pin being pulled.

Most grenades detonate about 3-5 seconds after the trigger is released, giving you a few critical moments to react. The kill radius from a grenade's explosion is about 15 feet, and the casualty radius is about 50 feet, though pieces of shrapnel can still fly much farther than that.

Anastasia moved at superhuman speeds.

Five.

She changed direction, pulling on the rope and running toward the far side of the cathedral simultaneously.

Four.

She picked up speed.

The headlamp of her enemy lit up the bridge.

Submachine gun fire began to trace her direction.

The flash of light lit up the cathedral, revealing an alcove several feet to the right of the bridge, back from the chimney, and a little lower down, too.

Three.

Bullets raked the entrance to the chimney.

Her attacker wasn't aiming directly at her. He wasn't going to risk shooting a moving target. Instead, he was going for a sure thing. He kept the burst at fully automatic, running at 600 rounds per minute, at the entrance to the chimney.

A place she needed to pass to get out of the blast radius of the grenade.

Do or die.

She was trapped.

No matter what she did.

Her eyes darted across the landscape, taking in all her options in a millisecond. Anastasia wrapped her hand around the rope and swung off the ice bridge.

Like a pendulum, she traveled across the void.

Two

She lifted her legs to clear the barrier of ice...

...and landed in the little ice-cold alcove.

Anastasia turned to lie prone on the ice and covered her ears.

One.

The grenade exploded.

Whoosh.

A blast-wave riddled the cathedral.

Hot air whirled and blew about the chamber. The ground shook. For a moment, Anastasia worried that the frozen outcrop upon which she'd taken refuge might crack and collapse. The violent ring of the blast echoed for what felt like an eternity.

After several seconds, Anastasia sat upright.

Her eyes snapping around, landed on the ice bridge.

A massive crack had formed in the middle of it.

The crack spread like a lightning bolt, searing a jagged scar throughout the icy foundations. The bridge shook. For a moment, she thought it might stabilize and hold. Then, one by one, the crack spread, causing large chunks of ice to fall. In total, the bridge held for another ten seconds before it too succumbed to the effects of gravity.

The foundations gave way.

The bridge dropped a half a foot, opening up one main crack.

Then, within seconds, the entire ice bridge shattered as though a massive giant had struck it with an equally large fist.

The ice bridge fell into the abyss.

Taking with it, Anastasia's only chance to escape her ice-cold confines.

Chapter Twenty

The hovercraft crept along the alien landscape.

With the blizzard raging, Sam wished the US Air Force Lockheed C-5M Super Galaxy had been able to drop them closer to Vostok. What should have taken no more than an hour was looking like it would take the better part of the day. Better yet, he should have had the pilots of the Super Galaxy drop him off upwind, so that instead of fighting them, their progress would have been helped. Instead, they had been dropped east of Vostok, and now had to battle those same winds back to the research station.

He only hoped they'd brought enough fuel for such a long trip.

It was like flying into the wind.

Which they kind of were.

Only right now, those winds were far more lethal and unstable than normal as they were katabatic. That is to say, they were filled with fast moving, high-density air.

The hovercraft's engine whirred in time with the howling winds, giving that tell-tale grunt of an engine under distress. Like an overloaded truck struggling to grind its way up a steep hill. It was still turning over, just working a hell of a lot harder than it should have been.

They had been going at it for six hours now.

The scenery hadn't changed all that time.

Looking through the windshield, the world was nothing but darkness with a soft blue snow, interspersed between an infinite display of stars littered across a velvet, black sky. Snowdrift pummeled the windshield. The wipers, were set at maximum speed, fighting to keep up with the constant barrage of ice.

It might as well have been the world's widest highway with zero other vehicles to contend with, yet no one was sleeping. All eyes were glued on their narrow window into the inhospitable environment ahead, or the various instruments, designed to keep them alive.

Sam kept his hands on the controls. He wasn't making many

adjustments, and the hovercraft might as well have been on autopilot. Other than that, from the tension in his body, he looked like anything but a relaxed driver out for a Sunday drive.

The Polar Plateau was pockmarked like the moon, riddled with deep ice crevasses, each one capable of swallowing the hovercraft whole.

Sam preferred that his vehicle remained on solid ground.

In the front passenger seat, Tom kept his eyes on two instruments. One was a ground penetrating radar, which kept a constant evaluation of the depth of ice beneath them. If it began to thin out, chances were, they were approaching an air-pocket or the top of a crevasse.

The second instrument was 4D Radar. 4D radar, like traditional radar collected data through an array of antenna elements, each with a wide beam. They were then digitally combined to create an array of narrow beams – through a process known as digital beamforming – which improves the resolution of the resulting image. The difference between 3D and 4D radar was in the arrangement of those antenna elements. A 3D radar system has antennas arrayed horizontally, whereas 4D radar has elements arrayed both horizontally and vertically. The result was the 4D radar provided a clear mapping of the landscape ahead, including the height and depth of the ground.

On the back seats, Genevieve, Elise, and Hu all looked alive, as they scanned the landscape.

Hu sat forward, craning his neck to look up through the windshield. "What is that?"

"What's what?" Sam asked, tilting his head upward.

A burst of light began to erupt into a radiant display of green, red, and blue hues dancing across the permanent night, wintry sky, pierced by the light of more than a thousand stars.

"What?" Sam grinned. "Those streaks of color, dancing like flames across the Antarctic clouds? They're part of the Aurora Australis."

Hu said, "The southern equivalent of the Aurora Borealis?"

"That's the one."

The sporadic phenomenon lasted just ten minutes, spurred on by the incoming solar wind. Then the light show drifted away into the night sky as quickly and mysteriously as it had arrived.

A moment later the constant drone of the hovercraft's engine changed as it began to cough and splutter. The eight-foot tall, four-bladed propeller slowed to a crawl, and the churning air inside the machine's inflatable skirt slowly evaporated. The cushion of air dissipated until the hovercraft dropped to the ground.

The engine cut out.

The hovercraft was stuck.

Everyone sat forward, cocking their ears, and trying to make sense of what was happening. Engine problems in most places in the world wouldn't be an issue. Parts could be repaired or replaced, lubricant sourced, or the vehicle towed. Unfortunately, in Antarctica during winter, a problem with one's transport spelled death.

Only Elise seemed unperturbed. She was still laying back in her chair with her legs crossed, and a pair of Air Pods playing God knows what, seemingly oblivious to the disaster unfolding.

Hu looked up. "That sounds bad."

"It sure isn't good," Sam agreed, studying a series of display instruments in the dashboard.

Tom, too, ran his eyes over the various engine displays. He said, "Uh. Sam? We have a problem."

Sam's eyes landed hard on the one gauge, which now flashed with a universal red light. He drew in a deep breath. "All right, I know what's going on."

"Oh. My. God!" Genevieve said. "Tell me what I think just happened, didn't happen!"

Sam shrugged. "All right, I won't tell you that." He paused. "Hey, Tom?"

"Yeah?"

"I'm afraid we just ran out of fuel."

Chapter Twenty-One

Sam adjusted the first gear lever to his left, cutting power to the main propeller which generated forward propulsion. The hovercraft immediately slowed along the barren floor. He then used his right hand to reduce the revolutions of the impeller which was the downward facing propeller used to generate lift. Thirty seconds later the hovercraft slowed to a complete stop and sank gently to the ground.

Elise sat upright. Took her Air Pods out of her ears. Her eyes wide with sudden concentration, she asked, "What did I miss?"

Genevieve turned to face her with a teasing smile on her face. "We ran out of gas."

"Really?" An incredulous smile crept in Elise's eyes. "That's funny."

"Not particularly," Genevieve said, "It's a long, cold walk to Vostok."

Elise sat back, unperturbed. "If you want to walk, but I'll take the hovercraft when you're ready."

Genevieve looked at Sam. "Did you bring more gas?"

"No." Reaching for his orange exposure suit with a suppressed smile, Sam nodded toward Elise. "She did."

"Leave it to the computer geek to calculate wind into the fuel equation." Then, turning to Elise, Genevieve said, "Thanks for getting us out of this mess."

"No worries. Don't thank me, thank Sam." Elise laughed. He's the one going outside to fill up the tank."

Sam grinned as he pulled the top of his exposure suit tight at the neck. "I thought it was time to get out and stretch my legs anyway."

Hu stared at the arid landscape; bitter in its hostility. "You want to go out here? The outside temperature is minus 110 degrees Fahrenheit!"

"All the same, someone needs to refill the fuel tanks." Sam began sliding each of his legs into the thick exposure suit, which more closely resembled a spacesuit than snow clothing. "Do you want to wait here, or come outside with me?"

"No." Hu shook his head. "I'm good."

"Any other takers?" Sam asked.

There was a collective murmur that unless he needed a second person, there was little need to submit anyone else to the freezing temperatures.

Hu said, "I thought gasoline freezes at minus 100 Fahrenheit?"

"It does," Sam acknowledged, unconcerned.

"So won't the gas be frozen solid?"

"The hovercraft has a compartment positioned next to the engine for the spare fuel tanks. The heat from the engine lifts the ambient temperature enough to stop the gas from freezing."

"Right, good to know."

Sam finished zipping up his exposure suit. He wore a thick woolen beany and then strapped the hood of the suit over the top as an additional shield from the elements. Over his eyes, the only aspect still vulnerable to the extreme conditions, he wore thick snow goggles which formed a perfect seal. His entire outfit was cumbersome but imperative to protect him from the otherwise deadly elements.

He then opened the hatch, and step by step, awkwardly made his way outside.

It only took ten minutes to fill up the tank.

Tom opened the hatch. "You almost there?"

"Almost." Sam stopped pouring. "One more fuel container to go. How come?"

"We've got trouble."

Sam connected the last container to the fuel tank. "Trouble?"

"This storm's about to get stronger."

Sam quickly filled the tank with the final container and firmly locked the fuel lid. He then placed the container back inside its cradle and tightened the strap.

He looked up, toward the Transantarctic Mountain.

A small tuft of snow rolled over the tip.

Known as a rain shadow effect, it was often caused by air rolling off the Polar Plateau being forced over the Transantarctic Mountains. This then cools, condenses, and deposits its moisture as snow, which dips down over the ice at the edges of the valley peaks. Such a formation precedes any number of meteorological events around the world. But in the dry Polar Plateau, it meant one thing only – an extreme wind was coming.

In 1805 Sir Francis Beaufort developed the "Beaufort Wind Scale," to measure wind. Using a scale of 1 to 12, it is still in use today. This looked anywhere between 9 (gale force) and 11 (violent storm). Either way, it was the type of wind that was capable of sending sand, ice, and grit along the plateau at such speeds it would tear holes through the hovercraft.

It could kill them all.

Sam checked that the last strap was secure. "Get the hovercraft fired up!"

Chapter Twenty-Two

Tom shuffled over into the driver's seat.

He hit the ignition button.

The engine whined as the thick rubbery skirt inflated, raising the hovercraft five feet on to a new cushion of air. He ran his eyes across the few engine gauges. Everything seemed within normal range. Sam scrambled in through the narrow hatch, locking its air-tight seal into place. He sat into the passenger seat and drew the harness across his waist.

Tom exchanged a glance with Sam.

Sam had once seen a similar weather event (storm winds – 10 on the scale) up close. He was in a hovercraft then, too. Crossing through the Taylor Valley that cut through the Transantarctic Mountains. Sam had described it to Tom like a Haboob, an intense desert dust storm carried on an atmospheric gravity current. Tom had never seen a Transantarctic Mountain gale, but he and Sam had once been caught out in the Sahara, under the deadly effects of a Haboob.

It had been terrifying.

Tom observed there was a fear in Sam's eyes that he hadn't seen many times before.

Shocked into action, he threw the left-hand throttle down to full, sending maximum power to the aft propellers. The hovercraft lurched forward toward the mirage in the horizon – at full speed.

Their vehicle raced along the stilled surface of the frozen world.

If they didn't reach Vostok in time, they might very well end up needing the Russians to rescue them if they were to survive. They had planned to use just such a story as a ruse to gain access to the Science Station. The irony of their situation was impossible to miss.

Tom kept the joystick straight ahead.

The real skill of piloting a hovercraft was predicting where you need to be, and then steering toward that place well before you get there. It was similar to driving a car on ice, with no means of suddenly changing direction, or braking.

Under different circumstances, it made for an active and fun driving experience.

Right now, it simply scared the crap out of him.

Beside him, Sam said, "We'll never outrun this thing. We need to find somewhere to take cover."

"Sure," Tom said, searching the icy landscape for any place to take refuge. "Do you see anything?"

Sam kept his eyes on the 4D radar monitor. "I'm looking…"

The hovercraft's aft propeller was turning at its maximum speed, but the hovercraft barely progressed at any more than a crawl.

Tom said, "Anything?"

Sam shook his head. "I got nothing."

Elise said, "I got something."

Tom said, "Where?"

"I'm looking at the real time satellite images," Elise said. "There's a series of deep crevasses about fifteen clicks back in the direction from where we've come, and then south."

Tom asked, "Do we want to go down a deep crevasse?"

"No. There's some undulating ground nearby. Large ice caves. Several places we can use to take shelter before this thing hits."

Tom exchanged a glance with Sam. "What do you think?"

"I don't have any better ideas." Sam turned to face Genevieve, Hu, and Elise. "I'm happy to backtrack, unless anyone's got a better idea?"

"Let's take what we can get," Genevieve said.

Hu said, "Agreed."

Tom said, "All right let's do it."

Elise read out the GPS coordinates to Sam, who put them into the hovercraft's GPS. The new mapping data came up through the driver's side HUD – Heads Up Display.

Tom eased off the throttle and swung the hovercraft around. The little machine shifted its position like a lumbering ballet dancer on ice, fishtailing around until it was facing 180 degrees.

Then he thrust the throttle all the way forward.

And the hovercraft took off.

With the wind on their tail, they sped up quickly, reaching 75 miles per hour. Tom struggled to keep control of the hovercraft. Without anything to slow the winds along the plateau, it ripped through unabated, and picked up speed.

Tom's hands tightened on the joystick as the hovercraft became difficult to control.

More like a kite surfer struggling to control his board in a powerful wind. The controls were becoming sluggish. Movements and changes in direction, cumbersome and unruly.

Sam said, "Ease off the throttle."

Tom reduced the main propeller's RPM down to 50 percent.

It took some of the proverbial wind out of the sails.

"That's a bit better."

Tom glanced at the anemometer.

It showed the wind gusting up to 140 miles per hour.

He pointed at the gauge. Then, to Sam, he said, "Is this thing likely to get much worse?"

Sam gave him a smile that he knew to mean, *You have no idea.* "This storm is just warming up."

They continued racing toward the ice caves.

A few minutes later, the true katabatic winds picked up.

The anemometer went berserk.

Tom adjusted the RPM down to 25 percent. It was like letting air out of the tire in a car. Instead of floating freely on ice, the hovercraft sank down into its rubber skirt.

The hovercraft slowed.

But then became even more cumbersome to handle.

Like a big four-wheel drive running on flat tires. It would be fine on sand at slow velocity, but deadly on the blacktop at speed.

Tom made careful, minor adjustments with the joystick.

The hovercraft struggled to respond, and he became worried the deflated skirt might dig in on itself, causing the machine to roll.

He gently increased the RPM up to 40 percent.

The hovercraft picked up speed again.

His eyes glanced at the anemometer.

It registered 160 miles per hour.

And still increasing.

Tiny bits of sand, gravel and pieces of ice, ripped across the Polar Plateau, forming lethal projectiles. They were deadly as any bullet. They pinged against the rear hull of the hovercraft, spreading out like hail against a car. A cacophony of ice and stone was hitting the metal alloy of the hull.

The winds gusted to 190 miles per hour.

Sending the speeding hovercraft up to speeds of 85 miles per hour.

Tom kept his hand firmly on the joystick, trying to keep them running in a straight line, while simultaneously battling to prevent the hovercraft from flipping.

He didn't know how long he could keep this up.

Sam turned around. "Elise, we're not going to make it to the ice caves. I need you to find somewhere else. Even it means abandoning the hovercraft, and taking refuge inside a crevasse."

"On it!" Elise said, her fingers already hammering her laptop, directing the satellites overhead where to search. "Okay. Head northeast, 45 degrees. There's a stream set of crevasses. I'm not sure if they're big enough to protect the hovercraft, but at least we can take shelter inside."

Tom began to make the course correction. The electronic compass set to 45 degrees. He straightened up. "All right, how far are we looking?"

Elise said, "Two miles."

Sam put the GPS coordinates in and began searching for the best place to pull the hovercraft into, while Tom continued to fight with the controls. Scrolling in and out of the mapping program, Sam needed to find a place with enough depth to hold the hovercraft.

They kept spiraling faster and faster.

Sam said, "One more mile to go!"

The wind roared with gusts up to 210 miles per hour.

A gravelly mixture of ice and sand skimmed across the hull of the hovercraft, sending sparks and flashes of light outside.

Tom slanted a wry glance at Sam. "Hey, at least we know what astronauts feel like during re-entry."

Sam grinned like a kid on a rollercoaster. "Just make sure we don't follow the same trajectory as the Columbia space shuttle."

"I'm trying my best."

"Never doubted it."

Astonished that his teammates were engaged in relaxed conversations, while somehow appearing to be having fun, Hu turned to Genevieve. "Is it always like this... I mean, is it always so..."

Genevieve laughed. "Insane?"

"I was thinking, lethal..." Hu said, "But insane works too."

Genevieve nodded. "Yeah, it's always like this."

Elise, in her most helpful voice, said, "This is actually fairly sedate. Quite often it's much worse."

Hu looked to Sam. "Are they serious?"

Sam turned the palms of his hands outward, offering an apologetic grin. "Afraid so. Did I fail to mention that when I offered you a job?"

Hu shook his head. "I guess so."

Sam said, "Do you want out... I mean, if we survive this mission?"

Hu didn't even hesitate. "No way in the world, just checking what I've gotten myself in for. That's all."

"Good man." Sam spotted the gap that led toward the crevasse. It was coming up on the GPS mapping monitor. "Okay Tom, off the gas. Our caves are coming up in about six hundred feet."

Tom reduced power to 20 percent.

Instantly, the joystick started to vibrate.

A strange shudder began taking effect across the entire hovercraft.

Sam said, "Keep it straight or we'll tip."

Tom's eyes narrowed. "I'm trying."

Elise said, "I don't mean to interrupt you gentlemen, but we need to start slowing the hovercraft down."

Tom said, "I'm open for suggestions."

"You can't cut the power anymore," Sam said. "This wind will tip us over as soon as the rubber skirt touches the ice."

Elise said, "All the same. There's a long, jagged crevasse that runs right through this section up ahead, so unless you're planning on trying to jump it, I suggest you come up with a plan."

Tom bit his lower lip. "We're working the problem."

"What about trying to change direction?" Sam suggested.

Tom gently maneuvered the joystick to the left.

With the powerful tailwind, the hovercraft refused to budge. It was on a straight course. "No good."

Sam said, "Try changing direction a little more aggressively?"

Tom gave the joystick a little jolt to the right.

Still nothing happened.

"No good!"

Elise said, "You're running out of time."

Tom's eyes landed on the GPS 3D map of the area.

The crevasse formed a long, jagged scar on the frozen landscape some 150 feet ahead.

Sam saw it too. "Okay, time for niceties is over."

Tom frowned. "What are you thinking?"

"Let's bring the RPM up to full power and slam the hovercraft around 180 degrees."

Tom shrugged. It was as good a suggestion as any. And like Elise said, they were out of time.

"All right," he agreed.

He pushed the throttle all the way forward.

The hovercraft rose high on its cushion of air, reducing the risk of the undercarriage getting stuck during the dangerous procedure.

Tom then jolted the joystick all the way to the left.

The hovercraft threatened to refuse to take the bait.

But after a split second, it fought against the airflow, caught, and spun around. He'd used the procedure to change directions plenty of times before, but this was the first time he'd even considered it at speed – particularly speeds like 90 miles an hour.

The hovercraft spun around on its cushion of air.

It didn't stop.

Kept spinning.

360 degrees.

720 degrees.

Tom stopped counting.

Sam said, "Other way now!"

Tom threw the joystick all the way to the right.

The hovercraft straightened up.

It was now running full speed in a backward direction.

Tom kept the forward thrust at full power.

The hovercraft was starting to slow down, but not fast enough.

Elise was sitting up, looking out the back windows. "Turn again, we're going to hit the crevasse!"

Tom jolted the joystick once more.

It swung around.

Another full 360 degrees.

He straightened up and powered forward again.

It looked good.

The spin slowed the hovercraft a good deal.

Then the back part of the deflated hovercraft's rubber skirt, dug into the undulating ice. Tom tried to adjust the joystick and keep in control of the machine, but in an instant, he'd lost all control.

The hovercraft began to roll.

From that moment on, despite being in the driver's seat, Tom was nothing more than a passenger on board the hovercraft.

The hovercraft rolled onto its roof.

It turned over several times.

Tom's harness went taut, but the rest of him kept moving.

The hovercraft slowed on the ice, sliding upside down on its roof.

Tom looked out the front windshield. They were sliding straight for the crevasse. There was nothing anyone could do about it.

The upside-down hovercraft crashed into the narrow crevasse, and fell through the ice, slamming to a complete stop several feet below the surface.

Tom hit his head on the side of the hovercraft's wall.

He blinked away the haze and turned around.

Taking in his injured team, Tom asked, "Everyone alive?"

There was a general and collective murmur that they would survive.

Sam tried to open the hatch. He said, "But we have another problem."

Tom frowned. "What now?"

Sam drew in a deep breath and sighed. "We're trapped."

Chapter Twenty-Three

Anastasia's world inside the ice cathedral filled with frozen, harsh darkness.

Shards of fractured ice permeated the air in a fine mist of splinters. Her head was ringing with the sound of the explosion. She blinked several times, trying to clear the ice which stung her eyes. She slowly fumbled inside her backpack and retrieved her flashlight. She switched it on to survey the damage.

The cathedral lit up.

The bridge was no longer there.

She was trapped.

Her mind quickly filled with the consequences of such a revelation. Unable to escape the ice caves, she would eventually freeze to death, well before the painful effects of starvation or thirst had their chance to inflict their pain on her. Not one to dwell on bad news, her mind quickly considered what other options she might take to escape.

There was still a rope and plenty of ladders on her side of the void...

Could she use those to form a makeshift bridge of some sort?

Without hesitation, she knew that she could. That was the solution. She would have to find a means of building her own bridge. She turned to the practicalities.

In her mind, she began to formulate a plan.

She was determined to get away. She had to. Not for herself. She still needed to escape the caves to contact her people to let them know about the attack. After that, she wanted to get revenge on the man who had done this to her, but at the very least, she had to reach the surface to make that single satellite call.

Her thoughts were suddenly interrupted by the sound of incoming submachine gun fire.

She ducked down behind the ice wall.

Bullets raked the wall behind her.

Anastasia stayed as low as she could, wondering how much protection a wall of ice might offer from the barrage of bullets that were raining down on her.

The wall was a little more than a couple feet thick. Not enough for lasting protection. The ice cracked, split, and began to shatter. The bullets ricocheted off the walls behind her.

Staying here was a gamble.

Anastasia shuffled into the back of the alcove. She listened intently, narrowing in on the shooter's position by observing the incoming shots. She drew a breath and made a silent prayer. Holding the flashlight along the barrel, she aimed the MAT-49 submachine gun in her attacker's general direction.

Then she squeezed the trigger and gave a short burst.

The bullets fell short of her attacker.

The man dived to the side.

She checked her magazine. There was only one shot left. She quickly replaced the magazine, pocketing the nearly empty one. She kept the crosshairs aimed at the location of her enemy. This was where he was most likely to be exposed when he made his next move.

Then she waited.

It only took a minute. Impatient bastard.

Anastasia saw his head pop into sight.

She squeezed the trigger and fired three 9mm Parabellums straight at him. The first two missed completely, but the third one struck his shoulder.

The man gave a curt yelp, like a wounded animal.

Then he swore at her.

When he finished cursing, he emptied an entire magazine of bullets in her direction. As he had been shot in his right shoulder, her enemy appeared to be right-handed, his aim was off. Anastasia smiled as she let him blow off steam.

When she heard the distinctive clicking sound of the weapon's firing pin landing on an empty chamber, she knew her enemy had no more chambered bullets.

Dry fire!

He's out of ammunition!

Anastasia looked out across the abyss, and aimed her weapon at him. Their eyes met.

He immediately began to run along the edge of the crevasse, partially protected by a broken wall of ice. Anastasia kept her finger gently against the trigger as she traced his projected movement. He was fast, and it was a difficult shot given the distance and poor visibility. There were multiple openings in the ice wall. The ghost of his silhouette kept passing through them.

She spotted his prize.

A gap at the end of the tunnel that led to the surface. That was his goal! She aimed at the last opening just before the end of the tunnel.

Last chance.

She had to make it a good one.

Anastasia waited.

The shadow of her prey's movement flickered through a small window in the ice, about three feet back from the exit tunnel.

She squeezed the trigger.

The barrel of the MAT-49 submachine gun flashed orange, as 9mm Parabellums fired at a rate of 600 rounds per minute, left the 9.1-inch barrel at a speed of 1279.53 feet per second.

Each one imbedding in the ice wall just back from their intended target.

Anastasia kept the trigger engaged, and gently shifted her aim to the right.

Her prey came into position, lining up directly in her crosshairs.

It was on track for a perfect shot.

Click.

Click.

The firing pin landed on an empty chamber.

She was out!

Anastasia fired again.

Click.

Click.

Her attacker began to laugh.

They looked at each other, meeting each other's eyes.

Her attacker shrugged, turning the palms of his hands outward. He grinned at her. In his soft, almost sensual, French accent, he said, "It looks like we are both out of ammunition? No?"

Anastasia laughed at the ridiculousness of it all.

Then she shook her head. "No."

Her attacker tilted his head. "No?"

In a well-practiced movement, she ejected the empty magazine and reinserted the one with a single round remaining.

She brought the weapon up into position, aimed, and fired.

The shot hit her attacker once more in his right shoulder, dropping him. There was plenty of blood. Maybe she'd nicked the subclavian artery. Or better yet, pierced and collapsed his lung. Either way, she hoped he was on his way to a painful death.

Her opponent rolled to his feet, grabbing hold of the wound, as he tried to stem the bleeding. "Hey, Anastasia," the stranger greeted her. The smile behind his eyes proclaimed his triumph. "Enjoy your stay. Think of me as you freeze to death… and remember," he laughed loudly, "I won!"

Then he turned toward the tunnel and vanished.

Chapter Twenty-Four

Anastasia watched him go.

The bastard would probably die out there when he reached the freezing cold surface. It was a small consolation, given that if she didn't get a move on soon, she would die down here, frozen and alone.

She dropped the MAT-49.

It was out of ammunition.

And besides, no one was coming after her anymore.

No longer concerned about being spotted, she tied her flashlight onto her backpack strap, so that it glowed forward. She then tugged on the rope. The same one she'd used to swing from the bridge to the alcove.

The rope came free.

She pulled on it, hand over hand, as the rope came effortlessly toward her.

Anastasia didn't stop until the end of the rope was in her hand. She brought up the severed tether to her face to examine it. The damned thing had been sliced in half by gunfire. The chance of this happening wasn't entirely unpredictable, but it was incredibly bad luck, nonetheless.

She slowly coiled the rope, measuring each foot as she did so.

All in total, the rope was still fifty feet long.

Anastasia figured that as a lifesaving asset, it wasn't much, but it was something. She ran her eyes across her surroundings, really taking them in for the first time since she'd landed in the icy alcove. The alcove, or what remained of it, was roughly ten feet deep, by three wide, and twenty feet high, ending in a series of ice dispersed windows in a large wall of ice.

The alcove was its own island in the cathedral.

She glanced downward.

The niche of space was perched on its own ledge, like an eagle's nest. She fixed the beam of her flashlight below. There was nothing but a vertical cliff face all the way to the bottom of the dark abyss.

Anastasia turned around.

Her gaze caught on the small, hollowed sections of ice high above. They looked like they had formed after several stalagmites had fused together over hundreds, probably thousands of years. The gaps were where warmer water – presumably in the summer – had managed to etch its way through the weaker points, forming gaps. The questioned remained, would those ice stalagmites be strong enough to support her weight if she could anchor a rope to it?

There was only one way to find out.

Anastasia's eyes narrowed. Formulating a plan in her mind. She picked up the French MAT-49, and fully extended its retractable wire stock, giving the weapon a total length of 28 inches. She then tied the end of the rope through the weapon's trigger guard. Finally, she tied the opposite end of the rope to her waist. The last thing she wanted to do was lose the rope and her machinegun.

She gripped the weapon-cum-anchor in her right hand, estimated the height and effort to reach the gap in the ice, and threw it up.

The MAT-49 hit the side of the ice stalagmite and bounced off.

Undeterred, she immediately tried again.

Same result.

She kept trying.

And on the eleventh attempt, she managed to throw the MAT-49 through the gap. She gently pulled the rope, hoping it caught, but the weapon fell upon her again.

She drew a frustrated breath and exhaled.

Anastasia paused to regather her strength and review her actions. She needed to find a way to pull the MAT-49 to the side somehow, once she got it through the gap.

It would be simple if she had a second rope.

But she didn't.

Frustrated, Anastasia pursed her lips considering other possibilities, but she had nothing. Failing to think of a better plan, she again tried to thread the needle. This time it took just three goes to get her weapon through the hole.

Hey, I'm getting better at this...

She gave the rope a gentle pull, and the weapon slowly, inexorably slid through the gap once more. Another failed attempt! So maddening!

That's when it abruptly clicked.

She knew what she was doing wrong!

When she pulled the rope through gently, she was giving it time to slip free. Instead, she needed to give it a sharp tug. Much like a captain laying an anchor gave the propellers a quick burst of power to cause the anchor to bite into the seabed. That's what she must do here.

Anastasia narrowed her eyes.

Focused on the gap, she threw the MAT-49 anchor toward the icy hole.

Again.

Again.

Again, until it went in. She stared at it.

Moment of truth.

This time she gave the rope a sharp tug and the MAT-49 caught on the ice! Then it flipped onto its side, becoming lodged in-between the two ice stalagmites.

Anastasia sighed a breath of relief. She kept pressure on the rope, scared that if she released some of the tension, her weapon anchor might dislodge.

Anastasia still didn't know if her improvised rig would hold her weight. There was only one way to find out. Thousands of years of solid ice. It would probably hold her weight. She wasn't heavy, but who knew for sure? Besides, it didn't matter. If she didn't try, she was as good as dead anyway.

She gripped the rope in each hand and put her weight on it. So far so good. Then she attempted to climb up the face of the ice-cliff.

Her feet kept slipping, and when they did, her hands slid too.

She remembered watching a team of Spetsnaz – Russian Special Forces – once climb an obstacle course. It was one of those feel-patriotic-about-the-Army documentaries. Something that showed how superior Mother-Russia's soldiers were compared to the rest of the world. She knew it was political BS, but she had to admit, having watched it, their Spetsnaz looked pretty damn effective.

Anyway, the part that stuck with her was how the big strong, men and women, of the Spetsnaz made it look so easy to climb a vertical rope. It wasn't that they were stronger, or better than civilians. Their ability was due to an unobserved technique they used to ascend the rope. Basically, they planted their feet together on the rope, then twisted the rope, to form a platform to step up on. Then they would lift their legs up again and repeat the process.

Anastasia gripped the rope with her hands, planted her feet on the rope, and twisted. It formed the first of what would need to be several stepping rungs of the rope ladder. She then tried to hold on with her hands and lift her feet up higher. As soon as she disengaged her foot-lock, her near frozen hands slid down the rope once more.

She tried adjusting the technique, but soon learned it wasn't going to happen. She was already in the first stages of hypothermic shock, and her fingers simply didn't have the strength needed to do what she was trying to achieve.

There had to be another way.

She looked at the remnants of the bridge's ice foundations and the start of the chimney, which she had clambered up not so long ago.

It looked to be about ten feet away.

Too far to jump, but maybe she could use the rope to swing across. It was risky, and a single mistake would mean that she fell to her death in that cold, dark abyss.

But what other option was there?

Inaction was the fastest way to death.

With that thought, she twisted her hands around the rope, almost tying them up, securing them so she couldn't slide off the rope entirely.

Confident that her hands had found their perch, she slowly leaned over the edge of the alcove into the open void below. She positioned her feet so they were perpendicular to the wall, like an abseiler. She began to walk side-to-side along the ice-cold cliff-face.

Like a pendulum, she picked up momentum.

Each swing was bringing her farther and farther along.

Her hands and wrists were aching, but she ignored the pain. By the fifth swing, her feet touched the remnants of the edge of the frozen bridge. It was all that she needed. Taking a deep breath, she released the rope, dug her gloved hands into the ice, and propelled herself forward.

Panting with effort and adrenaline, she didn't wait to catch her breath, but kept going, clambering all the way up the chimney.

At the top of the third chamber, she drew multiple, long, deep breaths of air, until her heart rate settled. She then backtracked until she found the gap with the MAT-49 anchor attached. She pulled the rope and the anchor through, catching them as they fell, in case she needed them. Coiling up the rope, she left it attached to the weapon, and placed them both in her backpack.

Anastasia then headed to the fourth chamber, where a series of ladders led to the bottom of the icy cliff. Her hope was to be able to remove one of them and use it to form a bridge across the cathedral abyss.

As soon as she looked at the ladder, she realized it wasn't going to happen.

The ladder was bolted into the ice in more than a dozen places. She didn't have a spanner, pliers, or anything to unbolt it. She stood there, staring at the embers of her last hope, shivering. Hypothermia was starting to affect her mind. She could feel herself getting cognitively slower.

She had to do something, but these ladders weren't it.

Anastasia returned to the main section of chamber three, which was the primary starting point for the entire ice cave system. She hoped that one of the scientists that helped set up the labyrinthian web of ropes and ladders, would have left a spare ladder or any equipment inside the initial chamber.

She was wrong.

There was nothing inside.

Just more frozen speleothems.

She returned to the chimney and gazed at the gap where the ice bridge once lay.

It didn't look far.

Less than the twenty feet as she had originally estimated.

Maybe as little as ten, if you consider the remnants of the bridge on either side of the void. She thought that, on a good day, she might even be able to clear the gap with a jump. Despite her small stature, she was surprisingly good at long jump. If it was all level, and she had the distance to make a run-up, she would even be confident enough to give it a try. But with the chimney blocking the lead up to the jump, there was no chance she could clear it.

She thought about making another pendulum swing.

It was no good.

If she tied the rope where she was, the pendulum would end up too far below the height of the old bridge. That meant no matter how good a swing she could achieve, she could never get it high enough to reach the other side.

No, to do that, she would need to start higher.

Her eyes drifted upward.

There was a ladder to what appeared to be a sort of crow's nest.

She climbed the ladder some thirty feet and reached a small air-pocket that extended out and over the cathedral chamber.

It was perfect.

She secured the MAT-49 anchor between two massive ice stalagmites.

This time, she tied a knot at the bottom of the rope. It meant that once she reached it, she could plant a foot inside, using it as a step, and preventing herself from simply sliding off the end of the rope to her death at the bottom of the void.

She quickly rubbed her hands together, trying to warm up the circulation. It didn't work. She was starting to freeze. Shutting down systemically. Her body shunting all her blood away from her extremities, toward her vital organs.

It was time to go.

Now or never.

Anastasia carefully crawled over the edge. She twisted her feet around the rope and gripped it with her hands. She then slowly released the pressure in her hands, carefully lowering herself all the way to the knot in the rope at the bottom.

Once there, she began the effort of swinging back and forth, developing momentum and swinging the pendulum from side to side.

This swing was big.

The rope was forty feet long and she was standing at the very end of it.

And swinging all the way in each direction.

The problem was she was swinging side by side, when she needed to leave this side, and reach the other side of the abyss.

To try and achieve this, she started to kick off the wall at the end of each swing.

It quickly changed the direction of her movements, adding an arc to her pendulum. She grinned. This was getting her in the right direction. But after half a dozen swings, she realized it was only ever going to get her halfway across the void.

Which meant she had to let go.

And she had no way to predict the outcome of doing so.

Chapter Twenty-Five

The pendulum kept swinging.

Her hands were freezing. Her vision was blurring. To top it off, her flashlight was starting to dim.

There were no other options.

Win or lose. Life or death.

She had to take the gamble.

Anastasia worked the largest of all the swings, and when she was at the peak of the upward arc, somewhere halfway across the void, she simply let go.

She flew through the air.

Climbing and gaining in altitude all the way.

And landed roughly ten feet up the opposite side of the bridge, on an icy slide.

Her hands instinctively struggled to reach out. To grab something for stability. But they couldn't find purchase on anything.

The upward momentum was overcome by gravity, and she began to slide backward – toward the destroyed bridge.

Her arms windmilled all the way.

As her legs slid off the pathway, her right hand caught hold of a stalagmite. Her feet slipped off the edge of the bridge ruins and dangled above the void.

She swung there for a second, then, using the last of her strength, she pulled herself up.

As soon as she was standing, she forced herself to scramble back out of the crevasse. She backtracked the way she had come hours earlier, until she eventually surfaced onto the alien world of the Polar Plateau.

With the bone-chilling wind, it was colder than ever. Yet between her unexpected success, her newfound sense of achievement, and the joy of being alive, the permanent darkness of an Antarctic winter enveloped her like a warm blanket.

She stared at the Vostok Research Station in the distance.

A single hovercraft seemed to be racing away toward the east.

A mixture of sadness and relief washed over her. It meant her attacker had survived, but it also reassured her that he wasn't still here, waiting to kill her.

Anastasia didn't have much more energy left.

She dropped to the snow-covered ground, opened her backpack, and retrieved the Iridium satellite phone. Then she dialed a number off by heart. Pressed the call button.

The phone went straight to voicemail.

Anastasia silently cursed.

Then she worried.

Anastasia's daughter Natalya was a university student. Like most adults, and all young people, she always had her phone in her hand or within arm's reach. Her offspring seemed to take the attachment to her phone to a whole other level. Natalya never let go of her phone.

Anastasia heard the confident, almost flirty sound of her daughter's voice on her answering machine. *Bad luck you missed me. Try me on messenger.*

There was no mention of leaving a message after the beep.

When the beep came, Anastasia said, "Darling. I want you to listen to me. This might be my only chance. I want you to run. Take the key to the safety-deposit-box… everything inside is yours. You must run like we've practiced since you were a little girl! Run baby, run!"

Chapter Twenty-Six

The blood rushed into Sam's head.

His vision blurred and darkened. He tried to blink away the fog of disorientation. He tried to remember where he was or how he'd gotten there but kept coming up blank. His eyes slowly came into focus. Everything was upside down. His entire world, inverted. Next to him he heard Tom asking if everyone was alive. His brain changed gears.

He had been in a crash. The hovercraft flipped, and now he was inside a deep, ice-cold crevasse. In response to a call of "Anyone need help?" there was a general murmur from everyone on board that they would live.

The beam of the hovercraft's twin headlamps shone on the chasm below. The warm glow radiating through the dark blue of the ancient glacial ice, showing a dark void. It looked like an abyss to eternity.

The seatbelt lap-sash was taut.

A revelation explaining his disorientation hit him as a tsunami of recent memories washed through his mind.

He was upside down.

Sam fumbled with the seatbelt. There was too much pressure on the locking mechanism, so he was unable to release it. He placed his hands on the dashboard and pushed, like one doing a handstand. The pressure came off his seatbelt, and he quickly unlocked it with his right hand.

His body fell forward in the process, like a sack of potatoes.

He tried opening the hatch.

It didn't shift at all.

He gave it a push with his shoulder, but the thing was stuck. More than stuck. It was wedged between two sides of an ice chasm.

Tom frowned. "What now?"

Sam drew a breath and sighed. "We're trapped."

Tom arched an eyebrow. "Are you sure?"

"Yeah, pretty certain."

Elise slanted Hu a wry, knowing glance. "Now *this* is more like how things generally go around here."

Hu performed the delicate handstand-like maneuver, unclasping his seatbelt with the finesse of a gymnast. He nodded. "I'm starting to get the picture."

The rest of them followed suit.

Tom said, "Any chance more hands on that hatch is going to get it to open?"

Sam studied the doorway wedged hard against the icy fissure. "No chance in hell."

"We'll need to shift the hovercraft somehow…"

"Agreed," Sam said. "Do you want to try to start the engine.

"Sure." Tom hit the engine start.

It fired, but quickly coughed, and choked. At a guess, it wasn't designed to be used in an inverted position.

"No go."

No one said a word as they all contemplated their cold, dark tomb.

Chapter Twenty-Seven

"All right," Sam said, breaking the silence.

Behind him, Hu sat with crossed legs like some sort of yogi monk, his face set in bemused curiosity. "Tell me, when you all end up in these sorts of scrapes... how do you generally manage to get out of them?"

Sam said, "Luck."

"Luck?" Hu tilted his head to the side. "That's the best you can do?"

"You'd be surprised how useful it is. I'd much rather work with someone born lucky than with natural talent or a high IQ. That's not to say that natural talent and intelligence isn't important. We need those things too. Being lucky is really important."

"Right," Hu nodded. Resting back, ready to just wait it out. "So we'll just wait around here and hope to get lucky?"

Sam grinned. "Sometimes we have to work on making good fortune happen."

Hu smiled. "That's more what I'm looking for."

"We need to change the weight in the hovercraft." He switched on his flashlight, pointing the beam down toward the infinite void beneath them. "If we can rock this thing forward a bit, we might get lucky and slide down there."

Hu stopped smiling. "That's your plan?"

Sam turned his head to face him. "Yeah, what do you think?"

"I think..." Hu swallowed hard. "I'm pretty certain we're all going to die."

Tom grinned. "There you go... now you really are part of the team."

"I'm serious!" Hu argued.

Tom nodded. "So are we."

Sam said, "It's all right. Something down there will arrest our fall. It will be fine. Anyone got a better idea?"

Nope. Zip. Nada.

They came to a consensus to shift the hovercraft forward.

Sam said, "OK. We're upside down, but on the count of three, we need everyone to move forward to where the front seats are."

"Ready," came the collective agreement.

Sam said, "One, two, three…"

Everyone shuffled into the forward compartment, squeezing in on top of one another between the driver and forward passenger seat wells.

The hovercraft creaked as all their weight shifted to the front.

Sam said, "Now back."

They all clambered across the length of the ceiling, toward the back of the broken vehicle.

The hovercraft grunted.

"Forward, but faster this time!"

Everyone, getting the hang of the concept, jumped enthusiastically into the front of the hovercraft.

The hovercraft creaked loudly.

Then something happened. Ice, wedged between the skirt of the hovercraft, broke free, sending small chunks of ice falling into the seemingly endless cavern below.

Hu said, "Are you sure we want to go down there?"

Sam watched a large chunk of ice fall away.

It flickered like a diamond beneath the hovercraft's headlamps, before disappearing into the distant darkness.

He swallowed. "It does seem like a long way down…"

It was too late for further discussions.

The hovercraft jolted forward. With nothing to hang on to, everyone slid toward the front. And in another second, it moved, picking up speed.

Then it was flying, dropping straight down the crack in the ice, plunging toward the bottom of the open chasm.

Chapter Twenty-Eight

Then it rolled.

Everyone tumbled as the hovercraft tilted, turning right side up.

The hovercraft slammed into a frozen ledge.

It sent a plume of fine ice shards into the air, like a gentle mist. When it settled, Sam drew a deep breath. It wasn't as far or as bad as one might have expected. The hovercraft was now in a near horizontal position instead of upside down and vertical.

He looked around, trying to see if his team were all okay. At a glance they looked fine. Just shell-shocked more than anything else.

His eyes landed on Hu.

Hu's generally unanimated face wore a broad grin. "Oh, now I get it. I've joined the circus."

Tom nodded, patted him on the back. "There you go. You do get it!"

Sam reached up and opened the hatch fully.

"Hey, it worked!" he said, in a voice that sounded genuinely surprised.

Sub-zero air whooshed into the hovercraft.

Sam gently closed the hatch again.

Over the next dozen or so minutes, all five of them donned their exposure suits. With backpacks brimming with equipment, they headed outside to see if they could reach the surface.

His flashlight attached to his beanie, Sam pulled himself up and onto the top of the hovercraft. He looked up. The beam of the light showed where they had fallen into the crevasse. It was far less steep and less of a distance than it had felt when falling down the narrow gap.

How fortuitous. They had gotten lucky. Sam exchanged a knowing glance with Tom. "What do you think?"

Tom stared at the fractured chasm, nodded with a smile of surprise. "Not too bad."

Together, in very little time or effort, all five of them climbed out onto the surface.

The wind was still howling.

But already, it was abating.

These katabatic winds were renowned for disappearing as quickly as they arrived.

Still, the ambient temperature was around 100 degrees below zero, and with the windchill factor, that temperature was much lower and far deadlier.

Sam studied the bleak surroundings.

Elise's attention was caught by the nearby ice caves. "We might take refuge in one of those until the storm settles down."

"Yeah," Sam said, "But there's no way, even outside the storm, that we're going to be able to walk to Vostok from here."

"Okay." Elise looked at him directly. "You want me to make contact with Amundsen–Scott South Pole Station and get the ball rolling for a rescue mission?"

Sam shook his head. "We might have to, but not yet. I'd prefer to still try to salvage the mission."

"Salvage the mission?" she said. "How? We lost the hovercraft."

Sam shrugged. "See if you can get through to the Vostok Research Station. Let them know who we are, and that we've had an accident and need their assistance."

"Okay, I'll give it a go," Elise said, lifting the Iridium satellite phone's antenna.

Tom ran his eyes down at the crumpled wreck of the hovercraft down below, before turning back to Sam. He wore a suppressed grin. "Sam, when you came up with this plan of approaching Vostok under the ruse of having crashed the hovercraft, I didn't think you'd actually go through with it."

Sam looked at the mangled wreck. "Don't blame me. You're the one who crashed it."

Tom turned his palms skyward. "I take no responsibility for this. I was just piloting the hovercraft under your directions."

They walked around the crash site, surveying the area.

There were a few ice caves and whatnot in which to take some refuge in the short term, but the fact remained, without the hovercraft, they would need to be rescued.

Using hands, feet, and every part of his body to ascend, Sam reached the peak of the nearby ice mound, until he could take in the entire landscape.

He withdrew a pair of binoculars from his bag and fixed them to the west.

Vostok came into view.

Probably only a little over a mile away, but might as well be on the moon given that they needed to make the journey on foot, across multiple, large crevasses that would need specialized climbing equipment or ladders to cross.

Sam adjusted the binoculars, focusing in on the new research station.

It looked like something extraterrestrial. A frosty habitat on a distant, inhospitable world. *What were those two planets with temperatures of absolute zero?* Uranus and Neptune. The ice giants they were called. Both were rich in chemicals like methane, sulfur and ammonia in their atmospheres. Sam remembered learning in a high school science class that it's really cold that far away from the sun, so these chemicals were likely to be frozen or trapped in crystals of ice.

Breathing hard, Elise clambered up to the freezing plateau. Her face was unreadable.

Sam said, "What did the Russians say?"

"Nothing," she replied.

Sam frowned. "They're refusing to help?"

"No, they're not saying anything at all." Elise tilted her head, gave a sort of bemused smile. "It's like they're asleep over there. Hibernating for the winter."

"That's impossible. You saw the dossier on the base's winter team. There must have been thirty people working through winter?"

"Thirty-two," she said. "I know. Something's not right."

"Did you try any other numbers?"

"Yeah, I tried both. There's only one official one for Vostok, plus the additional – Russian only – number that we hacked earlier. Both just kept ringing."

Sam asked, "What about Moscow?"

Moscow University, in Russia, managed the offshore components of the Vostok Research Station. They had a direct line of communication with the Antarctic base.

Elise said, "I explained who we were and our situation. They advised that they tried calling the staff at Vostok but were unable to make contact with them. They suggested we contact the Americans at the Amundsen–Scott South Pole Station."

Sam said, "Odd. No one's home at Vostok?"

Elise shrugged. "There's no reason to think the Russians are telling us the truth."

"Why lie?" Sam asked, puzzled. "I mean, they must have looked us up already. They know who we are and that we're on a fund-raising exercise for South Pole research. We need their help. It's a humanitarian mission. The Russians would ordinarily jump at that. It's just the sort of feel-good story that projects in Antarctica like to promote. Russians coming to the aid of stranded Americans. I don't get it…"

Tom said, "Unless everything our spy has told us is true, and Vostok really did find a 15-million-year-old spacecraft beneath the ice?"

Sam said, "That's a definite possibility, albeit a far-fetched one."

Elise said, "You want me to contact Amundsen–Scott South Pole Station to arrange a rescue mission?"

Sam shook his head. "Not yet. We may still have to, but right now, I think I have an idea."

"Why?" she asked. "What are you thinking?"

Sam turned to the wreckage of the hovercraft, buried deep in the cold crevasse. Languishing in its unmarked arctic grave. Sam grinned. "I'm thinking, I wonder what it would take to salvage the hovercraft?"

Chapter Twenty-Nine

Anastasia was freezing to death.

She no longer felt cold.

It was one of the most dangerous signs of hypothermia. She knew that when a person begins to lose the ability to feel cold, their body is shutting down. Blood from the peripheries and extremities are shunted to the vital organs. It was an evolutionary technique, developed over the millions of years to protect a person and promote survival, but it had its limits.

Her vision was blurring. Kept fading in and out. Like one of those old video recordings that wasn't quite right. Her legs, freezing to the core, weren't quite working properly either. She tried to keep going, but repeatedly tumbled, falling over, and landing in the snow. Her face was raw from the impact with ice.

Yet something drove her forward.

One more step.

Then another.

And another.

Up ahead, she could see the outline of the door to Module E. She would reach it.

She imagined getting inside and having a warm shower. Slowly raising her core temperature. Thawing out and coming back to life. It was just enough motivation to convince her to keep going. Through the sheering wind, she slowly trudged through the ice, back to the door. She reached the entrance. Drew a deep breath. And turned the handle.

Nothing happened.

The door was locked.

She put her shoulder into the door, as though she might somehow, slam through the heavily insulated aluminum with her petite frame.

It didn't budge.

Anastasia had just enough strength to try again, so she did, but it was too hard. She barely touched the damned door, and then slid down to the icy ground.

She pictured her attacker's rueful, final act to ensure she didn't survive.

Anastasia considered slogging her way to the door in A module. It was the better part of 900 feet away. There was no way she could make it in these conditions. No, she had to accept reality. She was going to die out here.

She reached in and grabbed the satellite phone. Then she dialed a number she hadn't rung for a very, very long time.

A man answered the phone on the first ring. "Hello?"

"Hello Merc."

His tone showed the hint of concern, mixed with disbelief. "Anastasia?"

"Yes Merc," she said, her voice meek.

His voice hardened. "I thought I told you never to contact me on this number?"

"You did. But I need help. There was an attack on Vostok."

"Vostok was attacked?"

He sounded honest, but she didn't believe him. How could she trust him? After all that he had done to her? She said, "It's your fault, Merc. We had a deal. I did everything you asked. I left that life alone. I worked hard to make a new one. For God's sake… I earned a PhD in glaciology, so that I would move as far away as physically possible from my old life!"

"And I appreciated that."

"But it wasn't enough. Still, you found me. As I knew you would."

"No. That was just bad luck. And when we knew you were there, we needed you to keep spying for us. That was all. Imagine my relief when I discovered we already had the perfect spy in place?"

"I did everything you asked."

"And I kept my side of the bargain, too. I've funded Natalya's life, her university, everything."

"Then why did you try to kill me?"

He paused. "You think I'm responsible for the attack on Vostok?"

"Aren't you?"

"No. Of course not. I had everything I wanted right where it was. You were positioned in the best place to retrieve it for me, unchallenged, during the Antarctic winter."

"So who attacked Vostok?"

"I've no idea. But I promise you I will find out."

"I'm dying Merc."

"Just hang on. Where are you?"

"Outside the escape door in Module E. I'm trapped outside. I'm freezing to death."

"All right. I'll send someone from the drilling site to help. They can be with you within the hour. I'll let him know who you are. You can trust him to be your handler from here on out, until he gets you out of Antarctica."

"What about my daughter?"

Merc said, "Natalya will be safe."

"Don't you dare let them do anything to her, Merc."

"I won't. As long as you continue to cooperate, the two of you will be reunited shortly."

She was drifting off to sleep in the ice.

Anastasia, no longer strong enough to sit upright, slumped beside the door, awaiting the frozen death that came to greet her. It was strangely warm.

In a whisper, she said, "Ten years! I had to go to the ends of the Earth just to escape you, and you still have power over me!"

The Ghost laughed… "Funny how life turns out, isn't it?"

Chapter Thirty

Grenoble, France

Natalya Utkin looked like a movie star.

She had long blonde hair, set in an intricate Dutch braid, with several stray strands framing her pale, unblemished skin. She had a small nose, strong jaw line, and long neck. But it was her enigmatic, gunmetal gray eyes that immediately captured people's attention. She wore the casual attire known these days as "active wear," along with running shoes and a Nike hoodie pulled over the top. She was relatively tall, which she inherited from her father, with a slim and athletic figure, which she inherited from her mother.

Natalya crossed the Isère River along a footbridge, with a determined stride.

Its crystal-clear water looked as pristine as the glacier in the Vanoise National Park, from which it originated. The Isère snaked around Grenoble, a city in the Auvergne-Rhône-Alpes region of southeastern France, which sits at the foot of the mountains between the Drac and Isère rivers. It is known as a base for winter sports, and for its museums, universities, and research centers. Spherical cable cars called "Les Bulles," meaning "Bubbles" connected the town to the summit of La Bastille hill, named for the 18th-century fortress on its slopes.

She breathed in the fresh air.

The vibrant scent of flowers wafted through her nostrils as she passed *Musée de Grenoble*, heading south toward the Cathedral of Notre Dame. She kept walking, stepping into the main square of the old city. In doing so, she passed the dilapidated remnants of a Roman built wall. The city had been under Roman rule since 43 BC. During the upheavals arising in the late Roman Empire, a strong stone wall was erected around the entire township in 286AD. Surrounded by history, the city was now a mixture of ancient structures, post-modernistic buildings, and architectural marvels.

Just how she liked it.

She stopped at the Fountain of the Three Orders and gazed at it.

Natalya was an Arts and History student at the University of Grenoble. She stared at the bronze fountain, as she had done dozens of times before. The stone and bronze fountain was built by sculptor Henri Ding as a tribute to the pre-revolutionary events of June 1788 – AKA the French Revolution. The three bronze characters embodied the people of Grenoble.

"Is it raining?" enquires the third estate.

"Please heaven it had rained," lament the clergy.

"It will rain," proclaims the nobility.

Entire doctorial theses had been written on the French Revolution.

The First Estate was the clergy, who were people, including priests, who ran both the Catholic church and some aspects of the country. In addition to keeping registers of births, deaths and marriages, the clergy also had the power to levy a 10% tax known as the tithe.

The Second Estate consisted of the nobility of France, including members of the royal family, except for the King. Members of the Second Estate did not have to pay any taxes. They were also awarded special privileges, such as wearing a sword and hunting. Like the clergy, they also collected taxes from the Third Estate.

The Third Estate was made up of everyone else, from peasant farmers to the bourgeoisie – the wealthy business class. While the Second Estate was only 1% of the total population of France, the Third Estate was 96%, and had none of the rights and privileges of the other two estates.

Natalya's cell phone beeped with a voice message.

She glanced at the number.

It wasn't in her phonebook, and she didn't recognize the number. She put the phone on silence and continued staring at the fountain.

Historians believe that one of the reasons the French Revolution came about was the dissatisfaction of members of the Third Estate, who wanted a more equal distribution of wealth and power.

Her cell phone beeped again.

Several messages this time.

Each one from the same, unrecognized number.

It looked like the messages were sent earlier, or more likely, the phone calls had been missed, as she entered a cellular black spot coming down the Fort de La Bastille in the south end of the Chartreuse Mountain range and overlooking the city of Grenoble.

She frowned.

There were eighteen missed-calls in total.

It was probably a scam.

She nearly deleted them entirely, working on the assumption that anyone who had bothered to call eighteen times would probably be willing to do so a nineteenth time if it was really important.

But something stopped her.

She hit the voicemail button and retrieved the first message.

Natalya immediately recognized her mother's voice.

There was an elation to knowing that her mother, who she knew to be working all winter long in Antarctica, had made the effort to contact her. She loved her mom dearly. They had been very close once, when she was little, and then, one day her mother changed. Everything in their lives had changed. She remembered moving to a bigger house, a wealthier school, and better gifts at Christmas and Birthdays... but also, a much more distant mother.

She was too young to make any sense of it, but the closeness never returned. Natalya eventually mourned that relationship with her mother more than all the wealth that she'd gained.

Elation turned to trepidation as she listened to her mother's voicemail message.

From her first few words, she recognized the underlying strain in her mother's voice. In that moment, she knew that her world was about to change completely again.

"Darling. I want you to listen to me. This might be my only chance. I want you to run. Take the key to the safety-deposit-box... everything inside is yours. You must run like we've practiced since you were a little girl! Run baby, run!"

Chapter Thirty-One

Natalya's heart raced.

She carefully withdrew the pendant that hung around her neck. It was made of bronze and looked ornate. It had a decidedly historical appeal, rather than physical value. It displayed the image of a man with a golden sword, riding a unicorn

She'd had it for years as her mom gave it to her when she was thirteen years old. Even then, it looked childish and silly.

And that had made it more precious than any of the other worldly possessions she might have. But more than that, she recalled her mother telling her that no matter what happened she was forbidden from removing the pendant from her neck.

Hidden inside the uniquely crafted pendant, was a key.

Like the pendant, which served as its old and ornate home, the key appeared ancient. Like a fabricated historic piece, rather than serving any real purpose as a means of locking or unlocking secrets.

Yet appearances, like many things, were often deceptive.

Inside that elaborate pendant was the digital code to a fortress.

Natalya had been given the address of a bank and lockbox number and told to commit it to memory. That one day, knowing this information might just save her life. At the time, there had been big changes with her mom. and Natalya – even at the age of 13 – had a fair idea that her mother was having a nervous breakdown.

They moved from Berlin, Germany, to Grenoble, France, leaving behind everything she knew, from school to friends. The move was made unexpectedly. Like a dream, her mother had woken her in the middle of the night. Scooping her up, her mom had placed a teddy bear she'd been given at birth and hadn't cared for in years, in her arms as a cuddle toy to soothe her. While she dozed in that in-between space somewhere not quite asleep but far from awake, her world changed.

When she woke up, she was in a big Chateau in France.

Her financial fortunes had changed, too. Natalya went to a privileged private school, but she'd lost everything she'd known in Germany. Her life and her mother were forever different.

Now, after all these years, she learned that maybe her mother wasn't insane. Perhaps she had been involved with some very bad people, and had fled to survive and to keep her daughter safe?

Before she went to make a withdrawal, Natalya needed something to carry whatever was inside that safety deposit box. She stopped at a clothing store that sold athletic gear. Her eyes swept the row of small backpacks, followed by large, hiking bags. She picked a black North Face one. It was medium sized, nothing too big, and would blend in well with what the horde of tourists visiting the Alps used each day. She bought it with her credit card and left, making her way, quickly, toward her destination.

She headed south along *Rue de La Poste*, toward the banking district. She stopped at a large 16th Century stone building. It had a regal appearance, and she guessed the structure had once been owned by a part of the French Aristocracy once upon a time. Ironically, it was now home to a prestigious bank, so for all practical purposes, it was still part of the French Aristocracy, no matter what the Revolution thought about it.

Natalya had never stepped foot inside before.

Her mom had instructed her not to.

But that hadn't stopped her mother from making her memorize how to reach it from any point in the city of Grenoble. It had become a Sunday morning task for a while there. Her mother would take her someplace in the city, and then tell her to meet her as quickly as possible at the bank. Later, it became a game. Randomly, sometimes in the day and sometimes at night, her mom would simply drop her off somewhere and tell her to race her to the bank.

Her mother timed her.

Looking back, it was quite crazy.

These days her mom probably would have been institutionalized. But Natalya just put up with it. She loved her mother. Never told anyone about these crazy games her mom used to play. It was partly because her mom had warned her not to ever tell anyone about the secret key and the bank, but it was more than that. Somewhere, not so deep down, Natalya knew that what her mom was doing was crazy, and that if she mentioned it to anyone – a schoolteacher, a friend, a police officer – her mom would be taken away from her.

She definitely didn't want that.

So, she remained silent.

As she grew up, moved out on her own, and went to university, she had sometimes been tempted to take the key to the bank to see what the key opened. To discover what hidden secrets had been kept from her all these years.

But for some reason, she had never quite had the guts.

Something told her it was important not to, although she couldn't quite say why. Maybe it was just because it had been so crucial to her mother. Had Natalya felt it would be too strong a betrayal to break that trust and open the safety deposit box?

So, here she finally was.

All these years later...

She was going to find out what this was all about.

Natalya drew a breath and entered the building that had occupied her curiosity so much from her youth. She was greeted by a bank manager as soon as she walked through the door. The man was elderly, and spoke with the gentle, but formal, obsequiously polite language reserved for the upper-class. She thanked him and handed him her key, informing him she had a safety deposit box with the bank.

She took the pendant off her neck and removed the key.

He looked at the key.

The outside of his upper lip curled upward.

He studied her, behind bespectacled hazel eyes, taking her in with sudden respect, awe, and possibly fear. Something about his response to the sight of the key suggested that her mother hadn't just been rich, she had been important. As though, just looking at the key identified her in a class of her own.

He took her around the back of the commercial part of the bank, through a series of secure doors, leading to a vault. The bank manager glanced at her. "You know the number that belongs to?"

She nodded. "Yes."

"Very good. I'll leave you in here on your own. The door will shut to provide absolute privacy. There's a phone on the other side. Just pick up the receiver when you're finished, and someone will open the door for you. Is there anything else you may need?"

"No." She smiled. "Thank you."

Natalya slowly walked down another set of stairs before strolling through the main vault. She ran her eyes across the row upon row of safety deposit boxes with a reverent gaze. The boxes were stored in drawers. A single red light glowed at the façade of each one.

She followed the numbers and found the one that matched her key.

Carefully holding the brass key, she inserted it into the lock.

It didn't turn.

It wasn't supposed to.

The red light turned to green.

Nerves on edge, her body in a cold sweat, she slid out the drawer. It wasn't very big.

The greatest secrets hidden from her all her life were about to be revealed to her. She placed the drawer on the oak table that adorned the center of the otherwise empty room and looked down.

Natalya's eyes fell on the few contents of the box.

Her heart stopped.

She whispered out loud "What the hell were you involved in, mom?"

Chapter Thirty-Two

It's a strange kind of underdog story.

In Pop culture, the consensus is that international crime runs on the U.S. dollar. But for a short period before the introduction of Bitcoin, authorities will tell you that the Euro actually was the underworld's currency of choice. The reason was simple: it's easier to move stacks of 500 euros than stacks of $100 U.S. bills. The weight of $1 million in $100 bills is 22 pounds. The equivalent sum in 500 euros, a measly 4.4 pounds.

Natalya ran her eyes across the four neatly stacked piles of purple 500-euro banknotes depicting bridges, arches, and doorways in modern architecture. All were vacuum sealed in polyurethane. She picked up the first bundle of 160x82mm notes, gently peeling back the bundle. It consisted of 10 stubs of 100 banknotes with the same denomination. 1,000 banknotes in total. The bank safety deposit box contained four identical bundles.

She placed each on the table and did the quick arithmetic.

1,000 bundles of 500 euros times 4 bundles...

She whistled.

There was a cool two million euros in cash sitting here.

More than she'd ever seen in her life, and more than she'd probably make in a lifetime of hard, honest work, as an arts major.

Natalya cursed, thinking of all the years she'd slaved away as a waitress for minimum wage, while putting herself through university. She said, still in a whisper, "I knew I should have opened the damned safe years ago."

She returned to the box.

There were two passports.

One British the other for the United States.

Natalya opened the first one. It depicted an American Eagle on the top page and a typical passport sized photograph of her on the left. The date of issue, along with the image was recent. She checked the second one. Same story. It looked legitimate, was in date, and had her image.

They were real passports.

She now held passports for the UK and the USA, in addition to her French one. She presumably had a German one once upon a time and a Russian one for that matter, but she'd never seen them. Her mother had never taken her to Russia. But if she had citizenship in the UK and the USA, why had her mother never told her about it? And how did she get them? Did it have something to do with the father she had never met?

Her brain kept bombarding her with more questions.

Then it hit her. For these to be so up to date, it meant that someone had gone to the trouble of putting them here recently. Only her mother knew about the bank safety deposit box.

Ergo.

Her mother had been in Grenoble.

A pang of loss hit her like a knife to the heart.

Her mother had secretly made the trip to Grenoble and hadn't seen her. She hadn't been back to France for years. Not that Natalya had known about. Of course, none of that really mattered. If she was going down that line of thoughts, there was an endless number of things her mother had done which Natalya didn't know about.

She examined the photographs in each passport, her eyes landing on the names.

Alecia Yeager – the American.

Michelle Rigozzi – the Brit.

So far, the bank safety deposit box hadn't been much help in finding out her secret past. Natalya was finding two questions for every answer she discovered. She laid each passport on the table.

At the very bottom of the drawer was a gun.

She picked it up.

Her features held a mixture of stoicism and incredulity in equal proportions. She studied the weapon, cautiously being sure not to point the barrel in her direction. It looked like a standard, black handgun. No different to what you see some police carry, or the bad guys shoot in the movies. Etched into the side of the barrel were the following words:

Heckler & Koch GMBH.

Oberndorfin – Made in Germany – 9mmx19.

She turned it over and found three letters along the side of the butt of the weapon.

PSP.

There was a magazine inserted, and the weapon felt like it was full – not that Natalya knew anything about guns, let alone how to load or check if one was loaded – but it felt heavy for an empty weapon.

There was a single note, written in her mother's handwritten elegant, cursive script. Natalya picked it up with some sort of feeling akin to relief.

Finally, some answers.

She read the note.

Dear Natalya,

The gun you are holding is a P7M13 pistol. It has one bullet in the chamber and another 12 in the magazine. It is loaded, ready to fire. Just like the movies, point it at the bad people, aim for the chest, squeeze the trigger. It's that simple.

Leave your cell phone inside this box.

Don't go home to collect anything.

Run.

Start a new life and don't ever look back.

I will love you always, mom. xo

Natalya turned it over, expecting something more, but found a blank page. She then flipped it and re-read the entire note.

After all these years, her mom left her with nothing but a tsunami of questions.

Who was her mother and what was she involved in? Why was there two million euros, two fake passports, and a gun in a private bank's vault?

She swallowed hard.

And most of all, who was she supposed to be running from?

Chapter Thirty-Three

Natalya found herself holding the gun in her hand.

One thing was certain, she wasn't going to get any more answers inside this bank vault. She loaded the cash and two passports into her North Face backpack, and then looked at the handgun. She could hardly walk out of the bank carrying it.

Should she even take it with her?

Weren't there strict laws about owning or carrying a weapon in France?

Did it matter? She needed to protect herself… from what exactly? Her mom hadn't even told her who she was running from! Who was she supposed to shoot? How could she even work out who the enemy was?

She drew a deep breath, slowly exhaled.

Her mom might just be suffering from some sort of paranoid delusion. Was she willing to leave her entire old life behind on the weight of a note from her mother, who she'd known for years suffered from anxiety and attacks of paranoia?

Natalya tilted her head to the side, considering her decision.

Was her mother crazy?

Or did this vindicate everything?

Two million euros certainly went a long way to suggesting her mother was involved in something illegal. She was a glacial scientist, with no connection to her own parents back in Russia. It was impossible to accept that she'd managed to save so much money with financial diligence and frugal living.

Okay, Natalya could work out all these things, she thought. But first, she would give her mother the benefit of doubt, and run.

She could get out of Grenoble, hire a car, and disappear anywhere within the EU. Or she could catch an uber to the first airport and hop on an international flight to the US. Then she could just hire a car and just keep driving. Go on a classic American road trip, traveling like a backpacker until she worked out what she wanted to do.

She stared at her cell phone.

It contained all her contacts.

Her friends, work colleagues, emails, social media apps, everything. Her entire life. She could always return for it if everything turned out to be fine.

She carefully placed the phone in the safety deposit box.

Then she looked at the gun in her hand.

She could hardly walk out of the bank carrying it. She thought seriously about leaving it in the safety deposit box, but what good would that do her? If she really was in trouble, it might save her life. So, should she put it in the backpack? How will that save her life if she gets attacked? No, better to have it in the pocket at the front of her hoodie. Then it wouldn't stand out, and if she needed to, she could always use it.

Natalya returned the drawer to its alcove, locking it once again with the key. The green light, returned to red. She picked up the wall-mounted phone and the vault's heavy door opened electronically.

Natalya thanked the bank manager who wished her good day. Then she walked out of the bank, heading north toward the Isère River and more importantly, public transport. Her eyes darted furtively at her surroundings.

There were throngs of tourists and locals walking the streets.

They all belonged there.

She'd walked this city for ten years without ever feeling insecure.

But at the back of her mind, she kept thinking – *that was before mom's letter* – when the world was still a safe place.

Suddenly the ancient roman city, which had always filled her with joy and her love of history, was now frightening in every way. The people looked menacing, and deceptive. The previously well-loved architecture, like devious hiding places. Even in the warm sun, she saw shadows everywhere.

Natalya took the shortest way north, cutting through the older structures leading to the Jardin de Ville, an historic garden. That was where she would go. The buildings she passed had multiple laneways, terraces, and plazas. Everyone looked dangerous to her.

There was a postwoman on a bicycle who seemed to be waiting there, doing nothing, just staring at her. A delivery driver in a beat-up van with license plates barely visible beneath their dirt and grime. Two men wearing thick jackets approached her.

She tensed up, her right hand resting on the handle of the pistol in her pocket.

Both men kept walking, passing her without any hint of interest.

Up ahead, an Italian tourist with a thick overcoat ogled her without any attempt to conceal the lascivious nature of his interest. It wasn't the first time that someone had looked at her that way, but it was the first time that it had frightened her this much.

She picked up her pace, wondering if she was just stirring herself up into a frenzy of paranoia.

After all, what had actually changed?

She didn't even know who was after her, let alone what they looked like, or why? Even if they did want her, she was one person in a city of 160,000 people. The chances that they knew exactly where she was or could find her without her phone – *wasn't that how people tracked people these days?* – was absurd.

Making the conscious decision to take her pace a little slower, she forced herself to breathe and relax.

A few minutes later, she reached the edge of the Jardin de Ville, a famous garden which was formerly private property of the Duke of Lesdiguières. It was surrounded by 16th Century architecture. Through a subtle interplay of terraces, the garden was isolated from the Isère to the north and the Draquet to the west. The scent of fresh flowers filled the air. To the south, were several hectares of pine trees.

And all of a sudden, she found herself alone in the forest.

A place she'd spent countless hours having picnics or reading a book on her own, without incident, and yet now, the isolation filled her with abject fear.

Three male youths were listening to music. The music was loud and known as RnB – Rhythm and Blues – although even at 23, Natalya failed to recognize any of the rhythm within the music. It was French Rap. The men were probably somewhere between 18 and 20. They had the typically dark skin of French immigrants from Sub-Saharan Africa. All three were tall, more like basketballers. They wore dark, oversized puffer jackets, that looked decidedly out of place in Grenoble's summer.

They looked up.

Their eyes wide and suddenly interested in her.

"Hey, where are you going?" The tallest of them asked, running his eyes across her figure, making no attempt to conceal his lust. "Wanna come hang out? Party with us?"

Natalya had had her share of unwanted attention over the years. She'd learned the most direct route usually worked best. But she was rattled by her mother's note and wasn't sure how she wanted to play this one.

In the end, she went with keeping her mouth shut, and pretending she didn't hear him.

The three of them started to approach her. "Hey, I'm talking to you! Where are you going?"

Natalya picked up her pace.

At a glance, they were kids. Maybe a little rough. Definitely overzealous and a little creepy. But hardly likely to be the sort of enemies her mother had in mind when she warned her to drop everything and cut her entire life in order to run.

She stopped.

Holding her ground, she met the biggest one – and seemingly the ringleader – in the eye. She smiled. "Meeting my boyfriend. And I'm afraid I'm running late. He's meeting me just over there."

"Over there?" the man asked. He shook his head and grinned. Big, beautiful, white set of teeth. "I don't believe you."

Natalya tried to back away. "Fine. I don't care if you don't believe me. I want you to leave."

Another one of the men asked, "What's in the bag?"

She didn't answer.

The third one said, "Whatever it is, I bet she doesn't need it as much as we do."

She couldn't believe her poor luck.

These were petty thugs! Of all the days she was going to get mugged! The three men approached together. They walked slowly, but there was an intimidating, predator mentality about them. Her eyes darted toward the Isère River in the distance and the busy roadway at *Quai Stephanie Jay* that ran parallel.

She tried to judge if she could get close enough to the road to get help.

She was a fast runner.

It was a possibility.

Natalya backed away.

They sped up.

She turned and ran.

The tallest one of her attackers shouted, "Get the bag!"

Adrenaline flowed in her veins, her heart thumped in her chest, and her primitive fight or flight mode kicked in.

She was a quick runner, made faster by fear, and she thought she could make it.

The tall pine trees whizzed past her as she ran.

She was faster than them!

Another minute and she would have closed the gap between the busy roadway and the empty forest. Natalya rounded a tree and got tripped by something moving lightning fast. She fell forward, rolled, and picked herself up.

Her backpack had fallen in the process.

She stepped forward to retrieve it, but another person – a fourth person, the one who had tripped her – had already picked up the bag.

The tall guy who had started by asking her to join their party, said, "Well done man. She was quick, I thought she was going to get away!"

One of her attackers went to open the North Face backpack.

Natalya regained her senses. "Give it back."

The man holding it started to laugh. "You want it? Come get it!"

She shook her head. "Give it to me now!"

He shook his head. "Make me! Bitch…"

Natalya reached into her hoodie pocket and withdrew the pistol. She hoped to hell her mother was right, and she hoped even more that she didn't need to use it.

She aimed it at the man with the bag. "Drop it!"

The guy who held the bag looked defiant. He met her gaze, and said, "No."

Natalya aimed at the man's chest.

Squeezed the trigger.

The shot fired with a loud bang.

It landed on the guy's thigh.

So much for aiming for the guy's chest.

He cried out in pain. More like the yelp of an injured animal than the overconfident boy a few seconds earlier. All four of her attackers turned their hands outward as though they didn't mean to cause any offense.

Natalya stepped forward, picked up the backpack and threw it over her shoulders, still holding the gun at the guy closest to her.

The four men didn't cower.

Instead, they seemed to spread out, as though they still had the chance to overcome her. She didn't want to start shooting everyone. The last thing she needed was to get involved with the police and a team of homicide detectives with 2 million euros in a bag, fake passports, and a gun – none of which she had anything close to an adequate explanation for. No, she would kill her attackers, if need be, but hell! It would be easier if they would just give up and go home.

They were at a terrible impasse.

Behind them, she heard a car pull off *Quai Stephanie Jay* and drive into the secret garden grounds. It was a blue Porsche Cayenne. Expensive but not so much flashy. A man of about thirty got out of the car. He wore a Versace polo shirt and blue jeans. Both were plain, but clearly expensive and perfectly fitting. With well cut, brown hair, and intelligent deep-set eyes of pale green, with flakes of gold, he was good looking. He had the defined muscles of someone who trained. Not just in the gym pumping iron. But was active in sports.

He casually stepped around to the trunk, opened it like he had all the damned time in the world, and retrieved a baseball bat.

The newcomer gripped the bat like he was ready for practice.

He wore the confident grin of a man who was more than happy to take risks, but never lost. "All right, who here doesn't want to listen to this young woman?"

One of the men looked like he was going to tell the stranger to stay out of it and mind his own damned business, but there was something in the new arrival's determined face that suggested such a route was indeed a very bad one to take.

The rapper turned his palms skyward. "I didn't mean any harm. We're leaving boss…"

The three uninjured men helped the man with the bullet wound in the leg get up and leave.

Natalya exchanged a glance with the man who had come to her rescue. "Thanks."

"You're welcome." The man gave a self-deprecating smile. It was boyish and attractive, with just the right amount of humility and genuineness. "I'm sorry I didn't get here earlier."

"Yeah, me too."

Then, he glanced at the gun, as she quickly, surreptitiously tucked it away in her hoodie pocket.

He said, "Not that it would have mattered. You look like you can take care of yourself."

She nodded. "Yeah, I don't normally get into this sort of thing…"

The stranger lifted his hand to stop her, indicating she didn't need to explain anything to him. "It's all right. I can see you're just having a really bad day."

Natalya took a slow breath, exhaled. Met his handsome face, and those dreamy eyes, with a genuine smile. "You have no idea."

He looked at her with kindness and a warm smile. "Look. Can I give you a lift somewhere?"

She nodded without hesitation. "That would be great, thank you."

"No worries." He opened the passenger side door for her, like a gentleman.

Natalya climbed in, pulled her seatbelt over her shoulder and clipped the harness, placing her backpack at her feet in the footwell, and keeping her hand on the gun in her pocket.

The stranger pressed his key fob and started the ignition. He turned to face her. "I'm Oliver Leroy by the way."

"Natalya Utkin."

"Nice to meet you, Natalya." He flicked on the blinker and gently pulled into traffic. "Where are you heading?"

Where was she heading?

She made a weak smile. "Honestly, I don't know. Out of town somewhere. I just need to get away from this place."

"Things are that bad?"

"Worse."

"Bummer. Can I take you to the police?"

She shook her head. "They can't help me with this. I'm not sure anyone can."

"I'm sorry to hear that." He changed lanes. Turning onto A41. "I'm on my way to Switzerland. I'm not sure if that helps, but I'm willing to drop you off anywhere you want to go along the way…"

She looked at him, trying to read his kind face. If she'd met him under other circumstances, she definitely would have asked him for his number.

He took her hesitation for concern. He lifted one of his hands apologetically. "I'm sorry, you don't know me, I'm a complete stranger, and you've been attacked by a bunch of thugs. I get it, the last thing you're gonna want to do is go for a long drive with a strange man."

"No, it's not that. That sounds really good. I'm actually just trying to work out where I should go." She shrugged. "Truth is, Switzerland is probably as good a place as any."

He suppressed a smile. "That's great. So you will come with me?"

"Sure. I'd like that. Thank you."

"You're not afraid of me, because I'm a strange man you've never met?"

She looked at his kind face. She was generally a good judge of character. "No, I trust you. Besides, I still have a gun."

"You're right," he said, lifting his hands from the wheel in mock supplication. "A weapon like that helps with trust issues."

The Porsche cruised along A41 and the two of them talked. Mostly about nothing at all. Things that were trivial to her now. Her arts degree and majoring in history at Grenoble University. He talked about business. He was involved in importing and exporting digital technologies, such as electronics and whatnot.

At some stage he asked her why she was running.

Natalya filled him about the voice message from her mom who she hadn't seen for years. The fact that her mother had been away for work as a scientist for three years, but even before that she had been distant. She was careful not to mention the contents of the safety deposit box.

He asked her pertinent questions and seemed genuinely interested. Trying his best to methodically work through the problems, resolving the simple issues, and talking through the complex ones.

Where would she go?

How would she afford to live?

What sort of life would she like to lead?

She found herself enjoying his company, and feeling grateful to discover after all that had happened, she had some good luck today.

He looked at her, with something akin to fondness in his pale green eyes. "How long has your mom been at Vostok?"

"Where?" she asked, almost certain she had never mentioned Vostok.

"Vostok. You said your mom was a glaciologist at an Antarctic Research Station. You didn't say which one, but it was in the news recently that researchers at Vostok had finally drilled into the ancient lake – some 15 million years old – and were making phenomenal discoveries. Forgive me, but I assumed with your accent that your mother is Russian? It was easy to put two and two together. Vostok is the only Russian Antarctic Research Station I know of."

"Oh," she said, "Sorry, I guess I'm a little paranoid today."

Natalya searched her memories of their conversations, and was almost certain she hadn't said anything about Antarctica. Only that her mom had been away for three years doing research.

Up ahead, they approached the overhead tollway.

Leroy looked at her and said, "There's a toll-pass in your door panel. Do you mind passing it to me?"

"Sure," she said, reaching down. The door panel appeared empty. "It's not here?"

Leroy said, "My mistake."

Natalya sat up and felt something touch the side of her waist.

Two barbs of a taser prong touched her skin.

Leroy said, "I'm sorry. I was enjoying our conversation."

She tried to reach for the gun.

He depressed the trigger.
And she felt her entire body convulse with the electricity.
It only lasted a few seconds.
But when it was done.
All the lights in her world had gone out.

Chapter Thirty-Four

Charles de Gaulle Airport – Paris, France

The Ghost seethed with anger.

He knew he couldn't trust that asshole Leo Green. The man was losing his instincts in his old age. He was no longer effective. There was a time when Green brought a certain level of credibility and government backing. But these days, he was more of a liability than an asset. He would have to deal with the man. It wasn't an insurmountable problem, but then again, Green was no fool.

The Boeing Business Jet 777X taxied its way toward runway 08R/26L.

Within minutes it had completed its takeoff roll and the private jet was in the air, climbing solidly. The jet had a range of 11,645 nautical miles, giving it the greatest distance of any other private aircraft, capable of reaching just about any location on earth in a single flight.

The Ghost dialed another number.

A man answered. "Yes?"

"Listen to me… you made a mistake."

"A mistake?" The French mercenary tsk, tsked. "I don't think so."

"You were given a damned manifest!" The Ghost made a theatrical sigh. "You said that you'd be methodical, tick off each name on that list. It's Antarctica, in the middle of winter. It's not like anyone's going anywhere. Come back to me when every name on that list is dead."

"I believe there is some mistake. Every name on that list is now a ghost."

The Ghost sighed. "Some people think I'm a ghost, but I'm telling you, I'm very fucking alive."

"Listen to me, sir… everyone on that list is dead."

"So then tell me why a pretty little afterlife spirit just picked up a satellite phone and called me directly?"

The mercenary said, "She called you?"

The Ghost shook his head. It was hard to find good workers these days. But the French team were meant to be the best. Besides, how hard could it be to kill a bunch of defenseless scientists, isolated in the most remote part of the world?

"Right, so now I've jogged your memory about who you left behind?" The Ghost's lips twisted into a malicious smile. "You wanna tell me why? Were you just too damned lazy to kill her?"

"Look. She's lethal! In fact, the bitch cut me with a medical scalpel. Just missed my artery."

"So why didn't you kill her?"

"She got away. Ran to some ice caves in a nearby crevasse."

"And you didn't think of following her and finishing your damned job?"

"Sure. We did, but she was ready for us and she managed to kill four of my men in the process."

"I thought your guys were the best?"

"They were. I recruited them personally from the French Special Forces."

"And what... this defenseless glaciologist took them out?"

"Something like that. I don't think she was just a glaciologist. This woman didn't move like a scientist. And she sure as hell didn't fight like one. I wouldn't be surprised if she wasn't ex-special forces herself, or maybe a spy?"

The Ghost smiled at that. The man would probably never know just how close he came to guessing the truth. It also made him laugh at the thought of Anastasia being activated again, after all these years. "So where did you leave her?"

"Outside Vostok. I locked the doors. There's no way in."

"And what, you thought she'd just take it sitting down and freeze to death?"

"There's a blizzard here. It's probably the worst one for the season and that's really saying something for an Antarctic winter. I left her out in the ice caves. I didn't think she could even climb out of them, let alone get back inside Vostok."

"Well, on that score, you're right," The Ghost admitted. "She's still trapped outside. You apparently successfully locked her out of her own research station."

The mercenary said, "So what do you want me to do about it?"

The Ghost shook his head. There was a time when all he had to do was pick up the phone and the deed would be done to his exact requirements. So much for progress! "Go back and finish the damned job I paid you to do!"

"She won't be alive in another half an hour, let alone an hour."

"No?"

"Yeah, no way. She'll be frozen solid by the time I reach her."

"Good. That will make it easier for you to finish the job and kill her properly."

"All right, all right. I'll turn around."

"Good man. And one more thing…"

"Yeah?"

"Don't ever lie to me again."

Chapter Thirty-Five

Sam Reilly stared up at the brightly colored spinnaker.

It was meant to be part of the ruse.

Their hovercraft, as part of Global Shipping's Antarctic Relay Team carried a spinnaker to help drag their team across the Polar Plateau using the assistance of the strong winds that hounded the region.

He watched the nylon balloon sail quickly inflate.

Ordinarily designed for light winds, this spinnaker was heavily reinforced and engineered. The 100 plus knot winds common in Antarctica, would shoot them across distances at speed.

Next to Sam, Hu asked, "Do you think it will work?"

Sam shrugged non-committedly. "Maybe?"

Tom was more confident. "You'd be surprised what things tend to come together for Sam and me. Especially when a top-notch team like ours is backing us."

Hu looked at the nylon sheets, that were guiding the spinnaker. The big balloon was flapping in the wind. His eyes narrowed. "So why isn't the hovercraft moving?"

Sam grinned. "Wait for it…"

An intricate aluminum frame had been erected and a series of pullies set to provide a mechanical advantage to the system in order to lift the hovercraft out of its frozen tomb. A spinnaker pole had been bolted into the solid ice, along with two winches. One was used to tighten their grip on the balloon, trapping more air inside, while the other dipped the curvature of the spinnaker, releasing the air, and with it the strain on the nylon ropes.

Tom sat on the crystalline surface of Antarctica with both hands on one of the winches. "Ready?"

"Let's do this," Sam said, managing the second winch, which kind of acted as a brake.

Tom slowly rotated the crank, tightening the spinnaker's sheet. The colorful spinnaker immediately thundered outward in the incredibly strong winds.

The ropes went taut.

Nothing happened.

Tom adjusted the winch, giving it another couple of full rotations.

The spinnaker ballooned... then and caught hold.

The ropes began to move.

The pullies were spinning as fast as an engine's flywheel.

Within seconds, the buried hovercraft escaped, flying out of the dark crack of the glacial surface. The spinnaker, no longer having to overcome the resistance of the hovercraft inside the crevasse, broke into a gallop. It snapped both winches, which had been bolted into the ice.

The hovercraft began its movement south.

Starting at a crawl, but quickly picking up speed, it took off like a runaway horse.

Seeing their lifeline literally springing away, Sam and Tom exchanged a stunned look.

"Quick!" Sam shouted, "Get on the hovercraft!"

Chapter Thirty-Six

The hovercraft shot across the ice.

Sam ran beside the vehicle that was being dragged along by the spinnaker. He felt like a cowboy in one of those old western movies, who has to catch up with, and board the speeding train. He had just one chance to reach it. It whizzed past. Sam tried to catch the side of the hovercraft, but he couldn't get enough grip to pull himself up.

He ran alongside it as fast as he could, but his stamina was fading. He had no purchase on the hovercraft to pull himself up on to the deflated, rubber skirt.

Tom was running behind him.

Playing catch up.

Unless he could sprint the 100 meter faster than Olympian Usain Bolt...

Tom was already out of the race.

It motivated Sam to run just that little bit faster.

There was nothing but ice for hundreds of miles. If Sam couldn't reach the hovercraft, the spinnaker would drag it away until it was lost from sight, probably never to be seen again. At the very least, it would be the end of their mission, and possibly their lives.

Sam's gaze locked onto a small support handle, like an upside down "U," it was designed to be held by people on top of the hovercraft.

He forced his legs to move as fast as possible.

And jumped for the handhold.

His gloved fingers gripped the edge of the handle, caught for a split-second, and then slid off the hovercraft's railing.

Sam hit the ice-cold surface, rolling hard.

It was over.

They'd lost.

Then inside the sound of the wind, he heard the whip.

He looked up.

Tom had thrown one of the spare coiled ropes over the back of the hovercraft. His very own, makeshift lasso.

Sam grinned.

I really am living in an old cowboy movie!

He looked behind him to the source of the lasso. Tom called, "Yeehaa! Round 'em up!"

His friend was holding onto the back of the rope, keeping his feet shoulder width apart, and hanging onto the line like a water-skier – or, keeping up with the cowboy analogy – a man holding the reins of a horse as it tried to buck him free.

Sam was back on his feet, running at full speed.

Tom shifted his position slightly to the left, swinging around to catch Sam in the process.

The rope swung toward Sam.

He gripped it with both hands and joined the wild ride.

Tom dipped his head, in a mock greeting like a cowboy doffing his hat. "Hey Sam, great to see you joining us."

"Glad to be here," Sam said.

He pulled himself up the rope, hand over hand. Slowly but surely, he approached the cabin of the speeding hovercraft. Sam's boots were slicing the icy landscape like a pair of ice-skates. He slowly narrowed the sixty or more feet, to zero. Eventually, he reached the runaway vehicle. His chest pounding with the fatigue of heavy breathing, and a hammering heart, Sam pulled himself up onto the back of the hovercraft.

His exhausted gaze drifted back to Tom, who was just about at the back skirt of the hovercraft.

Sam gripped the hold bar at the back of the hovercraft with his left hand and offered Tom his right. Tom took it, and with one quick movement, scrambled up and onto the hovercraft.

Their chests burned.

It was a mixture of laughing and hard work, and the simple ridiculousness of their lives.

Sam drew a deep breath, looked at Tom, and said, "Let's go stop this runaway beast."

"Agreed," Tom replied. Then his eyes landed on the giant crevasse coming up in the distance. "Sam!"

Sam's eyes snapped around to where Tom was looking.

It was an ice canyon some fifty or more feet wide. Just like in the Wild West, this was the part of the movie where the movie stars had to slow the wagon or fall to their deaths.

Sam said, "Tom, get inside the hovercraft and get the engine started, and the controls ready. Let's see if this thing's still going to run."

Tom looked at him. "What are you gonna do?"

Sam grinned. "I'm going to cut the horses loose."

Chapter Thirty-Seven

The wind ripped across their faces.

They worked hard, holding onto the grab holds, as they maneuvered their way to the forward section of the hovercraft.

Sam held open the vehicle's hatch.

Tom dropped inside, folding his large, muscular frame into the narrow confines of the hovercraft.

Sam yelled, "Get that engine started. We're going to need control as soon as you can possibly get it."

"I'm on it," Tom replied. "Go! Cut the ropes!"

Sam let the hatch close and focused on the prize. Up at the very front of the powerful hovercraft, was a small steel eyelet. It formed a sort of towbar that could be used to pull it off a trailer. Currently, the four ropes connecting the spinnaker balloon to the hovercraft ran through the eyelet.

Cut the ropes, and the power goes.

Sam carefully crawled to the very front of the hovercraft, leaning down to try and slice through the rope. He had a Halcyon titanium dive knife in his right hand. Razor sharp. He reached down. His arms weren't long enough to reach the rope.

He heard the hovercraft's engine start up.

The thing was an amazing piece of engineering. Simple but evidently as near to indestructible as one could imagine. The massive propeller began to turn. Tom began trying to adjust the controls, fighting against the potent spinnaker. It made no difference. The balloon was simply too effective.

But the ropes needed to be cut.

Sam kept hold of the last grab bar and struggled to extend his reach. He just about fell forward, but managed to catch himself with his left arm, expanding his reach.

It still wasn't enough.

The thick rubber skirt inflated. Unfortunately, the hovercraft, no longer causing as much friction, increased its speed over the ice.

They were racing toward the giant ice canyon.

He thought about letting go, and reaching all the way over, but a single bump and he'd be dead, crushed to death by the heavy vehicle.

No. He needed help.

"Tom!" he shouted. "Get up here!"

Seconds later, Tom's head popped up. "What do you need?"

"I need you to lower me down here so I can reach the ropes."

Tom's eyes darted between the canyon that rushed closer, back to Sam. His pupils dilated like dinner plates, but he didn't miss a beat. He pulled himself up through the hatch and grabbed Sam's legs.

"Go! I've got you!"

Sam didn't need to be told twice.

He leaned all the way out, across the hovercraft's rubber skirt, and all the way down to the steel eyelet. In one quick movement, he sliced. The titanium blade carved through each layer of the rope.

The cord made a springing sound, as it came free.

And the spinnaker opened, spilling air out of that side of its balloon.

Sam didn't wait to see if it was enough. He sliced through the remaining three ropes. One by one they popped off, until the spinnaker – now free from its earthly confines – shot off ahead of them, and further up into the air.

"Pull me up!" Sam shouted.

He and Tom stared at the upcoming canyon.

Without the spinnaker, the hovercraft was no longer picking up speed, but it was still flying over the ice with very little friction, and no real sign of slowing down.

Sam and Tom exchanged a glance.

"Get on the controls and turn us around!"

Tom didn't need to be told twice. "On it!"

Sam clambered back to the hatchway and climbed inside.

The cliff veered toward them.

Tom shoved the joystick all the way to the side in a sudden jolt. The hovercraft spun round 180 degrees. He eased the throttle all the way forward. The hovercraft skimmed the rim of the cliff.

Teetered on the edge.

Then shot back the way they had come.

Sam grinned. "Nice save."

"Thanks."

Sam's lips firmed. "Now let's get back there and get the hell to Vostok."

Chapter Thirty-Eight

Sam parked the hovercraft outside the entrance to Module A.

The thing looked like a giant spacecraft. Although it started its life in Moscow, the new Vostok Research Station looked decidedly more like something out of Star Trek. Of course, that seemed fair given that he felt like he might as well have been flying across an alien icescape in the hovercraft, for all the similarities Antarctica shared with the rest of the globe. Flying from the top of the first module were the distinctive tricolors, white, blue, and red of the Russian flag.

At the front of the first module, were a large set of stairs – three flights to be specific – that led to what appeared to be the main entrance to the Russian research station, perched high above the freezing landscape. Sam, Tom, Genevieve, Elise, and Hu climbed up the stairs.

Tom swung the side of his big fist into the door.

It made a large echo in throughout the engineering module of the Vostok Research Station. He waited, tried again.

Genevieve pointed to the doorbell. "Want to try that?"

Tom's eyes landed on the doorbell. It was one of those electronic ones with a camera and the ability to ring directly to any one of the five modules. He looked at Genevieve with affection, and genuine love. Tom pressed the ringer for the first module. "Thanks darling."

"You're welcome," she replied.

Sam listened to the distinctive ring. It seemed to keep going indefinitely. He waited a minute or so. After all, they were in the middle of Antarctica. It's not like they get a lot of visitors in summer, let alone in winter. Done with waiting, Sam walked up and pressed the call button to all five modules.

After two or three minutes, Sam exchanged glances with the rest of his team. He shook his head. "Would you look at that... nobody's home."

"You want me to get the C4?" Genevieve asked.

Sam shook his head. "Let's give them another few minutes, then you can go get your toys and kindly do the honors of opening this door for us."

Tom pulled his jacket in tight. "I might wait in the hovercraft."

Sam said, "Good point. I'm done waiting too. Genevieve, go get the C4."

Hu said, "May I make a suggestion?"

"Of course, Hu. Speak up. What do you advise?"

"How about I use Dragon's Breath?" Hu had a grin on his face like a kid waiting to play with his new toy at Christmas. "It will be a lot quieter than C4… in the off chance, we have company inside Vostok?"

Genevieve said, "The scar from Dragon's Breath might be a bit hard to explain to the Russians?"

Sam lifted his hand. "It's all right. I don't think they're going to be any more stoked about C4 remodeling their door." He turned to Hu. "Go ahead, open it your way."

Hu nodded. "Very good."

Hu drew Dragon's Breath.

The ancient sword was stolen from Emperor Qin Shi Huang, the first emperor of China. The weapon was forged by a master alchemist – Hu's great ancestor, who had crafted it for the First Emperor.

Like a transparent bubble in the sun, the blade glistened with iridescence.

The weapon was tinted with the rare element Dragon's Breath. The mysterious material caused a molecular implosion. Left unchecked, this sort of chain reaction could destroy unbelievable amounts of land, turning stone to dust. Hu's weapon held the very last known piece of Dragon's Breath in existence. Unlike the rest of Dragon's Breath, which could, conceivably destroy an entire continent, Hu's sword had a special limiter built into it by the ancient alchemists who forged its blade, thus preventing its chain reaction from expanding any more than three feet in any direction.

Hu stepped up, and dug the blade into the thick, aluminum doorway.

It created fine particles.

Sam's eyes narrowed, as he watched Hu's sword make contact with the aluminum door. Having seen the effects of Dragon's Breath on stone, he half expected for a moment that the weapon would slice through the cavern like some sort of Jedi lightsaber.

Instead, Hu began etching away at the soft aluminum. The sword chimed as the ancient weapon cut a fraction of an inch into the soft alloy, slowly forming the shape of a small opening. Just big enough for all five of them to climb through.

A moment later, the aluminum began to disassemble at a molecular level.

Then a small gust of air whipped around, and the doorway imploded, turning to dust particles containing the elements of copper, magnesium, manganese, silicon, tin, nickel and zinc.

Hu grinned. He put Dragon's Breath back into its scabbard on his back, held out a hand, and said, "Come on inside, the door is open."

Chapter Thirty-Nine

The stench of death wafted through the air.

Sam frowned. "Oh... that's not a good sign."

Tom said, "Someone's bad cooking?"

"I doubt it," Genevieve said, extracting her Heckler and Koch MP5 submachine gun. "Change of plans. We're no longer coming in under the ruse of adventurers trying to cross Antarctica in a hovercraft and needing their help. Someone's beaten us here, and by the smell of things, killed everyone inside."

Sam reached for his own submachine gun. "Agreed. Everyone, there's a potential race on for control of a 15-million-year-old alien spacecraft. Even if it's unlikely to be true, someone has enough evidence to believe it. Technology like that could completely alter the landscape of war and global power. Be sharp. Whoever's tried to reach it before us, aren't going to give it away without a fight."

Everyone armed up. Hu, keeping his sword in its scabbard, drew a QSZ-92 semi-automatic, removing the dual stack magazine. Inside were twenty rounds of proprietary 5.8x21mm Chinese-made armor-piercing rounds with bottle-necked case and pointed bullets, closely resembling the Belgian 5.7×28mm format. There was a distinctive absence of a star on the handle, indicating this was the military version, not the one used by the Chinese Police.

Elise caried an Israeli Uzi submachine gun, and a Glock 10 mm pistol with a 15-round magazine for backup. Tom carried a Mossberg 590A1 pump-action shotgun, popular with most armed forces around the world. With this, he carried a Glock 10 mm pistol for a backup.

Together, they made a scouting formation, and systematically cleared each section of the research station, with Genevieve in the lead.

They opened the second door – a sort of vacuum seal – designed to keep the heat in when people transition from inside the Vostok Research Station to outside and vice-versa.

The first module seemed to be the engineering module. With its labyrinthian network of metal steps and platforms that spread in a spider-like lattice over the electric generators, boiler, and water treatment systems.

The engineering module was unoccupied.

Next, they entered Module B.

According to the schematics they'd reviewed on their flight over to the sub-zero continent, this was where the bulk of the research took place. It housed the scientist's lodgings, living quarters, showers, medical, computer servers, and biolab.

They made their way through the computer lab.

Three people lay dead at their desks.

Genevieve glanced at them. "Two bullet holes each. Head shots. Whoever did this were professionals. This is Special Forces. A Tier One level hit."

Sam asked, "Or someone close to the scientists?"

Genevieve tilted her head, considering the question. "You mean, did our spy, having learned that there was indeed a spacecraft hidden down there, decided to execute the rest of her team?"

Sam shrugged. "Did he or she?"

"It's possible," Genevieve admitted, "But I doubt it. I mean, she might have been able to take out one or two of them like this, but not three in the one room. No, this was done by multiple people."

Sam stepped toward the next module. "All right, let's keep going, see if we can find anything else about what happened here."

"Agreed," Genevieve said, leading the way.

They kept heading south, through to Module C. This was the leisure quarters of the research station, with the food mess hall, dining room, kitchen, gymnasium, sauna, and storage facilities. Spoon in his mouth, someone was killed mid-bite. They found another person slaughtered while doing bench-presses, and a third dead in the sauna. The heat in the sauna had sped up the process of decomposition. Sam was happy to leave the door firmly shut.

Sam stepped into Module D, the second engineering module. There were a few more dead people and a duplication of much of the engineering equipment and power generators found in Module A. They moved on, entering Module E, which basically consisted of an oversized garage, that housed Vostok's entire fleet of polar vehicles.

His eyes landed on the Kharkovchanka. He remembered reading about it in the first Soviet-led expedition to the South Pole. The machine was an historic relic from the Cold War. The door to the driver's cabin was open. There was blood on the handle.

He gestured with his gun to the door, indicating to Genevieve to check it out.

She nodded. Whispered, "The blood mark shows that he or she, was leaving the vehicle at the time."

Sam's eyes swept the rest of the row of polar vehicles. "Where?"

Genevieve's eyes narrowed. "I'm not sure."

"There," Elise said. "Blood heading out that door."

Sam said, "It looks like someone might have got away. Find them and maybe they can shed some light on what happened here. Perhaps they know what Vostok really found at the bottom of their ancient, frozen lake."

"Maybe," Genevieve said, noncommittally. "If they did, there's a good chance they're dead by now. These people look like they've been dead most of the day, if not longer. I doubt anyone could have stayed alive in the outside environment for very long."

Sam followed the blood trail. "Well, there's only one way to find out."

The door was heavily barred.

Someone had gone to the effort to place a heavy snow plow up against the exit.

Sam looked at Tom. "You want to see if you can move it for us?"

"Sure," Tom said.

He stepped up and into the driver's cabin. As expected, the key was in the ignition. Tom turned it, and backed the snow plow up several feet, away from the door. Then he switched the engine off again.

Sam opened the door.

There was nothing but icy-cold darkness outside.

No way they were going to find anyone alive out there.

He turned to come back inside.

And came face-to-face with a dead woman lying in the ice.

Chapter Forty

Sam fixed his flashlight on her stilled face.

A second later, he swore.

The woman was still breathing as the water vapor in her breath condensed into lots of tiny droplets that Sam could see in the air, similar to fog.

It was shallow, and barely visible. But there was no doubt in his mind it was there. She was still alive. He said, "Quick, let's get her inside."

Sam picked her up in his arms.

She was short and petite, with a slim figure. He took her body weight in his arms with ease, quickly moving inside of Vostok.

Tom said, "I'll get back to Module C and get a warm bath going."

"Good plan," Sam said, following him.

Elise said, "I saw a medical facility back there. I'll go and see what they have. She's lasted this long. We should be able to keep her alive."

The woman started to speak. It was mostly delirium, but at least her eyes were open, and she was breathing. That had to be a good sign.

Sam carried her up the stairs, through Module D, and into Module C.

Tom came out to greet him. "I couldn't find a bath. There's a shower running hot in that room."

Sam put her gently on the ground beside the shower.

Genevieve started to undress her. Sam helped until they got her down to her underwear.

He then said, "Maybe we should get Elise to help."

Genevieve shook her head. "Sam. This is no time for gallantry. The woman's dying. Help me get her undressed so we can warm her up."

Sam nodded. "Okay."

It only took a few more seconds, and she was completely naked. The woman's skin was a horrible shade of blue, and ice cold to touch. It was hard to believe she had maintained the stubborn will to survive.

Genevieve and Sam lifted her into the shower, and sat her on the floor, with her back against the shower's wall. Sam adjusted the temperature, making it warm, but not too hot that it scalded her.

Elise came back in a few minutes.

Sam asked, "Any luck in the medical center?"

"No. It looks like any medical kits they had have gone missing." Elise shook her head. "Besides, I've racked my brains, and I don't think there are any drugs that can help with hypothermia. I suppose if she goes into cardiac arrest, or her heart slows right down, we could use atropine or adrenaline… but we've failed if she reaches that point."

Sam nodded. "So, what do we do?"

"All that we can do. What you're doing now. Just warm her up."

"Will it work?"

"I have no idea."

For a few minutes, they simply watched, helplessly, as the warm water flowed over her bare skin. No idea whether they were saving her life or speeding up her inevitable demise.

Suddenly, her eyes opened again. They locked on Sam's face, with a certain type of clarity.

She tried to lean closer.

Sam said, "Just wait there. We've got you in the shower, warming up."

She tried to talk.

Her tongue seemed dry and stuck on the top of her mouth. She tried again. In a whisper, she asked, "Are you my handler?"

"Are you our spy?"

The woman nodded.

Sam said, "Then yes, I am."

A moment later, she lost consciousness again.

Chapter Forty-One

Anastasia opened her eyes.

There was steam all around her. She was sitting on the floor of a shower in Module C. Everything hurt. There was an unfamiliar woman sitting next to her. The stranger hadn't seemed to notice she was awake yet. Anastasia remembered everything.

Vostok had been attacked.

She tried to escape and had been followed out into the ice caves. She'd killed four of her attackers, but the last one – if not more of them – had gotten away.

She'd called Merc.

Her damned past had finally caught up with her.

He'd promised to protect her Natalya, so long as she continued to work as his spy. It was Merc who vowed he would send someone to rescue her. A spy handler to retrieve her. She was to do what he asked and offer whatever assistance he needed. Then Merc would make everything all right. Do that, and she and Natalya would be free to live.

Then she was dying in the snow, trapped outside Vostok. That was the last thing she remembered. She didn't even have the strength left to try and make her way to the stairs outside Module A. It was just too far a journey for her in her condition.

So how did she get here?

In the shower.

Anastasia fought to shake the fog and disorientation from her mind, but it wasn't going to happen. Her brain wasn't just struggling to connect the dots. There were definite periods missing from her memory. Most likely, she guessed, she was unconscious when she'd been brought into the shower and warmed up.

She tried to stand up.

A woman watching over her, smiled. She had intelligent blue eyes, and brown hair, cut short like a pixie. Anastasia attempted to read the woman's face. There was plenty of kindness there, but there was also a certain type of hardness too.

Like a cold-blooded killer.

"It's okay. You're safe." The woman spoke in perfect Russian. "You were outside freezing in the snow. Hypothermia had kicked in. We didn't know if you were going to pull through, so we took you in here to thaw you out."

Anastasia frowned, the shadow of fear rising in her throat like bile. "You're Russian?"

She nodded. "I am. I grew up in Saint Petersburg. But I haven't lived there for many, many years. My name's Genevieve."

Anastasia exhaled.

This wasn't someone from her past.

"Thank you, Genevieve." She drew another breath, savoring the sensation of being alive. "For saving my life."

"You're welcome."

Anastasia asked, "Are you in charge?"

"No."

"Who is?"

"A friend. Sam Reilly. You'll meet him soon. Once you've had time to warm up, dry off, and get dressed."

Anastasia noticed that she was naked. It wasn't that she hadn't noticed before, but she felt so little, that it hadn't registered as being a problem.

Now, she seemed strangely aware of it.

Genevieve noticed her embarrassment. "We've brought you clothes. I'll leave and let you get dressed, if you like?"

"Yes, please."

"Are you feeling all right?"

"I'll live."

Anastasia ran the shower for another few minutes, savoring the warmth, and feeling her body regenerate. She turned off the shower, picked up the towel – warmed by the heating rack – and wrapped it around her body. She briskly dried herself.

At 49 years of age, she had retained much of her athletic physique from her previous life. She was short and petite, without an ounce of fat on her. Her muscles were small, but they were still well-defined, and powerful. Created from use and physical exertion, they had never been there for show.

Nearly fifteen years had been spent training.

She'd become an expert in killing people. She was naturally good at it. And what's more, she enjoyed it. If she was honest. And if you can't be honest with yourself, who can you be honest with?

She stared at herself in the mirror.

There were faint lines around her eyes.

Those enigmatic, gunmetal gray eyes had been the source of so much of her strength and equally as much of her problems. Those eyes alone, had seduced many men over the years, and a few women. Behind them, her mind was racing to find a solution out of the mess.

Anastasia got dressed.

She opened the mirror and retrieved a single shaving razor-blade. It was one of those flip open, straight-cut, throat blades, with a wooden handle. The same as the old barber's used to use. Or maybe still used? It wasn't like she'd ever been to a barber for a shave.

Anastasia folded the blade in on itself and pocketed the razor.

She then stepped out the bathroom and prepared to meet her handler.

Chapter Forty-Two

Sam studied the woman before him.

She looked a hell of a lot better than when he'd left her in the shower with Genevieve. He was blown away by her rejuvenation. Less than an hour ago, he thought she was dead. Definitely unlikely to survive. Now, she seemed quite well.

"Hello," she said. She smiled, but it seemed somehow withheld or restrained at least. She had an attractive face, blonde hair, and penetrating gray eyes. There was a confidence about her that was hard not to admire. She met his eyes directly. "You must be my handler."

Sam nodded. "Yes. That makes you our spy."

She blushed, as though the word was abhorrent to her. "I have a PhD in glaciology, but yes... I've been taking money to pass on our progress reports."

Sam lifted a hand. "It's okay. We all do what we have to do."

Her mouth twisted in a wry crooked smile, that kind of suggested he had no idea what she'd gone through to reach this point in her life.

Sam took a different tack. "My name's Sam Reilly."

"I'm Anastasia Utkin."

"Good name."

She looked confused. "Come again?"

"Your name. It means Resurrection. It was the Russian female form of the Greek name Anastasios from anastasis, meaning 'resurrection.'" Sam gave a soft chuckle. "I guess it's kind of apt given how close you were to dying from hypothermia."

Anastasia's smile turned mischievous, revealing nice teeth and supple lips. "Don't read into it too much. My surname refers to a duck."

His eyes widened; his mouth opened into an "O" of incredulity. "Really?"

She shrugged and laughed. "Afraid so."

"All right. It will be difficult, but I'll try not to read too much into that!"

She said, "Thank you for coming back for me. I appreciate it."

Sam wondered what she meant by "coming back," but decided not to question her. "You're welcome. Do you want to tell us what happened here?"

She tilted her head. "I don't know that there's much to tell."

"Go on, anything you can remember."

"We were attacked. They were professionals. Very efficient. Came through room by room, executing everyone inside and moving on."

"Do you know why they attacked Vostok?"

She looked up at him. "You don't think it's obvious?"

Sam said, "I only just got here. I'm not sure about much."

"It was concerning the spacecraft. They came to get it before we could retrieve it."

Sam said, "Wait. You were going to send someone down to the spacecraft?"

"Of course."

Sam asked, "How close were you?"

She shook her head, "No. You misunderstand me, Mr. Reilly... we just put someone down to the spacecraft."

"What?" Sam was incredulous. "How is that even possible? I thought it took you two decades to reach Lake Vostok? Now, you're telling me in just six months, you've sent a man down there?"

"No."

"No?" Sam cocked his head to the left. "But you just said..."

"We sent a woman. Maria Vassiliev, Astrobiologist."

"How?"

"There's a series of deep crevasses that lead to the bottom of the ice covering Lake Vostok. Over the past six months we have a high-powered, heat-driven drilling system to expand the opening, making room to bring down diving equipment to reach it."

Sam's eyes narrowed. "What are you saying?"

"Lake Vostok was teaming with thousands of different marine creatures unique to this one lake. Its own habitat."

"That makes sense. The place has been isolated for fifteen million years."

She shook her head. "No. You're not following me."

"Go on," Sam said.

Anastasia's eyes were expressive, communicating something important. "The life-forms we found… they haven't just been trapped beneath the ice for 15 million years…"

"Go on."

"They're aliens."

Chapter Forty-Three

Sam drew a breath, letting that sink in.

It was no longer a matter of finding material known to be used in aerospace, or marine creatures that aren't observed anywhere else on earth. Now it was in the realm of fact, and the race was on to secure the spacecraft.

The question remained, if someone else had already attacked the scientists at Vostok to gain first access to the machine, what was he going to do about it?

It's one thing trying to get a head start on finding if there's any validity to the rumors, but another thing completely to secure it with force, and potentially risking starting World War III in the process.

Sam said, "Backtrack me a bit. You said someone's actually seen the spacecraft?"

"Yes."

"This isn't a hoax?"

"No. We've put someone down there to examine the spacecraft after we found the lifeforms didn't originate on earth." She tilted her head and looked him directly in the eye. "I thought that was why you were here?"

Sam said, "To protect the alien spacecraft?"

"Yeah. As we both know, its technology will be priceless."

Sam was going to argue the point, but then realized the Secretary of Defense's spy clearly knew more than what he did. He just couldn't work out why the Secretary kept him in the dark regarding the spacecraft?

His mind changed gears. "How many people were in the team that attacked Vostok?"

"Five."

"Okay. So they have five fighters. We have five fighters. That's a fair fight. A little bit on our side because we know they're here and they don't know we're here."

"No. There's only one left."

A puzzled expression crossed Sam's face. "Four?"

"Yeah, I killed four."

Sam opened his mouth to say how, but then closed it again. The Secretary of Defense had kept him in the dark about the name and details of this spy, and he knew he wasn't going to get any more out of her than the Secretary wanted him to get. Obviously, in addition to being a glaciologist, she was trained to fight.

Anastasia tried to explain. "I was forced to. I didn't have a choice. It was self-defense."

Sam's eyebrows shot up. "Four times?"

"Nearly five. I shot the fifth one and sliced his wrist with a medical scalpel. I know I cut him deep. Thought he'd bleed to death, but then I spotted his hovercraft speeding away."

Sam lifted his hand to prevent her from continuing to apologize. "It's okay. I don't blame you."

"Thank you. That's good to hear."

Sam said, "Okay, so now it's six on one. I like those odds better and better. We should be able to secure the spacecraft until reinforcements can come in and work out how we're going to get it out of its ice-covered vault."

"I'll leave that to you to work out." Anastasia looked at him. "You wanna see the spaceship?"

Sam said, "Yes!"

"All right, we can go now."

"Where?"

"The entrance to the tunnels is below the former Vostok Research Station."

"How far is that?"

"Just under a mile."

"Okay. We'll get the team ready and take the hovercraft." Sam said, "We'll be ready in case the remaining attacker is trying to protect the place on his own."

"Good idea."

Sam quickly briefed the rest of the team.

Elise brought up the current satellite overhead, and directed it to look down near Vostok, in an attempt to find the second hovercraft.

There was no sign of it.

The French mercenary must have gone to ground, somewhere.

Sam opened what remained of the second vacuum sealed door at the front of Module A. His eyes scanned the area leading through the remnants of the first door, destroyed by Dragon's Breath.

His heart stuttered, then stopped.

For a second, he thought he was seeing double.

There were two hovercrafts parked outside the front of Vostok.

His eyes narrowed.

A split second later, someone fired a submachine gun at them.

"Take cover!" Sam said, grabbing Anastasia, pushing her to the floor, and covering her with his body.

Chapter Forty-Four

An array of bullets ripped through the entrance chamber of Module A.

Sam shielded Anastasia with his bullet-resistant-vest covered chest. The burst finished and he heard the distinctive sound of empty magazines being swapped.

"Go!" Sam shouted.

They shuffled their way back into the main engineering room in Module A, taking refuge behind the large, iron boiler used to heat the entire facility. Genevieve and Tom spread out, taking protective cover at each end of the room. Hu waited behind the generator at the back of the Module, covering their six, along with Elise, who was positioned at the opposite end of the Module.

Sam looked at Anastasia. "Are you hit?"

"No."

"Hurt?"

"No. I'm fine."

"Good." Sam kept his MP5 submachine gun aimed at the entrance. "I thought you said we were down to one shooter?"

"I thought we were!"

"There's at least five people outside."

"I counted seven."

"All right, seven. What the hell happened?"

She shook her head. "I don't know. My guess is they must have a base nearby. Maybe they've been trying to drill and reach Lake Vostok on their own."

"Is that possible?" Sam said, "I mean, to do that undetected?"

"Sure. This place is riddled with massive crevasses and caves that sink deep beneath the surface. If someone else knew about the spacecraft, it would make sense that they would try and reach it through an alternative route."

"But could it be kept secret?"

"Of course, it could. Hell, we did. We drilled from underneath the abandoned Vostok Research Station – the one built in the 1950s. That way no one watching on satellites could spot it."

Sam's eyes narrowed. "Did it work?"

She arched an eyebrow, grinned. "Did your people find out about it?"

"Touché. All right, so there's a French base out there somewhere, trying to reach this spacecraft before us – and before everyone else."

"It seems so."

Two people approached.

They were shooting French MAT-49 submachine guns. Each of them were wearing Kevlar vests and special ops gear. They moved in with the coordinated attack typical of Special Forces around the world.

Genevieve engaged in a short firefight with the assailants.

Sam stepped out and fired a short burst in their direction.

Anastasia exchanged a glance with him. "I need a weapon. Give me your pistol."

Sam said, "What makes you think I've got a backup?"

"Because only an idiot would try and secure a spacecraft with just one weapon. Give me your gun."

Sam handed her his Glock 10. He didn't ask if she knew how to use it. She'd already proven that somewhere along the line, she had learned as much about being a spy as she did about glaciology. "Here. Take it."

"Thanks."

The two attackers stepped into their line of fire again.

The second one provided covering fire in their direction.

Sam and Anastasia kept every part of their bodies behind the boiler. When the burst of enemy shots paused, they peeked out from opposite sides of the boiler, firing several short bursts. One of them hit one shooter in the chest, knocking him backward. With his vest, that had to hurt, but it wouldn't kill him.

Anastasia stepped out for a split second.

Fired twice.

One shot hit the target in his neck.

The second one, right between the eyes.

Then, Anastasia satisfied, Sam astonished and impressed, they retreated behind the boiler.

Sam shot her a look, admiration in his ocean blue eyes. "You can shoot."

It was a statement, not a question.

She nodded. "I've done a little over the years."

Another one of their adversaries moved toward his downed teammates.

Tom fired the Mossberg pump-action shotgun. The 12-gauge shot erupted out of the barrel. It struck the man on his Kevlar protected torso, but the spread ripped into his neck and eyes. The man clutched his face and screamed.

Genevieve slipped out into the line of fire and squeezed off another burst from the submachine gun. A small grouping disintegrated the man's forehead.

The screams went silent.

Out in front, Sam could hear a rapid exchange in French. Something about someone being dead and to leave the body. Followed by someone being told to protect the front door, while they come around the back.

Sam said, "Hu and Elise, they're coming around on your six!"

"We're on it," Hu and Elise replied.

Everything went quiet and still for the next eight minutes.

Then the silence was abruptly ended by a cacophony of noise, as simultaneous gunfire ripped into Module A from all directions.

Chapter Forty-Five

To Hu the first shots appeared to be coming from Module B.

He dropped down, taking cover behind the large generator in Module A. Gripping his QSZ-92 semi-automatic, he aimed at the doorway. Elise sprayed the incoming invaders with a quick burst of 9×19mm Parabellums.

In the other direction, a round of heavy machine gun fire erupted from the entrance to Module A. Someone had brought in an M2 Browning and set it up. 50 caliber rounds were slicing through the interior of the module, turning anything that wasn't behind solid steel into mincemeat.

Sam yelled, "Take cover!"

He heard Genevieve and Tom drop to the ground, along with Anastasia.

Elise exchanged a glance with Hu.

They moved from behind the boiler at the same time, shooting dead the only remaining attacker from Module B, sending multiple shots through their opponent's head and torso.

Elise shifted her position forward, taking up a defensive position between Module A and B. Hu was about to follow her when he heard an explosive blast erupt behind him.

Someone had used C4 to create their own entrance.

The blast wave knocked Hu to the ground, sliding him across the steel-grated platform of which most of the engineering workshop was built upon. He rolled off the raised surface, falling onto the steel grate directly below with a loud, metallic clank.

The fall hammered his ribcage.

Above him, a big guy stepped inside. Hu's foe was a veritable giant. At least 7 feet tall, and solid muscle. Damn, the guy could have easily played Center in the NBA. Instead, he was walking into Vostok, striding through a doorway he'd just made out of C4, carrying a M134 Minigun and looking exactly like the Terminator.

The renowned weapon fired American 7.62×51mm NATO cartridges from a six-barrel rotary machine gun. It had a high rate of fire via a Gatling-style rotating barrel assembly, with an external power source, fed by a disintegrating M13 linked belt feed that drew from a large backpack.

The Terminator guy pressed the trigger.

His monster gun opened fire.

The maw of the weapon erupted, spewing smoke and red flashes of fire. 7.62×51mm NATO bullets burst out of its six-barrel gun at a rate of 2,000 rounds per minute, and speeds of 2,800 feet per second.

Anyone within the line of fire was going to be ripped apart within seconds.

Hu's massive enemy stepped forward, gun swiveling back and forth, as he sprayed everything. He was walking on the platform above him, moving directly over Hu's head.

With a determined expression on his face, Hu drew Dragon's Breath. Tracking the man's movement, he drove the iridescent blade up through the gap in the steel grate. The razor-sharp point stabbed through the invader's Antarctica SWAT boot as easily as pushing a spoon into ice cream.

The giant cried out in pain.

The man's gatling gun fell onto the platform, its ammunition belt continued running until the weapon's hammer landed on empty space.

The big gun went silent.

The attacker reached down to protect his leg. He touched the boot in his right hand, clasping at the searing pain.

Then his fingers fell straight through the boot, as though it was liquid.

All appearance of restraint was broken. The mercenary rolled onto his back and stared at his disappearing limb in abject terror. He turned the fingers around the palm of his hand as one would trying to roll a marble, and then, one by one, his fingers began to disappear.

Followed by his forearm.

The big man howled as his torso and his 7-foot body was snatched away.

Inch by inch it vanished, until all that was left was a kind of hollowed dust upon the ground, a misty shroud of darkness. Fueled by the heat of the explosion, like a miniature tornado, the strong, well-formed, and presumably short-lived whirlwind stood a shadow of the man. It spun rapidly, catching dust particles in its upward circular motion.

Hu looked on at the evil he had created.

The fire devil looked more like a living specter than a natural weather phenomenon involving a vertically oriented rotating column of wind. This one was nearly translucent, but as light from Vostok's overhead LEDs cast down upon it, the storm reflected all the colors of the rainbow. The sight was a mesmerizing prism, magnified by intermittent bursts of red, orange, blue, green, and even white flames.

Then the malevolent vortex imploded upon itself.

Toward the door the sound of heavy footsteps running on the metal entrance grate to Module A echoed through the engineering module.

Genevieve shouted, "They're retreating."

Hu returned Dragon's Breath inside the scabbard on his back, gripped his pistol, and casually walked toward the front door.

The hovercraft was already speeding away.

Genevieve strolled toward their damaged hovercraft, opened a side compartment, and retrieved a Mk.153 SMAW. The Shoulder-launched Multi-purpose Assault Weapon was the primary infantry anti-tank weapon of the US Marine Corps. It was loaded with a single High-Explosive, Anti-Armor (HEAA) rocket, designed to be effective against current tanks without additional armor. It utilized a standoff rod on the detonator, allowing the explosive force to be focused on a small point, for maximum damage against armored targets.

A portable RPG for the modern soldier.

She lined the digital sight up on the hovercraft that was disappearing into the distance.

And pressed the fire button.

Chapter Forty-Six

The rocket flew straight and true.

An orange flame trailed the HEAA missile.

Some 900 feet away, the hovercraft made a sharp turn, but it was too slow for a rocket traveling at 720 feet per second.

Sam drew a breath and waited for the explosion.

Then a sudden gust of katabatic wind swept the rocket off course.

It wasn't much, but it was enough.

The missile exploded into the icy landscape, sending a plume of snow and frozen spray some thirty feet in all directions. Sam's eyes narrowed, focusing on the ice cloud.

When it settled, the hovercraft disappeared into the distance.

Genevieve swore.

She looked at reloading another rocket, but already the hovercraft was out of effective firing range. Knowing it was just a waste of another valuable missile, she put the weapon back inside the hovercraft.

Sam said, "I have a feeling you'll get another chance."

"I will, but they won't," she said, emphatically.

Sam turned to Anastasia. "Where are they heading?"

"How should I know?"

"Well, they must have a base nearby!"

"Possibly. Like I said, I assume they've been trying to drill down to Lake Vostok to reach the spacecraft too. Their base could be in several different locations."

"If they were doing that, where would they try?"

"It's hard to say."

Sam held her gaze. "If you were to guess?"

"Somewhere to the north." Anastasia thought about it for a second. "There's a series of large gorges and ice caves. That's where I'd look."

Sam said, "And we can reach this spacecraft by descending beneath the original – now retired –Vostok Research Station?"

"Uh-huh."

Sam turned to Elise. "I need you to set up a connection with any satellites overhead and see if you can find this French base."

"I'll try, Sam. But it's unlikely to do much good."

Sam asked, "Because of the weather?"

"Yeah."

"What about Google Earth or something? Surely with updates you may be able to at least see signs of large earthworks?"

"It's not gonna happen."

"Why not?"

Elise sighed. "You've never looked up Antarctica on Google Earth, have you?"

"No. Why?"

"Most of it is blurred out so much to effectively render it useless. The vast majority of Antarctica is also in low resolution due to the bright, often featureless, ice and snow. That makes high-resolution imaging both difficult and largely unnecessary. There's also the other issue of map scale. Because there aren't many permanent features to map near the poles, Google Maps doesn't show anything beyond 85 degrees and the poles are at 90."

"All right. See what you can do. Maybe we can get lucky. Failing that, we'll just have to make sure we're prepared when the next attack arrives."

Hu was already cleaning the blade of his beloved sword with a special silk.

Anastasia's eyes darted toward Hu and Dragon's Breath. To Sam, she asked, "What's the story with the Samurai?"

Sam grinned. "Don't ask. He likes that sword more than any modern weapon, despite what I might suggest."

"Samurai?" Hu feigned indignation. "I'm Chinese, not Japanese. My family come from the ancient band of Youxia."

Anastasia nodded. "Okay. But you like to play with swords?"

Hu grinned. "My toy happened to save your life back there, when that giant walked in carrying a damned rotary machinegun!"

Anastasia laughed at that. "Okay, that I'll give you. And thank you for saving our lives."

"You're welcome."

Sam said, "Do you need to grab anything before we head to the abandoned Research Station?"

"No. I have everything we need."

"All right, back into the hovercraft everyone. Let's see if we can retrieve and secure this spacecraft before World War III starts."

Tom dropped down into the pilot's seat.

He flicked on the ignition.

Nothing happened.

He tried a few more times, and then turned to Sam. "We have a problem. Our ride is dead."

"It's done well to get this far." He turned to Anastasia. "How far is it to the old Research Station?"

Anastasia said, "No more than a mile. But that's a long way on foot in this weather. I should know, I just about died trying a much shorter distance."

"All right. What do you suggest?"

"That depends." She grinned. "On whether your friend's Jedi Lightsaber can cut through an aluminum doorway."

Chapter Forty-Seven

Former Vostok Research Station

The Kharkovchanka made its way over the undulating ice.

Without missing a beat, its seventy-year-old Malyshev V-12 diesel engine groaned as it made its way across the frozen, alien world. It pulled up outside the front of the former Vostok Research Station, a derelict from the 1950's Soviet Union.

Sam climbed down from the massive Kharkovchanka. He ran his eyes across the horizon, before landing on the original Vostok Research Station.

It wasn't much to look at.

In fact, it wasn't much at all.

There was a large spherical, orange and white dome, which might have once been anything from a primitive radar device, meteorology building, through to a massive fuel storage depot, for all he knew. In addition to that, only a couple feet of various building structures were still visible. There was an old drilling tower, a communications tower, and a giant mound of ice.

Sam turned to Anastasia. "What happened to it?"

Anastasia grinned. "Antarctica happened to it."

"Really?"

"Sure. It's been languishing here over seventy years. That results in a lot of snow and ice that was never removed. When our people used to work there permanently, one of their biggest jobs was to eliminate the snow regularly. Even with the constant effort, it was a losing battle. Like fighting an incoming tide." She smiled and began walking toward the relic. "And since it was retired, that tide quickly enveloped all that remained."

Sam looked at Elise. "Are you sure our new friends didn't take refuge here?"

"Certain. I've had a satellite fixed on this station since we left Hawaii. No way have they come through here in the past two days."

"All right, Genevieve. I want you and Hu to sweep the old station, then secure topside so we don't get any uninvited guests."

Genevieve said, "I'm on it."

Together, they followed Anastasia down a narrow path that carved its way deep into the ice. They were all armed to the teeth, and hyperalert. Memories of the recent firefight with the French forces were fresh, especially as their bodies still hurt from hitting the deck.

The pathway continued for twenty or so feet at a gradual gradient, before disappearing into an underground passage. The tunnel opened another hundred or so feet when it reached the main living quarters of the now retired Soviet Era Antarctic research station. The power had been left on from a previous visit. It was running from an old diesel generator, but the lights flickered dangerously. It was a good thing they had flashlights.

The team spread out, securing the old base.

There weren't a lot of rooms, but by being so completely buried with few entrances, it was easy to protect from future intruders. Sam finished his quick survey of the old base.

He said to Genevieve, "Bring in whatever weapons you need to secure this building. No one comes in or out without my say so. Understood?"

"I'm on it." Genevieve gave a smile that suggested she would love to see someone try. "I brought that giant's M134 Minigun. I figure we can set it up behind a barrier at the start of the tunnel. Anyone who comes knocking will get turned to mincemeat. Hu can run it. It only seems fair given that he was the one to take down that huge guy."

"All right, sounds good." Sam leveled his gaze on her. "Tom and I are going to go take a firsthand look at this thing. Make sure we don't have any trouble while we're down below."

"No problem," Genevieve said, her voice sounding like she was looking forward to it. "Let them come."

Sam turned to Anastasia. "So how do we reach the spacecraft?"

Anastasia said, "You have to remember, this was all supposed to be kept secret until we could find a way to extract the ancient machine."

"Before news of its existence reached anyone?"

"Exactly."

Sam nodded. It made sense. "So how do we get there?"

She grinned. "I'll show you. Come with me."

Anastasia brought them to the old sleeping quarters. There were six sets of bunkbeds in a rectangular room with only one door – the one they had entered through. An old 44-gallon drum rested in the middle of the room. Perhaps the inhabitants once burned paper and other bits for warmth? There was no chimney, making Sam wonder where all the smoke must have gone. A casual glance at the ceiling revealed a thick layer of soot. Sam glanced inside the 44-gallon drum. It was still full of charcoal ashes.

Sam and Tom exchanged a glance.

The room appeared to be sealed and empty with only one door.

Anastasia stood in hesitant expectation, waiting for them.

After a full minute, Sam asked, "Well… where is it?"

Anastasia pulled back the 44-gallon drum, which was built onto a hidden sliding hinge. It revealed a concealed ladder, and a secret passage.

Chapter Forty-Eight

It was absolute darkness below.

Sam switched on his flashlight, velcroing it onto the side of his beanie. Then he swiftly climbed down the ladder, two rungs at a time. It was another one of those Silence of the Lambs type moments. The ladder dropped nearly thirty feet, before opening into a small landing section.

He turned his head, seeing the subterranean ice tunnel lead to a surprisingly large metal door. The beam of his flashlight darted across the room, casting a shadow on a small alcove just a few feet back from the entrance.

Anastasia moved into the alcove, pulled some sort of large electronic switch. The sound of a distant diesel generator starting up echoed throughout the cavern. A few seconds later, the downlights flickered, and came on.

They were standing beside what appeared to be an industrial-sized elevator. Two lights next to the door glowed blue.

One pointed up.

The other down.

Anastasia glanced at Sam and Tom and said, "One of you gentlemen mind hitting the down button?"

"Sure," Tom said, ducking under the narrow ceiling and pressing the button.

The elevator must have already been at their level as the elevator door opened. All three of them stepped in. Anastasia pressed the down button, and they began their 2.2-mile descent beneath fifteen million years of ice.

Sam grinned. "You have an elevator that reaches the sub-glacial lake?"

"Yeah. Why? What did you think we would be doing, climbing about a million rungs of a ladder to reach Lake Vostok?"

Sam shook his head. "I don't know what I thought. Honestly, I just assumed..."

"What?" she asked, her lips parted in an impish and mischievous smile.

"Well, you've only known about the spacecraft for a little while. It took you twenty years to drill down through 2.2 miles of ice with a 3-inch-thick drill head…"

She lifted a hand. "I know. It's a little unbelievable. I could tell you that we Russians have better technology than the West, but the truth is, we started building this twenty years ago."

"Why?"

"Platinum," she said, emphatically.

Sam's ears popped as the elevator descended. "Come again?"

"When we began drilling, geologists discovered a section near the base of the lake was rich in the rare element."

"Why all the cloak and dagger…"

She smiled. "You mean, why all the secrecy?"

"Yeah."

"For starters, under the Antarctic Treaty, mining of any sort is forbidden in Antarctica. And second, there was still risk of contaminating whatever microbial life we might find inside the lake."

"So, the entire thing was mined in secret?"

"Yes." Anastasia said, "And this elevator was used to reach the main mining site, which now sits on top of Lake Vostok."

The elevator came to a stop.

The doors opened.

A well-lit room opened up.

Unlike the building structures on the surface, which were decidedly Soviet era construction, this was futuristic and almost surgically clean. It was filled with modern computers, scientific equipment, and whatnot.

Sam took a breath, noticing the temperature change. He said, "It's warmer down here."

Anastasia nodded. "Just above freezing. That's why Lake Vostok is still liquid."

Sam said, "Ah, just above freezing. My favorite temperature."

"It's better than minus 110 which is closer to what it is topside right now." She kept walking, following one of the offshoots of the main room. "Not *my* favorite temperature, but a close second."

Sam, curious, asked, "What's your favorite temperature?"

She shook her head. "Don't worry about it. You'll just laugh at me."

"Now I have to know!"

Anastasia paused. Stopped walking. Met his eye. "Really?"

"Sure."

"Minus forty."

"Really?" Sam tilted his head. "I mean, why's that embarrassing? Actually, no, scratch that… why would anyone's favorite temperature be minus 40 degrees… Fahrenheit or Celsius?"

Anastasia laughed. "Exactly!"

"Exactly what?" Sam asked.

"Sorry, it's the science nerd in me." Her voice had a teasing lilt to it. "Minus forty is the exact point where Fahrenheit and Celsius intersect."

"Meaning?"

"Minus forty is the same irrespective of whether its Celsius or Fahrenheit. If you don't believe me, try calculating it!"

Sam tried to make the mental calculations, recalling his early primary school math. To convert Celsius to Fahrenheit… minus 32 and then multiply by 0.5556… or something…

Anastasia looked at his face. "Math not your strong point?"

Sam shrugged. "I'll take your word for it."

"You should, because it is the same." She turned to Tom. "Isn't that cool?"

Tom smiled. "Definitely cool."

Sam agreed. "You must be very popular at parties."

Anastasia ignored his jibe and led them to the end of a long corridor. She opened the door. Switched on the lights.

This room had a diving platform that opened straight out into Lake Vostok. The water was so crystal clear it looked like it had been distilled. Above which, was a small chamber of air, carved into the 15-million-year-old layer of ice. The entire chamber glowed with the most stunningly vibrant blue Sam had ever seen.

He turned around, taking in the rest of the space…

And came face-to-face with two giant mechanical monsters.

Chapter Forty-Nine

Neumayer-Station III – German Antarctic Base, Atka Bay.

The German Neumayer-Station III station was in a constant state of flux.

Situated on the Ekström Ice Shelf, lying between the Sorasen and Halvfarryggen Ridge, on the Princess Martha Coast of Queen Maud Land. It was first mapped by the Norwegian–British–Swedish Antarctic Expedition (NBSAE) (1949–1952), and named for Bertil Ekström, a Swedish mechanical engineer with the NBSAE, who drowned when a track-driven vehicle he was driving plunged over the edge of Quar Ice Shelf on February 24, 1951. The Ekström Ice Shelf occupies an area of 3,400 square miles. It is 520 feet thick at the edge, and rises 50 feet above the sea level.

Since 2007, the German base had moved along with the ice shelf roughly 660 feet toward the open sea. Along with previous Neumayer stations, it had been the center of continuous research since 1981. Currently, it focused on research areas of meteorology, geophysics, and atmospheric chemistry, along with infrasound and marine acoustics since 2005.

Axel Hoffmann stopped his snowmobile.

He looked through his binoculars, scanning the area off the Weddell Sea, across to the coast of the Atka Bay. There, thousands upon thousands of Emperor Penguins were congregating, huddling together against the bitter cold of Antarctic winter.

In the past few months, he'd grown to love the unique creatures with a passion that surprised him.

Emperor penguins were the largest of penguins and the most dedicated of parents. The colony of 11,000 birds gather on the newly frozen sea ice in Atka Bay every year to face the Antarctic winter. They form one of the strongest pair bonds in nature – vital if they are to raise their single chick in the most hostile nursery on earth.

His eyes landed on the new parents who were in the delicate process of transferring their one and only egg for the season from mother to father. It was a yearly dance, made famous in the Disney movie, Happy Feet.

After laying, the mother's food reserves are exhausted, so she very carefully transfers the egg to the male, then immediately returns to the sea for two months to feed. The transfer of the egg can be awkward and difficult, especially for first-time parents. Many couples drop or crack the egg in the process. When this happens, the chick inside is quickly lost, as the egg cannot withstand the sub-freezing temperatures on the icy ground for more than one to two minutes.

When a couple loses an egg in this manner, their relationship is ended, and both walk back to the sea. They will return to the colony next year to try mating again. After a successful transfer of the egg to the male penguin, the female departs for the sea and the male spends the dark, stormy winter incubating the egg against his brood patch, a patch of skin without feathers. There he balances it on the tops of his feet, engulfing it with loose skin and feathers for around 65-75 consecutive days until hatching.

Axel shifted, lowering the binoculars.

He was part of a secret operation, put together by Mykel Zimmerman, MP in the Bundestag and German Minister of Defense and Aerospace. His team included nine persons assigned to Neumayer-Station III under the auspice of research into the impact of iceberg collisions on the Ekström Ice Shelf.

In 2010 the iceberg B15-K collided with the Ekström Ice Shelf in Atka Bay. B15-K was 33 miles long by three miles wide, and a fifth of a mile thick. It hit the shelf in the vicinity of Neumayer Station III. The event caused damage to the ice shelf, equivalent to 50,000 tons of explosives being detonated. This altered the natural erosion and sped up the demise of the Ekström Ice Shelf.

As a result, logistic experts and scientist have completed thousands of hours of research into the event. A unique interdisciplinary compilation of data obtained from remote sensing, geophysics, meteorology, oceanography and ocean acoustics now provides new insights into the mechanics of the ice and crack propagation in the ice shelf.

Then, three months ago, a smaller iceberg hit the same region.

And Ekström Ice Shelf began to shift even faster.

The event was the perfect pretext for Axel's team, who were assigned to research the long-term ramifications of such collisions from icebergs. It was routine work and easy to perceive why Germany would be interested in sending such a crew to do the research. Better yet, it was easy to believe that they would need to work autonomously from the rest of the scientists at Neumayer-Station III, as they needed the ability to fly and take aerial surveillance through LIDAR and other processes.

It was also, entirely a lie.

Only one person from Axel's team knew anything about glaciology, geology, or Antarctica for that matter. The rest of them were specialized soldiers, recruited from the Kommando Spezialkräfte – German's Special Forces – and sent there for a very specific mission.

They were all under Axel's command.

So far, it had proved one of the easiest operations of his career. He'd been tasked to retrieve something of extreme technological and military hardware value by force.

Yet so far, the hardware hadn't been located.

Ergo.

He was sitting here watching the strongest family bonds of any creature in God's great animal kingdom. Just like David Attenborough, he was simply enjoying the day, observing these remarkable penguins survive. That level of trust and commitment between the male and female mating, in which both mother and father are needed equally in the success of their child-rearing and parenting process, was something that humans could learn from.

Of course, the more he'd read up about the magnificent creatures since arriving on the frozen continent, and with all the time in the world to kill, he discovered they're not as faithful mates as Disney might have us believe. Contrary to popular belief, Emperor penguins do not mate for life; they are serially monogamous, having only one mate each year, and remaining faithful to that mate. However, fidelity between years is only around 15 percent. The narrow window of opportunity available for mating appears to be an influence. There is a priority to mate and breed which usually precludes waiting for the previous year's partner to arrive at the colony.

Axel thought about that.

Then shrugged it off.

He'd like to see any man or woman, given their harsh lives, maintain such fidelity. It was an idle thought of course.

Axel wasn't Attenborough, nor was he a relationship counselor. All he could see were some of the cutest, most wondrous animals alive, and just how hard and diligently they worked seamlessly together as parents. They did all this to ensure their children would live and grow to maturity.

His thoughts were interrupted by the sound of his satellite phone. Axel picked it up within seconds. There was only one person who had this number.

"Sir?"

"Axel, we've located the machine."

"You want me to retrieve it?"

"No. Everything's changed. I want you to destroy it."

"Destroy it?" he asked, incredulous. "Are you sure. I thought…"

"I know what I previously said…"

Axel asked, "So what's changed?"

"That was before."

"Before what?"

"That was before they came after my daughter…"

Axel swallowed hard. "They came after Hannah?"

Zimmerman said, "Yeah. Nearly killed her too, but some hot-shot criminologist and a local detective found her first. The criminologist was killed, but Hannah survived."

Axel said, "What do you want me to do?"

The voice came back as cold and hard as the Antarctic winter. "Destroy it… and kill them all."

Axel hesitated, then asked, "Is that the best option? I thought we wanted the hardware?"

"We do, but then they attacked my daughter."

"What will destroying the hardware achieve?"

Zimmerman laughed. "Obliterate every inch of the hardware and The Ghost's own men will come after him. They can reach him where I can't.

Given what they've lost, they will hurt him far worse than I can."

"Understood, sir. I'll make it happen."

Then he thought…

Now there's a parent who's willing to do what it takes to protect his kids.

Chapter Fifty

Trapped Inside an Unknown Dungeon

Natalya opened her eyes.

She was surrounded by walls made of solid sandstone blocks. The ground was cool, but dry. The paved sandstone blocks fitted perfectly together. It felt like the basement of a medieval castle. Yet, in stark contrast, almost a jarring anachronism, the arched, stone masonry ceiling had a row of LED downlights.

She blinked and rubbed her eyes.

Where the hell am I?

Her head hurt. It was like one of those hangovers where you can barely remember what happened the night before. Then, slowly, as your brain fires up, and you return to some sort of level of coherent consciousness, bits and pieces come back to you in dribs and drabs.

Her mother had left a voicemail.

That was strange.

Her mother hadn't spoken to her in years.

Then, the voicemail told her to run. Open the safety deposit box, take it, and run. She probably wouldn't have believed her, had it not been for the two million euros, US and British passports, and the gun.

Ultimately, it had been the cash that had made her run.

No way her mother could have accrued that sort of wealth legally within her lifetime. The passports and the gun her mother could have secured through illegal, black-market means. But the cash? It meant she was in deep with bad people.

So, she ran.

Natalya remembered leaving the bank. Making her way north, through the historic gardens, Jardin de Ville. There, she was accosted by three… or was it four? Thugs. They were kids. Probably smoking weed, or ice. Idiots driven by pride, male aggression, and group mentality to steal from easy prey.

But she wasn't easy prey.

She had a gun and had no regrets using it. She shot one, and then the other's had attempted to attack her… but a good Samaritan intervened.

Her mind zeroed in on that memory. The good Samaritan had come in threatening to swing a baseball bat. She didn't even know the French played baseball. But there was something else that didn't make sense at the time. She had a gun. It was loaded and she'd even shot their friend – or at least partner in crime – and yet, they weren't scared of her. They didn't run.

Apparently, the thugs were so desperate or stupid, they were willing to risk their lives to continue their attack.

Yet the good Samaritan with a baseball bat…

What did they say?

Sorry, we didn't know she was yours. We're leaving boss.

At the time, she thought it strange, that the man wielded so much fear, and respect. But now it made sense. He wasn't just a tough guy with a bat, protecting a damsel in distress, he was their manager. The top of an organized crime syndicate, or maybe a drug cartel.

The words came back to her again.

Sorry, we didn't know she was yours.

Natalya remembered chatting to him on the way to Switzerland. She was enjoying the drive, the conversation with the good-looking man. She was even trying to work out if there was a way of keeping his number. Maybe one day meeting up once she'd established herself in a new country.

And then everything went blank.

They were approaching a toll, and he'd asked her to pass him his toll pass.

She leaned over, and when she sat up again, he had tasered her.

And now, she was waking up in what seemed to be a medieval dungeon. Strangely, her mind instantly pointed out that if she was still within France, she was technically being held prisoner inside an oubliette. The newfound trivia didn't fill her with joy.

The French word, *oubliette*, meant *to forget*.

Victims in oubliettes were often left to starve and dehydrate to death, making the practice akin to – and some say an actual variety of –

immurement. Natalya didn't understand. Why some guy she didn't even know would want to leave her to die in a dungeon?

She ran her eyes across the rest of the room. It certainly looked like an oubliette. A reasonably large, circular room, with a vaulted ceiling. There was a toilet and a water faucet at one end. Chain and manacles at the other end. Maybe she was going to be tortured?

Then, as if in answer to her question, her eyes landed on three cartons of water bottles, a box of sports protein bars, and a box of canned food. None of it looked particularly appealing, but she could survive on it for quite some time if need be.

On top of the pile was a single note.

Natalya read the note –

This needs to last you a week. It should be enough if you're careful. Also, there's a toilet and washbasin. So if you run out of water, there's always the faucet.

One week from now I'll come back.

If your mother keeps her end of the bargain, I'll open the door, and you can walk away.

Good luck.

She noted he kindly neglected to mention what happened if her mother didn't keep her end of the bargain.

Natalya began casually inspecting the cans of food. There was tinned spaghetti, minestrone soup, beef soup... she put them back down, and stopped looking for others. They would make do for seven days and nights. Her abductor had been thoughtful enough to leave her a fork and a spoon. She picked up a protein bar that advertised 30 grams of protein and zero sugar. It claimed that it tasted like a Butterfinger.

She took a bite.

It didn't taste anything like a Butterfinger.

She ate the rest of it anyway, chewing through the thick, gluggy protein, and washed it down with a bottle of water. Next to the pile of food and water was her North Face backpack.

She guessed it would be empty.

But she guessed wrong.

She slowly unzipped it. The cash was still there. So were the passports.

Her eyes narrowed as they landed on the pistol. She picked it up. The weapon seemed lighter. She wasn't an expert with guns, although she had done some shooting in a range previously with friends. She'd never shot a Heckler and Koch PSP pistol, but she knew her way around a handgun.

The pistol was fed from a single-stack box magazine with a capacity of 8 rounds. She searched the handle, and found a release inside the firearm's frame with another located at the heel of the grip. After the last round has been fired, the slide will remain open thanks to a slide catch that could be released by pulling the slide further back or pressing the squeeze cocker.

She released the magazine. It was empty. She looked in the slide catch, and found the chamber was, unsurprisingly, empty too.

She heard the sound of feet scurrying on the sandstone tiles.

Her eyes traced the sound.

There, in the middle of the room, a rat came for her protein bars. It actually managed to grab one. Natalya shouted at it. The rat turned to face her, nibbling away at the disgusting food bar, giving her that look that suggested, *What are you gonna do about it?*

She then tried swearing in both French and German. And when that failed to deter the rodent, she swore in her native Russian.

Eventually, the rat got the idea.

Carrying what was left of the protein bar in its mouth, the rat scurried across the floor, before squeezing its head beneath a gap in the masonry between two sandstone blocks. Its little clawed feet scurried away along what sounded like a tunnel on the other side of the wall.

Natalya worked the mortar around the stone using the back of the fork her captor had kindly left her, until it came free. The sandstone brick shifted a little bit. She worked it for several more minutes, and then it broke from the mortar and she was able to coax it out.

One down, about a hundred to go before she could squeeze through.

It wasn't much, but it was something. And besides, what else was she going to do with her time down here? She reached inside the opening, through the gap with the brick. It was wide enough that she could bring her entire arm through the gap up to her shoulder.

She felt around.

It was a large space. Probably a tunnel or maybe even the runoff for some sort of waterway. A latrine perhaps?

Wherever it was, it had to be better than where she was currently trapped.

She began pulling her arm out of the gap, motivated by her finding to keep going. It would take hours if not all day to release enough stones that she could squeeze her entire body out, but given her captor's note, she had the better part of a week to escape.

Her hand touched something on its way out.

It was metal.

A latch of some sort.

Her brow furrowed and she closed her eyes, trying to imagine what it was she was feeling in her hand.

Bewildered, she pulled the latch.

A series of creaks filled the chamber. Metal cogs began to turn, and for a horrifying moment, she suddenly regretted her decision.

Then a whole section of the wall swung open…

Revealing a secret passageway.

Chapter Fifty-One

The atmospheric diving suits were Russian.

Each one more than ten feet tall.

To Sam, it looked like a cross between a space suit and a medieval knight in shiny armor – on steroids – which was basically what it was built to be. A one-person, self-contained, articulated submersible. It resembled a knight's armor, with elaborate pressure joints to allow articulation while maintaining an internal pressure of one atmosphere. The two Russian atmospheric diving suits had twin propulsion systems on the back, and large, robotic grippers that resembled a pair of oversized pliers at the end of each hand.

Sam was well aware of the capabilities of atmospheric dive suits. They could enable diving at depths of up to 3,000 feet for many hours by eliminating the majority of significant physiological dangers associated with deep diving. The occupant of an ADS does not need to decompress, and there is no need for special gas mixtures, so there is little danger of decompression sickness or nitrogen narcosis when the ADS is functioning properly.

Anastasia said, "Have you ever used one of these?"

Sam suppressed a big grin. "Yeah, I've used one once or twice."

Tom said, "Maybe more. Sometimes, it even goes okay for him."

"You've had accidents with atmospheric diving suits?" she asked, her voice suddenly full of concern.

Sam dismissed her concern with the wave of his hand. "I'll be fine."

She persisted. "But you've had accidents inside them before?"

Sam nodded. "I got attacked once."

Tom said, "There was that other time that idiot fired a torpedo at you!"

"Oh yeah," Sam said, his voice seemingly surprised by the revelation, like someone revisiting a fond memory. "I remember that one."

"Oh, and of course, let's not forget when that old Atlantean underwater temple collapsed." Tom showed his white teeth beneath a boyish smile. "This game's fun."

Anastasia said, "Are you sure you're the right person to do this? I mean, we can find other professionals to work out how we're going to remove the spacecraft from Lake Vostok."

Sam shook his head. "Tom and I are teasing you. We're professional maritime salvagers. If anyone's going to be capable of pulling that thing out of the water, it will be us."

"Right," she said, in a voice that suggested she felt very much not all right. "So it was just a joke. You've never had an accident with these atmospheric dive suits?"

Tom laughed. "No, that part was right."

Over the next fifteen minutes, Anastasia ran Sam and Tom through the fundamentals, controls, and procedures of using the Russian atmospheric dive suits. They were basically mini submersibles, capable of reaching depths far greater than Lake Vostok's seabed. Each suit provided six hours of power and twenty-four hours of life-support.

Both the arms and legs could be shifted naturally with one's own arms and legs. The internal movements triggered the mechanically assisted external movements of the machine. In addition, there were controls to maneuver the pincers and clipping devices. In an emergency there was a bailout system, a single lever that drops a series of lead weights, causing the submersible to become buoyant.

"Questions?"

Sam said, "Yeah, any chance you can get a message topside?"

"You want to talk to your team?"

"Not now, but I need to let Genevieve know where we are in case they get attacked or need to send a message through."

"Not a problem. I'll take care of it."

"Thank you."

Sam opened the access hatch at the back of the atmospheric dive suit. He carefully maneuvered his body up and into the one-person submersible. He pulled the hatch closed behind him, and carefully turned the lock until it made a seal.

Tom pressed and pulled himself into the second atmospheric dive suit. It was a little small for him, but, as with caving, he somehow managed to fold his body in all the right places to squeeze into it.

Once inside, Tom adjusted his position, and said, "Sam, you're not gonna believe this."

Sam swallowed. "What is it?"

"This atmospheric dive suit is too small for me."

"I know. It looked cramped. Good thing we're not going to be down there too long."

"No. You misunderstand me, I can't even bend or straighten my legs inside the machine."

Sam was taken aback. Tom was always too big for things, and generally he just managed to perform some sort of magic, folding himself to meet the environment. But not this time.

"What are you saying?"

"I'm sorry Sam. You're on your own for this dive."

Sam looked at Anastasia. "I don't suppose you want to come with me?"

She glanced at the robotic submersible that looked like it belonged in an old 1960s horror film about alien invasions. "No thank you. I get claustrophobic. Submersibles aren't my thing. Anyone topside capable of making the dive?"

Sam shook his head. "Tom and I are the only ones who have ever used an atmospheric dive suit."

Her brow furrowed with concern. "Can you make the dive alone?"

Sam nodded. "Yeah. It'll be fine. After all, there's a reason they call it a one-person submarine."

Sam switched on the electrics.

A timer showed a countdown for remaining life support.

24 Hours.

Then a second one for electrical reserve.

6 hours.

But that could be quickly reduced if he used the electric propulsion system too much.

Anastasia checked him over. "Good to go. Any last questions?"

Sam said, "Yeah, which direction is the spacecraft?"

She smiled right at him. "It's directly below us. You can't miss it."

Chapter Fifty-Two

Lake Vostok had a depth of 2,198 feet, making it a significant dive, even if he had been in the ocean or a normal lake.

A lake which, unlike this one, wasn't buried under 2.2 miles of ice.

It took nearly twenty minutes for Sam to climb inside his diving suit, secure his harness, lock his watertight seals, and run-through the start-up procedure using a checklist that made piloting a helicopter seem simple.

Powerful spotlights fixed to the ceiling of the dive platform shone down on the lake. The beams of light were traveling hundreds of feet in the crystal-clear waters below.

Sam gave the good-to-go symbol with his robotic hand and Anastasia lowered the advanced atmospheric diving machine into the water. Sam watched as the fresh water of Lake Vostok rushed over the dome-shaped viewing port. A moment later, he released the tether, and took control of his submersible.

Sam adjusted the ballast, slowly taking in water until the heavily modified atmospheric dive suit became negatively buoyant. At a depth of thirty feet, he brought it back to neutral buoyancy.

He ran his eyes across a series of gauges, confirming that his power and life-support systems were all functioning correctly. Happy with the results, he depressed his radio microphone and said, "How am I looking, Tom?"

The Russian dive machine used a combination of UQC and 27 KHZ Acoustic which were heterodyned. This was a radio technique used to shift an inputted frequency from one to another through modulation in order to achieve successful transmission – to a high pitch radio frequency for acoustic transmission through water.

"Everything's looking good from above," came Tom's reply. "You ready to descend?"

"Yeah, I'm good. All right, I'm starting my descent, now."

Sam opened the ballast tanks farther, and water flooded in while large air bubbles were expelled, until his dive suit began its continuous descent to the seabed below. He dived in the dark, knowing from sonar and bathymetric mappings of the subterranean lake that there was nothing between the surface and a depth of 2,000 feet. With power a valuable commodity, he kept the LED lights switched off until he got much deeper.

Sam recalled that more than 3,500 different DNA sequences had been identified in samples extracted from layers of ice that have built up just above the surface of the lake. About 95 percent of them were associated with types of bacteria, 5 percent of them had the hallmarks of more complex organisms known as eukaryotes, and two of the sequences were linked to a distinct class of one-celled organisms called archaea.

The sequences included close matches for various types of fungi as well as arthropods, springtails, water fleas and a mollusk. What's more, some of the bacteria from the sample were typically found in fish guts – suggesting that the fish they came from may be swimming around in the lake. But for all that, the beam of light coming from the top of the diving platform made the water appear infinitely clear, like distilled water. Completely devoid of any life – marine or other.

Sam glanced at his depth gauge.

He was already at a depth of 1,000 feet.

"Still good, Tom?" he asked.

"Yeah, everything's working just fine."

At 1,500 feet he switched on his overhead LED lights, providing a thick stream of light ahead. Sam glanced across at his depth gauge. He was coming up on 1,600 feet. His eyes turned to the bathymetric sonar array, which gave a colored delineation of the seabed far below.

At 2,000 feet the seabed became a series of undulating submerged valleys and hills. The crests were at 2,000 feet, while the troughs were up to 2,200 feet.

Sam adjusted the buoyancy control, and the mini submersible slowed its descent to a crawl, before leveling out completely. He said, "Nearly at the bottom, my suit is working well. Gauges within normal parameters."

"Excellent," Anastasia said. "Tom is on the phone right now."

"Oh, yeah? How's the rest of the team on the surface?"

"They are all fine."

"All right. I'll keep you informed when I've found somewhere to hook a cable onto the spacecraft, and when we're ready to start hauling it up to the surface."

"Okay, we will be here when you need us."

Sam's eyes swept the seabed. Nothing but gravel.

He turned around.

Still nothing.

He depressed the mic on the radio. "No sign of this thing on the seabed."

Anastasia's calm voice came back normal. "You must have drifted somewhere. It should be directly below you."

"Maybe I got it wrong?"

"Got what wrong?"

"The directions?" Sam asked. "Maybe the spacecraft isn't directly underneath the diving platform, or possibly I've drifted on descent?"

"No. It's definitely directly below the dive platform. Could it be possible you drifted?"

"Drifted?" Sam asked. "How could I have drifted? The entire lake is locked in ice that's 15 million years old."

Anastasia said, "I don't know what to say, but the spacecraft isn't here. It must be there."

Sam turned around, turning in a slow, 360-degree arc. He pinged the sonar, trying to get a better bathymetric image of the seabed.

The mapping showed the lake's bed was completely empty.

In all directions.

There was no sign of any structure, let alone some sort of aircraft.

"I don't know what to say. According to my sonar, I'm all alone down here..."

"That can't be!"

Sam made a ninety-degrees turn to his left.

"Whoa!" He said, over the radio. "Where did you come from?"

Anastasia asked, "Where did what come from?"

Sam's eyes lit up in wonder.

The beam of light from his domed helmet, like an oversized spacesuit's visor, shone on the darkness.

Something seemed to be swallowing the light...

No, not swallowing it... more like... absorbing it.

Sam's eyes landed on a dark image straight in front of him.

It looked just like a spaceship.

"Never mind." He grinned. "I just found it."

Chapter Fifty-Three

Tom asked, "Where's the phone that communicates directly to the topside?"

Anastasia pointed to the wall in an alcove just inside from the diving room. "It's over there. Just pick up the handset."

"Okay, thanks."

Tom walked to the end of the diving platform, through the doors that restricted the movement of moist air off the lake from entering the main internal rooms and workspaces of subterranean Vostok.

He found the alcove.

There was a standing desk with a laptop, next to a single, wall-mounted phone. He picked up the headset.

There was no dial tone.

Tom tried pressing 0...

Then 9...

Weren't those how people generally got an outside line in a hotel?

No luck.

He walked back into the dive platform.

Anastasia met him with her cheerful demeanor. "Everything okay topside?"

Tom said, "I don't know. I couldn't get through. Do I need to press something to connect to an outside line?"

She shook her head. "Not usually."

"Hm. That's strange."

"You look worried, Tom," she said, walking toward the phone. "I wouldn't worry too much. Sometimes part of the line freezes, or moisture gets trapped in the line."

"And that cuts out a communication cable?" Tom asked, incredulous.

"Sure. Why, does that surprise you?"

"Yeah. In this day and age. I mean, you work in Antarctica. Your engineers have seventy plus years' worth of experience in running cables in a subzero environment."

Anastasia shrugged. "I don't know what to say?"

Tom watched her pick up the phone. She tilted her head to the side, her eyes narrowed. She tried a couple numbers. Nothing seemed to happen.

"No luck?" Tom asked.

"Nothing. Weird."

"Is there another phone?"

"Yeah. Just at the bottom of the elevator. I'll show you."

Tom followed her to the base of the elevator.

He picked up the phone.

No dial tone…

Tom passed the phone to Anastasia, who took it, listened, and then shook her head. "So weird."

"How often do both lines go dead?"

"Down here?" She arched an eyebrow. "Never."

"Is it possible someone topside cut the cable?"

"Anything's possible, but that's highly unlikely."

"Why?"

"Well, the cable runs alongside the elevator shaft, through to the internal living quarters of this building. The only way for someone to destroy it would be if they had overrun your people on the surface, and then cut the cable."

Tom swallowed hard. "Let's hope that's not the case."

She asked, "Do you want to go check?"

Tom said, "I'd better."

"Do you want me to come?"

"No. Stay here and wait for Sam. He's going to need your help to winch the atmospheric dive suit out of the water when he returns."

"All right. Good luck."

Tom pressed the up button on the elevator. The doors opened, he stepped in. The doors closed automatically, like any modern elevator in the world. The up and down buttons glowed blue. He pressed the up button again.

The elevator began its 2.2 mile journey.

Smooth and efficient.

Five to ten seconds in, he opened his mouth and shifted his jaw, trying to equalize the pressure as the elevator ascended.

Fifteen seconds in – roughly halfway up the marathon elevator climb – the elevator slowed, then came to a complete stop.

The lights inside the elevator flickered and died.

Oh, that's not good...

Tom switched on his flashlight.

He tried pressing the up button again. It no longer glowed blue or any other color for that matter. It was as though the power had been cut completely.

There was another phone on the wall.

He picked it up.

And swore.

Because he was trapped a mile beneath countless tons of ice...

Without a single way to contact anyone.

Chapter Fifty-Four

Sam fixed his overhead LED lights on the spacecraft.

It was smaller than he was expecting. Only big enough for one, maybe two people inside. That was, assuming aliens were anywhere near our size, which there was no logical reason to believe to be the case.

More triangular than a traditional rocket, it reminded Sam more of the old, original stealth aircraft. Kind of a cross between the Lockheed F-117 Nighthawk, and a miniaturized version of NASA's Space Shuttle.

Sam adjusted the joystick that controlled the atmospheric dive suit's propulsion. The rear mounted thrusters whirred as he surveyed the unique spacecraft, maneuvering the submersible around its fuselage. His face-shield mounted camera recorded everywhere Sam looked.

The spacecraft was covered in what appeared to be a light absorbing material, similar to the F-117 Nighthawk. Sharp angles rendered it virtually undetectable to sight, radar, or infrared sensors. He pinged his radar once more.

Nothing came back.

Yes. It was as if the spacecraft didn't exist.

Much like modern stealth aircraft that relied on skin that is radar transparent or absorbing, behind which are structures termed reentrant triangles. Radar waves penetrating the skin get trapped in these structures, reflecting off the internal faces and losing energy.

Only this vessel did exist, because he was seeing it with his own eyes.

Sam searched the machine, looking for signs of damage. Anything that might suggest why it had crashed or how it had gotten where it was, but the structure looked entirely intact. Not a scratch on it. The aerospace vehicle looked like it could be taken topside and flown.

He examined underneath the aircraft.

The bottom of the ship was smooth. It either didn't have landing gear, or if it had, the equipment was currently retracted, leaving a perfectly smooth undercarriage. He circled around in the massive diving suit, positioning himself directly above the spacecraft.

There was a barely perceptible outline of a small door.

Sam stared at the faint lines at the back of the spacecraft. He was certain he was looking at an exit hatch or possibly the only hatch. Either way, his eyes were nowhere near powerful enough to make sense of what he was seeing.

His gaze narrowed, focusing in on a digital image of what he considered could be the hatch. He stared at the computer monitor that showed the visual images taken from the visor mounted camera. He digitally zoomed.

His heart raced.

There, right there, was something he had seen a hundred times before.

It was an exit door… to what appeared to be a modern commercial airline… and on the back of which, something that sent chills down his spine…

An image he recognized at a glance…

And why shouldn't he?

Those series of stars and stripes represented something everyone born in the USA knew –

It was the flag of the United States of America.

Sam swallowed hard.

What the hell is an American experimental spacecraft doing buried beneath 15 million years of ice?

Sam depressed the mic. "Anastasia… you're not going to believe this…"

There was no response.

Only static.

He tried again. "Anastasia?"

Still nothing.

Something. Or someone. Was blocking their radio comms.

Sam attached the harness to a small eyelet at the top of the craft. He had seen similar hooks on a number of modern space-vehicles such as the one used by Virgin Galactic owned by Richard Branson, or Dream Chaser, owned by the Sierra Nevada Corporation. Both were towed up to 20,000 feet before launching.

He was ready to head toward the surface, with the cable trailing, but he didn't move.

Behind him, something glowed bright yellow.

Sam turned around.

The beam of light was blinding.

"What the hell is that?"

A machine moved quickly, and menacingly toward him. Its quad-propulsions systems were whirring powerfully.

Sam's heart began to unpleasantly hammer in his chest.

He was no longer alone.

Chapter Fifty-Five

Submachine guns crackled in the distance.

Genevieve listened to the echo of 9mm Parabellums being imbedded into the snow-covered mound above the former Vostok Research Station. If she had to guess, the shots sounded similar to the rat-a-tat-tat of the French MAT-49 submachine guns used earlier.

But that didn't make much sense.

Strike that.

It didn't make *any* sense.

The French attack force knew there was only one entrance to the former Vostok Research building. It was heavily protected and easily defended. So why bother with an assault on it all? Were they just testing to see what their defenses were like? Or was it something worse?

Genevieve brought up the schematics of the retired Soviet era base. She scanned through the iPad, searching for information from the original specs. Something that might reveal a second tunnel or something that the invading force might know about and be trying to back track and access.

Were they aware of a second way into the base?

The shooting kept going in various intermittent bursts of gunfire. There was no way that novices, let alone military professionals, would think that such random shots would serve any purpose at all. No, the gunfire seemed like an attempt to distract them…

But the question remained…

From what?

Elise had her laptop open at one of the old workstations, and had hacked into Vostok's original communications tower, which was still fully functional, and connected to satellite feeds. Her fingers, working as hard and fast as the submachine guns outside, were tapping away at her keyboard in a dramatic staccato as she connected to the US owned satellites above. She was still trying to find the destination of the disappearing French hovercraft.

"Any luck?" Genevieve asked.

"Nothing."

"Got any guesses?"

"Yeah. Our targets have gone to ground."

"In another ice cave?"

"No. I think they have a base somewhere nearby."

"A base?" Genevieve asked. "Why?"

"I don't know. If I had to guess, I'd say it's the same reason we've got a spy in Vostok. Someone talked, and now everyone knows there's a 15-million-year-old spacecraft resting at the bottom of a subglacial lake."

"And everybody wants it," Genevieve said, finishing her words.

"Exactly."

Genevieve looked at Hu and Elise. "Make sure no one gets in here."

Elise asked, "Where are you going?"

"I want to find Sam and Tom. Give them the heads up that there's a few things we don't understand. For a start, the French know something that we sure as hell don't."

"All right. Good luck, I'll keep looking for them, and I'll let you know if I come up with any answers."

"Thanks."

Genevieve headed down the corridor leading to the sleeping quarters. She circled around the small research base. It was always underground – although never quite this far underground. She couldn't imagine how difficult it must have been when the original scientists lived there.

She looped around twice.

Came back.

And said, "We have a big problem."

Hu and Elise turned to greet her. Together they replied, "What?"

Genevieve swallowed. "Sam, Tom, and Anastasia are all missing…"

"Missing?" Elise folded her laptop down and stood up. "Where?"

Genevieve shook her head. "Beats me. I've just checked the entire compound and couldn't find them. It's like they've vanished."

Chapter Fifty-Six

Sam studied the mechanical beast approaching.

It was fifteen feet tall and equipped with quad-propulsion thrusters. Instead of one person being at the controls, there were two sets of eyes staring at him behind the massive, partially domed viewport. Two sets of arms and legs, and two minds to work the intricate controls of a submersible robot, designed to work in one of the harshest environments on earth.

The machine looked like an oversized arachnid, with eight, articulated limbs. Each one equipped with what appeared to be titanium pincers, capable of cutting through metal. It was moving toward him in a horizontal position rather than how a traditional bipedal atmospheric dive suit moves. Its four propellers were whirring.

Then, simultaneously, all eight limbs began to open, spreading out, with an eerie and spine-chilling whine of sixteen hydraulic pumps being activated. This gave it the distinctive appearance of a giant, mechanical spider.

Sam guessed the strange machine had been purpose-built to retrieve the spacecraft, which meant that whoever was behind the controls had some other means of reaching the subglacial lake. He thought of the French base that Elise had warned him about, most likely hiding somewhere beneath the surface of the Polar Plateau. They had probably spent the last year tunneling through, hoping to steal the spacecraft right out from under the Russian's nose.

He thought of all of this in a fraction of a second.

None of it mattered.

Right now, he needed to get out of town.

The giant mechanical spider was every bit as terrifying as anything one's imagination might conjure up. Plus, there was no doubt in his mind that its pilots' intentions were anything but friendly. His only option was to escape before they could reach him.

There was no way he could beat them in a mechanical battle. And equally as little chance he could outrun them. Not horizontally, but there might still be a chance to outpace them vertically.

Sam yanked the joystick backward.

He dropped his emergency ballast weights. His buoyancy changed in an instant.

The Russian atmospheric dive suit shot upward.

The hovering spider increased its speed, racing toward him. It zoned in, making a beeline for him.

Sam made the mental calculations.

The spider submersible was quick, but it was just a few seconds behind. With the ballast dropped, it would never make the vertical ascent fast enough to keep pace with him, much less catch him. This was because there was no way they would want to drop their own ballast, and surface inside the original Vostok diving chamber where he had dived from.

He met his enemies' eyes as he floated past.

Sam grinned and gave them a mischievous wave. "Goodbye!"

Their eyes flashed anger.

And a split second later, Sam's heady elation turned to terror as he stopped ascending with a sudden jerk.

His submersible was still tethered to the spacecraft. He'd forgotten to cut the nylon cable. Now he was trapped. The few precious seconds it would take to sever the cable was all his attackers needed.

He tried to squirm out of the way.

The submersible's eight arms spread out, surrounding and entrapping his atmospheric dive suit. He tried to shift the joystick. The twin propulsion units whirred, but the enemy submersible was nearly twice his vehicle's size.

The mechanical arachnid had him trapped.

No matter what he did, he couldn't coax his submersible to pull away.

One of his adversaries met him in the eye. He made a condescending wave. Sam swallowed, licked his lips, and ran out of ideas. Now what?

Then he heard the high-pitched whine.

A single, articulated drill started to spin.

It was slowly moving right for his half-domed viewport. The diamond tipped drill head lined up to his face. Sam inadvertently pulled back. It was ridiculous. The second that drill pierced the 7.8-inch-thick acrylic viewport, his atmospheric dive suit would implode.

Sam struggled to move his head backward.

At first, it worked. But then the pilot controlling the drill, simply extended it farther.

With some sort of morbid curiosity, Sam watched the head of the drill slowly begin to turn. It scraped his acrylic half-dome.

Not the way he was expecting to go.

But hey, he'd had a good run.

The drill took a little while to bite. Mostly it kept slipping off the smooth viewport. On the third attempt, it caught hold. Then it began its drilling process in earnest.

Sam drew a deep breath.

And thanked his lucky stars for the life that he'd been fortunate to have.

A moment later, there was an earth-shattering bang.

The explosion ripped through the seabed of the subglacial lake, echoing in Sam's ears.

Chapter Fifty-Seven

I'm still alive!

For a split second, Sam couldn't understand how he was still conscious. If the atmospheric dive suit had been pierced, he would have imploded. In fact, he should be dead. His life would have ended in the tiniest fraction of seconds.

Not a bad way to go really.

One second, you're there. The next you're not.

A second blast wave struck him. The spacecraft, the mechanical spider, and his own atmospheric dive suit began to roll, and twist in the turbid water, spiraling out of all control. He was still tethered to the spacecraft, but the attacking submersible wasn't. The two submersibles lost sight of each other.

That's when he pictured it.

The scientists from all over the world had gotten it wrong.

Lake Vostok wasn't entirely closed off.

There was an underground river that once flowed beneath the lake. The US spacecraft, most likely performing experimental tests over Antarctica, away from prying eyes, must have somehow become submerged below the ice. There it floated down river and became trapped inside Lake Vostok. Sam's attackers had probably entered through the same river.

So then where did the explosion come from?

Sam mentally tried to picture it.

Someone had attempted to drill into the lake from the opposite end. While the robotic spider came from upriver, someone else was trying to come from downriver. They might have been tunneling for more than a year. And now that time was a significant factor in their mission, they had used explosives to destroy whatever section had long ago frozen solid!

He spun for nearly a minute, before everything seemed to stop.

The water became deathly still, like a slack-tide.

It lasted just a few seconds.

Like pulling the plug of a giant bathtub, Lake Vostok began to drain for the first time in years.

Sam, awkwardly riding on the back of the spacecraft, began to circle the whirlpool, in ever extending circles. The lake dropped its level quickly. He swiftly scanned the chamber for the spider-like submersible, but it was nowhere to be seen.

Perhaps it had been dragged under earlier?

He imagined it taking hours, if not days to drain the lake, with him in it. But just as he thought that a vortex opened up into a deep spiral.

Sam and the spacecraft dropped off the edge of it, where they were both perched, free-falling all the way to the bottom.

In one hell of a turbid rollercoaster ride, he was sucked through the artificial tunnel, and flung through the secret mineshaft.

The ride seemed interminable.

But then it was over.

Sam broke free from the thin nylon that tethered him to the spacecraft, and the two machines finally separated.

The mined tunnel widened to a natural ice chamber, and a gravelly beach.

The turbid water washed him high up the beach, before receding, leaving his atmospheric dive suit on dry land, laying supine.

Sam had a good view of the entire chamber.

He saw the spacecraft, but to his surprise, he also saw two people clambering out of their own atmospheric dive suit at the far end of the beach. They walked past him, undeterred. There was nothing they could do to hurt him now. Not once they were outside their own machine which appeared to be damaged by the explosion. They mostly ignored him.

A massive Tucker Sno-Cat 743 with four caterpillar tracked wheels motored down into the ice chamber. It turned around and several people, all speaking in French, worked a series of nylon harnesses and chains to hook up with the spacecraft.

One of the French mercenaries approached Sam with his pistol. He aimed the weapon at Sam's acrylic half-dome viewport.

Shaking his head in disgust, the man put the handgun away.

Sam was impervious to such weapons while he was inside the massive atmospheric dive suit. Afterward, the French team clambered back into the Sno-Cat 743 and drove away, disappearing up through a wide opening in the distance, along with the spacecraft.

Sam watched them leave.

When he was confident he was finally alone, he repositioned himself so that he could release the hatch at the back of the atmospheric dive suit. He turned the locking mechanism, releasing the air-tight seal, but there wasn't the traditional tell-tail *whisp* of air coming and going. He fiddled with the latch, but the door wouldn't budge.

How could it? There was nearly 900 pounds of titanium alloy pressing down on it.

Sam tried to get the machine to move, but whatever electric motor worked the hydraulic actuators that controlled its arms and legs, was now fried.

He was trapped.

Sam studied the gauge of the life-support system.

It registered 18 hours.

Less than a day to live.

Sam shook his head at the irony.

Trapped and sealed in an impervious suit, designed to keep him alive at unimaginable depths. The machine that had kept him safe, was now going to be the death of him. It was his permanent tomb because of a coin-flip. Fate had him wash onto the shore and land on his back instead of his front.

He wanted to scream for help.

But who would hear him?

Nobody, because no matter how much he screamed, no sound would be free to escape the near impenetrable armored suit.

Chapter Fifty-Eight

Natalya stared at the surprise secret passage.

Unlike the oubliette, which was surprisingly well-lit with LED downlights, this new tunnel was completely dark. The sort of thing cavers referred to as absolute darkness. What she wouldn't give for a simple flashlight. Even the phone she left behind, with its narrow, dim flashlight, would have provided enough by which to see. She could hear the sound of feet scurrying along the passageway and imagined dozens, if not more, rats making their way somewhere.

The question was, where were they going?

And could she come too?

Natalya looked both directions along the tunnel. The dim light from the oubliette only permeated fifty or so feet in either direction, before being enveloped by the narrow tunnel. She thought about leaving the passageway open, but then she worried that her captor would come back – and seeing the open door, immediately come after her.

No. She felt for the same metal latch that had opened the door. To prevent herself getting lost, she would keep her right hand on the wall. Then, when she turned around, she would keep her left hand on the wall, so that she would inevitably find the same spot again. Then, she could always open the hidden door to the oubliette.

She closed her eyes and imagined the absolute darkness that would soon follow. Her heart picked up its pace, several notches. Her hands became shaky and sweaty.

Natalya found the metal lever and pulled it upward.

The series of machinery began its movements in the background, finally culminating in the secret door closing. Natalya watched as all signs of light disappeared with it, leaving just the faintest glow where she had removed the single brick twenty minutes earlier.

Natalya drew a breath and began crawling through the subterranean passage. She had no means of discerning which direction she was traveling. No compass, no moonlight or sunlight to guide herself. Nothing but a narrow crawl space, a small creek, and a lot of time.

Which was good, because it would take plenty of time to get anywhere.

It was a slow process crawling on all fours. Trying to keep her right hand on the wall proved much harder than she first imagined. Several times she tried to find it again, only to worry that she had somehow turned all the way around and could no longer be sure that she was facing the right direction.

Natalya continued for what felt like hours.

The passageway seemed to continuously split into two distinct passageways, which then led to another split passageway. Sometimes she reached a sort of T-intersection, sometimes they simply formed a sort of dogleg, other times they looped in on themselves, like one of those spiral mazes, that eventually reached another dead end.

It seemed to open out to an outside well.

Natalya looked up.

It was a long way and the sky above seemed dark, with just dappled moonlight. It wasn't much, but she felt pitifully grateful for the simple knowledge that it was nighttime.

She stared at it for a while, trying to work out if there was a way to climb out, but it seemed impossible. The diameter of the well was too wide for her to push off in the climbing process of stemming the walls. She searched for a sort of hidden ladder somewhere but couldn't find anything.

Natalya gave herself a good hour, simply to enjoy it.

Then, she tried to reverse her trip, heading back to the original oubliette. Twice she checked the mental map she built in her mind, trying to imagine where she was, or how to get back to the start again. At times, she thought she knew exactly where she was, and how close she was to reaching the original chamber, only to find herself in a dead end.

This went on for what must have been hours.

Possibly even longer.

Eventually, purely by chance, rather than any skill, she reached a metal lever.

Natalya drew a breath.

Home sweet home.

The same series of mechanical systems played out in the background, before the hidden door finally swung open.

She blinked as her eyes, used to the absolute darkness, adjusted to the bright LED downlights.

A woman stared back at her.

She was a twenty-something year old brunette.

Natalya said, "I'm sorry. I didn't mean to. I just found this opening and thought I'd try to escape. I'll stay here now. Please forgive me."

The woman said, "Have you been kidnapped too?"

It was the first time Natalya noticed that the woman's hair was tussled, she wore jeans and a comfortable blue blouse. But she looked disheveled. There was a pile of water bottle, protein bars, and cans of food at the center. The pile looked a little smaller than her own one.

Had she returned to the wrong cell?

"Yes. I was abducted yesterday, by a man with hazel eyes with golden flakes."

The woman said, "I've met the creep."

Natalya ran her fingers across her forehead and through her hair. "I actually thought he was quite handsome, pleasant to chat to, until he tasered me and dropped me in the oubliette."

"Oubliette. Nice word. Sounds much more pleasant than dungeon. The French have a way of making everything sound better." The woman gave that some thought, and then asked, "Are we in France?"

"I don't know, to be honest. I was on my way to Switzerland when I was abducted. What about you, where were you taken from?"

"Germany."

"Germany and France." Natalya frowned. "Who is this guy and what does he want with us?"

The woman shook her head. "I don't know, but I intend to make him pay one day."

Natalya gave her a 'I wish you luck with that endeavor, but you might be setting your goals a little high given where you are' kind of look. "Good luck with that."

The woman looked at the open, hidden door. "Where does that lead?"

"A labyrinth. I might be wrong. I'll keep trying, but as far as I could tell, this place just keeps on circling back in on itself. There's my little chamber, and yours, but I haven't found any others."

"Right, then we'd better get started."

Natalya grinned. Happy to have company. "Started with what?"

She grinned. "Planning our escape." Then her tone turned deadly serious. "And our revenge."

"All right. Count me in." Natalya shook her head, surprised to find that she was actually smiling. "I'm sorry, I don't even know your name."

The woman held out a hand. "Andrea Jordan."

Chapter Fifty-Nine

The little red de Havilland Twin Otter flew along the side of the Transantarctic Mountains. When it reached the US base, Amundsen–Scott South Pole Station, its pilot banked left, taking it onto a straight line toward Vostok.

Axel Hoffman looked out the port window.

Far below them, a massive Tucker Sno-Cat 743, with four caterpillar tracked wheels towed a black spacecraft. It was heading north, along a narrow ice escarpment, as it negotiated its way around a thirty-mile crevasse.

At Vostok, the de Havilland Twin Otter circled the area, flying over the top of the former Vostok Research Station. Then it landed on the blue-ice runway, coming to a complete stop ten miles ahead of the French team.

Axel Hoffman opened the tailgate of the heavily modified aircraft.

Inside, were five Yamaha snowmobiles. Each one was quickly offloaded by a nine-man team who wore tactical gear and were armed to the teeth. All were recruited from the Kommando Spezialkräfte – German's Special Forces – and sent there for this very specific mission.

They loaded up onto the snowmobiles quickly. Four riding tandem with Axel on his own in the lead. They headed along the deep crevasse, until they reached a section of ice that stood above the rest of the landscape. It formed an excellent vantage point.

From there, they could look down upon a narrow section of the crevasse. One way. Very tight. A slow, five-point turn would be needed to change direction. And anyone transporting the spacecraft overland would have to go through this bottleneck.

It was the perfect place to set a trap.

Axel stopped his snowmobile.

The team set up.

They weren't taking any chances.

Two men were armed with German M3 Heavy Machine Guns. Their tripods were extended, and the big guns mounted. Another two carried

RPG7 rocket launchers. The rest of them carried Beretta PMX submachine guns.

Axel smiled.

It felt good. After months of waiting and boredom, he and his men were finally going to see some action.

What's more, his enemies were driving into a deadly trap.

It was going to be a bloodbath.

Chapter Sixty

Genevieve listened.

The gunfire had finally gone silent.

Outside, there was a new sound. This one was more like the constant whoop, whoop of an aircraft propeller. She took a pair of binoculars, and carefully edged out through the ice tunnel, until she could get eyes on the craft.

It was a red and white de Havilland Twin Otter.

The aircraft was banking hard, and setting his plane up to land on the blue ice fields to the north of them. Who was aboard the Otter was anyone's guess. But at least their French assailants seemed to have moved on.

She ducked back into Vostok.

Hu, still guarding the entrance, said, "Are they leaving?"

"Looks like it."

"Does that mean they got the spacecraft?"

Genevieve shrugged. "Probably."

Hu asked. "But how?"

She recalled the explosion they had all felt earlier. "They must have blown up part of the tunnel they'd been mining to reach Lake Vostok."

Hu said, "If that's the case, that aircraft overhead must be for their exfiltration!"

"You're right." Genevieve said, "Come, let's go."

"Where?"

"We need to find Sam and Tom. Anastasia too."

Hu stood up, no longer worried about guarding the entrance. The French were in the process of exfiltrating. They were no longer a threat. "When we find them... what are we going to do?"

Genevieve grinned. "Isn't it obvious?"

Hu shook his head. "Not really."

Genevieve set her jaw firm, an impish glint to her eye. "We're going to have to steal that spacecraft right back."

Chapter Sixty-One

Rhys Jones slowed the Polar PistenBully's 600hp engine.

The massive British Research Station, Halley VI being towed behind, reduced speed, then stopped. Each section began gently easing together like the carriages on a long railway train.

From behind him, Rod Jenkins climbed forward into the main driving cabin. His eyes were wide, and there was a curious expression on his lips, as he swept the empty landscape. There was nothing for mile upon miles.

Jenkins exchanged a glance with him. "Why have we stopped?"

Rhys gave a noncommittal shrug. "This is it. We're here."

"Here... where?" Jenkins frowned. "I don't see anything for miles. I thought we were supposed to be helping with an unfolding emergency at Vostok?"

"I don't know what to tell you. These are the GPS coordinates the British Ministry of Defense sent us."

"Right." Jenkins reached for the satellite phone. "I'm going to make a call and find out what's going on."

Rhys said, "I don't think that will be necessary."

"Of course, it's necessary. There's got to be some sort of mix up. If Vostok needs help, we should be heading in that direction, not over here to the north of it."

Rhys shrugged. "Suit yourself."

Jenkins began scrolling through the satellite phone's contact list, searching for the MoD.

Rhys reached into his concealed holster and withdrew a Browning L9A1 Hi-Power. The single-action, semi-automatic was chambered with .40 Smith & Wesson.

At the sight of the gun, Jenkins cocked his head to the side. His face wore a mixed expression of confusion, curiosity, and finally realization, and abject fear.

He opened his mouth to speak.

But Rhys squeezed the trigger.

Two bullets.

Both head shots.

Rhys then pulled his thick, exposure suit over his body, opened the door, and stepped outside. He walked around to each of the other polar vehicles used in the tow. One by one, he executed every one of them. It was time consuming work, but it needed to be done.

When he was finished, he climbed the series of steps and knocked on the door of the first pod of the Halley VI. The Research Station was meant to be empty for the cross-continental transfer, but a team of twelve men were inside. They were all ex-military. British Special Air Service or Special Boat Service predominantly. They quickly severed the large cables connecting the polar tow vehicles to the research station.

Rhys said, "Look alive gentlemen. We're about to become the proud new owners of one of the most advanced spacecrafts ever made."

Chapter Sixty-Two

The Tucker Sno-Cat 743 crawled along alien landscape, pulling the spacecraft they had recently retrieved from Lake Vostok 2.2 miles below. The Cat's four massive caterpillar tracks were crunching ice as it progressed. The awesomely powerful machine looked unstoppable.

From his high vantage point, Axel Hoffman grinned.

He could stop it.

He lifted a hand, a signal urging his men to wait for it. Not a shot would be fired until his mark.

Filled with Frenchmen who were celebrating their latest triumph, the Sno-Cat edged forward… right into the line of the crosshairs of his RPG-7. He aimed for the weakest spot of the machine, between the wheels and caterpillar tracks.

Axel squeezed the trigger.

Flame expelled from the aft of the high explosive anti-tank – HEAT – round fired.

The rocket landed in the soft spot right between the front right wheel and metal caterpillar tracks. The explosion, big enough to take out an armored tank, disintegrated the wheels and split the track.

The driver, realizing he was under attack, tried to turn the massive vehicle.

The tracked wheels kept spinning, further stripping the caterpillar tracks from their rails. Next to Axel, the second HEAT round was fired. This one landed right beneath the Sno-Cat's driver cabin. The explosive blast erupted.

Axel had another round loaded.

He aimed and fired the third RPG strike.

It hit the same wheel, only this time, it was enough to knock the entire machine over. The other three tracks kept spinning. In its death throes, the monster arctic vehicle looked like an upturned insect.

As if exiting an ant's nest, armed elite soldiers began spilling out of the lethally damaged machine. That's when the two M3 Heavy Machine Guns opened fire.

As expected, it was a bloodbath.

All in total, the entire fight was finished within 90 seconds from the detonation of the first RPG.

Using hands and feet for balance, Axel scrambled down the hill. He had dropped the RPG and now carried a single Berretta M9 semiautomatic. He made his way down to the spacecraft. Sporadic shooting took place, as his men walked around the battlefield, intermittently putting additional rounds into each victim's head.

Nothing quite like being killed by a ghost.

Axel climbed onto the purpose-built sled that cradled the spacecraft.

He pulled himself up and into the ship. His eyes narrowed as he depressed the safety-release for the hatch. It had a pull-out lever – which looked similar to a commercial aircraft's throttle – extending from the dark, stealth skin of the craft.

Axel pushed the lever all the way forward.

The air-tight seal for the spacecraft, opened with a whisp of dank air.

One of his men said, "I thought Zimmerman wants the spacecraft destroyed?"

"He does," Axel acknowledged. "And we'll set up some C4 and destroy it from the inside shortly. Just give me a minute. There's something I have to do."

"Roger that. We'll finish securing the scene."

Axel pointed the Berretta inside.

The dead, frozen body of the experimental pilot was still in the pilot's chair.

Axel took a seat in the spacecraft's second chair. It was surprisingly roomy for a two passenger, ultra-small spacecraft, and theoretically the fastest aircraft on earth. His eyes swept the confines of the entire cockpit. There were two seats, an array of digital controls, and a pair of spacesuits hanging from the back of the cockpit. The machine was automated, and capable of flight without anyone on board. Yet like all living creatures, humans needed complex life-support systems in place for suborbital flights.

He turned to look at the dead pilot.

There were two bullet holes to the back of his head.

Now that was unexpected.

The man had been executed.

Someone must have wanted to stop the sale of the experimental, stealth spacecraft to Germany. There was no way to really know who, but at least that answered the decade old question of why the aircraft crashed.

For a moment, Axel toyed with ignoring Zimmerman's orders, and keeping the potentially still functioning spacecraft. But then he recalled the man's cold voice when he said he wanted The Ghost's own men to do what none of them had been able to do, and that was to kill him.

No, you don't screw with a man whose daughter's been hurt or get in his way of gaining revenge.

Axel switched on the main power switch.

More than a hundred small lights lit up the spacecraft's advanced control system. It didn't surprise him that after more than a decade, the machine started, its batteries fully charged. After all, that was one of the greatest benefits of running a ship on nuclear power.

The spacecraft was an illegal experiment. Originally it was an American project with DARPA. The Defense Advanced Research Project Agency determined that the project went against fundamental international agreements for the use of nuclear power in aircrafts. The data was then unlawfully sold to The Ghost, who set up a research facility in Antarctica to complete the project.

As far as Axel knew, this was the holy grail of aerospace.

A nuclear-powered aircraft.

Its twin jet engines were driven by compressed air with heat from fission, instead of heat from burning fuel. During the Cold War, the United States and Soviet Union researched nuclear-powered bomber aircraft, the greater endurance of which could enhance nuclear deterrence. Yet neither country created any such operational aircraft. Americans scrapped the project entirely with the advent of nuclear submarines. From what he'd read about the project, this was some miracle spacecraft, capable of leaving the confines of the earthly orbit for short bursts and allowing it to travel at speeds impossible to achieve while still in the atmosphere. The result was a spacecraft capable of traveling point to point, anywhere on earth in under two hours.

Axel shrugged. What did he care about stealth aeronautics? He was about to become the richest man on earth. The first trillionaire.

He ran his eyes across the computer module, finding the USB access port.

Very circa 2010.

He plugged his external hard drive into the computer.

It contained the Private Key to the final payment for the spacecraft. Half a billion dollars in Bitcoin. Hard, untraceable, cash. A bargain for such an aircraft. The Ghost could have made ten times that amount if he'd been able to legally sell the hardware.

Axel extracted the Private Key to half a billion dollars of Bitcoin, shifting it from the spacecraft's onboard computer – where it had been hidden all those years ago – through to his own external hard drive.

He shook his head staring at the hard drive.

Half a billion dollars.

It was a lot of money on its own.

But that was based on Bitcoin value circa 2010, when Bitcoin was still a social experiment on cryptocurrencies, used by computer hobbyists. In a time when the value of a single Bitcoin was less than a US dollar.

At today's prices, even at the most conservative sale's price, Axel's newfound hoard of early Bitcoin was worth somewhere in the vicinity of 1 trillion US dollars.

Money, he thought...*That's what it all comes down to.*

He heard something move from behind one of the hanging spacesuits.

Axel turned around and was greeted by a man with a Glock pointed straight at his chest. The stranger looked disheveled, with a large cut to his left forearm, and a limp.

The man lifted the Glock to aim at his head. "Bonjour. I'll have the Bitcoin, thank you."

Axel realized the leader of the French team was traveling inside the spacecraft.

"Clever," Axel said, with a certain level of admiration and professional respect.

The French commander squeezed off two shots.

Chapter Sixty-Three

Rhys Jones stared through the crosshairs of his high-powered rifle scope.

The German forces had just annihilated the unsuspecting French forces. He grinned. They had just done half his work for him. He laughed. Now, if only they would only feel guilty about their line of work and commit suicide, he would have achieved his mission.

The Germans had done well.

Not the way he would have done it anyway. Far too much big bangs for show. No, his British team would do things in a more respectable, classic British way. His men were lined up across the natural undulations of the snow. They were armed with L115A3 Long Range Sniper Rifles.

He'd handpicked his team for their backgrounds as sharp shooters. Their bolt-action weapons, chambered in 338 Lapua Magnum, had an effective range of close to a mile. Put in the hands of expert marksmen, who employed a Schmidt & Bender 5-25x56 PM II 25x magnification day scope, with its big magnification and comprehensive total adjustment range, it was deadly from a distance. Each of the men wore VOX – voice activated radios – so that the entire team worked in perfect synchronicity.

There were six German targets alive.

Zero French.

The Germans were working their way through the wreckage of the Tucker Sno-Cat 743, executing any of the French special forces potentially still alive. None of them were expecting enemy combatants further afield.

Rhys assigned dedicated targets for each of his men.

When they came together on the VOX, he said, "Are your target's locked?"

"Confirm," came back the unanimous response.

He gave the order. "Fire."

The battle was over in less than fifteen seconds.

Not that Rhys counted it as a battle. It was more like long range target practice, with very life-like dummies. He ran his rifle across the battlefield, searching for any survivors. One person, shot through the chest, tried to make a move for his submachine gun. Rhys fired another round through the mercenary's head.

It turned the snow red with a fine mist.

"All right," Rhys said, standing up and dismantling his sniper rifle's tripod. "Let's go secure the spacecraft..."

They disconnected the ski-trailer that cradled the space craft from the damaged Tucker Sno-Cat, and re-connected it to the PistenBully 600, via the world's largest towbar. Once he'd confirmed everything was secure, his men climbed on board their small convoy of arctic vehicles.

Rhys patted the side of the PistenBully 600 as he climbed aboard. He looked at the second driver. "Next stop, Davis Station, where a cargo ship is waiting for us."

Chapter Sixty-Four

Tom felt a jolt.

The elevator began moving again.

It took a full minute to reach the top, before the doors opened as naturally as any other elevator in a posh hotel in New York. He stepped out, only too eager to escape.

Genevieve threw her arms around him.

He hugged her back.

Tom said, "What happened?"

"I don't know. There was an explosion. The French mercenaries who were attacking us look like they've been attacked by some other military group. We think someone detonated an explosion down below."

"Okay. So, let me get this straight. We're not being attacked by anyone just this instant, but there's a second group of mercenaries fighting over the spacecraft. And so, even if no one's shooting at us right now, our overall enemy number has increased."

"That's about the gist of it."

"So everything's pretty much status quo in our universe."

Genevieve nodded. "How's Sam and Anastasia?"

"Oh shit, Sam. I don't know. I've been trapped in this elevator for hours after the power went out." Tom frowned. "How did the power come back on?"

"After we found the hidden entrance to this tunnel – nice trick with the 44-gallon drum and sliding hinge by the way – we came down and found the main power switch to the elevator and turned it on."

Tom said, "The main power switch was off?"

"Yeah. Why?"

"I don't know. It doesn't make sense. The power was on when we took the elevator to the bottom. And I'm the first person to come up."

"So what does that mean?" Genevieve asked.

"I don't know. I hate to think we have an enemy inside Vostok?"

Genevieve shook her head. "Doubtful. We've searched every inch of this base trying to find you and Sam. If there was a mole, we would have found them."

"So then what caused the power outage?"

"I haven't a clue. Let's go find Sam and Anastasia and find out."

They left Elise and Hu to guard the top of the elevator, while Tom and Genevieve descended once more all the way to the lake 2.2 miles below.

Anastasia was waiting for them at the bottom of the lift.

She had tears in her eyes and threw her arms around Tom with as much, if not more, enthusiasm than Genevieve had. "You came back!"

Genevieve gave her a direct look and said in a low voice, "Yes, we came back."

Anastasia got the hint. She had to as it was about as subtle as a poke in the eye. Yet whatever she'd been through was far more frightening to her than inadvertently stepping on Genevieve's toes – although Tom thought, she might have felt differently if she realized Genevieve was once an enforcer for the Russian mafia.

Anastasia said, "I thought you weren't coming back, and I'd be trapped down here alone forever."

"Trapped alone? Where's Sam?"

She tilted her head, her expression furtive. "Sam… didn't you hear the explosion?"

Tom said, "Where's Sam?"

"He was diving in the lake."

"What happened to Sam!" Tom asked, his tone intense, his voice louder than he'd meant.

"The explosion must have knocked out the tunnel that drilled into the ancient lake!"

Tom shook his head. "What happened?"

"I'll show you…"

Tom and Genevieve followed Anastasia to the dive pontoon.

Where it had been previously built right on the water, it now hung by its ropes over a deep precipice. The lake was still visible far below. A large whirlpool still sucked away at the water.

Anastasia looked up, meeting Tom's gaze. Upon seeing Tom's abject terror, she said, "Like I was trying to tell you, Sam's lost."

Tom's voice took on a new hardness. "Then we'll just have to go find him."

Chapter Sixty-Five

Sam whistled a somber tune to himself.

It was *Clair de Lune*...

Which meant *Moonlight* in French. It was the third segment in Suite bergamasque, a four-movement composition for piano by French composer Claude Debussy.

He didn't know why he thought of the song on his death bed.

If anything, the whistling only hastened his demise, given the increase to his respiratory need. But what did it matter? A few minutes here or there, didn't count.

The tune seemed doleful and poignant.

He'd learned to play it on the piano as a child.

Trapped and sealed in an impervious suit, designed to keep him alive at unimaginable depths. The machine that had kept him safe, was now going to be his eternal tomb, all because of a coin-flip, that had him land on his back instead of his front.

He stretched out and looked at his surroundings.

The chamber with its dark, volcanic gravel beach, and infinitely rich blue ice was really quite spectacular. There wasn't much light. Just the dappled glow of moonlight. Like the song, it provided just enough light to see his surroundings.

It was beautiful.

A smile spread across his lips.

Always been the luckiest bastard I knew. Lucky in life... lucky in death.

He glanced at his life-support system that ran a digital countdown.

Zero.

There was a flashing red light next to the number.

Sam drew in a breath.

It didn't feel any different. If he had to guess, it probably contained more carbon dioxide than was recommended, and almost certainly contained less oxygen than needed to keep him alive. At least it didn't hurt. He could think of far more painful ways to go.

He'd had a really good life.

No regrets.

He thought of his family.

His brother who he'd lost years ago, and who had set him on the direction of his life. Then, he thought of his colleagues. The quirky, ramshackle team on board the *Tahila* who had become every bit like a family to him.

Then he thought about Tom.

Poor Tom...

He would take it the hardest.

Tom would blame himself for not being there to save him. He would think, if only he'd somehow squished himself to squeeze into the Russian atmospheric dive suit, maybe he would have saved Sam's life.

Sam shrugged.

Took another deep breath.

Lightheaded, his heart was speeding. He was short of breath and the headache he could feel coming on had forcefully made its presence known. Now his vision was starting to go.

This was it...

"It's okay, Tom..." he said, staring vacantly out into the chamber. "You saved my life more than anyone could have ever expected."

Sam blinked back the tears that formed. He smiled. "More than that, Tom. You helped me truly live..."

Through the haze of his vision...Sam imagined Tom outside, looking in on him. His face, full of worry. He said, "Don't worry, Tom."

It's true... Sam thought with genuine interest. *You see those who meant the most to you in your final seconds on earth.*

Then he could see Elise, Genevieve, even Hu, and Tom...

They were working frantically to release him. It was confusing.

Sam said, "It's okay..."

A moment later he felt like his world was spinning. He turned over, and over. Then the ghost of Tom was yelling at him. "You have to open the hatch! We can't do it from out here."

Sam nodded. "Look... Tom... don't you think I would have opened it, if I could?"

Tom shouted, "Just try!"

Sam, not wanting to upset even the ghost of Tom, tried turning the water-tight latch. This time it kept turning. After a few seconds, he was rewarded with the hiss of fresh air.

Then the hatch was open, and Tom was dragging him outside.

Sam looked him in the eye. "Oh Tom… I could have used you hours ago. Of all the adventures we've had together, what a stupid way for me to get myself killed."

"Hypoxemia," Hu said with a knowing nod of his head.

Tom looked at him, gave him a big hug, and said, "Sam… you're delirious, and you're rambling… but it's okay, because you're alive."

Chapter Sixty-Six

Sam listened as Tom brought him up to speed.

His headache finally dissipated.

"Okay, so let me see if I've got this right. The French blew up a tunnel and stole the spacecraft from me. Then the Germans blew up the French and stole the spacecraft. Then the British killed the Germans and stole the spacecraft..." Sam paused, cocked his head and asked, "By the way, how do we know they're British?"

"We don't," Tom admitted. "But they were towing Hayley VI, the British research station to Davis Base."

"Right." Sam grinned. "Then there's really only one option left for us."

"What's that?" Tom asked.

Sam grinned. "We're just going to have to steal it back again."

Tom said, "They have a twelve-hour head start."

Sam chuckled. "They're towing a spacecraft with a Polar vehicle on tracked wheels. How fast can they go?"

"They're a long distance ahead of us. We'll need to find some way to catch up."

Genevieve stepped in and said, "I might have a suggestion."

Sam asked, "What have you got?"

Genevieve said, "The Germans left a de Haviland Twin Otter behind."

"Oh, yeah?" Sam stood up. "All right. Let's take that and go get our spacecraft."

Chapter Sixty-Seven

Sam flew the de Haviland Twin Otter.

Over the years, he'd racked up more than a thousand hours in command of that type of aircraft. Tom flew in the copilot seat, and kept a constant eye on him, half expecting him to pass out at any moment.

Snow pummeled the windshield.

Darkness reigned supreme in the wintry landscape.

It would be impossible to follow the British assailants, but five large arctic bulldozers, fortunately, left one hell of a trail to follow. Elise was able to easily pinpoint them from satellites overhead, and then follow the path they made, until she reached the location of the convoy towing the spacecraft.

Tom asked, "So, how do you want to play this?"

"Genevieve told me how the British used sniper rifles to take out the Germans," Sam said, his voice almost wistful, as though he were imagining the sequence in his mind. "Maybe we should borrow a page out of their book."

"I'm sorry, I don't follow."

"Well, instead of going in guns blazing. Let's get ahead of them, and do it a little differently."

Tom looked worried. "Without guns?"

"No, we'll have guns. We're just not going to go in with bazookas blazing."

Ten minutes later, they were on the ground.

Sam and Tom were riding tandem on a snowmobile. Beside them, Elise and Genevieve were riding tandem on a second snowmobile. Both were white and electric, making the vehicles silent. Not that it mattered much. Given the extreme weather, the noise of the wind and blizzard, Sam figured he could just about drive a Mac Truck without a muffler up to the arctic bulldozers and get away with it.

There were five bulldozers in total.

The PistenBully 600 was number four in the convoy.

Their snowmobiles skied up to bulldozer number five – the last one in the convoy. With the snow it was nearly white-out conditions. Sam could barely see where he was going. He hoped to hell the driver of the truck felt the same way. If he did, he would leave the technologically advanced machine in tracking mode, automatically set to follow the vehicle in front, treating the entire convoy as a collective rather than individual machines.

Sam pulled back the throttle and raced alongside the massive bulldozer last in line. The roar of its oversized diesel engine and metal caterpillar tracks overwhelmed any sound Sam or Tom could make with the snowmobile's engine.

Tom patted his shoulder to signal, then he jumped off and onto their adversaries' bulldozer.

Sam stayed behind the convoy and waited.

It didn't take Tom long to send him the message he was free to do the next step of the mission. Sam watched as two bodies were unceremoniously thrown out the door of the bulldozer.

Sam swerved the snowmobile to avoid hitting them.

A second later, Tom stepped out onto the driver's platform, and gave him the thumbs up.

Sam nodded, and sped up.

His turn.

He brought the snowmobile around to the back of the trailer that had the spacecraft on board. Bringing it in as close as he dared, Sam reached across, and climbed up. The trailer had a wide platform all the way to the back of the PistenBully, making it easy to make the traverse from trailer to bulldozer.

Just before the driver's cabin, he withdrew a Glock 10 from its holster.

He knocked on the passenger's side door.

Confused, the driver turned to look at him.

Sam opened the door and shot the driver.

The relief driver sat up from the bed in the back, and reached for his weapon. Sam hadn't managed to stay alive this long by being slow. He immediately turned his aim toward the man, and shot him twice in the chest.

He threw the driver and his relief driver out the side doors.

Then he took a seat in the big, springy chair.

Two more minutes later, Sam watched another two bodies fall from the bulldozer ahead. Elise and Genevieve had also achieved their goal. Number three on the convey no longer had personnel on board As he watched the British mercenaries body count climb, Sam began to wonder just how much better his current plan was, compared to being trigger happy with a bazooka.

Up ahead, Elise and Genevieve would have set their bulldozer to tracking mode by now, so that number three kept following the convoy. Elise and Genevieve jumped off the back of their bulldozers, rolling in the ice as they hit the ground.

Sam and Tom slowed their two respective vehicles.

Elise climbed aboard the PistenBully 600, while Genevieve joined Tom in the bulldozer. Sam said, "Welcome. Where are you headed?"

"I'm thinking the Australian Antarctic research station, Casey."

"Sounds good."

Sam slowly turned his bulldozer around. Together, they drove back to the de Haviland Twin Otter. When they reached it, the cockpit exploded.

Hu and Anastasia joined the Convoy in the PistenBully.

Sam looked at Hu. "What's with the explosion?"

Hu said, "I left a grenade in the de Haviland Twin Otter. I figured given how things generally go for you, I didn't want to give the British a chance to come after us using the aircraft."

"Great idea!" Sam patted him on the back. "See? You're getting the hang of being part of the team already."

Sam then set a course for the Australian Casey Station.

That was where the *Tahila* was hopefully waiting for them.

Chapter Sixty-Eight

The next two days went by slowly.

Nothing happened quickly when crossing even a small part of the Antarctic continent. Anastasia passed the time, along with the rest of the small, motley group of adventurers, taking turns driving the massive arctic vehicles.

But despite the monotony of the landscape, she wasn't bored.

How could she be?

She didn't have much time to do what she had to do to save her daughter's life. Somewhere between now and the time they reached the coast, she needed to gain access to the inside of that spacecraft. It was the only way.

The question was, could she get away with Sam in charge?

Each day they would stop, stretch their legs for a few minutes, and sometimes swap over drivers and who would travel with whom for the day.

On the third day, the solution kindly presented itself.

The bulldozer always drove first, with the PistenBully 600 and tractor trailer three or four hundred feet behind. This wasn't an antisocial thing. It was fundamental safety 101 in Antarctic travels. If the forward vehicle drove across thin ice, or fell into a crevasse, it was vital the second one would have enough room to stop and render assistance. What's more, in this case, given the trouble the spacecraft had caused, it was imperative that it was able to reach the harbor where it could be transferred to a secure facility.

The two arctic vehicles slowed to a stop.

From within the bulldozer, Hu came out with a chess set. "Look what I found! Who wants to play?"

Genevieve said, "I'll skip it."

Hu looked around. "Tom?"

Tom said, "I'll pass."

"Wow. You guys are no fun. Elise?"

Elise pursed her lips then shot him a coy look. "I don't know."

Sam and Tom exchanged a knowing glance.

Anastasia watched the scene unfold, trying to make sense of the hidden meaning behind consenting to play a game of chess. She didn't expect Tom and Genevieve to emphatically rule out playing a simple boardgame to pass the time.

"Come on Elise, please!" When she tapped her lips with a finger, still thinking about it, Hu turned to Anastasia. "What about you?"

She smiled. Sensing the chance to possibly have enough alone time to enter the spacecraft, she said, "At least you can tell that is not a Russian bulldozer."

Sam paused what he was doing on his computer tablet and looked up. "Why? Russians don't like chess?"

"No. Russians love chess. But it's banned in all of our Antarctic research stations."

Sam said, "Get out of here… really? Why?"

Anastasia relaxed. "It goes back to one of the original team of scientists at Vostok."

Sam said, "Go on. What did they do?"

"In 1959, the Vostok station was the scene of a fight between two scientists over a game of chess. When one of them lost the game, he became so enraged that he attacked the other with an ice axe. According to some reports, it was a murder, though other sources say that the attack was not fatal. Afterwards, chess games were banned at all Soviet Antarctic stations, and the game's never been allowed back."

Hu said, "Well… I guess I'm just going to have to play myself."

Elise drew a big breath, exhaled slowly. "Look, if you want to tell me the rules, I suppose I'll give it a go."

Hu lowered his gaze to meet Elise. "You've never played?"

Elise made an innocent smile. "Does it surprise you that I don't play a lot of boardgames?"

"Actually, yes."

"Okay. I've played chess before, but you'd better refresh my memory."

Hu said, "I warn you I'll go easy on you to begin with, but I'm more than a little good at the game."

"Modest too, I see." Elise gave a half-shrug. "We'll see."

Sam stood up. "This could take some time. Shall we get back on the road?"

Tom said, "Sure, but I'm staying in the bulldozer. This game I've got to watch."

"Me too," Genevieve said.

Sam looked around at all the faces lit up and eager to watch the game of the century. He turned to Anastasia. "You want to keep me company or am I all on my own?"

Gotcha… Anastasia thought.

"Sure. I'll travel this section with you."

Within minutes they were back driving on the ice. The two arctic vehicles had picked up and were now at their maximum speed, which wasn't very fast. Roughly 15 miles an hour. The bulldozer settled in about four hundred feet ahead of them, and the PistenBully 600 slowly settled.

Anastasia said, "So… I take it Elise has played chess before?"

Sam nodded, suppressing a big grin. "A little."

"She's not bad at the game, is she?"

Sam kept his eyes straight ahead, watching for deadly crevasses hidden in the sea of ice. "No, I haven't personally played against her, but I can tell you now, she's going to win."

"Have you ever seen Hu play?"

"Nope."

"Maybe he's really good."

"Probably," Sam agreed without hesitation. "Hu's one of those people who expects the best out of everyone in everything they do – especially himself. He comes from royalty in the Youxia, a type of ancient set of warrior guards who originated in China. One of those people who has read Sun Tsu' *Art of War* cover to cover many times."

"But you think she will win?"

"Definitely."

"Why?"

"Elise isn't just one of those really smart people…" Sam paused. His face twisted as if he were trying to think of a good analogy. Failing, he simply said, "Look. It's like this. If you were to live to a hundred, and spend that entire time traveling the world and visiting the top universities where the brightest minds thrived, Elise would still be the smartest person you ever met."

"That smart?"

"Smarter."

Anastasia said, "So she's gonna beat him."

"Yeah." Sam gave a satisfied grin. "She's going to absolutely smash him."

Anastasia laughed. "Now I can see why everyone was chomping at the bit to watch the game."

She stood up. "You all right here?"

Sam looked at the controls. The PistenBully 600 was set on automatic, tracking the identical trail of the bulldozer up ahead. He could practically go to sleep. "Yeah, I'm all good. You want a break?"

Anastasia shook her head. "No, I think I'll have a walk around the back and take a good look at this spacecraft everyone's willing to kill for."

"Enjoy and stay safe." Sam handed her a radio. "Here take this."

Anastasia looked at the radio. "I'm not planning on going far."

Sam nodded. "I know. That's just in case you slip. I'd hate to reach Casey Station only to find out you fell off hundreds of miles earlier."

She smiled. "Okay. I'll take it, and I'll try to stay safe."

Chapter Sixty-Nine

Anastasia carefully stepped out of the driving cab.

A railing protected her along the length of the PistenBully but then there was a gap between it and the purpose-built sled that cradled the spacecraft. They were traveling at roughly fifteen miles per hour. It was hardly racing. Even if she fell, she figured she could probably run fast enough – at least over a short period of time – to catch up and climb on.

Then again, maybe she was fooling herself?

She was careful as she took the big step across the gap, and onto the spacecraft's cradle. She slowly made her way around the stealth vehicle. From what she'd heard, it was a nuclear jet, capable of suborbital flight. That made it the fastest jet on earth.

She ran her gloved hands around its smooth, light and sound absorbent skin. Anastasia was a glaciologist and an assassin by trade, but even she could appreciate the technological marvel's intrinsic beauty. Somewhere in the back of her mind, she recalled that there was a fully functioning nuclear engine running silently inside.

The thought made her draw her hand back again.

It seemed stupid.

The thing had survived being buried nearly two thousand feet beneath a lake for nearly a decade. There was no way it was going to be leaking nuclear radiation now. And even if it was... so what? She still needed to do what she'd come here to do.

Natalya's life was far more valuable than her own.

No question about it.

She came to the back of the spacecraft, and looked around, her eyes furtively darting toward the Pistenbully up front. There was no sign of Sam and even if he did come out, what was he going to say? She'd already told him she wanted to get a good look at the spacecraft. Although he'd be a little shocked to discover that she knew exactly how to get inside it.

Anastasia glanced up at the PistenBully.

The ice was thick in the air, sort of a frozen mist that enveloped everything. It was a perfect shroud of cover for her illicit act. She quickly clambered up onto the spacecraft. Her eyes narrowed as she located and depressed the hidden safety-release for the hatch. A pullout lever, similar to a commercial aircraft's throttle, extended from the dark stealth skin of the craft.

Anastasia pushed the lever all the way forward.

The air-tight seal for the spacecraft, opened with a whisp of air. She immediately climbed in, pressing the close button, to seal the hatch closed behind her.

Her eyes swept the high-tech cockpit.

Its main power was switched on, and more than a hundred electric lights were lit up. It made it look to her every bit as much a futuristic spacecraft as one could imagine. Even if its origins were decidedly earthly.

In the pilot's chair was the frozen remains of the original test pilot. Two bullet wounds showed that he was executed. She wondered if Merc or his secret partner was responsible for that? Next to him, there was a second deceased person. This one, decidedly recent.

A tendril of icy fear made its way up her spine.

She turned around.

A Glock was pointed right at her.

Her veins turned as cold as the temperature around her.

It was the French commander who had nearly killed her inside the ice caves. She noticed with some satisfaction, the red stain on his jacket where she had sliced his wrist with the scalpel.

Shame she hadn't cut deep enough.

Chapter Seventy

Anastasia turned the palms of her hands skyward. She asked, "Now what happens?"

The French commander's lips twisted into a malicious smile. "Now, I kill you like I should have from the start."

"Not with that you won't," she said, in a voice she hoped didn't betray her terror.

"Why not?"

"Two reasons."

"Go on."

"One. You shoot me, Sam Reilly and the rest of his team come out and kill you."

He shrugged his shoulders. "Sam Reilly? Never heard of him. Is he MI6?"

"No."

"Bundesnachrichtendienst?"

"No, he's not German Foreign Intelligence."

"Who is he?"

"Some American."

"Ah, CIA!"

She shook her head. "Maritime archeology."

"An archeologist?" He sounded surprised. "What's he doing in Antarctica?"

"Research."

"You expect me to be afraid of an archeologist?"

It was her turn to shrug her shoulders. "This one appears to have watched Indiana Jones a little too much. Instead of the nerdy intellectual you're picturing, imagine one of the hardest fighters around."

"All right, so Sam Reilly – the fighter – will come after me if I shoot you."

"You have to admit, the noise will attract unwanted attention."

"I agree." He lowered his Glock, replacing it with a large blade. An

Ontario Knife Mark 3 Navy Dive Knife. It was identical to the one the US Navy SEALS used. Strange given he looked like he'd come from the French Special Forces.

His eyes lit up. "You like knives, don't you?"

Anastasias said, "You don't want to do this."

"Oh, but I do. Ever since you cut me, I've been fantasizing about this moment. And now look at us. Here I was going to waste this experience by shooting you, but thanks to your helpful advice, now I'll get to repay you for slicing my wrist." He grinned.

Suddenly remembering that she had offered two reasons why he didn't want to shoot her, he said. "What was the second one?"

"Come again?"

"You said there were two reasons why I shouldn't shoot you. We've already overcome the first. I'll use a knife the same way you used one on me. So, what was the second one?"

"I could make you richer than your wildest dreams."

"I doubt it."

"No, I can. I could make you the richest man on earth."

"I do like the sound of that." He seemed to turn to the practicalities. Tossing over the fact that he knew she was just trying to buy time. "How?"

"When this aircraft was first to be sold to the German military in secret, a deal was brokered involving the majority of the amount to be paid in untraceable 500-euro notes. But the last of the fee, half a billion dollars, was to be transferred via Bitcoin."

"Half a billion dollars is a lot of money. To be honest, more than what I have any real purpose for, but alas, we must talk in specifics. And you said, I could be the richest man on earth. Half a billion dollars won't make me that. Deal's off!"

"No wait!" She started breathing hard, working to control her rising panic. "This deal happened in 2010. It was supposed to be half a billion dollars paid for in Bitcoin. This was at a time when Bitcoin was worth less than a dollar. I don't know if you've looked at the price of Bitcoin lately…"

He gave a smile that indicated he knew a little about Bitcoin. "Peaks and troughs."

"Right. Even the troughs are about US $30,000. Do the math, and any way you look at it, you're the richest man on earth."

The man edged the blade of his knife closer to her chest. "And you can get these... Bitcoin for me?"

"Yes. I'll show you. But you'll need my help to transfer it, and also to get out of this spacecraft and away."

"Okay," he said. "But if you're lying, I will kill you and I will take pleasure in making you suffer in the process."

"Agreed."

She sat down in the copilot chair and searched for the USB slot for the main hard drive. Finding it, she plugged her external hard drive into the USB slot.

Working on the computer, she searched for the hidden Bitcoin wallet. She frowned.

It wasn't there.

She kept searching.

Her heart racing ever faster.

The French commander said, "I'm waiting. What is taking so long?"

"I don't know. It's meant to be here. I just can't find it."

She kept clicking, and searching for more data, but nothing was coming up.

Behind her, the French commander began to laugh. The sound of it was big, boisterous, and snide.

Anastasia slowly turned around. She looked at him. "What's so funny?"

He held up an external hard drive. "Are you looking for this?"

She arched her delicate eyebrow. "You knew all along?"

"About the Bitcoin?" He nodded. "Of course. Do you really think anyone would be fighting this hard over some state-of-the-art experimental jet from a decade ago? The reason we haven't progressed with nuclear powered jet engines is that the international community disapproves of them. No one would have died for this stupid aircraft. It's like you said, the goal of being the richest man alive is that it makes people go crazy."

She tried to smile to match his insanity. "Why did you let me search for the Bitcoin?"

"Because I just had to see your expression when you realized the truth. When you knew how completely you failed."

Anastasia started to laugh with him. In her right hand, she felt for the scalpel blade that she had hung on to since she'd used it to slice his forearm.

She moved closer to him, speaking in a soft, seductive voice. "Tell me, what's a girl gotta do to make the world's richest man happy?"

"You wanna make me happy?"

She nodded. "Sure."

His expression was cruel, but it was his voice that chilled her completely. "Then die."

She watched him thrust the knife, throwing his entire body weight at her. The attack was clumsy. He was letting his hatred for her get in the way of years of training. It showed his lack of professionalism deep down. No wonder he quit being a soldier to become a mercenary.

Anastasia shifted her position to the right, using her left arm to deflect the knife attack.

At the same time, she slid the scalpel up and across the side of his throat. It severed his carotid artery, muscles, tendons, and windpipe in one go.

The commander lifted his arm to stab her again. But half-way through the motion, he seemed to suddenly realize what she had done to him.

He opened his mouth to speak, but only blood came out.

The commander dropped the knife, and used both hands in the vain attempt to stem the blood. It was pitiful. Not even a child would imagine one could survive such an injury. His eyes rolled back in his head, and he collapsed.

Anastasia picked up the fallen external hard drive. "Thank you."

She then stripped, and using her singlet, carefully wiped the blood off her wrist. This was where the first shot of dark red, arterial blood had landed when she severed his carotid artery. She got redressed, opened the spacecraft's hatch, and returned to the PistenBully's driver cabin.

Sam looked up at her. "What did you think of the spacecraft?"

Anastasia smiled. "It was highly rewarding."

Chapter Seventy-One

They were nearing the Australian Antarctic base along the coast.

The twin machines followed the thick icesheets. They were only a half a day out from the harbor where the *Tahila* was waiting to meet them. The bulldozer stopped up ahead. Sam frowned. It happened frequently on their journey across the icy continent, but something about this stop made him worried.

He radioed Tom who was driving the bulldozer. "Everything all right, Tom?"

"I'm not sure," came Tom's crackled reply. "The engines overheating."

"In Antarctica?"

"I know, right?" Tom said, "I think something's happened to the oil. I'm gonna need to stop and check it out."

"All right, I'll come give you a hand."

Sam parked the PistenBully a hundred feet back from the bulldozer. He climbed up into the bulldozer's cabin. Tom was going through a series of onboard internal, digital diagnostic tests. Ironically, the heating unit for the oil had seized, meaning the incoming oil couldn't be kept warm, and was starting to freeze. Without oil, the engine would begin to overheat.

Sam frowned. "Think you can fix it?"

Tom nodded. "I'm just going through the spare parts list on the iPad. The bulldozer seems to have duplicate spares for most components."

"That makes sense. Given that you're hard pressed to get external help here in summer, and almost impossible in winter."

Tom put the iPad down. "Yeah, we've got one."

"Any idea how to change it?"

"By the looks of things, it's typical throw away stuff, meaning you slide the old one out and the new one in."

"Great. I've got to make a satellite call. I'll do that while we wait."

"No problem."

Sam walked back to the PistenBully and grabbed the satellite phone. Anastasia asked, "Is everything all right?"

"Yeah. Some issue with the oil warmer or something. Tom's got the replacement part, he's just sorting it out now. I've got to make a call. Feel free to stretch your legs."

"No worries, will do."

Sam got out and walked back toward where his friend was working on the bulldozer.

Tom slid out from under it. He handed the oil component to Sam. It reminded him of one of those old electric heaters that had rows and rows of oil piping that were heated electrically, and then maintained their heat for hours. It was a horribly inefficient way to heat the house.

Tom said, "Any guess what might have caused this?"

Sam studied the oil heater, noticing several puncture sites. No wonder they were running low on oil. "I suppose we could have driven over any number of rocks or even the frozen ground could be sharp enough to do this."

"Really?" Tom asked, his eyes squinting, as though the thought of believing such a story seemed physically painful to him.

"You got a better idea?"

Tom said, "If I had to guess, I'd say someone's put a knife into this thing."

"Sabotage?" Sam said. "By whom?"

Tom arched an eyebrow. "Do you really have to ask?"

"Anastasia?"

Tom said, "Look. I don't have anything against her, but let's face it, everyone else here is part of our team. We know them. We've worked with them. They're not going to sabotage our bulldozer in antarctica."

"We don't know Hu that well," Sam said, simply playing Devil's advocate.

"Well enough to know he wouldn't betray us."

"I agree. So that leaves Anastasia."

"Afraid so."

Sam said, "I'll talk to her."

On that note, Sam picked up his satellite phone. Walking back toward his vehicle, he scrolled down through the contact list, and hit the call button for the Secretary of Defense.

She answered on the third ring. "What do you have for me, Mr. Reilly."

"Madam Secretary." He greeted her formally. "We have the spacecraft, but it has come at a cost."

"What was the price?"

"A lot of people are dead."

"Was that necessary?" she asked, sounding like an adult chiding a child.

"We weren't involved in much of it. Vostok was attacked by some French mercenaries, working for who knows who, then they in turn were attacked by some German mercenaries, who were eventually attacked by British mercenaries."

"Good God!" she said, "Mr. Reilly, do you mean to tell me you have inadvertently started World War III with the Europeans?"

"No ma'am."

"But who do you think they work for, and how did they know about Vostok's worst kept secret?"

"I don't know." Sam paused. Drew a breath. "Ma'am…"

"What?"

"You should have told me it was one of ours."

There was a time she would have tried not to answer such a direct question from Sam, but she was past that now. "I didn't know for certain, but it had entered my thoughts as a possibility."

"You lied to me. I don't say this to blame you. Simply to point out that it makes it harder for me to do my job if I don't have all the correct information. The US built a nuclear-powered jet engine."

"No, on that score, I can defend myself. DARPA began building a prototype. From what I heard; it was damned good too. But the project got canned after the international backlash and poor sentiment toward nuclear powered jet engines."

"Then where did this spacecraft come from?"

"I don't know what to say. DARPA definitely canned the project. Unless…"

"What?"

"There's always a chance that someone from DARPA sold it to a foreign party. They built it based on our designs, and then tested it in

Antarctica, where they could do so without prying eyes."

"I guess the test failed."

"I guess so." The Secretary hesitated. "I'd like to get to the bottom about how this thing leaked to the French, the Germans, and the British for goodness's sake!"

"I don't know how you're going to find out, ma'am."

"Put my spy on. I'd like to hear from him."

Fear started to hit him like heavy raindrops. Big thuds of fear. "Ma'am... our spy in Vostok was a woman. Her name is Anastasia."

"No, Sam. Our spy in Vostok was named Constantine Orlov."

Sam swore, thinking back to his first conversation with her. She was the one who said you must be the handler they sent to get me... and he replied, she must be their spy. It was an honest mistake among enemy spies. "Oh no! Anastasia wasn't our spy. She was one of theirs!"

"Sam... What are you talking about?"

From the ground, Sam glanced up at Anastasia who had moved into the driver's seat of the PistenBully.

He said, "I have to go."

"Where?" asked the Secretary of Defense.

The PistenBully started up.

Anastasia put it into gear, and made a bee-line straight out across the ice sheet, toward the Southern Ocean.

Sam cursed. "To save our spacecraft from being stolen."

Chapter Seventy-Two

Sam started running toward the PistenBully 600.

Anastasia turned the arctic vehicle a full ninety degrees and was heading straight out to sea. At this time of the year, thick ice-sheets ran another twenty or so miles.

He stopped after fifty or so feet.

Even if the trucks seemed slow at fifteen miles an hour, they were still much faster than what he could dream of running on ice to catch up. No, his only hope was to follow on the bulldozer. He changed his direction and ran toward, Tom.

"Tom, tell me you got that oil thing fixed!"

"Yeah, I just need to put the cover back on and tighten everything up."

"Don't worry about it, we need to go!"

Tom followed Sam's gaze out toward the distant sea.

"Anastasia making a run for it..."

Sam said, "Get in the bulldozer, I'll explain on the way."

The bulldozer was a crowded house with Sam, Tom, Genevieve, Elise, and Hu all squished in together. Sam brought them all up to speed about Anastasia being the wrong spy. They kept going. Slowly gaining on the PistenBully which was slowed by the heavy spacecraft.

They were closing the gap, but not fast enough.

At this rate, she would probably reach the ocean before they caught up with her.

Then, like a piece of good luck, the PistenBully began to slow. Its caterpillar wheels began digging deeper into the ice. Sam felt his heart leap to his throat.

Thinking of Anastasia, he said, "Oh no!"

A moment later, the entire front end of the arctic vehicle fell in through the ice. The PistenBully's crevasse bars – tubular bars that extended its length, caught on the ice. This prevented the entire truck from disappearing.

Sam said, "Bring us up close, Tom... but not too close. We don't want to go in."

Anastasia opened the door to the truck's driving cabin.

She got out and began running toward the sea. Leaving the spacecraft attached to the sunken PistenBully.

Tom said, "The sea's at least another ten miles away. No way she's going to make it."

"I know," Sam said, "But I'm still stuck, trying to work out what she knows that we don't."

Tom shook his head. "No idea."

Sam said, "We've got to go after her."

They opened the door to the cabin.

Sam said, "Genevieve, take Hu and Elise and see if you can save the PistenBully. Failing that. Be sure to save that damned spacecraft. Right now, it might be the only way we're ever going to find answers."

"I'm on it," Genevieve said.

Sam and Tom were already out the door, running full speed toward Anastasia. They were both taller, and faster runners than her.

But she had a much greater head start.

Still, they would catch her well before she reached whatever rendezvous she might have along the coast.

They passed the stricken PistenBully.

Up ahead, Anastasia tripped. Immediately picking herself up, she looked over her shoulder, and kept running hard. Spurred on by their pursuit, she seemed to pick up speed.

Tom was a fast runner.

He was pulling away from Sam and closing the gap between them and Anastasia.

Another five or ten minutes, and they would have her.

Then they would finally get some real answers.

In the distance, a shadow seemed to pass beneath the ice. It looked like a cloud had just passed overhead.

Sam cursed.

The ice was cracking.

Sam shouted, "Come back here, before you fall into the water!"

She shot a glance over her shoulder, and kept running.

"The ice water will kill you!" he begged, as he kept running toward her.

Suddenly a large, dark, metal object broke through the thin layer of sea ice. Sam watched it protrude higher and higher out of the frozen ground.

That's when he realized it was the conning tower of a nuclear submarine.

Sam and Tom raced faster.

The submarine didn't surface above the ice.

Just its conning tower.

The hatch opened.

Anastasia climbed the ladder.

A man from inside grabbed her wrist and pulled her up. A moment later, she disappeared into the submarine.

The hatch closed.

Tom reached the conning tower, clambering on board. He tried to open the hatch, but it was sealed from the inside. Sam reached him a few seconds later. They both tried to open the external hatch. Nothing happened.

Sam banged his closed fist on the hatch.

It seemed a futile effort.

A second later, the submarine retreated below the ice. Taking with it, any chance of ever finding answers, as Sam and Tom jumped off the conning tower and ran back to solid ground.

They were both breathing hard, struggling to catch their breaths in the icy cold.

After a minute or two, Tom asked, "What the hell just happened?"

Sam shook his head. "I have no idea."

Chapter Seventy-Three

Leo Green was in serious trouble.

His efforts to resolve the problem in Antarctica had failed. He reached for a grab bag in his apartment. All good spies kept one. They included cash, legitimate passports with new identities, and some sort of weapon. There was still time. He was done with the Ministry of Defense.

He could still run.

It was a lot of money to lose. More than any man had ever lost in the history of currency in civilization. Then again, what good was it to him, if it was going to get him killed.

That thought made him think of The Ghost.

What would he do?

The Ghost was known for being unforgiving about such matters.

Leo shook his head, attempting to push the thought aside.

He'd been a spy a lot longer than that man, and he hadn't lasted this far in the game by being stupid. No, he would leave. He'd exit the game and run. Start a new life. A third age. Retirement. Not much different than most people his age, and some a little younger.

If he couldn't lose himself in the entire world, who could?

Besides, it wasn't like he had any of the grand notions to spend his money, or flaunt it the way much of these younger spies did these days.

No, he would find an isolated island, preferably somewhere warm with a nice climate, where he would live out his days fishing and sailing. Not watching his goddamned back for once.

The thought appealed to him.

He would leave tonight.

No, not tonight.

Immediately.

With that thought, there was a knock on the door. The first two were gentle, the third one originated from an iron battering ram. The door splintered and two men stepped into the small apartment.

Leo spread his arms, adopting an appearance of elderly outrage. "I demand to know the meaning of this intrusion!"

"You wanna know?" the younger of the two thugs said. "The Ghost is disappointed, and he wants to have a little chat."

Leo shrugged. "So tell him to come have a chat in person. Like we've been doing for thirty years."

The younger thug said, "That's not how this sort of conversation works."

Leo slowed his voice, like someone used to being pedantic. "All right. I'll come with you. I just need to get my insulin from the fridge."

"Forget it."

Leo arched a thick, bushy eyebrow. "Forget it? Easy for you to say, but if I don't have it, I'm gonna die."

The guy shrugged in such a way to suggest, an issue with his blood sugar was the least of his worries today.

Leo changed tack. "Did I mention the first symptom of hyperglycemia is vomiting?"

That riled the thug.

Everyone hates vomiting.

It gets everywhere.

And you never fully get rid of the smell.

"All right, all right." The younger thug pointed to the taller one. "Get his damned meds."

The guy opened the fridge, his eyes scanning the top shelf, and that little tray where people store butter. "It's not here."

"Of course, it's here," Leo said. "What would I do without it?"

The thug, already frustrated, said, "Look for yourself."

Leo opened the vegetable drawer, parted several carrots and a head of broccoli, and retrieved a sawn-off shotgun.

He grinned. "You're right, it's not here."

"I told you..."

Leo didn't let him finish.

He squeezed the first shot.

It was loaded with a 12-gauge slug of lead shot. He didn't need to see that the recipient was dead. He pumped the shotgun, cocking it again, and fired at the second thug.

Then he picked up his grab bag, and casually strolled out of his apartment.

Leo shook his head. "Goddamned newbies."

Chapter Seventy-Four

Sam watched as the spacecraft disappeared inside the *Tahila*.

He was looking forward to getting some rest on board, and also taking the time to make sense of what just happened. His chief engineer – okay, his only engineer – Veyron took a look at the spacecraft, trying to find out how to access its internal cockpit.

Sam watched as he worked his way around the machine's stealth fuselage. He was about to go back up to the bridge to catch up with Matthew and see how the *Tahila* faired in the Antarctic Sea, when Veyron said, "Ah... there it is."

"What did you find?"

"I don't know yet," Veyron said. "I pressed this hidden button here, and this latch popped out of the radar absorbent skin."

Sam's heart hammered in his chest.

He was about to find some answers.

Veyron pushed the latch downward, and the entire hatch opened with a hiss, revealing a putrid smell.

Sam coughed.

He went and grabbed one of the many facemasks. The one and only benefit of surviving a pandemic. He put it on, tightened around his ears, making sure the N95 microfilter formed a good seal around his nose.

Then he switched on his flashlight and entered the spacecraft.

"What the hell?" he said, to no one in particular.

There were three dead bodies.

One, the original pilot, was still frozen. He had two headshots. To the side of the copilot's seat, was a second man. He had a single gunshot wound to his chest. Instantaneous death. If Sam had to guess, the man was killed in the past few days. Then there was the third one. The most gruesome of the lot. Sam recognized the man as the commander of the French mercenaries.

His left forearm had a deep laceration, where Anastasia told him she had cut her opponent, while trying to escape. It seemed the man had bigger problems now. There was a new wound, starting just below his ear, and ending somewhere just past his windpipe.

The fellow probably bled out within minutes if not seconds.

There was a note on the main dashboard, next to the computer controls.

It was addressed to him.

He picked it up and quickly read it.

I'm sorry, Sam.

They have my daughter.

Anastasia.

Sam sighed. He at least had one of the answers he was looking for, as much as he didn't like it. He didn't think Anastasia had intentionally betrayed him. Now he couldn't blame her. What wouldn't a parent do to protect their child?

He climbed out of the cockpit.

Elise handed him his cell phone. It was connected to the *Tahila's* wireless system, rather than satellite or a cellular network.

Sam looked at the name, and said, "Madam Secretary?"

"Hello Sam. I have some news. The person who is behind this is called Merc… no surname. AKA The Ghost. He's a high-end European Arms dealer. We've had some dealings with him over the years."

"Dealings, ma'am?"

"Governments throughout the world who like to sway the outcomes of various wars."

"Even the ones we're not involved in?"

She spoke like she was telling the truth about Santa Claus to a child. "Especially the ones we profess not to be involved in."

"Right. So, our arms dealer friend is behind this."

"I never said he was our friend. Only that such a man is often used as a go between for governments who want to provide assistance to achieve certain outcomes in various wars…"

"That we don't want to legitimately partake any active involvement?"

"Exactly. I'm glad to see you're still a fast learner."

"Ten years ago, The Ghost tried to sell the nuclear-powered suborbital spacecraft to the German buyer."

"Privately?"

"No. The German Department of Defense were interested."

"What went wrong?"

"The Ghost's partner, Leo Green, a British spy and counterpart in the arms dealer game, got cold feet."

"Why?"

"Why does anyone do anything? Apparently, he decided that giving the Germans the technology that could easily be reverse engineered to create a fleet of nuclear-powered suborbital jets, was a bad idea. There are a number of reasons why such technology should absolutely be avoided. But I feel that Leo Green's concern was far less about altruism, and more about history. His father served as a pilot during World War II, and in the process was shot down. In his records, there's something about being rather unimpressed by the way the man was treated as a German POW, having come back with significantly less digits than when he'd crashed."

Sam said, "Leo Green found his scruples because his father was treated poorly by the Germans as a POW?"

"Hey, the important thing is that he did in fact, eventually find his scruples. He stopped the transfer of the spacecraft, killing the original pilot and burying the spacecraft in a deep ice ravine. Little did he know the damned thing would resurface a decade later when Vostok began its drilling project."

"Okay, so everyone died... it was all a race to gather decade old nuclear technology?"

"It was meant to be very good technology if my intel from DARPA is to be believed. But no, according to Leo Green, this had nothing to do with technology and everything to do with money."

"Money? Because of the sale?"

"Not exactly. What do you know about Bitcoin."

"Not much. Why?"

"Well, because of the difficulty tracing them, they're popular among criminals."

"Sure."

"In this case, a lot of money was set to be transferred via Bitcoin, the private keys to which were stored inside the spacecraft's hard drive."

"Okay," Sam said, still not following where this was going.

"Apparently this was roughly equivalent to half a billion dollars in 2010. Now, imagine this was a share in a company... say, Tesla. Since 2010 the value has gone up substantially. Now that half billion dollars is worth a lot more, and in the case of Bitcoin, that half a billion dollars is worth closer to a trillion, making whoever can locate and access those private Bitcoin keys, the richest person to have ever lived."

"And that sort of cash is enough to get a lot of people killed."

"Right."

"So, you think Anastasia already retrieved this Bitcoin thing?"

"Not Bitcoin. Just the private keys to them. We won't get into how block-chain technology works. Elise can probably explain it to you much better than me."

"Okay. But you think Anastasia stole it?"

"I know for a fact that she did."

"How?"

"Leo Green told me."

"And you trust him?"

The Secretary said, "You're not the only spy I've developed a relationship with over the years."

"I thought you said he was British?"

"What's the point of having an American spy who only stays in America?"

Sam shook his head. It was dizzying trying to keep up with the ins and outs of international espionage. He said, "So what did Leo Green tell you?"

"That his partner, The Ghost was hellbent on finding the spacecraft, and retrieving the coins. He recently got them from Anastasia, and having done so, cut Leo out of the equation."

"How?"

"He sent two hired hitmen to try and take him out."

Sam said, "They didn't succeed?"

"No. Leo's an old man, but he's been involved in the game long enough to know how to get out of trouble when it comes looking for him. That's why he's come to me, and why I'm coming to you."

"Go on," Sam said, still, really not following very well.

"Leo needs us to kill The Ghost. Otherwise, he will always be looking over his shoulder."

"Sure. You probably owe Leo that. So, what makes you think we know where he is?"

"Not us. You Sam."

"Me? Kill some spy called the Ghost? Why would I do that?"

"Anastasia reached out to Leo Green. The Ghost has her daughter held captive. She's transferred part of the code to the Bitcoin's private key, so that The Ghost needs her to unlock it. She then contacted Leo Green and told him that they would be most likely flying to Switzerland, where her daughter was kept, and she wants to make a deal. Leo's given us a description of The Ghost, along with a list of real estate holdings, vehicles in his name, and whatnot. So far, we haven't gotten lucky, but we will."

"Does Anastasia know where her daughter's being held captive?"

"No. Just that there's a castle in Switzerland where The Ghost used to keep prisoners, slaves, and anyone who betrayed him. She used to work for him, a long time ago. About a decade to be exact. When things went bad with the spacecraft transfer, something went wrong, and she got out."

"But she can't tell anyone where the castle is?"

"No. Never knew the address. She's given us some nearby sites, but The Ghost was always careful not to let her know its exact location. She would be brought in for certain purposes, but never allowed to know where she was." The Secretary drew a breath. "We have people working in Europe and back here, trying to put everything together. We now know what he looks like, and a rough idea of where they're heading. You just need to get lucky."

"As I mentioned before, me?"

"Yes, didn't I make that clear? You're off to Switzerland."

"How? I'm in Antarctica."

"Not for much longer. I have a jet landing within the hour, ready to pick you up at Casey Base, and flown directly to Switzerland."

"Why me?" Sam asked. "I mean, I'm not involved in law enforcement.

I'm happy to help, but I can't see how I would be any more useful than say a police detective."

"Anastasia asked for you, specifically. She said she wouldn't trust anyone else."

"So we're all heading to Switzerland?"

"No. Just you. There's not a lot of room for you on the aircraft, let alone the rest of your team."

"What sort of aircraft?"

"I have a Rockwell B-1 Lancer. The supersonic variable-sweep wing, heavy bomber is the only craft capable of getting you there in time."

"Time for what?"

"Oh, didn't I mention. Anastasia says The Ghost is going to kill her and her daughter within 24 hours if she doesn't hand over the keys to the Bitcoin."

"So, I alone am supposed to rescue her and her daughter?"

"And hopefully get access to a trillion dollars' worth of Bitcoin for the State Department. I'm afraid it won't go anywhere near as far as it used to, but it will help with the deficit."

"Spoken like a true bureaucrat, ma'am. But basically, I'm on my own."

"Not entirely."

"How so?"

"There's a detective meeting you at the airport. Detective Tobias Fischer. He's been hunting this guy for more than ten years. He has an intimate understanding of the man and the way he operates."

"And yet he hasn't caught him in a decade?"

"The Ghost is one of the best." The Secretary added, "The detective will have a helicopter meet you at Switzerland's main airport."

Chapter Seventy-Five

The Rockwell B-1 Lancer touched down at Zurich airport.

It was nighttime locally.

Sam stepped out onto the tarmac. In the distance, a black Eurocopter EC635 with the words *POLIZIE* on its fuselage stood on a landing pad, its rotor blades turning.

A man in his late fifties approached. The man said, "Sam Reilly?"

"Yes, sir," Sam replied, offering his hand. "You must be Detective Fischer."

"Tobias," the Detective said, with a firm handshake. "You have anything?"

"No. I'm good to go."

Within minutes they were airborne.

The detective brought him up to date. They had a massive manhunt out for anyone fitting The Ghost's description. Main arterial roads were being monitored and roadblocks were in place with checkpoints. They had four helicopters out searching for his vehicles.

Sam said, "We know what cars he owns?"

"No," Tobias admitted. "But we know he has a predilection for high-end European cars and because of his work and where he travels, he always drives an SUV."

Sam suppressed a smile. "Wow. We're looking for a high-end European car in Switzerland. That's gonna be difficult."

"No, I don't think you understand. We're talking about very high-end cars."

"Such as?"

"Think Porsche Cayenne on steroids and then go up in value. Think, Bentley Bentayga. Lamborghini Urus. Rolls-Royce Cullinan Black Badge."

"Okay, I'm getting the idea. So much for The Ghost trying not to stand out."

"Oh no. This guy likes to stand out. He wants to be seen."

"All right, so what's the plan?"

"We're gonna find this guy. We have his description; we have Anastasia's description. We know they're in the country."

"Do we? How?"

"Anastasia messaged her contact, who passed it along."

"Okay. So now we just have to get lucky."

"Really lucky." Tobias said, "Did you bring a weapon?"

Sam nodded. "Yeah, a Glock 10. No one even checked me at the airport."

The detective smiled. "Yeah, well, we've been hunting this guy for years, and if you're the only bait we have, we're happy to take risks to get you here on time."

"Thanks."

The helicopter banked, following highway ten into the thick forest of Doppleschwand.

Sam stared at the window. "What about that one?"

"The Mercedes Maybach SUV?"

"Yeah. It looks expensive."

"Not his style."

"Right. How do you know this?"

The detective shook his head. "I can't say. I just do."

"He wants something flashier, a little more flamboyant. Something that says 'I have so much money, I don't care about wasting it on a car that's worth more than your house.' Maybe a new Ferrari Purosangue – Ferrari's first SUV."

"Like that Ferrari down below."

Detective Fischer looked out the window. "Yes! Absolutely." He leaned forward to the police spotter next to the pilot. "Hey Anya, can you get a closer look in on the Ferrari?"

"Sure," Anya replied, zooming in with their digital camera.

The image was displayed on a monitor in the back of the helicopter.

The detective looked at the driver. His eyes narrowed and squinting, he tried to compare the image with the description that Leo Green provided.

Sam skipped the driver and looked at the zoomed in image of the passenger. It was a woman. He took one glance at her and shouted,

"That's her! That's Anastasia."

Tobias leaned forward, spoke to the pilot. "That's our target. I want you to back off, but keep contact with it using FLIR. We need to know where it's going. We'd still like to rescue Anastasia's daughter if it's possible."

The pilot banked the helicopter, adding a little more room between them and the vehicle they were now going to be trailing.

Anya changed from visual imaging to FLIR.

FLIR stood for Forward Looking InfraRed, and provided an excellent tool for tracing people in the dark, fog filled environments.

Tobias handed Sam a VOX – voice activated radio – to put around his neck, and a pair of earpieces. One let him talk over the radio, the other let him listen.

Anya said, "We've got him, Toby."

"I sure hope so," he replied. Then looking at Sam, he said, "There's something else I need you to know."

"What?"

Tobias drew a heavy breath. "My last partner, Andrea Jordan, was recently killed because of that man."

Chapter Seventy-Six

The Ghost kept the Ferrari Purosangue within the speed limit.

It was a difficult task in a SUV equivalent of a Formula One race car, with a naturally-aspirated V12. But rules were rules, and the last thing he needed was to get pulled over by the police for speeding. He glanced over at Anastasia. He couldn't believe she'd managed to get the best of him.

There was no reason he should have had to come back here.

She should have transferred the nearly 1 trillion dollars' worth of Bitcoin into his digital wallet. He should have shot her dead and left her damned daughter to die in that oubliette. But instead, the bitch double-crossed him, quickly transferring the access codes to the Bitcoin to an outside server, where no amount of torturing would provide him with what he needed.

Oh well... he was close to his goal now.

In twenty minutes, they would reach his castle.

Once there, the police couldn't touch him. He would trade the daughter for the Bitcoin. Once the transfer was complete, he would shoot them both, and walk away. He would never be allowed back to his medieval home, but what did it matter? With the sort of money that he was going to have, he could buy an entire island and build a new castle – and we're not talking about some little Caribbean thing. A trillion dollars will get you a significant country!

Above him, he heard the familiar *whoop, whoop* sound of a helicopter's rotor blades beating the air. He looked up. It was a black police helicopter. He watched it for a minute. The chopper had been climbing for a while now, gaining altitude, but what did that mean? They had plenty of technology that could close that gap.

Were they following him?

He turned to Anastasia. "How long has that helicopter been tailing us?"

"What helicopter?" she asked, innocently.

"The black one. On my right. Don't tell me you haven't seen it?"

She said, "I haven't seen it."

The Ghost frowned. "You can wipe that smile off your face. Don't forget, if I get caught, you will never find your daughter, and we both know she'll die in that oubliette. So you had better start praying that we make it."

She closed her eyes. Her body was trembling, sweat was dripping from her face, despite the cold mist. "All right, all right. Remember, I'm on your team. As much as I don't like it, I know what has to be done."

"And don't you forget it!" he hissed.

Six more minutes and they would reach his castle.

Once they got to his place, it would all be over. Too late for the police to do anything about it.

In his side mirror, he caught the glimpse of that helicopter again.

It had dropped down too low to be unintentional.

A police helicopter.

It *was* trailing them!

He floored the accelerator, quickly overtaking the other vehicles in his lane.

The Ghost looked at Anastasia. "Quick, transfer the Bitcoin codes now!"

Anastasia looked scared. For the first time since he'd picked her up in Antarctica, she seemed properly rattled. But her eyes remained defiant. "No. When I get my daughter, not before."

He swerved off the highway, pulling onto a dirt road.

The Ferrari didn't slow down.

He kept his foot hard on the accelerator, and the powerful SUV kicked dirt up, as it wound around the thick pine forest, skidding into the open garage.

He quickly stepped out of his car.

The police helicopter flew overhead and began lowering itself toward the ground.

The Ghost reached into the car and retrieved a hunting rifle. He pointed it at the tail of the helicopter and fired several shots until the firing pin in his weapon landed on an empty chamber. He was no sniper but heard the distinctive ping of a round hitting somewhere around the tail or the engine. The helicopter spun, its pilot trying to avoid clipping the nearby pine trees.

The Ghost turned and sprinted into the house, already feeling a little happier at having seen the helicopter struggling to lower itself onto a nearby clearing.

He closed the garage door, and ran through the 16th Century castle.

Anastasia knew where she was.

That was good. At least he didn't have to fight with her.

She would have headed to the library.

An empty fireplace stood before a couple comfy leather chairs and a couch. It was overlooked by a big oak desk that had been in his family for more than three centuries. On the walls were thousands of leather-bound books, many 1st editions, spread out over rows upon rows of bookshelves.

Anastasia said, "Where is she?"

The Ghost said, "Transfer the Bitcoin codes."

"Open the damned door."

He shook his head in frustration. Then he walked over to the last bookshelf. He reached a book three from the end of the shelf. It was an old Australian classic called *A Town Like Alice*, by Neville Shute.

He pulled on the book.

The whole bookshelf opened up, as though it was a heavy door. He pulled it all the way open, perpendicular to the wall. Even upside down, all the books remained fastened to the shelf.

Through the gap, Anastasia spotted the elevator that must lead to the oubliette.

He pointed the rifle at her. "Give me the Bitcoin keys!"

Anastasia pressed the down button.

The elevator asked for a code.

"No. Give me the code!"

"All right, all right. Suit yourself." He typed the code into the elevator. The doors slid open.

He kept his rifle aimed at her. "Now transfer the damned money!"

From her position in front of the elevator, she chucked him her cell phone. "Done."

Picking it up, he looked at it.

Relieved, he saw that the transfer had gone through.

The Ghost raised his rifle, increasing the pressure on the trigger, intending to finally end Anastasia once and for all.

Bang!

The sound of a bullet and breaking glass made him hit the floor. In a state of shock, The Ghost took a moment to think. Before he could get off a shot, some bastard had fired at him through the windows! The round had missed him, but it was close. The near-death experience transformed him. His primitive fight or flight response slammed into action.

He needed to get out of the house.

The Ghost fired at the elevator as the doors were closing, but already, Anastasia was gone.

Finding the alarm system on the wall, he opened it up and pressed a red button. Then he grabbed the remote next to the TV. It didn't belong to the TV, but he was going to need it where he was going.

The castle was set up with several different escape routes.

On all fours, careful of snipers, The Ghost made his way over to take a turkey peek out the window.

The helicopter was already landing there.

The Ghost moved to the back of the house. Grabbing a rope that was tied to a tree outside, he swung into the darkness, toward his freedom.

He landed heavily.

Got up and ran into the thick pine forest.

Where his escape was waiting for him.

Chapter Seventy-Seven

Sam felt the Eurocopter spin and yaw.

The pilot showed his experience as he fought to regain control, keeping them upright and in the air. He had lost tail-rotor control. Expertly though, he managed to wind the helicopter down onto the patch of gravel outside the house.

As soon as its skids barely touched on the gravel, Sam swung the helicopter's door open, and was running toward the house, his Glock in his right hand. Right beside him, moving like a man half his age, detective Fischer had his pistol drawn.

Sam tried to kick the door in, but it was too strong.

He stepped around the back of the house.

A big, solid oak door was partially open. As though someone had run out of it so fast that he or she didn't have time to close it. Sam's eyes locked on it. Then, out the corner of his eye, he spotted The Ghost running off into the forest, like some sort of Olympic sprinter.

The detective exchanged a glance with Sam. There was no way the older man was going to be able to catch up to The Ghost on foot.

He said to Sam, "Go after him. I'll get the girls."

Sam hesitated, then thought better of it. He ran after The Ghost, who had already disappeared into the thick forest of pines, and the enveloping mist. He sprinted toward where he saw The Ghost enter the woodland area.

There were no trails, only dense pine trees.

He kept going for a minute or two and then stopped. There was no point. He couldn't see the perpetrator, or even which direction he went.

Sam turned around.

Again.

And again.

His Glock was drawn, ready to shoot.

Above him, he heard a second police helicopter approach.

Sam said, "Pol Air, please respond."

"Go ahead, Reilly," responded Anya, the police spotter who must have climbed on board after her helicopter crashed.

"I've followed the suspect into the forest, but have lost a visual." Sam was glad Anya was in the air above. "I can't see anything down here. Can you pick him up on the FLIR?"

He took out his flashlight in his left hand.

It barely penetrated the mist.

"Copy that Reilly. He's heading due south."

Sam spun around, his eyes darting up toward the stars.

They were all concealed behind a thick blanket of fog.

With nothing to reference, he had no way of knowing which direction was due south. He got on the radio again. "Sorry Pol Air, which way is south?"

"Take a couple steps forward."

Sam took three steps forward.

The spotter on Pol Air said, "Okay turn to your three 'clock."

Sam carefully turned. "I'm there."

"Good. Now just keep going straight ahead. We'll be your eyes."

In the distance, Sam spotted something that looked like a light.

Gotcha…

Then he heard a sudden explosive blast. It was coming from the castle!

He turned to see a giant mushroom cloud of fire rising up like a mini-nuclear explosion. Disappointment and sorrow sent him into an unhappy head-spin, as he knew in a heartbeat, that Detective Tobias Fischer couldn't have survived the blast.

Chapter Seventy-Eight

Anastasia switched on her flashlight.

The oubliette was empty.

A shadow of fear flittered across her heart.

Where was Natalya?

Had Merc lied to her again?

She cried out, "Natalya!"

No response.

She scanned the dungeon. The pile of food and water was still intact. That was a good sign. If she was still alive, where was she?

Her gaze landed on the opening in the wall.

Right.

Then it all came flooding back.

She switched on her flashlight and entered the narrow, secret passages.

Anastasia quickly made her way through the labyrinth.

It was specifically there to make people struggle. As a sport it was cruel and sick. A game to play with the unfortunate's head. Played so that someone like Merc, with his unique depravities, could enjoy watching his victims suffer.

She sped through it.

Hit a dead end.

Back tracked and continued again, until she reached the second oubliette.

There, she heard whispers. Anastasia came through the door and found Natalya talking to a brown-haired girl in her twenties.

Natalya called out, "Mom!"

Anastasia wrapped her arms around her daughter. "It's all right. You're safe now."

Natalya introduced her mom to Andrea Jordan, who, she explained, was a cop who had also been kidnapped.

Anastasia said, "Pleased to meet you. If it's all the same to you, I'd like to get out of here."

Andrea said, "Sounds great."

They backtracked to the first oubliette, but the elevator had automatically gone up. Of course, Merc would have never allowed them to go free. The Ghost wanted her, and her daughter, dead.

Natalya burst into tears. "Oh mom, I've got you trapped here too…"

Anastasia shook her head. "Have you been through the entire labyrinth?"

"Hundreds of times."

"What about the spiral maze?"

"The one that comes up to a sort of well?"

"Yes!" Anastasia said. "Great! So, it's still here. That's how we're going to get out."

"We can't," Natalya said.

"Why not?" Anastasia asked.

"The walls are too wide and smooth to climb."

Anastasia said, "Leave that to me. If you can get me to the center of the spiral maze, I can get us out of here."

Natalya guided them through the series of tunnels and passageways until they reached the center of the spiral maze.

Anastasia fixed her flashlight on the smooth surface, counting each large, sandstone block that made up the walls.

On the fourth stone, she pressed it in.

The stone depressed three or four inches.

It wasn't much, but it was big enough to hold onto, or to place your feet on. She then moved up and pressed the next one four above. She continued this process until she reached top of the well.

Andrea followed directly behind her, and then Natalya.

All three of them looked at the stars above.

Free at last!

And then the ground shook, and the castle exploded into a ball of fire.

Natalya said, "Do you think they will catch him?"

Anastasia shook her head. "I doubt it. He's been planning this for a very long time. But I know where he's heading."

Andrea said, "Really… where?"

"I'll tell you, but I'd like your help."

Andrea said, "Sure. What do you need?"

Anastasia made a theatrical sigh. "I'm gonna need a car, and a gun."

Chapter Seventy-Nine

The Ghost kept running.

He was in the race of his life, against a much younger man.

There was no trail, but he instinctively knew where he was going. He'd practiced this route dozens of times. Practice, practice, practice. That's how he'd managed to stay alive in this game for so long. Leo Green taught him that.

Long before the man betrayed him.

The Ghost was breathing hard.

He had to take a break.

Had he lost the determined American yet? He turned his head. Behind him, he saw the gentle glow of his pursuer's flashlight.

Damn, the man could move quickly.

The Ghost looked toward the clearing up ahead. Unsure that he would even make it. Every fiber in his body wanted him to rest. To take a seat. To stop and suck in some more oxygen. But if he did that, he knew he would be dead, or worse – stuck in a prison for the rest of his life.

This thought spurred him on toward the clearing.

Reaching into his pocket, he retrieved the cell phone and pressed the call button.

A man answered immediately.

The Ghost said, "Oliver. They're on my tail! Get the helicopter warmed up. We'll takeoff as soon as I reach you."

"Understood boss."

In the distance, he heard it start up immediately. The Ghost grinned, as he listened to the soothing sound of an engine and the rotation of the rotor blades.

Behind him, Sam was moving fast.

Fast enough that the Ghost knew it was going to be a problem reaching the chopper first.

Chapter Eighty

Sam kept chasing The Ghost.

His radio was crackling, but he couldn't quite make out what Pol Air was saying. He could barely see anything, but he could hear the man thrashing through the forest and see the slight movements of nearby branches and trees where he brushed passed them.

There was a faint glow up in the distance.

He just had to reach it.

In the distance, he heard the gentle *whoop, whoop* of a small, single engine helicopter warming. Sam shook his head and tried running harder. Faster! He cursed. How could The Ghost have gotten so far ahead of him, to reach the helicopter?

His cell phone buzzed.

It was an unknown number.

Sam hit the answer button. "Yes?" he panted.

Like the radio, it was a broken communication, with more static than clear words. Even when he heard the words, it was only every second or third one that came through. Still, he heard enough to know it was Anya, the police spotter from the downed chopper. She's in the twin-engine Eurocopter overhead.

He tried the radio. "Reilly to Pol Air. Transmit?"

"– turn your radio up!"

"... forget... helicopter."

Sam aimed his Glock at The Ghost's getaway helicopter in the distance. He could now see that it was a Robinson R22, a two-seat, two-bladed, single-engine aircraft. He was getting close enough to take a shot.

He could just make out the blurred shape of the pilot.

The chopper began to rise slowly. It rocked back and forward. It was no more than ten feet off the ground. Sam planted his feet, ready to take aim at the helicopter's cockpit.

His phone started to ring again.

Sam hit the answer button. "What?"

Anya shouted in his ear. "He's behind you!"

The words didn't register in Sam's mind straight away, but through luck or instinct, his body reacted.

Sam dropped to the ground.

Three shots whizzed past him in an automatic burst.

Sam rolled to the side, taking aim in the direction the sound had originated, and squeezed the trigger.

Once.

Twice.

Anya spoke into his earpieces. "Sam! Listen to me. Don't talk."

Sam kept down on the ground.

"I've got The Ghost on FLIR. He's lighting up clear. I'll direct you exactly to where he is. He's at your nine o'clock!"

Sam looked toward his nine o'clock.

It was in the direct opposite direction to the Robinson R22.

He took a quick shot.

Nothing.

Anya said in his ear, "The man's laying prone. Taking cover behind that log."

Behind Sam, the small helicopter rocked and rolled, before hovering just a few feet off the ground. The pilot was obviously waiting for The Ghost.

Sam took stock of the situation.

The Ghost needed the helicopter to escape. Sam was in his way. Sam was protected behind a series of trees and logs where he was. The Ghost was covered where he was. Nobody was moving. But Sam had the advantage.

He had all the time in the world.

There were three helicopters hovering overhead, more than a dozen police cars, all wailing lights and sirens. All speeding to this spot right here. Every one of them were intending to capture or kill The Ghost. If he could just hold out a little longer, the police would be at his side.

Sam shouted out, "It looks like we're at an impasse."

"Not from where I'm standing," The Ghost replied in a voice, much too confident for Sam's liking.

"Oh yeah… how do you see it?"

The Ghost said, "The way I see it, I have just one choice."

Sam took a quick furtive look at the helipad in the clearing up ahead, trying to get an idea of what The Ghost was planning to do.

Behind him, The Ghost fired three rounds in quick succession.

Sam retreated and kept his head down.

No way was this dirtbag going to hit him.

The pilot in the Robinson R22 looked horrified and betrayed. He pulled back, trying to escape the attack.

Sam heard the *ping* of bullets striking the helicopter. In an instant, Sam understood what his enemy intended. He rolled over and began crawling as fast as he could. He got fifteen, twenty feet away, when one of those shot landed right where The Ghost wanted.

It hit the fuel tank.

And the helicopter erupted into a ball of fire.

Chapter Eighty-One

Anastasia had to run to keep up with her daughter and the cop. Andrea reached the first police cruiser. It was parked fifty feet away from the burning castle. Even at that distance, the air was hot and stifling to breathe.

Natalya said, "Look!"

Anastasia followed her gaze. There was a man in a detective's uniform. Even from where they were, they could see he was severely burned.

Andrea swore and ran to help. "Toby!"

Toby looked up at her and muttered a curse under his breath. "Am I dead?"

She smiled. "No."

"But Andrea... I saw you in that house back in Germany. I saw it explode. You got blown up so completely there was no body. There was no way you could have survived."

"Yeah, well, I did. I've been The Ghost's prisoner all this time." Andrea's eyes landed on his torso. There was a large branch sticking through his lower chest. "Are you in much pain?"

Toby shook his head. "No. They say it doesn't hurt when you're gonna die."

Andrea grabbed his radio. "We have an officer down at the castle crime scene. We need an ambulance here."

There was no answer.

The radio was dead.

Toby looked at Andrea. "It's okay. Look at me. I'm dying. There's nothing any doctor is going to do. I just want to make sure we finally get this bastard!"

Anastasia said, "Hello. You don't know me... I'm..."

Toby managed a crooked, pain-filled smile. "Anastasia. And your daughter, Natalya. At least you two are safe."

"I don't know if The Ghost has escaped, but I do know where he's headed. And what's more, I know how to stop him."

"Good. Go! Leave me and do that!"

"There's just one thing," Anastasia said.

"What?"

"I'm gonna need your gun."

Toby drew a breath. "Are you sure you can get this bastard?"

"Certain."

"OK." Toby lifted his pistol and handed it to her. "Then for me, please make sure you put two bullets in his head."

Chapter Eighty-Two

Sam felt like he was in Dante's Inferno.

Heat from the blast seemed to radiate in every direction. The fire, spreading out in a wide arc, parodically triggered small brush fires in the trees nearby.

A painful combination of steam, mist, and smoke flooded his nostrils.

He couldn't see anything, and he could barely breathe.

Into the radio, Sam said, "Anya, tell me you have him?"

"I'm sorry Sam, the heat has flooded the FLIR – it's a complete whiteout. You're on your own."

Sam tried to make his way out of the fire, over into the clearing in the distance. He saw a small garage near where the Robinson R22 had taken off, and made his way to the garage.

The roller door was shut.

He walked around to the front.

Inside the building, he heard the electric starter motor of a motorcycle engage. Was The Ghost planning on using a motorbike? Sam came around, just in time to see the motorcycle ride straight through the back door, and through the fire.

The bike shot off through the woods.

He drew his Glock and fired multiple shots until he emptied his magazine after it.

He then swapped it over with a fresh one.

But it didn't matter, his enemy had already ridden away.

Sam looked around.

There was no other vehicle inside the garage, and no way for him to follow. Once again, The Ghost had simply slipped away.

Chapter Eighty-Three

The Ghost grinned from ear to ear.

He felt like a kid again riding the KTM 350 XC-F Enduro bike. Its 4-stroke engine was full of energy. Despite the power available at a touch, he carefully drove through the narrow bike path. He'd ridden the trail plenty of times before, but never in the dark, and when the forest was shrouded in mist. He had to consciously slow down, and make sure to take it easy. The fact was, a fall now or a simple mistake, could mean the difference between life and death.

It took roughly twenty-five minutes for him to carve his way through the forest and come out the other side. When he turned onto the main road, he half expected to run into a police roadblock. But there wasn't one.

He used the blinker and turned onto the thoroughfare.

It wasn't long.

Maybe another fifteen minutes, and he reached Buochs Airport. The little regional airport in Nidwalden in Switzerland catered to small carriers and private aircraft.

The Ghost pulled up at the private gates. Swiped his electronic key card and rode his bike into a private hangar.

Inside was an Eclipse 550 private jet.

The Ghost didn't waste any time. He unlocked the aircraft and began quickly working his way through the take-off checks, skipping any step that wasn't vitally important. He needed to get into the air. Fast, before the Police shut the damned airport down.

Within fifteen minutes, he was taxiing out onto the runway. He said a quick good morning to air traffic control and was assigned to takeoff on runway 24. He was asked by air traffic control to wait for a couple of minutes. There was some sort of emergency that took precedence.

He held his breath.

A knot of fear twist in his stomach.

A series of police cars, their sirens wailing, their red and blue lights flashing, approached the airport. The Ghost held his position and tried to imagine his options as soon as he was informed the police were after him.

Could he still takeoff?

Would they shoot him down?

If they didn't shoot him down… how far would he get?

There was a parachute on board.

If only they let him takeoff, he could set the aircraft up on autopilot and then skydive to safety. Then he could be a few thousand miles away before they realized his scorched remains were not on board the wreckage.

A commercial plane taxied to the terminal gate.

Nobody got out.

Police cars surrounded the aircraft.

Air traffic control thanked him for his patience and advised him that he was cleared to takeoff.

The Ghost exhaled.

He pushed the twin throttles all the way forward. The Pratt & Whitney PW610F engines roared, and his aircraft raced along the runway. It reached takeoff speed. The Ghost gently pulled back on the wheel.

The private jet gracefully left the ground, releasing its earthly restraints. The Ghost climbed high above the Swiss landscape. He'd always loved to fly. No matter how rich he got, or how successful he became, he loved to fly himself.

It was absolute freedom.

He set the autopilot up, made sure it was working correctly and went back to wash his face in the bathroom.

He was king of the world!

When he finished, he stepped out into the main cabin.

Anastasia and her daughter greeted him. There was a pistol in Anastasia's hand. It was trained on the center of his chest.

The Ghost's eyes narrowed. "What the hell is this?"

"Change of plans," Anastasia said, with a twisted smile. "Turns out I've reconsidered. I'd like a trillion dollars."

"It's not going to happen. We had a deal."

Anastasia laughed. "It has recently come to my attention that deals are subject to change. Traditionally by the person holding the gun. I thought you, of all people would understand that."

His voice turned cold and hard. "You're bluffing."

Anastasia pointed the pistol toward his kneecap and squeezed the trigger.

The Ghost fell onto a seat, cried out in pain, and gripped his leg.

"You know, I used to hurt people for a living." She pointed the pistol at his other knee. "I really enjoyed that job."

"Stop, stop... please!" The Ghost said, bringing his cell phone out. "I'll do it, I swear!"

"Text me the private key. All of it. I want every single Bitcoin. If you screw this up, even if by accident, I will take out your other knee, and then both of your elbows. We all know, you deserve it."

"I will, I will. Just wait."

A few seconds later, her phone buzzed.

She checked the message.

The transfer appeared to be complete. She handed her phone to Natalya. "Just double check that it went through, will you?"

Natalya glanced at it. "It's all good."

Anastasia smiled and exhaled slowly. "That's great. Really great. Now promise me you'll never hurt another living being."

The Ghost nodded. "I promise I'll never hurt another living being."

Anastasia said, "Excellent."

"So, we're all done here, right?" The Ghost asked, grimacing with pain. "You got what you want."

Anastasia said, "You didn't really think I'd allow you live after you threatened my daughter?"

He opened his mouth to speak.

She didn't let him. There was nothing he could say that she wanted to listen to. After all, protecting your child to the best of your ability is one of the greatest, most holy responsibilities shouldered on any parent.

Anastasia shot The Ghost in the head.

Two shots.

In rapid succession.

Classic execution style, double tap.

Anastasia looked down at his dead body. "You're right, Merc. You will never hurt anyone again. Know why? Because you threatened my daughter."

Chapter Eighty-Four

Private Airfield – Texas

Sam re-read the card, still unsure how Anastasia had even tracked down a postal address. The postcard showed a non-descript tropical island that could be found anywhere around the globe. Written in simple, flowing cursive, were the words…

Dear Sam,

I'm still sorry I betrayed you.

By the time you get this I'll have moved on, so don't bother trying to find me. I want you to know my daughter and I have a new life and for the first time in years we feel safe. And we owe a lot of this to you, so thank you.

Love, Anastasia.

Sam tucked the postcard away in his shirt pocket. Then he walked over to the inside of the hangar he had rented. There, at the center of it all, was an experimental suborbital spacecraft that nobody knew existed.

Elise climbed out of the newly cleaned cockpit.

To Sam, she seemed to be glowing. Something about the machine's intricate digital network made her appear particularly fascinated by the spacecraft.

He looked at her. "Well?"

Elise paused, like a child who wanted something, but was too afraid to ask.

Sam said, "Yes?"

Elise sighed. "Can we keep it?"

Sam grinned. "I don't see why not. Will you learn to look after it?"

"Sure. How hard can it be?"

"A nuclear-powered jet engine capable of suborbital flight…?" He shrugged. "I don't think that will be too problematic."

"So we get to keep it?"

"Yes, we'll keep it. Maybe don't mention it to anyone though."

Sam's cell phone rang.

He answered it. "Madam Secretary."

She began her debrief without preamble. "As I'm sure you're aware, a man was found in the Swiss Alps today, having fallen or jumped from an aircraft. It took some time to identify him, given the extent of his injuries. But they found a license in the name of Mercury Thompson."

"Interesting," Sam said. "Do you have any working theories?"

"I was hoping you might shed some light on the accident?"

"Afraid not, I missed him. I tried my best, ma'am but in the end, he got away."

"Well, I suppose it's for the best. Oh, one more thing."

"Yes?"

"Someone kindly and anonymously donated roughly one trillion dollars to a human rights charity, dedicated to ending modern slavery."

"Hey, a feel-good story for once."

"That's right," the Secretary said. "I just thought you'd like to know."

"Thank you, Madam Secretary. I appreciate that."

"And thank you, Sam. I mean it, this one could have really blown up in our face."

"You're welcome, ma'am."

"One last thing. If anyone asks, I most certainly didn't allow you to keep that damned spacecraft!"

Sam grinned. "Understood, ma'am."

The call ended.

Elise came up to greet him. "What did the Secretary say?"

Sam's set his jaw firm. "We have to deep-six the spacecraft."

"Will you?"

"I don't know yet."

Elise looked at him with her deep, purple eyes. "Sam, we can't destroy the spacecraft."

Sam tilted his head. "Why not?"

"The onboard computer was a massive experiment into Artificial Intelligence, designed to make the ultimate machine. Its internal silicon matrix was designed to build on itself, like a child's brain, it develops and expands with new conscious thoughts. After ten years, all on its own, the spacecraft's onboard computer never stopped learning and developing."

"How much learning can a computer develop stuck at the bottom of an icy lake?"

"You'd be surprised."

Sam bit his lower lip. "Elise. What are you saying?"

"I'm saying, Sam…" She paused, drew a breath and said, "We can't destroy this spacecraft because it's sentient."

Epilogue

Sam's cell phone buzzed.

He picked it up, expecting to hear the voice of the Secretary of Defense, congratulating him on his success. Instead, it was his father's voice. There was something unusual about it. A slight tremor or concern that was unlike him. He seemed shaken. His father was never shaken about anything. Nerves as cold as ice, and hard as steel.

Sam!" his father said, "I need your help."

"My help?"

Sam was taken aback. His father rarely asked him for anything. "What do you need?"

"The Texan Tanker, Global Shipping's super tanker just ran aground in the Suez Canal…"

"Where?"

"Six miles south of the Suez Port."

Sam pictured that part of the waterway. There were no roadways nearby. It was utterly isolated and would be a nightmare to bring digging equipment in. They would need to use a dredger, bringing it up through the canal.

He asked, "How bad is she stuck?"

"At a cursory glance, I'll be happy if we can get this thing moved in under six weeks."

A delay of that would cost billions of dollars in additional transport costs and shipping delays as the world's busiest shipping route was redirected around the Cape of Good Hope on the southern tip of Africa. "Tom and I will fly to the Suez Port today. We can be there in eight hours. We'll see what we can do."

"Sam…"

"Yeah?"

"I don't know if you realize how much is riding on this…"

Sam nodded grimly. "The blow out will cost billions of dollars per week."

James Reilly said, "It's more than that."

"What?"

"If we can't move that ship, we'll be sued for every single of one of those dollars."

"Can Global Shipping take the hit?"

"That big?" James swore. "Not a hope in hell."

"What are you saying?"

"Better buckle up, Sam." James Reilly's voice was hard and emphatic. "If you can't perform a miracle... this thing's going to bankrupt Global Shipping."

The End

Printed in Great Britain
by Amazon